Death of an Unnamed Girl

DAVID ROSE-MASSOM

DEDICATION

Writing is a lonely art and yet I have been surrounded by friends, and family, who have helped encouraged and sometimes driven me onward. To all of you a massive thank you and I hope I have lived up to the faith you all had in me and my adventure.

To Nicki, Ben and Harry – my family

DEATH OF AN UNNAMED GIRL

DEATH OF AN UNNAMED GIRL

DEATH OF AN UNNAMED GIRL

ACKNOWLEDGMENTS

All my friends and family.
To Tania Ball for the stunning cover picture.
Robin Weisz Design for the cover design.
Huge thanks to my friend Omar Abdel-Wahab for his invaluable help
and input. (I will be using you again very soon Omar)

And a genuine thanks to the coffee houses who have kept me fed and
watered throughout the process of writing this novel.

DEATH OF AN UNNAMED GIRL

CHAPTER ONE

Bending on one knee with his hand, resting palm down on her almost flat chest, he pressed down hard, rhythmically. She had already coughed her last breath and lay still beneath his touch. The body of the teenage girl felt cold through her thin woollen top; a skinny frame, his hand could feel the contours of her ribs. Her porcelain white, bony legs pointing off-kilter from the short, dark skirt. Her pale, slightly grubby underwear was on show and in a moment of caring, he tugged the skirt down over her straggly thighs that were painted even whiter by the soft light of the moon, thereby defending her dignity even in death.

Despite the shock of the moment and the confusion which covered his mind like an early evening autumnal mist, he looked upward, toward the cathedral spire as if in silent prayer; thoughts registering a pencil thin pair of white vapour trails that crossed between spire and moon separating the two like the sides of a fraction.

The spire, an ancient landmark of ash grey, reflected in the cold blue sky of an early sunset that ended an autumn day, pointed accusingly at the waning moon as if in judgement. The moon, off-white and soft as it rose in the last of the daylight, threw a beam of light into the shadows of the tower where a family of peregrines lived and hunted. It seemed fitting somehow that the fastest creature on earth, stooping at some 200 miles an hour should set up home in a tower that had remained motionless for a millennia.

From where he knelt in the Bishop's Garden, Lucas Tubb looked upward at the early evening moon as it made its way over the golden cockerel weathervane sitting atop the tall tower and glistening brightly in the remnants of sunshine; his eyes dropped from the religious skyline and viewed the growing shadows that were slowly emerging and spreading in the tranquil garden, his ears pricked at the sound of a small fountain with its

1

tinkling spouts of water as they fell and disappeared into the mother pool, confused he looked back at the girl that lay prone and broken in the damp grass beside him.

Furtively he scanned the gardens where one of summer's last bees flitted lazily between dying flowers, first darting in one direction then the other. The moonlight picked out the darkness under his eyes and the shadowy growth of the early onset of beard. Dark hair normally so well gelled and smartly combed was matted with perspiration and stuck to his forehead where small beads of sweat broke the skin's surface. With the finger and thumb of his left hand he pinched the bridge of his nose as if to stem a nosebleed. He was trying hard to think, to recall, what had brought him to this moment.

Again his right hand, with absence of thought, pushed gently and rhythmically down on her chest, a final and futile attempt at revival; knowing already that it was too late. The pretty blonde girl lay wide-eyed, her head twisted in such an horrific way. He knew that her neck was broken. Her face, still pretty despite the death mask, was now marred with an ugly circular wound that ripped her cheek apart just below a staring and cold eye. The wound was indented deep into the flesh and had seeped blood. It looked dark and ominous in contradiction to her pale and greying complexion.

A surreal image of himself, kneeling over her and frantically pounding her chest with desperate entreaties for her to stay alive, entered his mind, but perversely he realised at that moment that he could not even remember his own name, it was on the tip of his tongue, it was so close but he could not find the wherewithal to just pluck it from his memory.

From inside the imposing Cathedral and drifting across the surrounding city rose the warming and full sound of voices in harmony and song. He recognised it as time for evensong. The park would be closing its gate soon, and he needed to be somewhere, anywhere, other than here.

Briefly his mind wandered from his current situation. Following the musical notes that droned and floated on the evening air, his thoughts strayed into the cavernous and ancient interior with its crypts, stained glass and ornate pews. He imagined the colourful glass faces, inactive and staring for centuries; lines of lead surrounded them in the stained glass windows and they were looking down on him in judgment. His eyes, now moist with selfish tears, drifted guiltily from the body to spire and then from the brightness of the moon to the dullness of her grey pallor and bluish lips.

"Please, wake up!" A sob escaped his thin lips and a bloom of vapour drifted silently into the swiftly chilling evening air.

With one last self-protective look around, he stood, brushed the mud from the knee of his sharp blue suit, straightened his tie and absent-mindedly checked the zip of his pants. He noted that the toe of one of his highly polished tan shoes had a grey scrape that was ingrained with something dark on the otherwise faultless reflective leather, "Fuck it, look what you made me do!" he muttered. With his remaining perfect shoe he pushed the weightless body slightly deeper into the shadows, under the bench where he seemed to recall he had seen her sitting.

He now could not bring himself to touch the damaged girl with his bare hands so, his foot gently placed against her ribs, he gave her one last shove, she rolled unceremoniously under the bench as if she was hiding in a childish game of hide-and-seek.

He pushed his hands into his trouser pockets and with one last look around the park, crunched his way along the curve of the gravel footpath, he looked for the comfort of the moon but it was now hidden by a tree which held leaves of deep maroon. He passed under another with leaves of gold, brown and russet, the world around him was in the process of dying and life as he had known it was also about to expire, but there was no time to reflect on that.

He ducked his head under the low lintel of the red brick archway that separated park from path, walked out of the green sanctuary between an umbrella of palm trees alongside an ancient and castellated brick wall.

Leaving the Bishop's Garden the magnificent spire began to tower over him, imposing its history upon him, each step took him nearer until the cloisters surrounded him and, as if in premonition, he noted the barred, gothic windows that kept a small area of garden imprisoned. The voices of evensong were now loud and harmonious, the last encounter with a feeling of peacefulness and tranquillity that he would hold for some time.

Breathing a sigh of relief at leaving the unsavoury taint of death behind he exited the confines of the Cathedral and began walking briskly toward the town centre, where an ornate stone cross designated the midway point, the streets named for the points of the compass. His head hung low, his eyes averted from the crowds that were heading home with their shopping, or sitting around the ancient cross eating pizza from cardboard containers; dinner on the go. Without inviting a look or a glance from anyone he walked directly from North Street to South of the monument. On the far side he passed a rotund, female busker, her harsh soprano voice belting out 'One Fine Day' and murdering one of his favourite arias from Madame Butterfly. The cacophony created by her slightly off-tune voice gnawed at him, and yet, without thinking, he dipped into his pocket for a handful of coins and dropped them into the deluded diva's bucket with a generous clatter. The singer failed to notice the particles of blood decorating the silver coins. Lucas smiled at his philanthropy and nodded a good evening and accepted the nodded thanks of the singer who recognised his generosity without deviating from the discordant note she projected across the precinct.

He checked the Patek Phillipe watch on his tanned wrist, it felt heavy, the gold casing glinted expensively under the street lights; "Still time for a swift gin before home" he spoke out loud to himself as he straightened his jacket and pushed back an unruly lock of dark hair from his forehead, behaving now as if this were just an ordinary evening.

Once again, he noted the muddy-toed shoe, rubbing it on the back of his trouser leg in the hope of regaining a little shine. Redbrick cobbles of the street passed beneath his feet and being still damp from an earlier rainfall, they reflected the remaining lights emanating from the now closed and partially shuttered shops.

It was still early evening and the pub was reasonably quiet, however the walls were busy with pictures of an older Chichester alongside photos of a brutish looking bulldog, muscularly posing for the camera alongside posters advertising long ago played musical events. A man was perched on a stool, hunch backed, he leant on the polished bar, elbows spread to deter anyone coming near, staring unfocused at his partly drunk pint before him.

With short hair dyed jet black, framing a pale face, the barmaid also leant on the bar counter. A pink mobile phone between her fingers with diamante crystals stuck garishly to the casing. Using just her thumbs she typed a message into the screen as quickly as a typist with a batch of letters to finish at ten to five on a Friday afternoon. He noted, glinting under the bar lights, a loop of silver through the piercing in her nostril. She looked up at him with an insolent flick of her head and asked what was wanted. Her tongue stud shone brightly as she parted her lips, obviously severely restricting her vocabulary. "A large G & T please", he answered, his voice soft and almost unheard over the booming cacophony of the bar's sound system. "Bombay Sapphire if you have it, with Fevertree Tonic." With a carefree flourish she poured a double shot of Gordon's and half a mixer bottle of Schweppes over ice, the cubes cracking with anger at the intrusion of warm liquid. Lucas left a ten pound note on the bar and turned to sit on a rough leather couch. A solid looking brown and white bulldog, that had more than a passing resemblance to the dog he had spotted earlier in the photos around the walls, almost appeared to be melting into the couch' leather cushions. From heavy jowls a line of white spittle dribbled from the dog's mouth as he stretched, and farted into the antique leather, and with his tongue protruding from between his teeth it suspiciously eyed the new interloper, daring him to approach what was, most definitely, the dog's couch.

Lucas sipped his drink, immediately feeling refreshed from the fizz of the tonic and the juniper flavour of the gin, and deciding discretion was the better part of valour, chose to sit on a stool opposite the couch; the protagonists eyeing each other warily. Within seconds Lucas looked away, the dog winning the staring contest.

An hour later the dozing dog still retained ownership of the couch despite the bar becoming packed with young drinkers, many looking far too young to be drinking but served anyway, economics far outweighing the fear of the law. Familiar greetings indicated this was the usual early evening crowd looking to quench thirsts, get drunk and converse behind the roaring sound of the increasing volume of heavy indeterminate rock music. The dark haired barmaid now scooted up and down the length of the bar, ensuring everyone was served and increasingly happy, and those not so happy and argumentative were removed very swiftly from the bar to the street outside, by a thick-necked & shaven-headed bouncer wearing a dinner suit that appeared to be two sizes too small for his gym and steroid produced massive frame.

Induced by alcohol, time passed quickly for Lucas, it was now ten o'clock and a good few double gins had increased his unwanted advances toward the barmaid, who had grown more desirable with every visit to the bar, whilst he grew less attractive to her sober eyes with every double served. He'd gazed at the girl with clouded blue eyes, his baby face looking tired and pale, drink rendering him a drunken lout and no longer the handsome playboy. A lewd suggestion of carnal copulation in the car park was enough for the barmaid, as well as the watchful landlord and doorman and a simple nod from the former driving the latter into action. Lucas was not too gently, forced to join the legion of the ejected.

Outside and in the cool night air the effects of the alcohol hit him and he held onto the scaffolding that surrounded the pub walls for support; regaining his equilibrium before weaving across the green swathes of a park where he unzipped his trousers and relieved himself against an isolated tree, his free hand used against the smooth bark to keep him upright.

He woke with a start, and pulled the wrinkled blue suit jacket tighter around his frame, feeling the cold and dampness of the night on his skin which and through to his bones, as a deep voice gently but firmly suggested it was time he headed for home. Blurry eyes opened, eyelids flickering, the harsh light of morning leaving pin-pricks of pain, and as he allowed the light in, he saw the command had come from a police officer who towered over him. With surprising speed and supreme effort, he sat upright on the park bench, rubbed and dry-washed his face with the palms of both hands before looking around and feeling totally bewildered at the strangeness of his al-fresco surroundings.

Eventually, with a confidence he did not really feel, he looked the constable straight in the face and braced himself.

"Rough evening was it Sir?" Thumbs tucked into the front of the armholes of his stab vest, he smiled down at the dishevelled but well-dressed drunk. "It is time you were heading home I think, but I trust without driving!" He added more as a command than a question.

From his position on the hard, cold, wooden bench the park that surrounded Lucas slowly began to come into focus, there was a sudden realisation of the cold and damp that had been chilling him and there was a dull thumping ache above his left eye. He looked up at the officer, and softly responded. "I don't think it could have been any rougher".

The serious tone to such a simple statement brought a raised eyebrow from the uniformed man in front of him who, used to such dishevelled sights, kept his face passive, like a good poker player, and waited for the deal of the cards. His patience was rewarded.

"I think… I think I may have killed a young girl!" Lucas stuttered.

CHAPTER 2

At the same time as Lucas greeted the mist shrouded dawn's light with his abrupt confession a few miles along the attractive Sussex coastline, where it merged with the Hampshire border Gill Harmon paced the short hallway of her small Victorian coastguard cottage and waited for the post, as she had done every day for the past week or so. Bright green eyes, intense and gleaming, glared at the letterbox daring it to deliver her mail. Auburn hair, streaked with dyed hints of blonde and copper, crashed down onto her shoulders and she tucked a few of the unruly strands behind one ear, before flicking them free again, the whole remote operation like a nervous tic.

Her tiny upturned nose gave her face a cute profile and carried an expression that was normally full of warm smiles, but not this morning. This morning her demeanour was full of angst and worry.

She considered herself pretty, but not attractive or stunning; just pretty - and her face lived up to that billing. A baggy, white T-shirt stopped halfway down her thighs, showing off leg muscles toned and fit from regular gym visits and on her feet Danger Mouse slippers, the super-hero cartoon character well worn and comfortable.

The looseness of the slippers caused her to scuff along the corridor, ten feet, a turn, and another shuffling ten feet back to the door, gripping her coffee mug bearing a bright red logo, which stated she was indeed the World's Best Journalist, but yet to be proved in her mind and in deed. The remaining dregs of black coffee had long ago cooled, but such was her attention to the letterbox she failed to notice either the taste or the temperature.

"You had better bloody arrive today, three days you have had me pacing this bloody hallway, I knew I should have got a bigger place with more room for pacing..." she spoke out loud. She turned her back on the door and scuffed her way once again toward the bottom stair and no sooner had she turned away, as if to tease, the flap rattled and spewed forth the morning post.

A colourful advert sheet for the services of Royal Mail, a letter to The Occupier offering better internet speed and even more TV channels (that showed nothing new), and a crisp white envelope which clearly showed her name, Ms G Harmon, through the little plastic window.

She raced the few paces from stairs to door ignoring a row of framed and monochrome onlookers that hung on her wall, frozen portraits that had no interest in her hasty passing. The white envelope was then carried like a recently found treasure into the small and brightly decorated kitchen. Gill sat at the small oak table, rescued from a skip and lovingly restored.

"Well you have been waiting for it for long enough, now would be good time to open it." A knife left abandoned from last night's lonely dinner, now doubling as a letter opener, waved close to the flap of the envelope, eager to go to work and yet being held back. She thought, what if it says no, there is no job, then what! "Oh, for Christ's sake open the bloody thing!" She berated herself and the knife hovered for a few seconds more before, seemingly with a mind of its own, the tip dived under the flap and began to cut it away from its host envelope. Task done the knife was discarded and the free hand then pulled the letter from its paper cave; it remained still folded on the kitchen table, among the debris of the early morning breakfast of toast and peppermint tea. It lay stranded, like a fish landed on a riverbank.

Slowly Gill lifted the corner of one third of the folds in the paper, her address with the previous day's date clearly typed just below the flag that boasted 'The News' in a bold, blue, font. As the correspondence unfolded along its creases the body of text became clear…

Dear Gillian…

It must be good news if they are using her Christian name…

We are pleased to welcome you to the ranks of The News' journalists, we have received your college and work placement references and we are happy to inform that your application for the post…

Gill was no longer reading, her breathing had quickened and her heart was racing. Three years of college, a hard earned degree in English Lit followed by dozens of letters; a couple of not very satisfactory interviews and finally, finally she was to be a fully-fledged newspaper hound, a journalist!

Seeking out the big stories, finding scoops, interviewing stars of stage, screen and television all awaited her inquiring mind and rapid pen. It had taken her until her mid-twenties to decide what she wanted to do with her life, and a series of mundane, mind-numbing jobs in various shops and offices until the realisation of what she should do with her life hit her, and since she had worked day and night to achieve her goal and now it was finally here.

Of course she knew she was starting at the bottom in her chosen profession but glory would come! Tales from the police calls each morning, through the court cases of magistrate's hearings and eventually onto the big stories. Just for a brief moment she tried to recall if her sleepy home town that sat quietly and uninterrupted on the harbour side had indeed ever had a big story apart from last year's floods, nothing came to mind but nothing was going to divert her from journalistic greatness; there were always stories out there if you knew where to look.

She hugged the now crumpled letter to her chest and almost cried with joy. With a wage coming in it meant the worry of the massive student loan was no longer a concern, so she decided to treat herself to a lunch somewhere nice to celebrate. She put the letter to one side, in readiness to re-read its contents and digest them fully; before the day was over she would have read and re-read that short tome more than a dozen times.

Preparing to head out she noted that a baggy and unflattering T-shirt along with Danger Mouse slippers were not the way forward in the aim for a successful celebratory lunch; a change of clothes were needed.

Showered and now sparkling with vitality, tight jeans topped with a fresh white T-shirt, walking shoes on and a waterproof jacket to keep the chill autumnal day at bay, she locked the blue front door behind her and walked the few yards down the hill to the quayside where the views never failed to inspire her or hold her in their thrall. The tide was out, and a thin river was being fed into the harbour from a brick outlet under the yacht club, the old mill basin on the other side of the building continually feeding just one of the fingers of Chichester Harbour. The shoreline, enlarged by the ebbing of the tide, was littered with small craft that were chained to various points on the shore, and sometimes to each other, to avoid escapes on the unrelenting receding and incoming tides. Traditional wooden dinghies and small fishing craft lay lopsided keeping close company with moulded fibreglass vessels looking like plastic bowls of bright blues and yellows, garish against the misty morning scene. With the tide out Gill was able to walk along the shore, passing a rotting jetty, wood dark and seaweed covered with legs holding it above the stony and mud shore, the far end reaching forlornly for the water's edge, whilst the near end stopped short of anywhere in particular, leaving from nowhere and going nowhere it summed up Gill's life until the arrival of the morning post that day. Lost in thought, she walked into the marina where a balcony table looked out across a flotilla of luxury yachts and powerboats lined along the private pontoons that filled the pool of the marina.

On the land around the mostly ignored yachts stood square, block built homes that could have been designed by Lego so uniform were they in style. They all stood propped on tall, wooden limbs placed at each corner and in between them space and storage for a variety of small craft, windsurfers and the odd car. Strangely there seemed to be mostly bright coloured VW Beetles under each square house, all with even brighter flowers in their dashboard vases. A straggly line of ducks, a brown feathered mother with several little brown chicks, shuffled between the summer houses and Gill had to smile at the thought of new life that waddled before her.

Parked in a corner of the balcony, the tables no longer sporting gay umbrellas since the demise of the summer sun, and deep in thought she sipped a refreshing mint tea and dug into a brunch of soft, moist carrot cake, today was not a day to worry about calories, it was day to relish and enjoy, Gill Harmon had arrived, watch out world!

CHAPTER 3

Whilst Gill sipped her aromatic tea her gaze spreading out across the marina, in the nearby city centre of Chichester a growingly distraught Lucas Tubbs had exchanged one hard seat for another. First the Bishop's Garden with its tragic bench, the pub settle because of the bulldog hogging the comfy seat and then the overnight park bench which had held close council to his earlier confession. This latest in a line of hard benches was behind a cell door that had slammed closed with an angry metallic clang followed by a second lesser bang as the viewing window was closed, the prying eyes of the custody sergeant the last thing Lucas saw before his isolation. Claustrophobia crowded him while his thoughts journeyed back to the image of the bent and broken girl that he had so callously kicked into the dark shadows under the bench like unwanted rubbish. All within the gaze of the towering Cathedral spire and its resident peregrines; the fact that it was in the reassuringly named Bishop's Garden made his act even more of a sinful happening; the guilt was piling on and those moments of self-pity made that culpability an even heavier cloak to wear on crumbling and sagging shoulders.

It could have been minutes, an hour or an age before first the hatch and then the door were opened, by then Lucas had lost all judgement of time.

"Your solicitor has arrived Mister Tubbs." Lucas could not recall phoning for his solicitor; did he even have a solicitor? In the movies they always seemed to have a solicitor to call, but in real life?

Of course, there was the family solicitor who seemingly had been available for several lifetimes, but he was the man who handled simple family legal matters, he knew nothing about criminal law and he had obviously used him in the past, when settling his father's estate, the reading of the will, but he could not even recall the man's name who always appeared to have an abundance of hair creeping from nostrils and ears.

"I don't recall phoning for a solicitor." He said confused to the back of the police officer that led the way as he walked out of his cell.

"This isn't the movies," the officer said as if reading Lucas's mind; "You don't get to make a phone call but you asked us to let your housekeeper know where you were, and being the nice friendly service that we are in this fine hotel we got her number from your mobile, we assume she phoned him for you." The sarcasm was not missed.

"Have I been arrested?" It was becoming too much for him to take in, his thoughts a jumble of what had happened over the last few hours and the fear of what the next few would hold. He could think no further forward than that.

"Not as yet sir."

"Am I to be?"

"That's not for me to say Mr Tubbs." The politeness seemed incongruous with his surroundings or his situation.

The short walk along a dingy corridor in harsh need of a lick of fresh paint brought them into a stale, airless room with just a table with two hard and unattractive chairs on either side. From the far side of the table, with its scarred and stained top, sat a casually dressed and straight-backed visitor who spoke first, his voice rich and syrupy.

"Bit of trouble Lucas?" The voice warm and carried with it a hint of comfort. Without standing the elegant man offered a firm handshake and with its extra-long hold, offered friendship. With a look and stamp of a man of importance he could have been an MP or a high flying manager, the stately looking man's other hand clamped firmly on Lucas' shoulder with a strength that belied the owner's age.

"Take a seat my boy and let's get this sorted, shall we?" The hand on his shoulder gently pushed him down to emphasise the need to sit.

As if a portrait was being unveiled at a gallery opening, Lucas suddenly recognised his Godfather, Father's old golfing buddy. On the battle scarred and weary table that Lucas now sat behind, but avoided touching as if poisonous, sat a yellow legal pad and on top of that a meaningful, black and monolithic Mont Blanc fountain pen, Lucas had never seen Robert Berry QC with anything else; it was a pen that carried weight and purpose. He actually took a moment to wonder if Robert was even still practicing the law, believing he had retired to a life on the golf course and in the clubhouse some years ago.

Grey and distinguished hair filled Robert's head and swept back over his ears, perfectly coiffured. The lawyer's calm face boasted a sharp goatee, neatly combed to a fine point, salt and pepper colouring, but his overriding feature were the intense and keen green eyes, emerald like, jewels shining from a face that, although in its seventies now, was smooth and handsome.

Tanned skin, almost line free apart from radiating crows' feet of smiles creases in the corners of each bejewelled eye. It was the face of someone who at one stroke could demand respect and yet put those who it gazed upon at ease; it exuded confidence and a need to be heeded.

Robert was not dressed in what would be considered normal barrister garb, he hung his blue bespoke and pinstriped suits up along with his wig and gown on his seventieth birthday while swearing to himself that enough was enough after fifty years of the law. This morning he wore an open neck shirt, pale blue and with button down collar, and over it an antique leather blouson jacket, the leather soft, cracked and well worn, under the desk dark brown corduroy trousers with inch-deep turns-ups hanging over comfortable brogues that were as comfortable as the company of old friends, however such was Robert's demeanour and strength of character that he looked as imposing, sharp and dapper as if in one of those now retired suits. He was a man who did not need the accompaniment of wig and gown to demand respect!

"Excuse the informal attire dear boy, after forty odd years of suits and ties it feels so much more comfortable to be casual." He smiled a warm smile at Lucas. "You do know that it should just be a lowly solicitor doing this bit my boy, but it did seem serious enough to get me away from a morning of coffee and shopping with your Aunt and her offspring; my lovely stepdaughter Clarisse, who sends her regards by the way. You provided a lucky escape and saved me from an excruciatingly boring few hours." He paused for a brief thought to balance his words. "But, maybe not so lucky for you, eh?" The idle chatter served up, not as the ramblings of an old man but as a means to settle and relax the tired and fraught looking boy in front of him, who despite his 28 years had a cherubic face that at one looked frightened and lost; the child had returned.

As planned Lucas finally took some comfort in the soothing voice but still realised he had once again exchanged hard park benches and the rigidity of the cell bed for an equally hard and uncomfortable chair. Was this what life was going to be like from now on, one uncomfortable seat after another? He braced himself and tried to straighten his back, shaking off the weight he felt was dragging him down.

"Sorry Uncle Robert, everything is very confusing and clouded at the moment I don't remember asking them to call you, and, anyway, I thought you were retired, given up on the law."

"Well my boy, lucky for you Annie contacted me, she has been keeping an eye out for you boy and man so I guess she was not going to stop looking out for you now, as soon as the police contacted her she called me. But, enough preamble, right, to business, you look like shit and you seem to be up to your neck in the stuff so you now need to tell me what you have told the gentlemen outside of this room so far."

Lucas, still confused and feeling displaced, let it all out in one long breath. He explained how he had been woken, after an all-too-routine evening, for him, in some bar, by a kindly police officer and how stirred from his drunken slumber in the park, he initially confessed to the belief that he had killed a young girl and then proceeded to tell of his attempt to revive her as she lay beside him with her neck broken and her face bloodied and split. A tear escaped the corner of one eye, neither man was sure if it was for the situation or the girl.

Suddenly the young man became aware, rudely reawakened as he re-entered the real world into which he had been harshly thrust with the realisation that he had tears in his eyes, suddenly as if tension had been released the boy overtook the man as he began to sob uncontrollably. Apart from being informed of his father's death it was something he could not recall doing since his pre-teen years. Though the tears may have been, in some way, for his own predicament in his heart he knew they were more for the young life of the, as yet, unnamed girl that was crushed out before its time. He realised he felt no guilt about the harming of the girl, not out of being callous but because he had no recollection of any violence on his part, you cannot feel remorse for something you did not do. His only bad feeling was for just abandoning her already dead body and leaving her poorly hidden under the hard park bench.

Robert remained stoic, back ramrod straight, a strong presence in the room and waited for Lucas to regain a little composure, to finish his story without interruption, then gently asked "Let us take it back to a little earlier last evening shall we? Begin at whatever beginning we can reach!"

"I, I don't recall earlier, it's a blank!" A look of bewilderment confirmed the statement, his brow furrowed with effort of thought. "I remember sitting alongside the girl, I could hear a choir, or the organ or something coming from in the Cathedral, felt bloody spooky I can tell you. My being there with the girl and them inside singing something melodic, religious and Latin. I was just pushing down on her chest. Her head was crooked and at a strange angle and I remember thinking how skinny and white her legs were and wondering why she had no shoes, and why she had blood on her face." A moment of thought and he looked his Godfather in the eyes. "What have I done Uncle Robert?"

He struggled to think, Robert remaining quiet, a coherent thought process suffering from mental constipation! "I sort of thought she might be dead and so gave up, just stood up and tidied myself up a bit, I brushed the mud and grass off the knees of my trousers, the best I could, and I remember noticing my shoes had been badly scuffed; my favourite brogues." As if in realization he leaned back slightly and looked down at his feet, the shoes were still there, one shiny and one scuffed and dark with dried dirt, his laces were missing one tongue was poking out as if in a rude gesture

"Where are my laces?" Another vague moment, "It seems callous to me now but I was more concerned about ruining a good pair of shoes than the plight of that poor girl. Do we know who she is yet, have they told you anything, have I been charged…" The little composure he did have evaporated and the final words gushed out in a stampede of words.

Robert held his hand up, a silent command for Lucas to quiet himself, before laying it on top of his Godson's own trembling hand, the touch was gentle and softly said; "Calm yourself Lucas, all in good time. I am here now, we can take as long as we need, but at some time they will probably want to begin a formal interview. Assuming of course they find a body; which at the moment is still in some doubt as they have been searching the park where you were found this morning and as of yet, so they have told me, no girl, or indeed no body of any description." Lucas looked ready to interrupt but his question was answered before it could escape into the world, "If, or when they decide to start formal proceeding I shall be present of course, every step of the way, and you will say nothing without my say so. Do you understand?"

"Only answer questions when you say so!" Lucas breathed in deeply, and held it for a while as if to extract every molecule of oxygen from it.

"Exactly!"

The air rushed from his lungs, eager now to escape. "But, who was she, the girl, I cannot even remember what her face looked like, except she looked terrified and had this nasty looking wound on her cheek, I remember thinking that was lucky, whatever made that mark could have had her eye out. It's almost funny the things that go through your mind when situations like this arise; not that a situation like this had ever arrived before…" He realised he was waffling and apologised. The friendly man opposite had this manner of raising his hand communicating a plethora of meanings; an instruction to cease, there to be no need to apologise and just a simple comforting gesture; Lucas took them all in as a child would take visual commands from the teacher. Robert learned early on in his career that a courtroom lawyer needed to be a good actor.

"Let's go back to the start of the day, did you go to work, what did you do all day?"

The question was rewarded with nothing except a pained expression, as if his body were trying to give birth to a cognisant thought. Before the troubled expression could rise into sheer panic the soft voice interrupted, keeping command of the situation. "Take me back to last night, what did you do, it was a Friday?"

A light came on in Lucas' eyes. "The Park, I was at the Park…"

"The park where they found you this morning?"

"No, no, not a park, *The* Park, The Park Tavern, they had the first log fire of the year because it was so chilly outside and there were three or four of us hogging it, stood around the hearth. I remember not being able to sit on the couch because the pub's fat bulldog was spread out, he was sleeping with his tongue poking out and no-one had the heart to move him! I sat on a little stool opposite until some the regulars began to chat with me."

"Who were they, it may be important later?"

Again the strained look; "The usual regulars I suppose and, I think, I mean I seem to recall, that Jacob dropped by at some time." Lucas stole a glance at Robert to see if the information was important.

"Your brother dropped by? I didn't think you two were talking."

"We're not, not really but sometimes he just turns up at the house or the pub, usually when he wants something; but this time he just stayed for a couple of drinks and then drifted off again. I thought it was nice to see him without some sort of trouble between us rearing its head, he didn't even seem to want to borrow any money which is highly unusual for him, as that's usually the first thing he asks for."

"When did you last see him, before last night I mean?"

"Months ago, probably, I thought he was up in London. You know what he is like floating between his friends' houses in town and his own apartment in Southampton it was a real surprise when he ducked his head under the door last night." An afterthought! "Is that important?"

"Not really just trying to get your memory to work, my boy." He brushed aside the snippet but banked it in his memory and made a hurried note on the yellow legal pad, as history recorded that the two brothers rarely got on, in fact the opposite could often be said as growing up their dislike of each other often turned into rough confrontation. Jacob, the adopted son, always felt as if he was in the shadow of his older brother and fought for superiority at any chance he had. Lucas in return had offered nothing but love and protection to Jacob. That said, even he bit back on occasion.

There was a sharp rapping on the door to the interview room before it opened and in walked two men, importance and urgency stamped on their very presence, the crisp, white, uniform shirt on the custody sergeant looking bright and garish against the dull greyness in the room; he appeared like some advert for a whiter than white soap powder product, while the younger officer behind him still wore the full dark uniform that he had been wearing a few hours ago when he woke Lucas in the park, his shirt black and shiny, the collar zipped to his throat, added to the black combat pants gave him a menacing appearance, the cumbersome stab-vest was now missing from his dark ensemble; the fact the constable had nowhere to place his thumbs meant his arms now hung uncomfortably down his sides, and looking as if they needed somewhere to live.

The older man looked well-worn and comfortable, the younger man, in his mid-twenties with unruly blonde hair over a face not yet worn out by life, looked sharp and serious. It was the senior man who spoke to introduce themselves; he was balding, with a slight paunch that was battling to outgrow both trousers and that white shirt.

His face was like an ignored indoor plant and looked as if it could be improved with a few days of sunshine. It was pale and drooped at every corner, his mouth thin and lipless, his eyes dull and lifeless, he appeared to have served his own prison sentence in the confines of the station's cells. The energy had been dragged out them by a life of dealing with deadbeats, and even the occasional dead body!

"Good evening," a voice as gruff and worn weary as his face, "I am the custody sergeant David Grant and this is Constable Harry James, who you met a little earlier in the park I believe." He did not wait for a response to the rhetorical question.

Robert Berry, in full QC mode, was about to reclaim his right to talk, but experience told him that things had moved on and the inevitable was about to take place, he stayed the desire to control events and remained as quiet as his client. He placed a securing and comforting hand on Lucas' forearm.

The sad face of the sergeant took on an I-mean-business look and his voice gathered itself into a severe tone. "Would you please stand up sir...," The hand on his arm moved and now touched Lucas' elbow and both men stood, client and representative; Lucas looked from sergeant to Robert and back again, fear stamped on his face, "I have to inform you that following your earlier verbal and volunteered statement to PC James we have discovered the body of a young woman and following that discovery I am informing you, in the presence of your solicitor, that I am arresting you in connection with the, as of yet unidentified, young lady's death and that I must warn you..."

Lucas' legs lost all feeling, the wobbled and gave way, like a weak tree on a windy day, and he slumped back onto his hard chair, hardly hearing the rest of the warning, what had begun to feel just like a bad, and drunken, dream was now a definite reality, life would never be the same again; for anyone involved. Although he should have remained standing for the charge, they left him stranded on his hard chair, like Robinson Crusoe on his island waiting to discover Man Friday's footprints in the sand, a friend to rescue the lost.

"Do you understand everything I have told you?" He had missed, he did not know, how many words that had been spoken to him, Lucas remained quiet, stunned by what was happening to him; from his seated position he gazed blank of emotion at the three other faces that now seemed to be looming over him, he was a spectator in a slow moving film, not knowing what was expected of him next.

"He does Sergeant." Robert intervened calmly and with a certain amount of solemnity. "And I will explain it all again to him later."

"Sorry sir, as you know the prisoner has to tell me himself."

"Lucas?" asked Robert while gently shaking his arm.

"Yes, yes, I understand!" Lucas was not sure he did but answered anyway!

The process was about to get underway, everything up till that moment had been the introduction to the play, the overture to the drama and tragedy of life's opera, the tragic storyline was about to unfold.

"Would you like a few more minutes with your client sir, give him time to take this in? None of us, it appears, will be going anywhere soon." Despite the harshness of the crime there was a gentleness to the custody sergeant and his manner; he had seen it all before.

The small room descended into silence, the grey walls closing in around them, and the door closure echoed through Lucas's head his thoughts becoming fogged as if alcohol or too much caffeine had stolen its vigour.

"We have just charged him and are about to go in and hold the first interview under caution. His brief is still in there chatting with him." Harry James, explained to Kobie Kaan, the Detective Sergeant now leading the investigation.

"We searched the park and the surrounding area for a couple of hours before someone spotted a few flakes of dried blood left on the yellow foam, you know that stuff they wrap around scaffolding and that protects the drunks from the pub from walking into it; the scaffolding was surrounding the Park Tavern where the accused said he had been drinking, and we realised that the girl must have been in another park and not the Priory Park where we found him. Harry's head nodded backwards toward the cells, just in case the 'him', meaning Lucas, in question was in any doubt.

The constable was in his stride now, the initial anxiety he displayed when faced with his first proper murder, dwindling. "As we started searching the other parks in town they opened the gates in the Bishop's Garden and the gardener found the poor girl pushed under a bench, forensic teams are there now, Sir."

The experienced DS Kobie Kaan realised the young PC was looking for encouragement as he ceased his tale but remained standing in front of him. He would have to find it elsewhere, it was his job and should not need a slap on the back for doing what he was trained for.

Kobie, had that exotic, playboy, look in his eyes, dark almonds, brown and intense, and there was a dark and somewhat brooding softness in them; which meant many people just did not take him seriously – always a mistake; he was olive skinned and given his name he should have come with black, glossy hair that was tousled and straying down across his forehead, but instead he had a soft, round face that completed the dome shape of his shaved head. He was short, for a police officer, just five eight when most of his colleagues topped the six foot mark. But, there was something gentle and easy about the way Kobie Kaan looked, he was not handsome in the traditional sense but he did have a certain charisma about him. His name meant protected king, and he indeed seemed to lead a charmed life, good job, promotion on the cards and a good home life with a beautiful wife and two lovely children; Kobie always felt that he was a lucky man to have such a beautiful wife when he thought he was so average in the looks department. To his fellow officers he always seemed a little aloof and full of confidence, his intelligence seemingly a barrier between them, and yet there was nothing boastful about his manner.

In the harsh lighting of the interview room, with its grey walls and utility furniture, Lucas found his mind beginning to sink into the mud, he was a soldier in deep mental trenches. The floor beneath his feet flooded, the mud well-trodden and soft, the more he tried to move the deeper he sank. His feet were cold. He could hear the man alongside speaking and feel a tugging at his elbow. The icy, damp feeling was climbing his legs, numbing the nerves, numbing the thought process, he was waiting for the artillery fire of his situation to begin its powerful salvos, but instead there was silence. The guns were silenced, the mud was deeper, colder, his body damper, the weather greyer, the skies duller, he was shutting down; dying from the inside out and without a shot being fired. Finally he slipped down into the cold, ever deepening mud trenches of his mind...

Lucas, the real Lucas, playboy, confident, handsome, was gone!

CHAPTER 4

She had expected the large newsroom, vast like a factory floor with pounding machinery and full of important actions, to be as they were in the movies. Her work placement, while at college, had been on a small local paper which was one cramped office and lots of multi-tasking for the owner/editor/journalist and chief photographer. Gill's arrival and two months of placement had been a welcome relief to the overworked, grey-haired proprietor who curved vulture like over his keyboard as if in wait for the carcase of news. Now though, she stood in the newsroom of, aptly named, The News, overcrowded, stuffy and yet almost silent except for the workings of the news machine. The incessant hum of people working phones drifted across the factory floor of the newsroom; but mostly it was industrious heads down as her fellow scribes tapped away on quietly clacking keyboards, fingers walking out stories gleaned from a never ending supply of press releases, police calls and unseen informants and 'friends of the accused commenting'.

First task each day was to check her e-mails, press releases and information. Facts were never in short supply on a regional newspaper, except, she had been told, in August when everyone was on holiday and news seemed to be away for the month as well she was taught that she should always keep some less time-sensitive stories back in case of a shortfall – how could news be stored like food with a sell-by date and then pulled off the shelves when the news machine was hungry? She had to admit, being the runt of the news-hound litter was not as much fun as she had hoped, it was a mundane factory of cliché and few words, very little investigation and very little to be proud of at the end of each day when heading home and leaving the industrial output of the local news sweatshop. Her only escape from office drudgery was the universally hated Vox-Pops, which involved wandering the streets asking the public at large what they thought about any given subject of the day; but at least it got her out in the fresh air! The downside to the dreaded Vox-Pops were the catcalls and insults thrown by rowdy youths as she attempted to get brief quotes and soundbites, the soundbites were for the website, a journalist had to multi-task these days, but were usually unusable after some loud mouth or other had yelled obscenities into her microphone over the shoulder of the person being asked to comment on the latest local council scandal.

Gill's only escape from the frustration of sheer boredom and the tedium of her craft were her walks along the waterfront and around the marinas, she loved being at the water's edge, especially in a smart marina on Chichester Harbour where a new café had opened with views across a particularly beautiful part of the large harbour and conservation area. The Boat House, with the huge marina of leisure craft behind it, had become a haven from all that she disliked in the world and on those sunny autumnal days when she first joined the News team she loved to watch the hardier sailors take their shining craft in and out through the narrow lock gate. She would sit at an outside table, from where she could see close to the distant shore where the wind was more consistent, a flotilla of small dinghies, their white sails shining boldly against the golden leafed background, darted back and forth in an attempt to gain advantage over their opponent. Safe waters, calm this far into the harbour, rose and fell with the tides, leaving mud banks where feathered waders sifted for crustaceans with long, inquisitive beaks. Surrounding the harbour on all sides were deep woodlands of deciduous trees that changed colour with the seasons and reflected in the waters that lapped up to their exposed roots that trailed from eroded banks.

While sitting enjoying the last moments of a sunny afternoon and taking in her surroundings she had no hope of realising that she did have an instinctive nose for a story; and very soon it would smell success but it would change everything she knew, loved and hated about her life. What she considered the humdrum day to day chore of working local news was about to take a turn that would give her a ride of excitement, of fear and of change in everything she had planned to that date! The best laid plans of mice and men often go awry or just simply go to waste and the tedium of working for the local paper would be something, at times, she would long to be reacquainted with as the future unravelled out of control!

CHAPTER 5

The bass music pounded through his brain, flashing lights danced across his sensitive eyes, and Jacob Tubb cheered loudly in an effort to gain the attention of everyone around him so as they could see what a good time he was having. Hired for the exchange of a twenty pound note the lap dancer writhed and wriggled her near naked arse just inches from his lap. He noted the way the thin string of material that constituted her brief thong pulled tighter into the delicious crevice of her buttocks the more she writhed, most of it hidden as the fake tanned orbs closed in around it.

Drink, and some really good powder sniffed into his nostrils earlier in the evening, threw away any common sense he may have possessed, and he could not help himself, one hand grabbed one of the finely honed globes of her bum and squeezed hard while his free hand snaked around her lithe body and grasped a, surgically enhanced, and rigid, naked breast, he could feel the liquid sack mould firmly to his hand. With all his senses heightened by a mixture of white powder and several single malt whiskies that had collided with great effect in his system some time ago, the sense of touch took to the forefront at that moment, he registered that her nipple had hardened to his touch and now sat excited and erect in the palm of his hand. Taking this as a signal to grip the tit even harder, he did and squeezed with vicious intent causing her to screech in surprise and pain.

Sadly for Jacob; and in accordance with the dance club's strict no touching policy, the girl who just one moment before had been only too happy to tease and tempt her generous benefactor, leapt from his grasp, raised one hand to cup her bruised and injured breast while turning and raising her sharp, stiletto heeled, and fake Louboutin in one movement, before driving the rubber tipped and crystal covered dagger into his trousered and semi-erect cock.

His previous roaring of excitement became a cry of pain, which also disappeared as quickly as his lap dancing joy, as the young girl, dancing to pay her way through university, drove a clenched fist straight into his face and causing his nose to bend in a way it was not designed to do and in the process producing a down-pouring fountain of blood, that splashed hand-made shirt, furniture and floor in copious amounts of claret that picked up the flashing disco lights in gleaming body fluid. Numb in groin and face Jacob pondered that girls were not supposed to hit that hard!

As he tried to staunch the bleeding two pair of burly hands, which were joined to even burlier men in shiny dinner suits, grabbed each of Jacob's arms, forcing them backward, his face forced just inches from the ground that seemed to rush past his eyes as in a blur of pain and pouring blood he found himself lifted and dragged through parting ranks of jeering crowds before being harshly deposited without ceremony onto the hard and wet pavement outside the club. He lay there, humiliated, hurt. A passing police officer, upright and officious in his black military style uniform, looked down at Jacob, stricken, in pain, bloody and now wet, with a total lack of concern and quietly asked, "Did we ignore the no-touching rule sir?" before walking on with just a nod of recognition at the muscle bound doormen, their dark suits bulging with overworked and steroid induced physiques, in the lapels of their jackets bright red carnations.

From his position on the pavement, knees rent open in his trousers and a blood soaked body, there was not much of a retort available to Jacob, anything intelligent would have been wasted. "Fuck off!" he responded, knowing full well, that the police officer, probably nearing shift's end, was going to ignore the fallen drunk; unless he did something really stupid; Jacob had learned a long time ago when to ease back on the stupidity whenever liberty was at risk. Moving from supine to sitting Jacob felt the cold rain began to fall again and make him feel even more uncomfortable he was certain that he saw a small smirk of enjoyment on the officer's face as he took a moment to look back at the fallen reveller.

It felt as if he ached and hurt all over and Jacob did not know whether to grip his sore member, that was no longer sporting any sort of erection despite the drugs inside of him, or to hold his throbbing nose which was beginning to give him a raging headache while continuing to soak his white shirt with a rain-water diluted blood. He used the cold, dirty, water from a puddle to rinse his face and its coldness was a shock to his, already overloaded, system but it did serve to ease the dull aches that had been growing in his face. "Fucking stuck up bitch!" he muttered.

Attempting to stand, still under the piss-taking gaze of the doormen who were smiling benignly at his discomfort, was not as easy as he thought, his legs almost giving way and dumping him once more onto the hard and unforgiving pavement. With a final flourish of belligerence he flipped a 'V' sign with fingers that were blooded and grubby toward the uniformed guardians of the nightclub door and then tried to recall where he had parked his car looking around to see if it was near, before spotting it at the kerb just a few feet from where he had been left sitting bloodied and beaten on the cold, wet pavement.

As if in mockery at his own dirty, blood stained and dishevelled state the white Range Rover sat gleaming and sparkling at the kerbside, rain drops on polished paintwork glistening under the street lights. Jacob checked his pockets in search of the key. It took two circuits of jacket and trouser pockets before discovering the black fob and with all his delving into pockets the double bleep of the doors being unlocked broke the quiet of the night before the fob even left the dark confines of his jacket.

Not even considering what his wet and filthy clothes would do to the cream leather driver's seat, with its mint green piping, he shuffled his way into the warm and safe interior. Now out of the rain he grabbed a handful of tissues from a box that was sat on the console between the front seats and dabbed at his sore nose. Twisting the rear view mirror round a little he lifted his face to the reflection and examined the damage. He saw a blood-caked, blonde moustache, bushy and slightly curling at the ends, in what had become the fashionable style that he likened to the look of an Alexander Dumas musketeer and felt it enhanced his already dashing looks and gave him charm; he quite fancied himself as a sword swishing hero. Tightly curled blonde hair, that never gave him a choice in styling, had been scrunched even further with the effects of the rain and he was showing more forehead than he liked. Jacob hated that his hair was receding.

Despite the pain of his cleaning-up the bloody result of the stripper's punch he still thought that, with his powerful blue eyes, he was a handsome man, ruggedly handsome would have been his own vain description; "That dancing bitch was obviously a lesbian, don't know why they employ girls like that who tease you and then slap you down for appreciating what they had on offer." He said, muttering to his own reflection in the mirror he started the car, the big V8 purring, and pulled sharply away into the stuttering flow of late night traffic. A near miss announced by the loud blast of a car horn, followed by the sight of a small silver Audi swerving around close to the front wing of his Range Rover made Jacob realise that as he was driving stoned and drunk; maybe he should take a little more care.

A fine spray of late night rain flicked its way into the car after Jacob had cracked the window a couple of inches to ensure a flow of fresh, even if damp, air across his face to keep him alert. He pointed the nose of the Range Rover up the slip road towards the M27 and home. As he approached the link road there was an instant decision to be made, left to his crummy little weekend getaway penthouse suite overlooking a sad marina with its rowdy waterside bars in Southampton; or right, right towards Chichester and the family cottage; the cottage that his older brother

Lucas lived in, well did live in before his arrest. It was a warm and welcoming option and, more importantly, empty, apart from Annie the housekeeper, but she was only staff, the family retainer, and she would do as she was told.

Instead of dropping across to the west bound carriageway, the gleaming white vehicle ploughed on through the rain, sweeping up the curving ramp to join the road east. Jacob decided he was going to sleep easy in the family cottage tonight, it was a no-brainer really, and, who knows, it may end up as every other night if his darling half-brother got everything that was coming to him.

'I like a bit of rough sex Lucas, as much as any guy, but you took it a little far big brother.' The thought crossed his mind as if in personal conversation with his brother and his drug confused brain could not recall if he had actually said it out loud or just thought the words. Jacob was enjoying the drive toward, what he suddenly considered, his new home. "Well, you won't be using it for quite a number of years old boy; its mine now." He proclaimed out loud and smiling. The Range Rover hummed along the motorway, its broad tyres throwing rain from the deep tread, toward a place he had always despised because of the 'normality' that went with it. The neat, pretty, but spacious, English cottage with its rose beds and curving pathway that travelled from white-painted, picket gate to a creeper covered front porch, the attractive gardens dropping down to the ornamental pond and the summer house that at certain times of the day just flooded with glorious light. The once derelict, marina side, cottage where his father had built a home for his two boys, the elder always being the favourite, where he had his office, where, if his stories were to be told, he had begun the affair with Jacob's mother, the cottage where he had been conceived; by the Lord of the fucking Manor, as Jacob oft described him.

The old man had broken his mother's heart, despite promises; and she just left, never to be heard from again. The Old Man never recovering from the death of his wife, Lucas' mother meaning he would never marry or allow Jacob's mother to move into the house he had built. He had abandoned her and their son, for the love of a dead woman, to fend for themselves. Finally, and according to the old man himself, with mother apparently unable to cope, the old man had adopted his bastard son and bought him into the household. In his 25 years Jacob had never had the slightest inclination to find his birth mother, she had left him, abandoned him, signed him over to his father; his absent mother would have to live with the consequences of her actions, just as he had.

Now the story had turned full circle and the good son, and heir, was now disgraced and locked away, stuck on remand awaiting reports and assessed his mental ability and whether he was sane enough to understand what was going on with a trial, there was no escape or release; Jacob was convinced that the favoured son, Lucas, was never coming home. Now the family homestead was about to be taken over by the prodigal son; it held a certain irony for him.

A sudden outburst of laughter broke from Jacob's mouth but was just as swiftly caught as his big, white, beast of a car suddenly swung out of control across two lanes of the motorway. Narrowly avoiding ploughing in to the centre Armco barrier and narrowly missed by a speeding BMW that blew its horn long and hard in anger at the sudden diversion. Jacob straightened the car, checked his rear-view mirrors and wiped a bead of sweat from his brow, but did so forgetting his damaged nose and yelled to himself at his carelessness as the cuff of his jacket caught the sore and bruised protuberance. "That bitch is going to pay for doing that!" he cursed.

South of the cathedral city of Chichester is an area of outstanding natural beauty; the harbour shaped like the five fingers of a splayed hand. It is an area of strict conservation with wonderful watery inlets, wooded shorelines, marinas, monumental and keenly protected sand dunes and all holding a wondrous glut of stunning wildlife. It was the popular haven for sailors that gave rise to the family business of yacht brokerage, started by grandfather and then grown to great success by father but none of this beauty, or the family heritage, was given a second thought by Jacob, he preferred life in the centre of town, the noise, the bars and clubs, and, more importantly, the women. His, considered meagre, allowance just about financed a one-bedroomed semi luxury apartment alongside the Thames in a fashionable part of London; while a little bit of entrepreneurial drug dealing on the side paid for his own cocaine habit and extravagant lifestyle as well as another small apartment in Southampton, his bolt-hole, that few people knew about.

After the old man had died older brother Lucas was given the idyllic Bosham cottage and most of the old man's shares and wealth; Jacob, being the half-brother and the bastard son, in his mind had pulled the short straw and received just a healthy annual allowance and a, not inconsiderable, lump sum which had long since gone, wasted and frittered away, even though their father had only been dead for some 18 months.

But now Lucas was locked up, apparently as mad as a box of frogs, and not coming home anytime soon; the cottage was empty, apart from the sanctimonious housekeeper. However, she was not going to stop him; and Jacob was no longer going to miss out on living the country life and in a property more suited to his partying lifestyle; it had been wasted on Lucas! If Lucas was incarcerated then the yacht brokerage of Tubb and Son would have no one at the helm, so to speak, Jacob, as he drove toward his new home, recalled that one of the bigger brokerage firms had made a tidy offer for the family business, it would be his first job to contact them the next morning. Things were looking up for Jacob.

The Range Rover found its way without any further problems besides, Jacob in his arrogance had no doubt that even if he had been stopped by the police for his erratic driving he could have talked his way out of trouble; it was something he excelled at, mostly through practice, the talking his way out of trouble. A charming smile went a long way when used properly.

The White House, stood out from the half a dozen properties around it, and was suitably named with its whitewashed walls shining like fresh snow drifts on days of bright sunshine. Jacob pulled hard on the wheel to swing the Range Rover parallel with the white picket fence, the fat tyres of the Range Rover biting into the shallow layer of gravel that acted as the parking bay and spitting it out sideways, his headlights briefly lit the bright cottage walls. Grinding to an angry and crunching halt in the gravel Jacob reached across to the glove box and after some fumbling found his keys to the house. Keys that were hardly used although Lucas had always told him he was welcome to stay at the house whenever he wanted and for as long as he wanted, it was the family home after all and he had to have a set of keys. Lucas had tossed the bunch of three keys attached to a chrome fob across the kitchen to his brother and Jacob so wanted to let them just drop to the tiled floor, but, knowing he may need them one day, he reluctantly caught them while offering his brother a small, fake, smile of thanks. As the exterior security lights pinged on, making the walls even brighter, a now smiling Jacob walked the last few paces to the door and opened it with the broad grin of the victor plastered across his face. Slamming the door closed behind him, as if in a thumping fanfare to his arrival stood in the hallway his eyes taking a while to become accustomed to the dim hall lights when, from the top of the stairs, he heard Annie the housekeeper's voice call out.

"Mr Lucas, you are home, why didn't you call, I didn't know they were letting… you… go!"

The obvious excitement of her voice reduced in union with its volume when she noticed it was the bulkier form of Jacob standing in the low light of the hall with a faint shadow dark and ominous on the doorway behind him. It was not her Lucas.

"Hello Annie, make me a coffee there's a good girl, seeing as you are up now." Hands in pockets Jacob and with a jaunty stride headed for the library, where he knew Lucas still kept a stock of the old man's best single malt whiskeys.

Annie noted the blood stained shirt front but ignored it, instead she responded with a sternness she did not feel. "This is not your house to order me around Master Jacob…" Annie knew the use of Master instead of Mister always annoyed Jacob. "Mister Lucas will be home any day now and this   is   his   home   not   yours."

"It's the family home Annie, and I am one of the family, not like you, you are just staff! So if you don't like it you can always just fuck off and leave. Darling Lucas is going to be gone for some while so it's time for me to take over the ancestral home. Now either pack your bags and get out or make me a cup of coffee, sharpish!"

Annie knew she would win no battles by leaving what had been her home for the past 26 years or so, and where would she go? So, reluctantly, and with a head full of shame for not being more forceful against the interloper, she turned and moved toward the kitchen. The tough times, without Lucas around, the anguish she had been feeling, and the sheer stress of the last few weeks had now intensified and she would need all her will power and spirit to get through the days, weeks and months to follow, she said a silent prayer in the hope that the time would not drag into years.

In the shaded corner of the very manly room, it's walls lined with hardback novels mixed with tomes on yachting, sat a pair of grand, red-leather, winged armchairs, between them a dark mahogany table which held a deep glass ashtray that reflected, diamond like, the light that was thrown down by a single table lamp, its stainless steel base in the shape of a J Class yacht under full sail. Jacob dropped his backside into one seat, the rich leather squeaking as if in protest of the invasion; he, feeling more like the Lord of the Manor with every passing moment, pulled a plump, and firm, Honduran cigar from the shiny, wooden, humidor that sat on the table shelf beneath the rigid silver yacht that was sailing to nowhere. It astounded him that Lucas had changed nothing since their father's death by heart attack. Jacob could not understand that mentality, with more violence and pleasure than it should have received, he used the gold clipper to snip the end from the cigar before striking the match, holding the tall flame to the flat end and puffing on the sweet tasting tobacco, getting a real pleasure from the plume of smoke and the bright red glow that appeared six inches from his lips he would have changed it all; made it his domain. And it is what he now intended to do!

Leaning back into the chair, and crossing one leg over the other, with an air of superiority he took the cigar from his lips, blew out an impressive cloud of sweet smelling smoke, examined the glowing tip, before putting it back between his lips and puffing again as the match flame bit into the glowing ember end, causing the flame on the match to burst into a new round of activity. Annie came into the library carrying the tray of coffee, she placed it on the highly polished table, pushing the ashtray to one side as she did, before turning and walking out of the room without speaking a word. She knew her place; and closing the door to the library behind her.

With a heart as heavy as lead she climbed the stairs back to her room, hugging herself within the folds of her terry towelling dressing gown, which had long ago seen better days and was a threadbare version of its former self and now worn like an old and comfortable friend, her thoughts weighed down with foreboding. She would stay for Mr Lucas' sake, she had cared for him as a baby boy when she first joined the Tubb household as a nanny and she would not give up on him now, even if he did not recognise her during her one visit to the Remand Centre in Winchester Prison, where he now resided awaiting crucial psychiatric reports for the court; he was a dull shell compared to his former bright light of life. She would stay strong and resolute for Mr Lucas, this was his house and home and it would be again; of that she had no doubt.

If an archetypal nannie cum housekeeper had to be designed Annie would fit the bill. Quiet and unassuming she wore her shoulder length grey hair always neatly tied up in a bun, not a hair out of place. The only time her hair was allowed to fall was when she was alone in her rooms. Though she had a pretty smile, Lucas had always told her she had a smile that could charm angels, her face appeared to carry a serious and business like expression. Petite of build, Annie had the energy of a young fitness fanatic high on one of those energy drinks, although the years were catching up with her, tiredness hit her hard in recent months. She passed retirement age some years earlier, but the Old Man would never let her go and she always kept busy, she was indefatigable; although as she now climbed the stairs back to her little annexe she felt a weight and weariness she had never had to suffer before. Each stair was an effort, each breathe a strain, each step a step toward a future she did not hold in high regard.

Back down in the library Jacob, for his part, stayed wrapped up in the comfortable hug of the wing chair and puffed away, a slight sideways shuffle movement on the leather seat cushion eliciting a sound like a fart as the seat gave a sigh against his weight. His lips alternating between the kiss shape of the mouth's caress of the cigar and a smug smile as he blew out the clouds of aromatic smoke. He ignored the coffee that he had not really wanted, it had been a deliberate attempt to stamp his authority over Annie, and with that mission accomplished it sat cold and redundant, un-poured and unwanted in its cafetiere.

He knew he could be really charming when he needed to be and if he played his cards right Annie would soon be eating out of his hand. The cigar tasted good, the old man had never liked Cuban, said the flavour was too strong for his taste, always preferring Honduran and the extra sweetness that came with the smoke. It may have not been an estate or even a large house, but Jacob was now Lord of the Manor and Master of All He Surveyed! Life had just become good, and he was god in his little domain.

CHAPTER 6

Robert Berry QC looked anything but a serious barrister. In his traditional robes and wig, standing at the Bar in a court room he looked more comfortable in that role than in his street clothes. However, away from Chambers the pinstriped suit gave way, most times, for jeans and sweat shirts. The alter-ego away from the law was an accomplished musician who loved nothing better than letting his salt and pepper, perfectly trimmed, hair down and belting out some blues on his beloved red and white classic Fender Stratocaster that he had owned and played since the early sixties. His ever grey, closing in on a silvery white, goatee beard and moustache looked distinguished, giving him a studious and knowledgeable persona, almost professorial; but when in the corner of some pub bar with two other musical barristers, one a bassist and the other a drummer, he was just another struggling blues musician looking for his big break and happy singing about the woes and troubles of his life.

When he met with Lucas in that dank and dismal interview room, with its harsh and caged fluorescent tubes overhead, he kept the clothes smart but casual, in much the way he would for a golf clubhouse or a restaurant. Dressing down slightly so he could be Godfather and friend as well as legal counsel, he felt it would keep the young man at his ease, hopefully, and draw him from the torpor into which he had descended. When meeting with the Crown Prosecution Service and investigating police officers it was the intimidation that worked, the wearing of the well-cut suit, the crisp shirt and the club tie. Wear a good suit and stand up straight and everyone in the room will listen and pay heed to you.

When Robert had left Lucas late in the afternoon that first day he had insisted with the custody sergeant and the interviewing officers that before any formal questioning had begun he needed his client to be assessed as to his fitness to be detained for interview. The kindly godfather taking over from the experienced barrister for a brief moment while still not forgetting his craft.

Lucas' sudden, and dramatic, drop into whatever dark place he had fallen was now constituting a mental impairment; all in the room could see this was not a game. The troubled boy's godfather looked across the table with sadness as he explained to the round faced, serious but affable Detective Sergeant his concerns for his client's mental wellbeing; in turn the experienced officer realised this was not just a solicitor's ploy, but a genuine request, and anyway, with what looked to be a high profile case every care had to be taken to ensure fair and honest treatment of the prisoner; any lapse in procedure and there would be hell to pay.

"We will still need to get him checked for forensics sir. We will need his clothes and take some samples but I can arrange for a social worker to be here when we do that. But, you realise we do need to do that right away." Kobie Kaan was being as gentle as he dared

"He is family as well as my client Mr Kaan;" Robert let his professional side slip just a little, just for a brief moment. "So, do what needs to be done but take care of him please, I really do not think he is in a good place."

With no hint of an insult being felt. "By the book sir, by the book, you can be sure of that."

With one brief backward glance Robert glanced at his godson with worried eyes. "Try and be strong my boy, we will get you through this." He felt heavy of heart and foot as he left the interview room.

Over the next few hours, and a mere day since his story began, a silent, and almost still, Lucas was carried on a journey, over which he had no control whatsoever, toward total mental shutdown as he was stripped, his clothes exchanged for an unflattering, ill-fitting, white paper onesie, his smart shoes, one still exhibiting the scuff from the park, were exchanged for slippers; and finally hair samples were taken, DNA swabs were wiped around his mouth and indignity after indignity were inflicted upon the young man, now more of a confused boy, who had no idea what was happening or why.

It was early the next morning that Robert once again sat opposite Lucas, the young man now dressed in sweat shirt and jeans bought in by his godfather. Both men looked tired and drawn, the only difference was there was still the brightness in the QC's eyes, something that always shone like twin beacons whenever a challenge loomed; while Lucas held an expression that was usually reserved for the dead, or dying, his eyes were dull, lifeless, lacking emotion. They scanned aimlessly around the room, not registering a thing about the surroundings that were as grey as his memory. The normally well turned out, fashionable man-about-town, who always cared for his appearance looked dishevelled, disheartened and his normally shiny and dark flowing hair looked greasy and uncared for lank and hanging around an increasingly troubled and pale skinned face. Robert knew there was no point asking questions as he would get no response but he still spoke to the young man in quiet, reassuring tones, in much the same way as an adult would talk to a troubled child or pet to calm them; at times a quake of emotion caught in his voice and he coughed behind the mask of his hand to hide the fact. Robert was finding it hard to hide his caring godfather persona, even though he knew that Lucas needed him to be the strong lawyerly character that had won so many court battles.

The same custody sergeant who had been on duty the day before knocked and entered the room, his paunch arriving first as it always did. Pleasantries in the form of simple 'good mornings' were exchanged between the professional men, respect always a part of their dealings together. "We have had Mr Tubb examined sir and the doctor seems to agree with you and thinks that his poor state of mind is genuine and that he is not fit to be charged or questioned, so, unless you have any great objections, we intend to remand him on bail to a secure location where he can be further assessed. As you know sir the case will remain open and inquiries will continue but our Inspector; and the CPS think this is the best way forward."

Robert nodded his agreement; there was no other course open to him, or Lucas; and he gripped the young man's hand while knowing he had no comprehension of what had just occurred. "Has DS Kaan been informed and does he agree?" Inquired Robert. A nod and response from the portly sergeant in the affirmative seemed to end the terse conversation.

So, it was with those few sombre words Lucas Tubb had his immediate, and foreseeable, future sealed.

Broadmoor was as imposing as its reputation although on his arrival at the hospital for the criminally insane, Lucas never noticed the red brick façade with its towering walls hugging everything within the man-made barrier or the rain-grey slate roof, he missed seeing the cold, shining, coil after coil of razor wire that seemed to follow every inch of the wall ridges and roof line with its small sharp blades glinting in the sunshine, he never saw the huge double gates swing open to allow the van, with a tight squeeze, enter the strange half world of the maximum security hospital, although he did, somewhere in the small awareness that was left, notice the vehicle, with its hard bench seat in the cramped cubicle, had slowed down.

In his closed off mind, even those members of staff his unseeing eyes passed, he failed to acknowledge anyone who greeted him, processed him and then crowded round him, a burly watcher in each of the four very close corners of his world, as he was taken to his cell-like room, a burly male nurse either side, a hand on each elbow and another on each shoulder. It would be many months before he was ever in the company of just one person apart from Robert, godfather and legal counsel; but even then he knew, somewhere in the recesses of his damaged mind, that he was always being watched, always being checked. Every time he felt a tiny jolt of life returning to his thoughts, even the tiniest spark it would be subdued and kicked into submission by the drugs they would give him; once again dulling him down, always drawing a curtain across his consciousness and hiding thoughts, feelings and emotions away. The smiling, friendly Lucas, the charmer of women and one of the lads, was gone. Clear thought was something definitely not allowed or encouraged; it would be too easy to turn thought into action and cause his guardians and carers potential problems, he was not allowed to be a problem – ever again.

For Lucas life had become a simple round of simple things on a daily and hourly basis, tedium being the order of every day, wake for breakfast, exercise, but just a small amount, examination and questions, drugs to inhibit thought, desires and movement. Every time his cell door was opened it would begin with the small curtain being pulled back from the narrow window in the door, and a pair of eyes seeking his whereabouts; which always seemed pointless when he was confined to the ten by ten room, then the keys would clank the lock and echo the sound of imprisonment; a constant reminder. As the keys rattled in the lock, turned and released the deadlatch, that automatically relocked when the door is closed, and finally the gate to the grey corridors would be opened but a human barrier remained as three or four minders, nurses, would be crowding round the small portal; in this section of the hospital no staff member would ever be allowed to open a door alone, there was always a support team, numbers meant safety and control.

This meant for, what appeared to be, a fast ageing, Lucas life was one claustrophobic encounter after another. His room, small and sparsely furnished, its walls the same colour as the rest of the hospital, closed in on him the ceiling dropping by inches daily and the walls closing in toward him unseen during the hours of darkness after lights out, the door opened and a crowd of people pressing in on him, they would surround him, one on each imaginary corner again, as he was accompanied from his own small confine to another small room, all within his section of the asylum; never to wander for more than a few controlled and watched paces. Eyes and cameras watching his every movement.

Winter had arrived quickly, from that warm autumn evening when he had so callously shoved the still unnamed girl's body under the bench in the park; he barely noticed the October storms that howled around the tall walls and thrown hail over the razor-wire, missed the cold November nights that hung greyly outside the thick, towering, walls of Broadmoor. In the attractive village outside the walls life continued as normal as Christmas came and went, the festivities muted and strange within the hospital, and yet still celebrated, in such a non-festive surrounding. Santa, should he have been real, would certainly not volunteer to drop down this chimney, even if he could find his way beyond the sharp wire, the motion sensors and alarms.

January came and disappeared with its snow flurries and noisy wind that seemed to hug and scream at the walls, February with an unseasonal warmth and sunshine, then a wet March before finally the warmth of spring arrived in the exercise area – all went by mainly unnoticed, time was not a happy commodity in this place.

The mixture of therapy and the drug regime Lucas appeared to be waking from a clouded dream, finally beginning to feel and recognise the progress of day and night as well as the changes in the seasons. It was if the stopped clock of his mind had begun to tick again and show the passing of time; even if that time was slow and inhibited.

During this exile, his only visitors were Robert for an occasional update on his legal situation and Annie, but neither ever seemed happy to be there. Robert was all business, with just a show of affection on his arrival and his leaving, but when Annie left all Lucas could recall was the fact that she always complained about his brother Jacob. It had taken a few visits before he recognised what Annie was talking about and realising that his brother was now in the cottage, and worked out that Jacob was taking care of things while he was away. Lucas, ever the supporter of his younger brother, did not know the only thing Jacob was taking care of, was Jacob; and he was welcome to the cottage, it was his home too, as Lucas knew he would probably never go there again.

CHAPTER 7

Life had already changed irrevocably for Annie, with Mr Lucas locked away in that horrid hospital the White House, once a place of laughter and comfort, had become cold and unwelcoming, something it never was in the past. One night, with a restless wind blowing in from across the harbour, she had woken with a start, it had taken a while since Lucas' arrest but she had now become used to the house being quiet, it was dark outside and yet she was certain she had heard a car pull up, crunching across the loose gravel, the volume of the wind increased as the front door was opened and then allowed to bang shut seemingly sending vibrations through the whole house. Annie smiled broadly, had Mr Lucas come home? Why didn't he, or Robert, call to tell her something of the case, a call to say they would be arriving?

Ignoring her bedside clock and climbing from bed she pushed cold feet into slippers and grabbed her terry towelling dressing gown in one movement, thinking that Mr Lucas may be home she felt spry and lively despite the fact her age and the last few weeks had stolen much of her vigour.

She headed for the stairs and fixed a smile that actually made her face hurt, it had been a feature of her psyche that had received very little exercise of late; life had offered little to make her smile. A voice from downstairs caused her to hurry a little more, Mr Lucas was home, it was not a dream or over-active imagination. Reaching the top of the stairs her greeting was halted along with her downward progress; she tottered on the top step. "Mr Lucas, you are home, why didn't you call, I didn't know they were letting... you... go!" Her excited voice trailed off toward stunned silence.

Without warning she became as imprisoned as her Lucas. Master Jacob had arrived, full of his own self-importance, and ordered coffee that then went untouched and ignored, her life changed at that moment. Service in

36

the employ of Mr Lucas, and indeed his father before him, had always been a pleasant and happy experience, but now it was a life of bullying, horrid servitude at Jacob's beck and call. Annie was in the habit of keeping her thoughts, and indeed her opinions, under control, they all had their lives to live and she was in no position to judge, but Jacob and his friends, who always seemed to be changed as regularly as his cars, pushed her goodwill to its limits.

She was bullied, ordered to serve drinks and food like a common waitress, she had to ignore the barbed comments and the lewd suggestions. Annie knew she should have left when Jacob had first walked through the door, but someone had to care for Mr Lucas' left-behind life.

His house, the family home, his things were all important, but one day, and one day soon Annie kept repeating, Lucas would be exonerated and would come back to the family home. Here, more than anywhere else, was all that was dear in his life. It was more than possessions, it was more than ownership of the family home, it was the lives that were lived and enjoyed here the memories that had been made within and around the white walls, was the happiness that had become part of the bricks and mortar of the place. She still had total faith in her young charge and would be there when he came home, Mr Lucas deserved to come home to all that; and Annie would suffer whatever indignities she was forced to suffer by Jacob and his unsavoury friends to ensure that one day, one day soon, she would welcome Lucas back into the nest.

On a daily basis Jacob was feeding misery, anger and vitriol into the décor of the waterfront cottage; he was evil spawned and fuelled by the drugs, the drink and by the ill-behaved, hedonistic, lifestyle of his friends and the women they would bring back to be their slaves in debauched sex games. Girls that always seemed, even on arrival, to be in a constant state of undress and under varying forms of hyper excitement. The once peaceful cottage seemed always to be filled with high-pitched screeches of lust and it permeated into every wall, filled every room and were held in beneath the red-tiled roof and behind the white walls that seemed to be growing darker with age.

Annie knew she should have left months ago when Jacob first appeared at the foot of the stairs, but where would she go and who would take care of the home in readiness for when Lucas did return.

This was a constant battle, a war, and she was the one that had to fight it. Annie had to be the one that picked up the broken pieces from the floor, whether that be glasses, bottles, pottery or even people. Until common sense and Mr Lucas returned she was the sentinel, the guardian, it was her job, her vocation and, more importantly, her wish; she liked to think that in her 65 odd years on this earth she had overcome bigger problems than Jacob and his clan...

The door banged again Annie shuddering along with the cottage foundations. She waited at the top of the stairs, prepared for the call, no longer did she just head down to carry out duties that she had considered a privilege for all her adult life, now she waited near her rooms, confined in her upstairs domain, scared but determined to survive and outlast the bully downstairs, who now, as if on cue, bellowed her name!

"Annie, Annie..." and still louder, "ANNIE; where is that fucking woman." Jacob was drunk, or high, or both, as usual.

For her part she almost floated down the slightly curving staircase, on the outside she was serene, a debutante on her way down to the Deb's Ball to be welcomed into polite society; instead of her fading housecoat, she imagined she was in lace and petticoats, a Norman Hartnell designed gown that was only outshone by the grand chandeliers that hung over the ballroom's highly polished wooden and reflective dance floor. Instead of the obnoxious recently self-installed Master of The White House, waiting at the foot of the stairs it was the eligible son of some Duke or Earl, ready to step-out with and accompany to all the season's grand balls, parties, Royal Ascot and the polo at Cowdray Park, Ladies Day at Glorious Goodwood. Annie's imagination would keep the bully at bay. Not only that, the peaceful expression on her face was something that always annoyed Jacob and the serene expression had become part of Annie's armoury.

"What have you got to smile at you ridiculous old woman; it's about time you knew your place." Jacob angered quickly, in direct proportion to how drunk or stoned he was. The more drink or foreign substances that were in his system the quicker his temper revealed itself. Today must have been a semi-sober day, as his rage was controlled and short lived.

"I'm hungry, get me and my friends some food." She merely turned toward the kitchen and floated in her gossamer gown toward the 'downstairs' part of the house without comment.

Turning toward the kitchen from the foot of the stairs, Annie then spotted the two young girls, slim, slightly pretty with their short skirts, the hems just brushing the 'V' piece of cloth at the front of their G-strings, and cropped tops, that stopped just below pointing juvenile breasts, making them look slutty, they stood in the doorway of the library, the taller of the two black with pink hair, the shorter pink faced with cropped, greasy black hair; the opposites in appearance of the two child-like girls not lost on her.

They stood close to each other, holding hands, Annie was not sure if it was an attempt to look provocative or as a defence mechanism. She felt devilish but could not help but wonder how much they were charging for this evening's fun with Jacob. She looked back at, what she had come to think of as the wicked half-brother, and noted the lascivious intent etched into his face; he was enjoying this discomfort in her expression as the scene before her stole away the Debutant fantasy of 'his' housekeeper. A sadness crept across her face, Jacob saw the raw emotion but neither showed recognition or challenge.

"What would you like Master Jacob!" The *master* barb hit its intended target and the lust in his eyes turned to loathing, it was an almost daily battle that Annie continued to win; knowing that if he made a fuss of it in front of his guests he would lose face. She also knew that come the morning she would be made to suffer from a verbal assault; and although she would look a mixture of crestfallen and apologetic for the sake of her sanity as he ranted and raved about her insubordination, in her mind she would be thinking of him as a disturbed child with a bout of Tourette's Syndrome. He could try and beat her down but she would always be the better person and one day, one day very soon, all would be back to normal; the house would once again ring with normal laughter. The thought of a return to normality and happier times always kept her going and kept her ahead of her tormentor, she steeled herself and kept strong.

But, as Annie would discover normality or happier times were an unreachable goal.

As are we all, ignorant of the unexpected, Annie headed toward the kitchen while Jacob, with a huge, but very false laugh, walked into the library, the two girls turned tail and went in through the double oak doors with him. He wrapped an arm round the slim waist of each girl, they each in turn, knowing their job well despite their tender years, placed and arm around his waist, holding hands behind his back, and begun to nuzzle into his neck, their tongues tracing wet lines down his skin.

As they approached the brown, antique leathered couch, its skin well-worn and cracked, and which faced the huge mahogany desk, Jacob swung the black girl around to his chest and she wrapped her long slender legs around his waist, wrapped both arms around his neck and kissed him hard, pushing her tongue deep into his mouth and pulling his head even tighter onto her mouth. The dark haired girl watched without moving away from the tight grasp of her benefactor, then, as if in a choreographed dance scene, dropped to her knees and began to release his leather belt and unzip his trousers. Jacob, grabbing the kissing girl by the hair pulled her lips away from his face, he drew back to take a breath and was rewarded by having his bottom lip bitten, hard, hard enough to draw blood, once released he drew back his head and launched an insult, "You black bitch!" said with venom and lustful enjoyment. But she knew her role in the game they were playing and ordered him to just suck it up and kiss her again, he smiled and they mashed their lips together once again at the same time as his engorged cock was released from the confines of his trousers to be sucked and bitten my the third willing member of this wicked dance.

That was how they fell onto the antique and cold leather of the Chesterfield, the three a tangled mass of legs, arms, mouths and lust; this was how Annie discovered them as she walked into the room with a tray of neatly cut sandwiches and small, fancy cakes. Annie was serving tea for the vicar in a room that reeked of the aromas of sex. High tea being served to guests who were high on drugs, life and evil. She loathed the sight of the ménage-a-trois, that she was sure was being performed as much for her displeasure as it was for Jacob's warped pleasure but she, once again, failed to let it register in her expression which she knew would anger him. She was sorry that the two girls would be made to suffer but they had made their own bed, so to speak, and now must lie in it, they chose this life, or like her it chose them, and there was little she could do about that. Stoic, straight faced, calm and strong, she placed the tray on the green leather top of the desk, looked Jacob square in the eye and proved to be the stronger person.

Battle of wills won and without a word she turned away and gently closed the large duo of oak doors to, what was Mr Lucas' favourite room of the house, and as she did she knew that Jacob had either failed to notice, or chose to ignore, the tears that now rolled down her cheeks, Annie hoped it was the former as she heard another peel of lustful laughter echo around the ground floor of the house. Head hung low, an ache deep in her very soul and a mind that could see no more happiness in the future she silently climbed the stair back to the sanctuary of her attic rooms, each step heavier and more tiring than the last.

CHAPTER 8

Time was dragging for everyone, except maybe Jacob, and with him time meant nothing apart from where his next thrill, his next high and his next extreme sexual encounter would be coming from. Throughout winter months of short days, dark evenings and grey drizzly weather that seemed, in various guises, to echo the lives of Lucas, Gill and Annie; each stuck with daily routine that did not live up to the expectation of their youth. An expectation that is at some time enjoyed by everyone, dreams of freedom, happiness, laughter, love and success. With adulthood comes a huge reality check as plans seldom go as, well, planned; what was left now was the daily grind of just getting through the daylight hours without too much trauma and sadness. Seasonally adjusted disorder some call it, but it is just the greyness that descends on us all during grey, dank days when here is nothing to do except cogitate on life's foibles.

But, with spring comes new life, new hope, and new opportunities, as green leaf buds burst open into a lush new foliage that will change the landscape, so hopes and dreams explode with new beginnings. For two lives it would indeed be a new beginning but for one, to be ended before any master-plan had reached its original conclusion, spring would be short lived; and as the overweight but energetic, rock-troubadour, Meatloaf sang 'two out of three ain't bad!'

From his ten by ten world where the ceiling was the main focus of attention Lucas lay on his narrow, firm, bed and noticed the brief flash of a light from the corridor as one of the staff drew back the small door curtain, that flash, like a brief glimpse of dull lightening, was followed by a wrap on the metal door, "Can you stay on your bed please Lucas, we are coming in." Where was he going to go in ten by ten? Lucas, pulling his eyes away from the dream world of his ceiling, sat up but remained as ordered, it was spoken as a request but past infringements ignoring such requests always brought quick retribution where even the smallest of punishments brought about an even starker existence and so he now did as he was asked, he had been acclimatised to the regime. A key scraped its metallic way into the slot, turned in the lock with a heavy clunk that did nothing to relieve the feeling of imprisonment; even though Broadmoor, as they constantly reminded him, was a hospital and not one of HM prisons.

The door opened inward, so foreboding its motion that a creak such as heard in horror movies would accompany the swing forward into the room, and, once open, it was a second or two before the casually dressed nurse stepped into his room, his eyes not leaving Lucas propped up on his bed. Two other nurses took most of the light from the corridor as they blocked the doorway, the regular safety measure. All three burly men, toned and muscular biceps exposed by short sleeve shirts, watched him intently. The strength in numbers was supposed to be imposing and it almost forced Lucas to pull back and cower against the hard wooden headboard of his single cot bed, but a small remnant of strong willpower, plus the addition of regular doses of mind-sapping drugs, kept him still.

"Good morning Luke…"

"My name is Lucas, not Luke." There was no threat or tone of arrogance in his response, just simple statement of fact delivered in a cold manner; and seemingly daily since his arrival, some of the young man's former strength of independent mind had begun to return, despite the drugs and the confined lifestyle, he was beginning to remember who he once was. Although he was still a young man in years, 28, or 29 – maybe, if he recalled correctly, and simple memories of his age even that was now in doubt; he knew he looked older, skin had taken on a pallor and texture somewhere between grey and yellowing old parchment, dry and lifeless, like his eyes where there was no spark of the former man who once inhabited this body. His cheeks were puffy, the finely chiselled chin and angular cheek bones long since gone; Lucas had put on weight; one of the side effects of the cocktail of drugs fed him three times a day were hunger pangs, stomach aching pangs, coupled with an almost constant desire for sweets and chocolates, which, coincidently, was all that was on sale in the hospital shop .and where he was now allowed to attend each morning and spend the meagre pocket money he earned in the hospital's workshops. His hair, which was once slightly wavy, thick and shiny, and always cut with skill by his regular hairdresser, was now lank, long, hacked whenever cut by the hospital visiting barber, and like everything else about this place it just hung around lifeless and without a purpose for being smarter or neater as nobody would notice or comment.

"Sorry Lucas, have it your way, I was just trying to be friendly." Finally using his given name and Lucas smiled at his captor. The response from the nurse was tired, a reaction weary of confronting people he was just trying to help, there was no apology in the voice but it was a brief retreat, staff knew it was not best to antagonise but to be pliant while still being authoritative. The one overriding rule for the well trained, and professional, personnel was that their charges had a different interpretation of reality to the rest of the world, and that awareness often kept them safe from assault, verbal or otherwise.

The voice, pointed at Lucas, held a slight eastern European accent, Lucas wondered if it was Polish or Romanian, but then shrugged the thought away as, like everything else in here, it mattered little to him. The lead nurse in the room was a short man, just a little over five foot five, but he was stocky and powerful in stature, feet planted firmly on the floor but slightly on the balls of his feet as if expecting to react quickly, his shaven, almost hairless, head was separated into two halves by a very spiky, short and thickly gelled Mohican cut that reminded Lucas of a balding porcupine, silly to look at but still a little dangerous if approached in the wrong manner muscular arms, each carrying a colourful collection of artistic tattoos, he was not somebody you would take on willingly in a physical confrontation, plus he always had two others with him. Lucas was on the 'three persons' rule, his cell was never opened by just one staff member, nor would a single staff member approach him.

From his arrival through the daunting 150 year-old gate, over which stood the old, weather-worn clock made by Dent of London, the white lettering of the name and place still clearly legible, but the time stopped and long ago became still, It was a reflection of life the other side of the clock, where time itself stood still and not just the recorders of it. Lucas had been watched by security camera and attentive staff for every minute of every day, even when doing simple craft work, which would be sold to help toward his 80p an hour, he, as with every other patient, was watched closely and every moment reported on. Over the previous nine months of incarceration the staff of the secure wing had logged reports of his every movement but now he was heading for the Assertive Rehab Ward where there was just a little more freedom and the slightest hint of independence; but still under that constant and ever-watchful electronic eye.

He would still be monitored just as closely, every movement, shuffle of feet and blink of eye, he would still have the daily sessions of Psychological Therapy but he could mingle, even maybe make a friend and indulge in something he had missed more than anything, social interaction and banter! Lucas longed for the idle chatter of friend with friend, the inconsequential moan and groan about the things that made everyday life a little more bearable; what was life without a moan about poor service, bad Government and the prices of things. Even the freedom to do that was stripped within the strict walls of Broadmoor, every one of the million or so bricks that made up the towering fortress was another brick in the wall of confinement, not that moaning about anything would be productive within this Victorian edifice standing guarded and isolated behind the endless, bright loops of razor wire.

They stood to one side, guarded and ready, and the three nurses led Lucas from his room and through the corridors, the two silent assistants had a hand, gently and yet firmly, on each elbow, steering him, bringing him to a halt as key after key turned in innumerable locks and opened the procession of door after door, like a barge through various lock gates of a canal progress was slow. For their part the nurses always treated their patients, with the utmost care and respect. A respect borne out of the fact that at any moment, no matter how compliant or calm they seemed, an inpatient could turn and show the vicious, sudden and uncontrollable violence toward those around them, or even themselves , that they had exhibited and perpetrated before they were ordered to be detained in this place.

A man way out of his depth amongst the depravity and violence that haunted these halls Lucas had always been calm, from the day he arrived last autumn, hence why he was now being moved to a more open area where he would be able to join a small general population of fellow-patients for walks, talks and table tennis; but still the nurses were sensibly wary knowing full well from experience that a peaceful nature could turn to violence without a hint of its sudden and destructive arrival.

The main thrust of the continual and private conversation within Lucas' mind was, and always had been since that morning in the park, *'did I do it?'*

If truth be known, and that was a difficult concept in this place, the truth, he thought himself incapable of harming someone. Could never recall attacking the girl, his only memory of the events, and even that snippet had taken a while to rear its ugly head, was of pushing the young girl with the thin, bare legs, so white, pale and so slender, under the bench, in much the same way as picnickers in the park would have dealt with the detritus of their lunch should they be too lazy to take rubbish to the bin. That action, and its consequences, shocked the sensibilities of Lucas so much that it seemed only reasonable to assume that if he detested himself so much for that one moment of callous behaviour, how could have been so cold as to kill the unnamed girl. It was something to hold on to, to keep part of his brain within the realms of sanity!

Lucas had not seen many dead bodies, why would he have? He remembered well, the image clear as day, standing alongside his father's bed, holding the old man's bony and cold hand, while he breathed his last breath and that haunting sound as it rattled from his throat.

As for stranger's corpses they had thankfully always remained strangers;

out of sight out of mind. Despite lucid moments of thought on the matter that were so rare, Lucas had always assumed he was the cause of the battered girl's violent death, what other answer could there be, he was there, she was bent and broken on the grass at his feet and he was trying to hide his shameful act before heading to the pub. The coldness of his act disgusted him almost as much as the fact that it had been of his doing. His biggest recollection, to his shame, the scuff on the toe of his otherwise immaculate brogues.

Robert Berry, as barrister and not godfather, had fought hard to avoid the case ever going to trial and Lucas was forever grateful that the family name had been in the eye of the media for only a short while because of it, the press and the public had swiftly moved on to a new object of hate and anger, achieving boredom with the killing as other subjects and events took over their collective concerns. He, like his victim, now were interred, buried and forgotten, away from the intense gaze of adverse publicity. Throughout the months of incarceration whenever he was alone, Lucas would wonder what his father may have said, had he still been alive, about his actions and his 'illness', he could hear him now in his kindly and patient voice telling Lucas to 'pull himself together', it was not that easy for a broken mind. It had taken the few months of intensive and revealing therapy sessions but Lucas did now believe he was ill rather than mad or bad.

All these thoughts and more passed through his mind as the small entourage moved through the echoing hallways. The procession of carers and cared-for continued along one beige corridor after another, before the lead nurse, his muscular and colourful arms bulging in competition with his tight shirt sleeves, turned one last key in one last lock,

"Here we are Lucas, a more pleasant room for you, you have a view of some trees, it will be nice, the leaf buds are just about bursting open, it's spring outside now." The Mohican had turned from nurse and guard to tour guide. "At least you will not be looking at just your cream walls now," it was amazing how institutional beige had suddenly turned to a more acceptable 'cream, "and, don't worry about your belongings, we will move your personal things over later;"

It was like an hotel upgrade, efficient and almost apologetic for disturbing his stay, Lucas almost reached into his pocket for a small tip for the porter. Back in the real world of Broadmoor, the burly nurse stood to one side of the window that offered a view of tatty gardens and a clean, pale blue sky, letting the light of a spring sun pour into the room through the grill of thick bars on the window, to point out the new view, those thick white painted bars, peeling and showing hints of rust at the ends as they disappeared into the wall, that blocked out at least half of the light, had become virtually invisible.

Lucas was also aware that none of the nurses ever turned their backs on their patients. "You might even see the occasional squirrel or bird, but they don't seem to like being behind these walls either." He added with a laconic tone.

Then without ceremony the three left him there, the cell door unmanned and unlocked stood open and useless. His normal stoic, upright stance took a sudden, scaring, flush of fear that shivered through Lucas. He took on board the fact that the door remained open, which was a strange feeling, frightening, he felt like a child frightened of the dark and the Boogie Man that was coming to get it.

Had they forgotten to close and lock the door, were they trying to trick him, leave the door open and see what he would do? But even stranger was that for the next hour there was an even greater fear and that was the fear for Lucas as he tried, in vain, to face even walking over to the door, either to pass through it with, relative, freedom, or to close the portal and feel safe once again from the outside world.

Lucas tried to build up the courage to leave his cell-like room and just as he gained the strength to take that one step closer to the corridor, to pass through the open portal and reach into the relative freedom that stood the other side of his wall. Just as he was about to launch himself into that adventure, a figure, skinny but ramrod straight, dressed in neatly pressed jeans and T-shirt, stood before him. It was a single human being, no keys attached to his belt, no fellow hangers-on and no safety in numbers; it was just one person, come to visit! The visitor stood with feet shoulder width apart, his hands clasped behind his back as if some Sergeant Major had just ordered him to stand at ease! Lucas examined the interloper, took his gaze up from the slippered feet, the rounded nail of a big toe pointing through a hole in the right slipper, to the thrusting chest and on to the soft face where a hooked nose seemed harsh and strangely out of place, the blue eyes burned with intensity from beneath a sparse fringe of fine hair. "Welcome old chap, welcome to the comparative freedom of the Assertive Rehabilitation Ward;" The voice was clipped and sounded to Lucas as if it were quite well educated. "Colonel Drayton-Farlington," he snapped of a sharp salute, "at your service, and to whom might I have the pleasure of speaking?"

Lucas, felt a smile cross his face, just a small one, but it was the first one he had felt in many months, it felt like a warm bath on a cold winter's day as the bonhomie of the introduction washed over his entire body.

"Lucas Tubb, Colonel... Lucas Tubb..." It was also the first time he had heard his name said in a tone other than officious or angry for some time. It felt good. He offered his hand and it was shaken, the skin to skin contact and the warmth of friendship, even in that place, meant a great deal. Robert was the last person able to offer the warmth of human kindness and contact, small freedoms to an imprisoned soul mean such a great deal when the incarcerated is reacquainted with them.

Everyone on this planet has a trouble of some kind or other, most of them trivial but always full of importance for the trouble's owner. In another world just fifty miles or so away from Broadmoor, a disillusioned and thoughtful Gill Harmon scooped the last semblances of foam cappuccino from the bottom of the cup with her teaspoon, there were still traces of the chocolate powder that had been sprinkled onto the frothy cap, and she put the illicit beverage, too much caffeine and too many calories, remnant into her mouth for one last tiny hit of caffeine and flavour. Looking around the Boat House Café at the other customers she noted one elderly man, hair long and tied into a skinny ponytail, long at the back but balding across his pate, eyes intent on his task, coffee going cold on the table before him, as he pounded away at his laptop. Eyes glaring at the screen and a scowl of concentration on his face, his fingers moved quickly, occasionally taking short break so his brain could catch up with the story line on screen, before once again sprinting across the black keys, a well-rehearsed dance of fingers. Cafes, it seemed, the perfect place to find the next great writer, a new J.K. Rowling, so maybe instead of spending days writing magistrates cases, obituaries and tales of missing pets Gill, just for a moment considered that she should be sat there writing the best-selling novel that it is said we all have in us.

Through the café's large picture windows that gazed out toward to calm harbour waters where the sun was now shining, stealing away the last of winter's chills Gill could see an escape from her maudlin thoughts, leaving the drained cup on the table, alongside her newspaper with its completed crossword, she walked outside and breathed in the salty air that the fresh breeze was bringing in off the waters of Chichester Harbour. Bright yellow daffodils, scattered with organised randomness on patches of freshly mown grass, heralded a new and brighter season, a sharp blue sky, cloudless, brightened the almost blindingly white sails as they were hoisted by a yacht that exited the lock gate with purpose, all that glisters is not gold and the chrome of the pulpit on the bow was glittering brightly under the glare of the sun and pointing the way to an early season cruise. Behind Gill, as she walked, a seemingly endless row after row of redundant leisure craft tied by a selection of, depending on the age of the craft they held, hemp or nylon umbilical cords connecting them to the fingers of pontoons that struck out into the marina in uniform rows. Without exception they were all expensively built and expensively bought for one purpose and one purpose only and yet, tethered as they were like racehorses left at the gate, they seemed to be denied even that one task, they sat gleaming and abandoned;

loved yet ignored. Gill felt much the same way, bright, keen to rush through the waters of life, driven on by the elements, and yet denied the thing she had been put here for, stopped by unseen tethers holding her still with all her vast potential fettered and unleashed.

She mentally shrugged her shoulders. "And, of course, you are never going to find your big scoop that will change your career here in this marina Gill Harmon!" She was prone to mumbling quiet admonishments to herself while she leant on the rail that stopped onlookers falling into the dark grey marina waters sitting inert a few feet below, with fingertips she absentmindedly scooped a stray lock of hair behind her left ear, noticing a black smudge on her fingers where the ink had rubbed from the newspaper as she worked the daily crossword. It was her favourite spot in the marina as she could watch the comings and goings of both people and craft through and over the lock gate while enjoying the spring sunshine. On bad days she had even stood here in the rain gazing out, deep in thought, while the lockkeeper stood little-employed and sipping freshly brewed tea in the gatehouse above her.

Somewhere out there was the story or event that would change things, that one exciting scoop that she would find, the reporter's dream was becoming an obsession, she had even thought of a change of careers while standing there and often wondered how one become a lockkeeper. But, she was a writer, a journalist and like all in her profession she craved that big story, or at least a small, well written and reported story that would get her noticed. Every time there was a chatter of voices behind her, or from people walking near her, she would listen carefully, intent on picking up the odd word of sedition or criminal intent; the best she had heard so far was when two elderly ladies had been discussing one of their grandsons and his walking holiday in Scotland. 'Poor lad,' The old lady had intoned with a compulsory 'tut', 'it was not till he finished his walking holiday and took his boots off that he realised the skin graft on his foot hadn't taken!' Gill had imagined all sorts of ills and results for the poor lad's foot!

She continued to stare, almost blindly, across at all the craft that sat waiting for someone, anyone, to step aboard and bring them to life; "Like you are ever likely to see Mr Big the master criminal step aboard his luxury yacht, and signal for you to come over and interview him, or catch him in nefarious doings with his underlings…" She again muttered in low tones of self-loathing.

"Sorry did you say something?" Gill, startled, had failed to notice the young, good looking (she thought), man waiting to cross the lock gates once they had closed. He had an engaging smile, so much so that she had immediately forgotten her doldrums.

"No, no, sorry," she stumbled. "I have this horrible habit of talking to myself when I am feeling down; bad habit, I know."

"How could you feel down on a wonderful day like this," he responded waving his arm in all directions as if pointing out the obvious.

Gill felt like she was about to be hit upon, half hoped really, enjoying the distraction, she waited for an invitation for coffee. The gates thumped closed, the young man smiled and then walked on, calling over his shoulder, "Dog, Dog, come on boy." And a little terrier came scampering after him. The human of the pair looked over his shoulder at Gill, "Just don't start arguing with yourself or the men in white coats may come to take you away!" It was said in a condescending manner, and Gill poked her tongue out at the back of the man and his dog.

"Fuck off!" Gill barely uttered before turning and walking back to her car, her desire for continuing a springtime waterside walk, or an intimate conversation over coffee, now firmly dunked into the cold water that surrounded her. Like every other day off she had taken recently this was turning out to be a lonely, depressing, dead loss.

The worlds of the three main players on this stage were growing ever closer as just around the corner at another of the harbour's inlets and in the White Cottage, with its neat hedgerows surrounding the garden which lead down to the water's edge, Annie was finding it increasingly hard to keep her tongue still and her thoughts silent as Jacob once again treated her like his personal slave.

"Annie, ANNIE…" he shouted down the stairs. "Rustle us up some breakfast there's a good girl, need enough for two…" A moment's silence, a respite, the housekeeper not knowing if the shouted orders had ended or stopped for a brief thought; it was the latter. "Mind you we will need enough for four with all the shagging we did last night." Jacob's laughter was loud, raucous, but the shrieking cackle of his latest bleach-blonde and surgically enhanced companion overshadowed it and filled the once so peaceful waterside house with harsh sounds like the squeal of chalk on a blackboard.

Annie knew she should have vacated the house when Jacob first arrived and announced his intention to stay, she had enough savings to see her comfortable through the rest of her life, the boy's father had seen to that very generously in his will, but deep in her heart she knew that one day Lucas would be back, back in his rightful place in the family home. Until then she felt it was her duty to try, as best she could, to protect his home, well it was also her home and had been for a little over a quarter of a century.

The last few months, through the dank winter, had dragged with each day seeming like a lifetime, she was suffering her own form of incarceration, first there was the fear of what was happening to Mr Lucas, and then her own, very real, fear of Jacob and what he was capable of. She had always thought if anyone should be locked away it was the animal upstairs toying with his latest tart. These almost, never-ending, thoughts crowding in on her mind as she slipped four pieces of wholemeal bread into the gleaming chrome toaster, and then cracked four eggs into a bowl, mixing them vigorously with a little milk and black pepper, her anger dissipated slightly by the fury of the hand balloon whisk as she used it to whip the ingredients together. It was about the only thing the two boys, men now, had in common, their love of eggs scrambled rather than any other way. The rich aroma of coffee, one of those homely smells that always offers comfort, drifted across the kitchen as the filter machine began its morning task accompanied by a relaxed burbling and bubbling, and, as a distraction, Annie thought back to the first time she had walked through the rickety gate and down the path to the front door; it was an oft recurring thought that kept her spirits high.

Her finger had been mere inches from the doorbell when it was flung open before she could operate the ringing. Jonathan Tubb stood a tall and imposing figure of a man and yet the expression on his face, a serious face with a firm chin and heavy nose, his eyes sparkled though as if full of life and never likely to let go, was anything but, he looked panicked, distraught and quite frankly like a man who was drowning.

"Are you Annie?" The young girl on the doorstep, just in her early twenties and still not used to all the strange ways of the world, stuttered an affirmative answer to the handsome man before her, then mentally kicked herself for her nervousness.

"Yes sir, and you must be Commander Tubb…"

"Yes, and its Jonathan, Jonathan Tubb; forget the Commander bit, been away from the Navy for a while now! A pleasure." His hand shot forward for a brief but polite handshake. "Right when can you start, right away I hope!" He turned and walked back into the house from where Annie could hear the impatient screams of a young boy who possessed a fine set of lungs. She stood a brief moment and then realised he had intended she should follow; nervously crossing the threshold the thought crossed her mind that although this was the strangest of interviews, it was, by all accounts, going well so far.

Entering the attractive and ship-shape house she noted off to the right of the hallway was a wonderful room full of leather bound books, row after row of them, shining reds and browns like autumn leaves lined regimentally along deep brown and highly polished forest of book shelves, three walls full of them breaking only for a small bay window with a plump cushioned window seat, and a fourth wall which had a stunning brick fireplace over which hung a portrait of a beautiful woman dressed in a black cocktail dress; a dress that was only beaten for elegance by the even deeper, richer head of black flowing hair that tumbled down over a long neck and onto porcelain -white naked shoulders, both elegant and stunning.

As she stood, not knowing what to do next, on the uneven floor of the hallway she could see into, what she would later learn, was the library and in the middle of the room a huge desk, ornate, topped with green leather and suitable for a retired naval officer behind the desk a swivel captain's chair stood full of importance and waiting for its host. Either side of the fireplace sat a matching pair of red leathered wing chairs, deep, comfortable, manly, the seats worn into an antique patterned, bum shaped, scoop and the coffee table between them holding a glass topped humidor filled with the dark tobacco tubes of cigars. It was from one of these chairs that the wailing noise was emanating. As seen from over the curving arm of the chair a fine head of wavy black hair on a young boy, aged around four or five, matched him to the woman in the painting, she had to be the boy's mother, he her son.

The main difference was that while her face showed a calm serenity, a stunning beauty; the younger, male version showed childish rage, recalcitrance and, most of all stubbornness, something that Annie also recognised in his father; neither male was about to give in, father stood in front of son, one hand on a hip, the other brushing back thinning strands of grey hair, he stood feet slightly apart and he could have been speaking commands to a ship's company so harsh was his bark.

"Lucas, this screaming is getting us nowhere. We have a visitor and you are embarrassing the pair of us." The stern tone of one man who had commanded hundreds of hardened men under his command was being belittled by one four foot tall, immovable, individual. Annie felt the two may have been differing sizes but they were both from the same obstinate pod!

Jonathan turned to the nervous girl loitering in the doorway to the library. "There is your interview, Annie was it?" He questioned. "The spawn of the devil in that chair is my son, get him to stop and give me a breather and the job's yours. All terms and conditions for your employ already agreed without question." There was resignation and even a hint of begging in the tone. "To be honest I don't know what to do with him; he has already got through," a moment's calculation. "Must be a dozen or so nannies in his five tender years; and I thought these were supposed to be the best years!"

The father looked up to the picture over the fireplace and just for a moment the flare of light that Annie had noticed in his eyes disappeared.

"That's his mother up there," his gaze remaining on the face in the portrait and Annie could read the sadness in his eyes. "Laura had cancer but held on long enough to give birth to our son. That's Lucas, her beautiful legacy, the young man causing such a rumpus as he usually is so wont to do. He is so like his mother in every way, except for the tantrums, and I have no idea what to do with him, I suppose adoption is always an option, me or him. I don't care which" It was a hopeful face turned from portrait to Lucas and then to Annie. "Have you experience with young children? Please say yes!"

"Yes Sir, I was one myself once." A smile cracked across her young face and she hoped that the Commander had a sense of humour.

"So was I once but that was probably too long ago!" His smile matched hers "So what do we do, sell him to the gypsies, although what they have done to deserve him I shall never know, abandon him by the side of the road, or offer him up for the aforementioned adoption?" Annie liked the way the commander spoke, and feeling he was only half joking as he stood in front of the still yelling boy, feet still apart, now both hands on both hips as if he was still commanding a rolling ship!

"Well let's start by ignoring him, Sir!"

"Stop with the 'Sir' lark please, Annie" She nodded. "Its Jonathan, or Mr Jonathan if it makes you feel more comfortable, and this is young Master Lucas, master because I am certain he is already master of this house!"

"A ship full of men under your command and not one of them would dare to cross you no doubt, and then this mutinous young man has you at a loss as to what to do. Have you tried keel hauling?"

Finally a broad smile brightened the exhausted face. "I think you and I, and this little man, are going to get on just fine Annie."

"Well; let us leave him to his tantrum and head for the kitchen where I will make us tea and we can discuss terms." Annie said in a take-charge tone that she never really felt.

The two of them headed for the kitchen, and no sooner had they left the library via its heavy dark oak doors, than the pitch and the tone of the tantrum changed, Annie grinned but did not let Mr Jonathan see the small smile of victory. It had not taken long for the kettle to boil and the tea leaves to infuse their flavour in the pot, before a small face appeared in the kitchen doorway, his father started to turn to greet the boy but the fierce look from Annie stopped him.

"Do we have biscuits Mr Jonathan?" The title seemed to roll from Annie's tongue and it would stay that way for the next twenty odd years. He pointed to the cupboard above the kettle, Annie opened it and pulled out a half empty packet of Digestives, perfect for dunking. She tipped a few onto a plate and put them between the adult's cups on the refectory table; two more were placed on another plate and they in turn were placed next to a glass of ice cold milk that was already on the table, strategically placed in front of a stool.

Ignoring the young boy they began to sip their tea, dunk their biscuits and discuss Annie's salary and duties. Master Lucas for his turn, climbed up onto the stool and placed his elbows on the table, siting directly opposite the fascinating new Nanny, and in a copycat move dunked his Digestive into his milk, leaving it just long enough to go soggy but not too long for it to break and fall into his drink; already an expert.

"Elbows off the table young man, manners at all times please." Softly said the command was swiftly carried out as the young boy removed his elbows picked up his glass and sipped his milk.

Annie had fitted into the small family and their way of life from that moment, Lucas adored her and Mr Jonathan thanked all that was holy for her arrival. From that day, until the unfolding of current events it had, in general been a good life in the White House, and Annie, until now had known much happiness.

Her facial features now stern, her smile no longer in use, and a hardened heart, Annie laid the toast onto two plates alongside the crispy bacon that was already laying dark and reddish-brown against the crisp whiteness of the plate, and began with absence of thought to scoop the scrambled eggs into neat mounds. A sharp, painful, slap on her 'bony arse' as Mr Jacob referred to it; stole away the precious reverie and fond remnants of her arrival at The White House.

"That smells just right Old Girl." Jacob enthused, as his skinny companion sat at the table and the brief kimono she was wearing gaped open showing a glimpse of one small and pointed breast, the shiny bar of a nipple piercing catching the light from the overhead spots. "She knows how to cook a good breakfast does Annie; no wonder Luke kept her around for so long. That bacon better be crispy as I like it Annie old girl!" His laugh was forced and harsh, uncouth just like the man who emitted the sound that Annie had come to hate and dread. In front of his *'guest'* he performed like the loved master of the house but Annie knew the respite from his anger was only put on hold; she never could understand what one man had so much to be angry about.

CHAPTER 9

For an increasingly disassociated Lucas, one day continued on where the
last had left off, little change in everyday happenings within the walls of
Broadmoor, the norm of a controlled lifestyle and timetable within the
demands of a strict regime and institution, always being a safe option for all
concerned. The same dark grey, steel doors separated Lucas from each
room, each corridor and each concourse and he knew there were a dozen
or more such seemingly impenetrable doors between him and the outside
world, he was interred, almost buried but without the funeral where friends
could bid farewell over a sad tear or two, his real and previous life a world
away from the constant watching, and a universe away from, what most
would consider, a normality.

Although, in his newer, slightly freer confines, as one day bled into the
next he was becoming more aware of the surroundings, while the flip side
of the coin was that he was becoming less aware of what a normal life was,
he was forgetting more of his past. Things he previously had taken for
granted; TV where he could pick any one of a hundred channels or more; a
life where he could lay in bed at weekends and stroke the soft skin of a
woman's body next to him. Choosing whether to eat in or pop out to a
local bistro, a pint or a scotch with friends, oh, how he could down a pint
of foaming black Guinness right now or sip on one of his father's glorious
single malts, step by step he seemed to be forgetting the world that he
shared with Annie and everyone, even his annoying brother. A lost world
like lost loves where day by day their faces took on the guise of stranger and
faded in the memory.

The world of Lucas Tubb, before he so callously pushed that young
girl's scrawny body, with her white, thin legs sticking out from her short
dark skirt, under the park bench was receding from his memory, the faces
once so familiar fading from view; he realised that despite it being several

months on since that day, he could not recall her name, the unnamed girl. He puzzled, trying to remember; had anyone even mentioned her name; whenever anyone spoke of her, she was just referred to as the girl in the park, or the girl under the bench; or, even worse especially during the lengthy therapy sessions, the girl he had beaten to death.

He needed to recognise his crime and show regret for his actions, redemption could only come with acceptance. But, how can you accept something you cannot recall!

It not only saddened him when he thought of her in those terms, her neck at an awkward angle, her face torn and bloody, dank hair sticking to her forehead, but it also frightened him. It scared him to think that he was capable of such a thing, of such terminal violence, of beating a young girl to death, he could not recall hurting her, or, if it came to it, even seeing her alive and talking to her; but he was there in the Bishop's Garden with her among the dying flowers of autumn, and he did push her broken and lifeless body beneath the bench, that hard unforgiving wooden bench.

The bench where previously old men had sat reading their papers, school children had sat texting their friend just a foot away from them on the same bench, or lovers had sat holding hands and kissing, while the people of Chichester strolled past enjoying days of sunshine.

Lucas was burying himself, or just being buried by circumstance, away in a world of shadowed memories, half believed dreams of how life once was, even the brightest of thoughts of moments past painted in a layer of grey, he could not recall how long it had been since he had read a newspaper – they were folded and put down when he was front page news and could not take seeing his image and name linked with the death of a young girl.

When had he last texted a friend or held the hands of a kissed and cared for lover; with each thought of a life torn away his heart broke a little more. His only strong memory was of the painting over the fireplace in the library; his mother tall, elegant, beautiful and Lucas was sorry he had shamed her and glad she had not been alive to witness his downfall.

Behind the walls they spoke of time, there was little else to discuss apart from which chocolate bars to buy today; they said there was time, and then there was Broadmoor Time, the latter dragged day into day, night bringing no respite to the tedium, with little ever changing. Imagine waking every morning with your greatest hope and wish for the entire day to just be the chance to sleep again, to bury your head under the thin quilt, to sleep, aided by drugs, through the bad dreams until the next morning. This was the life of Lucas, and his fellow patients.

Now, he was out of the isolation wards where had been confined following his arrival, and into, what could best be described as general population. A place where he could mingle with others that were also deemed not to be so dangerous to those around him, or indeed themselves.

Many were in the confines of Broadmoor because of their self-harming, the scars and wounds on their arms and necks testament to their personal demons and troubles; others were there, just like him, for harming the innocents around them.

For the first time in, what felt like another lifetime, his was now a life of short scenes of sequences and cameo appearances in his own story, Lucas was dining in a room with others. Admittedly they all looked at each other with suspicious gazes, well those among their number who could at least catch the eye of their fellow inmates, most looked down at their food, or the floor eager to avoid the intimidating or accusatorial glare from drug-glazed eyes, but it was still a room with others just like him. Lost souls in a world of lost souls hidden away from so called 'normal' folk in the outside world; buried behind high walls and all but forgotten by the world on the other side of the brick and razor wire barrier. Broadmoor not only confined them but it also hid them from a world that held no truck with violence and did not want to be reminded of it.

Lucas, nor any other patient, knew it but such was the nature of the place that the staff, as well as forbidden to, chose never to speak of what they did behind those walls and the coils of razor wire. If asked they would respond that they worked for the NHS, which was totally true, but they never, to family or friends, divulged the true nature of their work or their damaged and dangerous charges.

A raised voice broke the revere, stole him from the enclosed life he survived in, it was imposing and full of self-importance, it roared and echoed across the dining room, bouncing off the beige walls. It came from a vulture like man at the next table, he sat in a stooped pose, the curved spine giving him the shape of a hunchback, but with his thin, bony features, balding head and pointed, sharp nose he looked every inch like the ravenous carrion bird looking down upon a tasty carcass.

The owner of the scraping voice pushed his chair back as he stood, its plastic legs farting against the polished floor, walked around the tables toward Lucas, the movement carefully observed as they always were by the on-duty, ever-vigilant, nurses. The human vulture wore a pair of loose-fitting jogging bottoms that were rolled up to his knees and Lucas thought they made it look as if the plumage on the legs stopped halfway down his bird-like limbs, looking lower he half expected to see claws of a vulture with sharp, menacing talons rather than feet. Thankfully he noted that the talons were encased in stained, off-white, fake Nike trainers, their instantly recognisable swoosh logo inverted.

The vulture reached its prey and the hawk like features suddenly loomed above Lucas and his lunch, harsh, sharp, features that seemed to fit right in with the surroundings, a predator among predacious prey. In corners of the dining room, nurses looked on, all eyes watching every movement but allowing the patients to socialise, but at the same time keeping a wariness brought about by experience.

"Good afternoon my good fellow." The voice, deep and sonorous, almost plummy, offered a clipped attempt at a posh accent that seemed alien given the surroundings. A smile filled the vultures face, softening the features; "Colonel Drayton-Farlington, late of her Majesty's armed forces, pleased to make your acquaintance." A hand was offered for a friendly shake, but was withdrawn before Lucas could accept or refuse. "Here, incarcerated in these hallowed halls, just like your good self, because of some damned awful clerical cock-up I am afraid, bit of a JANFU if you ask me." Lucas looked even more puzzled if that was possible given his surroundings; the madness of having met the Colonel at his room just a couple of hours before. "Sorry Old Boy, forces terminology, JANFU, Joint Army Navy Fuck Up..." The Colonel explained as if reading the puzzlement on Lucas' face. "Now, who are you and what have you been wrongly accused off?"

"We met a little earlier, Colonel." Lucas reminded him.

"No, I think not dear boy, I would have remembered." The hawk-like man replied. "Strange thing to say."

Lucas ignored the remnants of his tasteless hospital food, that had resembled bangers and mash to look at but he had no idea what they tasted of, and looked up into the broad and intense eyes of the Colonel whose Brylcreamed hair lay slicked down onto his bony dome of a head. The lanky man above him seemed to go on forever and Lucas was not sure whether to answer or head back to his room and close the door, which he was now entitled to do. The 'beak' of a hooked nose threatening as it hovered over him, waiting to peck and gouge the flesh of his prey; but a broad smile that was both genuine and warm, the first warmth Lucas had seen in some while, apart from Annie's all too brief visits, warmed him to this strange new character, who had the memory span of a goldfish.

"I'm Lucas, and I am not sure if I did what they say I did or not, so I can't say if I am wrongly accused, so it feels like I should be here, at least, just in case I did what they say I did!" His new best friend took a seat and settled himself alongside Lucas; still hunched, the curve of his spine still prominent making it appear as if he was always leaning in to hear better what his neighbour had to say; as he worked his way into the chair he noted that the vulture had moved with a pronounced limp, and, as his companion sat, he was obviously favouring a stronger right leg.

"Everyone calls me the Colonel;" he attempted to sit bolt upright, as when stood he had tried to stand at attention but the curved back had negated the attempt, now as he sat, in his mind's eye ramrod straight the curve took on a cartoon like comedy appearance. "But, there again everyone here in this dastardly place is someone other than they first seem."

The booming voice of moments before now took on a sad and low whisper as if the volume had suddenly been turned down by some unseen remote control. The hooked nose and the wary eyes scanned the room.

Not knowing what else to say, the art of conversation having died even before he had arrived in this place, Lucas enquired. "What happened to the leg, wounded in action were you, not one of those IEDs I hope?" Lucas may have joined the conversation but still he battled the depression driven desire to walk away and keep one's own council, but the draw of actually communicating with someone other than his captors was too much to ignore. He nodded down to the un-favoured leg and hoped he had not been too inquisitive too soon. The art of comfortable conversation, that he was formally so used to, had disappeared so very quickly in the 'hospital'. "Sorry, I shouldn't pry." The small amount of confidence he had felt suddenly drained from him. "The leg and you in here, maybe you don't want to talk about it, didn't mean to pry. Getting used to people again!" Lucas dropped chin to chest and kept his eyes looking toward the floor, which was dusty and scuffed.

"Not a problem Dear-boy," The curved back slumped just slightly, the head now hanging from an arched neck like a heavy apple on a thin branch, and the small hint of a confident poise left the Colonel; leaving Lucas, to imagine he resembled one of those angle poise lamps that stooped over the workspace on a desk and illuminating paperwork.

"Have to admit it is nice to have some civilised conversation for a change, it's hardly surprising, I know, but everyone in here, staff and all if you ask me, is barking bloody mad." The laugh sudden, unexpected, explosive, first startled Lucas but it then became infectious and Lucas began to laugh too and he could not recall the last time mirth had been one of emotions, so dull had the medication left him, but in that moment he also noticed the plum accent of The Colonel was beginning to slip. "Have to admit I am well and truly amongst, and on the side of the, barking." Laughter ceased as if a tap had been turned off and the lips instead took on a forced smile; and the eyes, in their dark hollow sockets, darkened and saddened.

A moments silence where Lucas did not know whether to up and walk away, to stay, to respond in kind; or even just to run away from the situation passed before the Colonel spoke again. "I failed a tank driving course, that's what finally got me in here." The dark yet sensitive eyes took in Lucas' facial expression, before deeming it okay to continue. "I can see the puzzled expression on your face, not surprising really given the situation." The Colonel scanned the room again, the predator wary of becoming prey. "Never was in the army; shocker right? - Although it was always my dream to serve." He slapped his bad leg on the thigh and the sound echoed around the common room; the Colonel held up his hand in conciliation to avoid one of the nurses coming and ordering him back to his room. "The limp comes from an accident I had when I was about ten or eleven, even then I had this heroic dream of being in uniform, from what my parents called an "overactive imagination". We were on holiday in Portland, down on the Dorset coast and I was playing at troop manoeuvres among the rocks, did a rapid turn to ward off some marauding pretend German troops and my foot slipped between the rocks and snapped in bloody half; left the family with a ruined holiday, me with a permanent limp and no chance of getting into a Post Office uniform let alone an army one."

A moment's silence followed and for a moment it seemed as if his friend was about to cry as his eyes began to fill. "So, I know what you are thinking, how come if no uniform, how did he get to take a tank driving test? No test, Dear Boy, I stole the bloody thing! Pinched a bloody great big Chieftain tank from the roadside, left with its engine running while the Captain commanding the machine stepped into a bank to cash a cheque, of all things. Rest of the crew stepped behind the beast to enjoy a smoke!"

"You stole a tank?" Lucas was sat mouth open, eyes spread wide and for just a brief couple of moments forgot he was in Broadmoor and wanted to hear the rest of this marvellous adventure; far better than his exploits of nicking the local copper's push bike; Lucas was in awe. "A real tank? How the hell do you steal a tank? Was it a big one?"

"I don't think they make small tanks!" He shook his head as if to confirm his knowledgeable statement. "It was a Chieftain, the real deal. I always like to go to those special open days that the Forces have and they had been doing a tank demo for the crowds in the town square when it stopped and the crew clambered out at the bank; I was fascinated to see it just parked there and left for anyone to steal. Then, as they lit up there fags behind the thing, I took a brief, very brief, look around me before I jumped in and took the bloody tank, just banged into gear, hit the throttle and I was off! Noise like bloody thunder in there, don't know how they stand it."

"How did you... how does anyone, know how to drive a tank?" Lucas was still amazed at the story being unfolded but this new companion was rising in Lucas' estimation; despite the madcap adventure and its outcome there was respect.

"Simulators Lucas, simulators. Spent a couple of summers down at Bovington Tank Museum in Dorset, not more than a dozen or so miles away from where I broke the leg all those years ago, they had one of these tank driving simulators; it teaches you like you were driving the real thing. Thing was once in the real tank going forward and getting the thing moving was exactly like the pretend ones and when you looked through the drier's visor it was like watching the view on a simulator screen; it was when I began to turn and manoeuvre the damn thing I had the real problem; not as easy as hose simulator thingies. Ended up ploughing through part of the grandstand into the car park and those things are really good you know; they just ride over the top of cars like a big boot crushing a tin can." Sadness now filled his face and the warming smile had gone as the incident was fully recalled; Lucas suddenly held the realisation that this tale had a bad ending otherwise why the incarceration.

"Surely nicking a tank would not have put you in here. I used to nick our local policeman's bike to get home from the pub and all I used to get was a telling off and on one occasion when he had had enough, a small fine and some Community Service." Lucas placed a hand on The Colonel's shoulder and offered a supporting squeeze.

"This pretend khaki Colonel drove the bloody tank over half a dozen cars," continued the sad faced man, the hawk like features now replaced with a look akin to a troubled child. "But, what I didn't know was that a family was still in their car, sat eating their picnic, enjoying a day out and not knowing what was heading their way. I crushed Mum and Dad's legs, left the dad with a permanent limp, mother in a wheelchair and rode straight over the two kids in the back seat as they tucked into their sandwiches; they never stood a fucking chance, only the family dog escaped unscathed. Fine military hero I turned out to be; killing kids just so I could live out my desire to be in uniform and be recognised for daring deeds instead of being a useless and clumsy cripple."

What could be said at that point? Nothing! The pair of them sat in silence but Lucas left his hand resting on his new companion's shoulder, tragedy it seemed was a good setting off point for a friendship!

A huge sniff, from the very large nose as the Colonel recomposed himself, broke the silence. "Anyway, I deserve to be in here and to be honest I hope they never let me out, still delusional of course which is why I insist on being called Colonel; but when it's just you and me Lucas would you call me Charles? I so miss my real name." Lucas nodded his assent. "When we are in a group if you could still go with rank it would be nice. If I am going to stay here need to keep up some pretence in case they think they have cured me. I don't want to go back out there, in the real world, too many pressures, too much danger for someone like me; I feel safer in here out of harm's way and no danger of hurting anyone else like those poor kids."

Lucas smiled a reluctant smile, realising the tragedy of the story and the torment his new-found friend was going through, it put his own troubles into a little perspective. "For my part, now I have begun to feel better, I cannot wait to get out, but I cannot see that happening anytime soon. No one is looking for anyone else with regard to the young girl who they say I killed and I have to admit now they have eased off with the strong doses of medicine I can neither remember, nor feel, as if I killed her. I still don't even know her name. I just have this gut instinct that all I did was hide her, which was bad enough but maybe that's why I am here because I did do it and I am just locking it away in my own mind. It just seems cruel to always think of her as an unnamed girl!"

"The Johnsons…"

"Pardon?"

Head hung low, chin on his chest, Charles, as Lucas now thought of his friend, responded. "The Johnsons, their two children were Jessica and Jenson." Sadness dissipated slightly and his head came up, eyes on Lucas and for a moment the tragedy of his actions dissipated from his gaze. "What's the matter with bloody parents, we are supposed to be the loonies and they go and call their kids, Jessica and Jenson Johnson; do parents not think when naming their kids; if I hadn't driven over them those two would have grown up into years of being bullied and having the piss taken out of them, especially poor Jenson Johnson! The kid would not have stood a chance with the bullies." Charles realised he had started to rant while hiding his crime behind glibness; suddenly stood and walked away. A brief moment to look over his shoulder. "Gotta go Lucas!"

And, with that the lanky, and stooped man, limped away to his room in a strange and one-sided loping, quick march and some thirty seconds later Lucas heard the metallic thump of, what must have been, Charles' cell door closing, with its closing air seemed to be taken, sucked, from the common room and corridor. Behind the closed door Charles, the Colonel, relived over and over the one moment of total madness in a life time of fantasy that had left two innocents dead and a family grieving. But part of him still blamed the parents for giving those lovely children such horrendous names.

Lucas remained in the common room, slumped in the armchair, thoughts running deeply through the confused forest that was his mind, there was darkness and no defined path to lead him from the midst of the imaginary trees that crowded in on him. Gazing without sight at the barred window that separated him from the outside world and in the midst of the troubled footpath that he was mentally following, every turn another tree blocked the pathway of easy thought, an organic maze that at first would lead to a clearing where his life unfolded in clear air and then suddenly back deep into undergrowth which confused and complicated.

With freedom of movement, even if there were still some restrictions, comes freedom of thought and Lucas began to realise for the first time since the events of that tragic evening in the Bishop's Garden; he had finally started to admit to himself, that there were the faintest of feelings telling him that the young girl's death was not down to him.

He still could not recall anything prior to pushing down on her chest in an attempt to pump life back into her broken body, and then the callous action of pushing her limp and lifeless body under the bench. Somewhere in the recesses of logical thought Lucas began to realise that he had never been a violent man, in fact he hated violence, hated bullies and loathed conflict of any kind; Annie had raised him to be a gentle soul and he would never do anything to let his surrogate mother down.

His father had always hoped that Lucas would follow him, and, indeed, his grandfather and his father before him, into the Royal Navy to be a ship's officer via the Naval school in Dartmouth where the Tubb ancestry was affixed to achievement boards on the walls of the distinguished college, but it was not to be. Unlike Charles, the Colonel, who would have loved to have his every waking hour predetermined and ordered for him, Lucas cherished his free will too much.

As a young boy, although tall and fit, Lucas had been badly bullied at school. He was not afraid of those that antagonised him, he just hated the thought of getting into fights, no hint of the cowardly but just a desire to be left alone and free from the pressures of how he should behave according to his peer's demands. So, whenever push came to shove, he just walked away and if they followed he would run. The only time he had fought back was when his younger brother Jacob had been subjected to the same taunts by the same gang of bullies and without a thought for his own safety Lucas just waded in among the six- strong gang and gave them, what his dad had referred to as 'a damn good thrashing'. Although both Tubb boys and an invited father had been brought before the school Principal, it had been the Head who took the verbal bashing from an irate Jonathan Tubb. Lucas smiled at the memory of his father vocally laying into the normally unruffled, normally aloof, Head.

"How dare you drag me down here and tell me how to raise my boys." Father had pinned the Head back in his leather swivel chair with just his steely glare that forced its way across the vast expanse of the huge desk, he was a small man protecting himself behind a big desk and getting smaller by the moment as the two brothers attempted to keep their faces with a serious appearance, "All my boys have done, it seems from what you have told me, was for one to suffer at the hands of school bullies while the other defended his brother. They should be commended, and backed by you, not pilloried or admonished by you. All you have done is perpetrated more bullying but this time from your official position and that is an abuse of your profession. It is this gang's parents and the bullies who should be sat here now and getting the rough part of your Head's scolding tongue! Not two boys who for once stood up for themselves and fought back!" Father was good at a rant when his boys were wronged and the Principal sat there, cowering, chastised and stuttering out a mixture of excuses and apologies.

In his early teenage years a spate of bullying had led Lucas to being enrolled into Judo classes by his father, something he railed against to begin with but within the first couple of lessons had begun to love the beauty and etiquette of the sport. He had gone through the student phases of the Judoka with skill and speed, quickly rising to a brown belt, the highest student rank; while the black belt he had worked so hard for had never happened, despite keeping his training up university and then girls and a good time had got in the way, Oxford as a university town had much to recommend it for a young man with no money worries. He found the peer pressure of copious amounts of alcohol and sex too tricky and tempting to avoid.

Toward the end of his university years, when exams beckoned he needed a diversion to keep him sober and directed and he returned to training three evenings a week, under a Sensei who he liked and admired, he even took to teaching the juniors on a Saturday morning for many years. Unlike other martial arts based on violence, Lucas liked the fact that the inventor of the martial art, judo, Jigaro Kano, developed the sport in the late 1800s after he had suffered bullying. Judo meant Gentle Way, and Lucas loved the artistry of the fighting art. As he turned 22 Lucas finally reached the rank of Black Belt First Dan and then fought his way to bronze medals in two successive National Championships. At 26 years of age he had retired from competition with a second Dan black belt and then as career demanded more attention he had gradually stopped participating altogether. Now being incarcerated he realised that after two years he had begun to miss the sport and promised himself if ever he got out of this place he would train for his Third and maybe even further Degrees, even if they were teaching grades rather than combat ones. His years of training and the demands of such an intense sport were about to help him escape the confined worlds of Broadmoor, and his mental internment, as he once again brought to the fore the techniques of meditation that he had learned over the years in the Dojo.

Shut in his sparsely furnished room, a single bed, bedside table and his one luxury sitting atop his bedside table, the I-pod with all his music; and a utilitarian chest of drawers with a plastic garden chair alongside it. Adjacent to this tiny room was the door-less toilet, with its wash basin along with a hanging rail for his few clothes. Not much compared to where he had come from but in his current situation it seemed almost palatial. Looking out of his window, between the broad and rusting bars, even with the restricted view he could only see tarmac pathways bordered by small areas of lawn with scruffy clumps of grass and weeds poking through them. From the outside when they were allowed their daily short walk in the fresh air, the wards took on the appearance of a rundown council estate, but to Lucas it was paradise, it was an oasis of green, it was the outside world. Lucas was beginning to feel the pangs for freedom! As he began to return to, some sort, of normality within his head he more and more took to meditating his way out of the room. Sitting cross-legged on his narrow, and firm, bed (he longed for a soft and luxurious seat), he would focus on a speck of black, not much bigger than a pin head, on the wall in front of him and slowly disappear into the hole that would emerge in his mind's eye. With this one action which he performed at least twice daily he began to escape the fog of the drug regime and the past two years of ordered and controlled incarceration.

Not only that, but by training his mind to think for itself again, he was gaining the real desire to either remember what he had done, so he could at least feel regret for his actions, while feeling as if he deserved to be locked away in this depressing place. But, how could he ever solve both problems? How could he either begin to show regret or, as he now firmly believed more and more he was, prove his innocence? The two things seemed like insurmountable mountains. Charles, the Colonel, may want to stay in here and keep the public safe from his crazy actions; but for Lucas' part, and during his increasing moments of lucidity, never felt as if he was a risk to anyone; nor, more to the point, did he feel he was ever a danger to anyone.

CHAPTER 10

He raised his hand in anger, the right fist clenched, its knuckles white with the pressure; face contorted, venom in hate-filled his eyes and standing just inches from the threatening posture Annie felt real and tangible fear, she wanted to pee, felt the pressure within and just wanted to let it go but she was made of sterner stuff. Still she cowered and backed away from Jacob who towered over her, her own arms raising to cover her face in a movement of self-preservation, his arm cocked, clenched fist loaded and ready to fire, to launch a punishing blow to Annie's face.

It was her own fault, in a moment of weakness she had raised her voice in anger toward him, a thing she had trained herself not to do however hard he pushed her or cajoled her; but seeing the meal she had prepared thrown at her and now running down the kitchen wall, bits of congealed food dripping down onto the freshly polished floor, this was the bridge too far. She always knew Jacob was capable of violence, and that given the right circumstances he would lose his considerable temper. Now she was about to feel the full force of that anger; and she was scared, trembling, leg weakening scared!

Annie had been about to call out for Jacob, and whoever his guest, or guests, of the day had been, when the two of them sauntered along the hallway into the kitchen. He in just a brief pair of black underpants, so tight that a semi-erection was in obvious view, as he knew it would be; and her, with long slender legs and hips wrapped in a cream towel, but from the waist up naked with her huge, surgically enhanced breasts unmoving on her chest, beneath the pink orbs the rest of her body lean and almost emaciated with rows of sharp ribs showing through almost transparent skin. Annie noted sores on the girl's lips and around her nostrils, the eyes were blurred and seemingly having trouble focussing, the hair was bleached blonde and hung in loose, straw-like, strands around her face.

Annie turned her back on them, not wanting to see their blatant exhibitionism, and she was rewarded with slap on her buttock. It was enough, it should have been enough months ago, but she was tired of the treatment and his need to attempt to shock her. Turning on Jacob she screamed at him to keep his filthy hands to himself. The moment her pent-up frustration escaped she also realised she had released more than her own

65

poison; she had opened the cage that would let a beast loose in her kitchen.

Jacob, in turn, reacted with swift anger as he noted the shocked look on his female conquest's eyes and the glimmer of an embarrassed smile breaking across her face. Nobody showed him up in front of his women, he felt belittled and was not about to be shown up by the hired help of all people, the house keeper should know her place and never speak to him in such a way, she was staff damn it, and he clenched his fist and raised his hand in readiness to mete out the punishment for such an indiscretion. He was blind to restraint, buried within a rage over which he had no control.

Only Annie's raised arms that deflected the blow, and her ducking away from Jacob saved her from a beating, backing up against the kitchen island she looked on horrified, as he picked up the fresh hot dish of lasagne. Such was his anger, or his drug ingestion, there was no sign that he felt the heat of the dish that had only recently been drawn from the oven where the Mozzarella cheese topping had melted to a slightly crusty perfection but still bubbled like molten lava. It flew across the room trailing steam, the dish exploding against the wall and leaving its mark deep within the plasterwork. Half the dinner stuck to the wall but the mixture of off-white cheese sauce and deep reddish brown Bolognese mixture had first splashed with the impact and then run down the wall like a Jackson Pollock masterpiece. Annie, a mixture of fear, anger and confusion all coursing through her mind, just turned and walked out of the kitchen, she headed upstairs to her room, all the while listening to the couple laughing uproariously at her departure. They could scrape the food from the wall and floor if they wanted to eat, or eat it where it sat like the dogs they were! She rubbed her forearm and checked for bruising while she walked away.

She wondered how much longer she could live with this ill-mannered and brutish behaviour and then on reaching her room at the top of the house she did something she had not done since childhood, she flopped down onto her bed, buried her face into the pillow so her sobs could not be heard and she cried, she cried until her eyes had no more tears to produce; and then she just heaved dry sobs into her sodden pillow. By the time she finished her bout of, what she would later refer to as self-pity, night had crept into her room and left her alone, in the dark and totally at a loss as to what to do next. She felt as imprisoned as Mr Lucas and was sharing his pain deeper than she had previously realised.

Annie wanted to move on, she could have and should have retired many years ago and settled in her own, little, dream cottage by the sea, she had the money, but at the same moment a lifetime of loyalty told her that she had to be there when, or if, Mr Lucas needed her, she had to be there when Lucas came home, but most of all she knew that there had to be a way to escape the anger and fear that Jacob was dishing out.

Chapter 11

Three lives were, for all intents and purposes, on hold. Lucas, shut away on a ward where he was deemed to be mentally ill and a danger to himself and others and given just enough drugs to keep his moods level and his potency for violence, or indeed any strong emotion, hidden beneath the chemical fog. Annie confining herself more and more to her attic rooms while counting down the days and the hours, doing her housework and daily duties and then locking herself away from anger and bile, the less she saw of Jacob, his obnoxious and loutish friends and the various sluts he brought home almost daily, the more she found staying in the cottage bearable; she felt as much a prisoner as her Mister Lucas.

And then there was Gill Harmon, although on the outside, and having the freedom to come and go as she pleased, in her mind she was entombed in a life and a job that did not live up to expectation, when not at work the small rooms of her waterfront cottage were closing in more and more, and her only break for freedom, mentally and in reality, was her regular visits to her marina café with its views across the harbour; her mental escape riding in and out with the vagaries of the tide. It was the only moments she felt at peace and felt like her true self.

Three different people with varied lives that were on hold, just waiting to be opened out, like spring buds waiting for a brief glimpse of sunshine before bursting forth, but with day after day of clouds the sunrise was just out of reach and with no real expectation of being able to take that huge breath of freedom that we all need to attain some level of happiness. They were all locked away in their own confined worlds.

Life is something that happens when you least expect it, and as history shows the best laid plans, etc. etc.

While Annie had lived a long, and mostly happy life with a thousand or more adventures, and Lucas had led a charmed life with a, mostly, privileged upbringing mixed with the adventures of privileged youth; Gill Harmon felt as if she had been treading water up until now and was still waiting for her life to start; everything it seemed was always on hold. The dreams and aspirations we all have as we move into the world of adulthood had been left hovering, uneasy, not yet ready to land and fulfil all those wonderful hopes. A few months ago when she ripped open the envelope from The News telling her that the dream job was hers, she felt that fresh horizons leading to a great adventure were about to begin but what she had not taken into account was the fact that she was going to work on the everyday production line in a "news factory", churning out unmeaning product after product. It was a factory with a ceaseless, pouring output of fine words, platitudes and cliché, and all produced for the lowest common denominator of their readership, simple phrases of easy reading. It fought the good fight for the local downtrodden masses tackling good cause after good cause, it supported fully the town's ever-failing football team which in just a few years had dropped from glorious cup triumph to lowly survivors in a far lesser league and playing small-town teams of little note and from places where none of the fans knew of their location upon a map.

As the voice of the surrounding populace The News chased down drug dealers and wrong doers and proceeded to name and shame them, they praised the successful and the charitable, and in Gill's case they paid homage to the dead, deceased and long forgotten heroes and every day folk. One day the police would be praised and hailed, headline heroes - the next vilified and beaten down as front page villains by the intense scrutiny of the press; it was the way of the modern media, build-em-up and then knock-em-down. Gill was disillusioned.

Day after day in the crowded newsroom it was her task to scour press releases for snippets of local news, Am-Dram groups, Round Table and Rotarians, Charity sales and bring and buys for mum and toddler groups; they were all in Gill's remit for reportage. Only the laborious output of the sub-editors seemed more tedious and soul sucking than hers, as they proof read every story and then placed other journalists' words into predetermined spaces within the paper. If the submitted pieces were too long they did not even get to re-write, they just snipped off the bottom paragraph to make the piece fit. Gill looked in envy across the newsroom toward the intense and always smiling character of Georgia May, she was what Gill had hoped to become from the moment she entered the hallowed halls of the newsroom, the star reporter, in her handbag business cards that read 'Senior Journalist'. With her pixie like face, cheeks like a hamster puffed up with all the smiling, only in her late twenties but traces of crow's feet already at the edges of each eye, another legacy of that perma-grin, the face framed by cropped boyish hair, dyed a rich and unnatural red, just sweeping with a small fringe from her forehead. In appearance a keen little eighteen year old kitten, butter unable to melt in her mouth, who, from just her looks, would not seem able to seek conflict with the smallest of adversaries. However, in reality this twenty nine year-old experienced journalist was a hard-bitten, well trained news hound who after years on the paper had become a magnet for the big stories, and, despite her elfin like features, nothing scared this woman. Once a sniff of a story came within her range she would circle like a ravenous shark before sinking her teeth in to her prey and shake the story out like a dog with a new toy, tearing apart the facts until the stuffing fell out. Gill envied the life of a senior journalist and her freedom to chase the big stories.

Gill had watched in undisguised awe one morning while she was in Portsmouth's main police station on the daily press call. Although much of what was being listed by the force's press officer and spokesperson she listened intently as tales of car break-ins, joyriders and a glut of pick pockets working the seafront stealing purses and wallets from unwary holidaymakers; as usual she was only paying scant attention to the monotone report, from across the room and standing behind the tall figure of a lad from the local free paper, unnoticed till she spoke Senior Journalist Georgia had appeared and began firing a salvo of highly explosive questions about a well-known local drug dealer and gang leader who had been released without charge yet again following a raid on his home and drug den the previous evening.

Jaws had closed on her uniformed victim resplendent in badges of office in an attempt to show a strong authority figure, the journalist's bite holding him firm, she was not accepting a no, or no comment, from the press spokesperson who now actually showed discomfort bordering on fear etched on his face despite the fact he stood a full foot taller than her and normally oozed intimidation from every pore. That intimidating look borne of years of experience slowly drained from him like honey oozing from the comb.

The reporter gripped him with her gaze, held on and harangued him, moved forward till standing toe to toe with him, he was looking down on the short reporter but she held the power and in quiet tones demanded he explain to her how anyone could sell powerful and illegal drugs to school children and then walk away from arrest. He attempted to stand his ground his face, with the dark shadow of beard growth darkening his demeanour, began to drain of colour and rage borne of embarrassment began to fill his eyes, but as the spokesperson he had to keep his cool and Georgia knew this. With the black look on his face at that moment Gill would have crossed the road to even avoid sharing a pavement with him, but it was the senior reporter's job to get the big stories and Georgia May was threatening to quote him whether he said anything or not. She knew she only had a few minutes remaining of the morning press call to get the news item she needed for that evening's edition from someone who was growing increasingly reluctant to divulge any further information about the raid or the dealer involved. Ultimately, either to shut her up and bring an end to the forceful questioning, or just because he felt beaten down by her insistent nature, he capitulated, took her to one side and gave her the story.

Less than half a working day later the presses began to run and the lead story splashed across the front page under a bold two-line headline was the story accredited with a by-line to Georgia May, Senior Journalist.

The drug dealers take was one of a deprived Childhood, abusive father, drug addict mother, then as a ten-year old a drug runner for the local gangs which he now ran as an hardened eighteen year old, an alpha male who would battle and best any young buck trying to take away his leadership, he was now the head of those same gangs he had run with as a child; the Portsmouth Don and still in his teenage years. The whole miserable story of his life was unveiled, and following the first lead story the dealer himself stepped forward and agreed to be interviewed by the tenacious and experienced journalist. Her scoop would be printed over two weekend editions of the paper; and, when later he was charged with a whole series of crimes from dealing to supply and the attempted murder of a rival dealer there would be further front page stories; the aim of every journalist and all because she would not let a press officer get away with a 'no comment'.

That kind of headline grabbing story was what Gill had got into journalism for but so far her only scoop, and a very minor one at that, was the discovery that a well-known local councillor had died suddenly from a heart attack, Gill had been first on the scene; but that was only because she lived next door and had seen the flashing blue lights as the ambulance pulled up outside her window.

With police on the scene and the councillor's widow so grief stricken she would, and did, talk to anyone about her loss and her husband, Gill was able to get plenty of quotes and for once instead of her words being somewhere between the TV pages and the sports' section she was elevated, or at least her words were to the dizzy heights of page five, but at least is was lead story on that page to add reward to plaudits. But, even then she still had the boring task to write a glowing obituary of both the man and public servant, fine words about a man she never knew.

Best efforts aside Georgia never, it seemed, got nearer to the front page than page four, and then only on a bad news day when little happened around the world or in Portsmouth, which the ace reporters never seemed to suffer with, even during the quiet holiday weeks of August when strangely 'news' was a rare item, it seemed that events went on holiday along with the local readership.

The only lightness in a seemingly dull world of disappointment was the regular trips to her favourite marina café, life for Gill Harmon would have been just one humdrum moment following another. Journalism had seemed like an exciting career move; a life of recognition, glamour, maybe, but certainly a life of discovery and the unravelling of thrilling stories that would move her while she wrote them and bring about a gamut of emotions to her readers as they moved past her by-line and into the thrust of her amazing news stories.

There would be plaudits, awards, grateful residents offering praise and thanks as her campaigning style of writing brought about a change in the minds of local Government or saw the downfall of another villain or criminal. Through her words and her investigative skills she would bring about change and a better life for those that read The News on a daily basis, living their lives through the stories that the local media would bring them. Instead the best she had received so far was a brief E-mail of thanks from the grateful family of the dead councillor for saying nice things about their recently departed.

Was it life in general that she was disappointed in, or herself, Gill had no idea?

All she knew as she sipped her coffee, a straight black Americano this afternoon as she felt the need of a caffeine boost, while gazing out on the calm waters of the harbour, was that life was not turning out as expected, did it ever, for anyone? Yet another change was not an option, what would she do, how would she explain yet another career move to friends, or her parents God forbid, why yet another switch of job was in the wind; she had to stick this one out, she had trained for two years and put everything into this, it was just such an effort to ride through the boredom.

Notwithstanding her disappointment, Gill knew deep down, in her heart and mind, that she had a talent for the written word. As a child at school if they asked the class for a two hundred word essay, she would give them five hundred or a thousand if the subject really moved her. It was always a disheartening moment when the teachers would mark her down for not sticking to the subject, or the word count, few praised her or noted her passion for writing, they had their curriculum that they had to stick to and by her writing double what was needed she was throwing the rigid curriculum requirements into the wind and her uninspired, jaded, teachers, suffering badly with low moral were being required to extend themselves into areas they did not want to concern themselves with. All they looked forward to were the weekends, the Christmas break skiing holiday, the inset days and the odd day or two of rebellious strike action to cry poverty and beg for even higher wages. Teaching, like many professions, had lost its passion, its calling, and was now just 'another job' to be moaned about and complained about!

Now here she was 28, and just a couple of weeks away from 29 (creeping ever nearer to the dreaded thirty when all life and excitement would surely be at an end) and stuck in a job that she felt more than qualified for but that held her in a constant hiatus of boredom and offered a distinct lack of personal achievement despite the passion she had initially put into her efforts.

There was a big story out there somewhere, one that would make her name, bring her the personal glory she craved, not for the plaudits, just for the satisfaction of a job well done. But, in the meantime life was stifling Gill Harmon and she needed to escape. She felt like the boats that surrounded her in the marina, moored permanently to the pontoons of life and just waiting for someone to slip the ropes and release the lines, to find freedom to achieve what they had been designed for, to enable her to sail off into the bright future she had been built for.

Chapter 12

Lucas looked down at his waistline, and in both fists grabbed a handful of loose flesh, wobbling it for a while, before trying to pull the T-shirt down over the bare skin that seemingly emerged of its own volition, while, for some strange reason, the errant piece of clothing would no longer reach the waistband of the grey and limp cloth of his jogging bottoms.

Jogging bottoms, sweat pants, trackies? It was not that many months ago that he did not even own such an item of clothing; Lucas always prided himself on looking smart, even when casually dressed, smart was always the key word. He was not as strict as his father had been with his personal appearance A trace of a smile crossed his face for just a brief moment, as he recalled that each evening at 6pm or eighteen hundred hours as his father was always keen to call it, on the dot, father would head for his dressing room and change out of his brown shoes, usually brogues and highly polished, and change into black shoes, plain and buffed to a reflective shine, before coming back down to dinner. This was always taken as the norm so neither of the boys had asked their father if this was a left-over from his days in the Royal Navy or if it had been something he had always done, he never wore anything but black shoes after six, it was not the done-thing and standards had to be maintained.

Lucas had let himself go, life in Broadmoor was not conducive to healthy living, nothing to dress up for and nowhere to go, except the common room, and he was gaining weight for the first time in his life and now wearing jogging bottoms, and trainers, without laces but with Velcro straps like the shoes of an old man; the realisation hit him that he was becoming just that, an old man, it was what life inside this place did to a person. He seemed to recall from his early days of incarceration someone pointing out to him that the prescribed drugs would make him feel constant pangs of hunger and the prolonged periods of boredom would leave him with little else to do other than eat. It helped very little that the hospital shop which opened daily for them to spend the little money they earned only stocked sweets and chocolates.

His new friend, The Colonel, walked into the common room and his skinny, stooped stature seemed to argue with the obvious overweight condition of everyone else in the room.

"Morning Colonel;" with that greeting the sad face of his friend looked across toward him and, as with modern tanks that once the gun is locked on the target it stays on the target despite the direction the rest of the armoured vehicle is going, so it was with his eyes locked on to Lucas. Head pointing in one direction, his body heading in another his lower half then diverted from its chosen course to the grey, plastic covered and high backed chair next to where Lucas sat.

"How come you remain so thin while the rest of us put on weight, Charles?" Now he was close enough to speak quietly and out of earshot of all the other inmates Lucas reverted to The Colonel's given name.

"Metabolism dear boy; metabolism. Inside this calm and slow moving exterior, inside the sloth beats the heart of a finely honed athlete that is rarely at rest and is always sprinting flat out and burning the calories!"

"Is that right?" Responded Lucas who was as surprised as he was doubtful at his friend's explanation. "Really?"

"No, of course not, total bollocks old boy... Just skinny, always have been, probably always will be now." Laughter was an alien sound and without exception every head in the room turned toward the two men as they shared a chuckle or two. For just the briefest of moments Lucas felt a brief spark of life explode back in to his dark world.

"Lucky bastard!" Lucas responded with a jiggle of his belly, both men smiled, their friendship secure; or as secure as anything could be in this place.

"Yes, lucky! That's me." The smiles gone as quickly as they arrived, "Broken leg, lifetime limp, career disappeared before I even had chance to start it, then I discover, all too late I might add, that driving a tank is not as easy as it seems. And, I have to kill two lovely children before their lives had ever really began. Just call me Lucky!"

Lucas looked crestfallen at putting his friend in that place with such a careless remark. "Sorry Charles, I didn't mean..."

A dismissive wave of the hand from Charles put the apology to one side. "Let's face it dear boy, I deserve to be here, and probably about the only place in the world where I would fit in."

"Nobody deserves to be in a soulless place like this!" Without thought Lucas pulled at his T-shirt again in the hope of covering his ever-widening girth.

"Well I have been thinking about that Lucas; and I think I may have a plan to get us both out of here." While trying to look casual Charles took on the look of a guilty man, he looked furtively around the room; too late if anyone had been nearby and listening.

"Not wishing to put a damper on any grand scheme you may have for escape, but we are under surveillance 24/7, there are a dozen locked doors to get through just to get from one ward to the next, let alone find one that allows us to step through those walls and into the outside world. Any escape plan you have would need more expertise than either of us have and, without doubt, a huge slice of good luck. Something that both you and I seem to be lacking in!" Another smile from Lucas. "Unless, of course, Colonel, you have an SAS squadron of elite and dedicated troops on standby ready to sneak in on a covert operation and spirit us away unnoticed in the night."

The Colonel took on a look of earnest seriousness. "Do you want to get out of this smothering place and discover the truth about what happened to you, and to your unnamed girl? Because, and I know we are all a little delusional in here; I have a feeling that you did nothing wrong, you may well be the only truly innocent, or sane, man in here, and have been wrongly incarcerated. I doubt there is anyone on the outside looking to prove your innocence, is there?"

"I doubt it!" Lucas felt depression cloud over him.

A silent few minutes passed while both men considered what had just been said, their eyes flickering from corner to corner of the bland room, but no one, crazy or sane, was paying them notice.

"How?" Lucas broke the silence first.

"How what?"

Lucas repeated, "How?" Looked at his friend with the seriousness that he felt was needed for the occasion. "How do you intend to get us both out of here?"

"Well, I still need to hone the final plan, and work out a few kinks, but I do have the makings of a really good strategy and although nothing is ever totally fool proof; I am beginning to believe it can work and we will both be free, free from everything in this place that holds us down and drags the life from us. I will disappear, I have a place to go, somewhere I have wanted to be for some time now, and you can head back to your close friends and family and work out what really happened to you and that poor girl under the bench."

Lucas was with him, wanting so hard to believe. Believe there was a way out of this living death, believe that he was innocent, but he could not see how any plot to escape these old and secure walls, to walk out beyond the bricks and the razor wire could ever work. How would he ever get to walk under that clock with the maker's name still clearly stamped on it? But, he now had one belief that was firm in his mind, he knew his only chance of regaining any sort of normal life, was to trust someone again, to rely on a friend. Was to escape!

Chapter 13

Although the first patient admitted, to what was then referred to as a lunatic asylum was a young woman accused of infanticide, in 1863, it was a year later the first male patients arrived on 27 February. If the two conspirators had known the facts they may well have rethought their plan as over the decades few had escaped the towering walls. One such character was John Straffen, who had killed two young girls in Bath, then escaped from Broadmoor in 1952, then, while on the loose, had strangled a young girl out riding her bike. That incident led to the installation of 13 sirens, known as the Broadmoor Sirens, which, with their wailing cries cover the surrounding towns and sound for 20 minutes when a patient escapes. The entire region would know, and be on the lookout, once the two men had negotiated their escape and the alarm raised. Based on the air-raid sirens of the second-world-war, the two-tone alarm sounds across the whole area in the event of an escape, every village with a certain radius would know. It is tested every Monday morning at 10 am for two minutes, after which a single tone 'all-clear' is sounded for a further two minutes. Following the murder of that small child in 1952 schools in the area must keep procedures designed to ensure that in the event of a Broadmoor escape no youngster is ever out of the direct supervision of a member of staff once the siren sounds.

Maybe it was better for the two inmates that they never knew of the alarm system, for it would surely have changed their thinking.

"Have you anyone special on the outside Lucas? Someone you trust." The use of his name alerted him to the fact that Charles was about to say something serious; he nodded his assertion that there was and the action made him feel like a secretive bidder at an auction. For his part, Charles was furtively looking back and forth across the room like a demented tennis spectator; as was the norm these days no one, except Lucas, was paying him any attention although he was well aware that the CCTV cameras, sited in every corner of the room and without a blind spot, all being monitored with a wary and well trained eye they would be watching them all at all times. "Someone who you can trust with your life and will be there for you no matter what?" He took another glance over his shoulder.

Time was something that was in good supply within Broadmoor and Lucas told Charles Annie's story, his once Nanny and now housekeeper; he had not talked much about his world outside the walls of Broadmoor, except in measured releases to his therapists where he knew he had to give them something even if it was only snippets, the highlights of, what now seemed, an unfulfilled life since being placed in the hospital he had thought it important to keep his world and this strange place, which was far removed from any sort of reality, as far apart as possible and until this moment had succeeded.

The story told, "I trust Annie with my life!" Lucas concluded.

"Good because you may have to!" More sly glances back and forth across the common room and Lucas found himself doing the same but was also aware that there was nothing more captivating for those that are paid to watch than two patients, both deemed dangerous to themselves and others, trying to act innocent and failing miserably. Two inmates of a mental institution sitting side by side watching an invisible Wimbledon final and trying to look inconspicuous.

While his head moved back and forth Lucas began to really look at his surroundings for the first time, taking in the sorry, monochromatic details, as he began to return from the dark place his mind had taken him; suddenly as if a light had been switched on there was a realisation of his surroundings, he even noted that it had now become part of his everyday life to be on hard uncomfortable chairs; was this part of his punishment, to never have another comfortable seat.

The room being scanned, every inch covered by Lucas with each head movement was cheerless and cold, grey chairs, plastic of course, flimsy tables, everything bolted down, even the walls a uniform, institution beige. Adorning the graceless walls for the entertainment of the inmates, pointless landscapes, Lucas assumed that they were of the Berkshire countryside and thought their addition a cruel reminder of lives lost. Lucas disliked all of them, apart from the image of a giant red stag, a magnificent beast with a full seven point set of glorious antlers being held proudly aloft, it stood atop a snowy Scottish peak, Lucas loved the freedom the stag had to roam his territory. He did not know a great deal about Berkshire but he was certain there were no snow-capped mountain ranges; if there had been he was certain they would have been visible from trackside during Royal Ascot, the only times he could recall entering the county. Lucas' mind wandered to Ladies Day, and the well-turned out women, champagne, caviar, the horse racing and tote.......

"To quote that funny little chap on Blackadder, I have a cunning plan!" The sudden statement from the Colonel shook him from his reverie and Lucas realised that Charles was no longer looking around the room, his eyes were fixed on him. The look felt unsettling as this was a place where no one looked anyone else straight in the eye; that would be inviting danger into the room.

Lucas so wanted to point out that Baldrick's cunning plans in the comedy TV show always, but always, backfired but he did not have the heart.

"Do tell!" He wanted to believe so much that there was a way out of this institution and its medicine fogged hell he was living in; he was willing to listen to anything; no matter how wild. It was akin to buying a lottery ticket, you had little chance of winning every Saturday night but the dreams of what to do with the winnings between buying the ticket and the actual draw made the entry fee more than worthwhile. Charles was about to sell him a lottery ticket and the jackpot prize was freedom, worth listening to the plot even if only for that short dream.

"Why the hell not Charles, as they say, shoot for the moon and even if you miss you get to dance among the stars for a while, let us at least have a moment dancing among the stars!" Lucas dug a gentle and playful elbow into his friend's ribs.

"Not here, not now, we both know we are being watched." Charles stopped the furtive flicking back and forth of his head, as if the tennis match had ended suddenly, but Lucas unaware of the sudden cessation of movement continued on for a few more rallies until, feeling embarrassed, he too stopped and just looked down at the table. The head may have been still but Charles' eyes continued to dart around each corner of the room and from camera to camera. "It will all happen this coming Friday, so be ready, I am going to write you a letter, you have to promise me you will not open it until the time it says on the envelope, that is a promise you have to make or none of this will work. I suggest you read it and then eat it so no-one will discover my cunning plan." The tone of voice had been low, just above a whisper, and serious and as he finished speaking, as if to put a stamp of authority on his words he looked Lucas square in the eye, daring him to ignore the Colonel's mission statement.

"Eat it? Really?" Lucas raised an eyebrow.

"Of course not, but it just sounded more, James Bond than, 'read it and stuff it under your mattress!' don't you think?" The Colonel smiling to show he had kept his own sense of humour.

In his dream world the Colonel had been recruited and moved from uniform branch of the services, joining the secretive ranks of MI6 (or maybe it was MI5, whichever was the home security branch, he could never remember), such was the mystery and clandestineness behind his plan, Lucas was more than aware of his friend's fantasy world and he tried hard to subdue a mocking, but friendly, smile that was spreading out across his lips. Was Charles about to spring Lucas from this court enforced trap, or save the free world from some tyrannical subterfuge or other? Only time would tell.

As he hatched the scheme for his friend to escape, Colonel Drayton-

Farlington, Charles, had no idea that he was about to put into action a series of events that would see four people in total find freedom. Two of those four would no longer be captive by their restrictive lives and surroundings, but neither would they be able to breathe the sweet fresh air of life for their freedom was brought about by their untimely death.

The regime on this ward was freer than the rest of the hospital, but free was a relative term when incarcerated in a hospital for the criminally insane, there would never be total freedom or even the ability to move about at will. Doors on their rooms would be under their own control until lights out, which was mid-evening but that seemed to be a moveable feast and most patients were in their rooms and settled long before the doors were locked from the outside. It was late that next Friday afternoon, just before lights out, Lucas was spread out on his bed reading an old Leslie Thomas paperback about a woman called Chloe who was about to go on trial for murder, the irony lost on him. The curtain that covered the narrow window on his door was drawn open, this was a glass covered hole in the solid door that could be used by the nurses to just watch their charges and Lucas had always hated the scrape of the curtain on rail across the hatch and the pair of eyes that would invade his space and glare into his room in the name of security, in olden days it would have been a hinged hatchway used to push food, drink and anything else that was needed through to avoid opening the full portal of the door to the most dangerous of patients. With no hatchway this time the delivery of a plain white envelope, was slipped under the door, adding to the covert feeling of the event. It entered the room with a secretive shove before fluttering across the floor like a white butterfly. Across the flap of the envelope, like a secret seal, was written in a scrawled hand, *'LUCAS, FIVE O'CLOCK AND NOT A MOMENT BEFORE OR AFTER'.*

With no watch on his wrist, a timepiece would have been totally redundant, even if he had been allowed one, time was something that all patients tried to forget, Lucas turned on his radio and awaited the five o'clock news.

On a long journey the more one looks at the road signs and the distance left to travel, the longer the journey seems, and so it is with time, the more you wait for it to pass the more it seems to drag. Like a kid on Christmas morning, if you are told to wait to open your present, the more it needs to be opened. Lucas had no idea how anyone could escape the confines of Broadmoor, or even contemplate such an audacious plan, and the more he had thought about it over the days since the cunning plan had been announced by the secretive Charles, the more ridiculous the whole thing seemed, so what difference would it make to open the envelope early. The heart pounded in Lucas' chest, he could feel his ribs throb and hurt with each beat, could hear the liquid pulse of blood through his veins thumping in his ears, a steady rhythm of a drummer beating out a march. Everything within Broadmoor was designed to relax and suffocate extreme feelings, the regime, the drugs, continuous control day and night; and now he was feeling a natural high, adrenaline coursing through his every fibre. Looking at his hands, which tightly gripped the envelope, he realised they were shaking with a mixture of fear and anticipation

What if, just *what if*, Charles did have a plan and, further-more; what if it was a viable one! Then what if, by opening the envelope early he had jinxed that plan. He waited, both because it was what his friend had asked and for the fact he was enjoying this natural high he was feeling!

Outside the tall walls and the razor wire in the villages and towns, a world away from where he sat, life was carrying on, folk went about their daily business, winding down from the working week and looking forward to the weekend, in the woodlands surrounding Broadmoor the footpaths were popular with walkers, their dogs and their young children.

The sirens were about to put on hold those peaceful and carefree lives.

"This is Radio 4 with the BBC, it is five o'clock, I am Corrie Corfield, and here is the news…" The voice was rich, succinct and clear, plummy tones eased their way from the twin speakers except Lucas heard nothing more of what had been happening in the world that afternoon as his attention was now totally on the letter as he tore open the flimsy envelope…

Lucas expected the hand writing to be a hurried scrawl, but legible non-the-less, instead it was a beautifully written letter, the text flowing as if written by an artist, or practiced calligraphist.

My Dear Lucas
Since your arrival you have made my life in here bearable, or at least tolerable, there has never been a friend such as you in my entire life as I have always lived in my fantasy world where few others were invited. You never queried or questioned my alter ego of the Colonel and for that I thank you.
I have had enough of living imprisoned in here, and indeed incarcerated in this fantasy world of mine which led to the deaths of two young innocents, and with a lack of guilt in mind, I also believe in your innocence. Someone as gentle and caring as you could not have done those horrid things to that young girl. So please take what happens in the next few hours as my gift to you, given in friendship and love, and given gladly I might add.

Although Lucas knew something bad was coming he could not stop reading, he had to discover all he could about this, so called, 'cunning plan' of Charles', but as he read on down the page alarms began to howl and echo, for a brief moment he was unsure if they blared in his mind or in reality but the sounds of shouting and running feet were coming from outside his room; something bad had happened in his Wing and he was torn between rushing out of his door, as anyone in normal surroundings would do at the impatient sound of an alarm, or continuing with the letter. The inbuilt and instinctive knowledge that with the alarm going no one would be allowed out into common areas made up his mind for him. His door was ajar and he could hear the alarm screaming its warning while many feet, all seemingly shod in trainers, squeaked their way in urgent runs across the polished corridor floor to the room next to his. Charles had indeed done something drastic. But, blind to what was happening outside of his room.

Lucas needed to read on!

My favourite book has always been the Count of Monte Cristo, loved it as a child and must know it almost word for word by now, well the author, Alexandre Dumas, had one wonderful quote, "All human wisdom is contained in these two words - Wait and Hope" *and that is what we all do in here; in fact it is all we do in here; just waiting and hoping for something different. We wait for freedom and we hope for a better life, and sadly for many of us poor demented souls it is never going to happen; but I digress dear boy.*

Dumas also said it is necessary to wish for death in order to know how good life is; so with that in mind our hero, Edmond, is wrongly incarcerated in the infamous Chateau d'If where he befriends a priest, Abbe Faria, and as the story unfolds, as well as leading Edmond to untold wealth and riches, the kindly priest also aids in Edmond's escape.

The alarm you are hearing outside your door now is because the staff have discovered my body, if my plan has started well they should have found me hanging from the light fixture; stay where you are dear boy and keep reading, it is too late for me and if you waste this opportunity then I have died in vain.

Lucas wanted to rush next door, cut his friend down, loosen the noose and resuscitate his friend, but, and more importantly, he wanted out of this place.

If I have worked out which day of the week it is correctly then the weekend is due and the staff should be switching over. All days bleed into one another here, week days and weekend are as one for us. It is shift change in just under an hour, you must use that time to take my place for the ride to the mortuary, while they change shifts switch yourself with me.

During my years here I have seen them work like this many times, they will sort everything out, slip me into a body bag (horrid thought having my face covered so you will be doing me a favour by removing me from it) or sometimes it is just under sheet, we can both hope for the latter, and then the outgoing team will leave it for the new shift to get me to the morgue, there I will be put in the mortuary fridge until Monday. I have no doubt that a keen mind like yours has seen where this is going by now. Vis a vis, the Count and his escape for the dreaded Chateau; I cannot lead you to any treasure but your freedom should be golden enough for you.

You need to hide my body in my own room, I have cleared the space under my bed, they will spot you if you drag me to yours; then you need to get into the bag, or under the sheet, in my place and lie as still as death itself.

One last thing, I have no idea how you will get out from the inside of a morgue fridge but if you manage it, and you have made plans as I suggested a few weeks ago, then your faithful Annie will be waiting for your call, ready to come and get you and take you to your freedom Lucas.

Get away from this place my dear, dear friend, have a wonderful life, remember me fondly and if you make it and stay away, prove your innocence. If you discover you are not so innocent I will leave it up to you to do what your conscience dictates.

Treat every day like it is a new life Lucas, be safe and be happy dear boy, it has been a privilege.

Goodbye dear boy, your friend
Charles, The Colonel…

As he lowered his hands, and the letter, to his lap Lucas noticed that tears were streaming down his cheeks, his only friend in the last year had just sacrificed his life in order to give freedom to his associate.

There was little time to ponder or tarry, he reached under his bed for his trainers and slipped them on before moving to his cramped wash area and rinsing his face, the cold water revived him and sharpened his thoughts

Gently he pushed his cell door outward, just inches, so he could listen before he looked, a few more inches and pushing his face into the crack between door and jamb he quickly scanned the long and brightly lit, broad corridor, the floor tiles highly polished and reflective as a still pond would be. On the pristine surface it was without sign of the myriad of trainers that had just been running over it! First one way then the other he watched, there was no one in sight. Hope alone said that those who carefully watch the monitors connected to the corridor cameras would be too busy dealing with a suicide to worry about keeping vigilant with normal tasks.

He stepped out, ensuring he pushed his door until the lock clicked home. No going back now.

Walking softly avoiding his shoes squeaking on the highly polished and well-worn floor, with a stealth he did not feel he moved toward Charles' room, each step soundless, each careful step one nearer freedom.

Behind him, and a little way down the corridor, he could hear the muffled conversation of the hand-over conference, their voices and odd ripples of laughter drifting out of the nurses' room some twenty paces away. The main topic of that talk would definitely be the body awaiting transfer to the morgue. He realised that, in the corridors and meeting rooms of the institution, Charles would no longer be a name or an alter ego army officer, but hereinafter known as just 'the body'!

The door to the Colonel's cell was left unlocked, there was no reason to secure the door on a dead body, it was going nowhere, thoughts of escape had already been carried out; the dead escaped imprisonment with ease. Under the bed was a long drawer where private belongings were stored in the compact quarters and as Lucas pulled it out he realised Charles had indeed already cleared it, in anticipation of his body being placed there.

Thankfully there was no body bag, just a thin sheet covered his friend and Lucas pulled it back slowly, holding the triangular corner he peeled the covering away from his friend's cold and impassive face, as if in the hope that Charles was just playing dead and his only friend would be alive and burst forth with much laughter, but there was no bursting forth and no laughter, only sadness and a greying stillness in the face before him. A red, harsh, welt from the improvised noose circled his grey-skinned throat.

There was not much time to grieve but Lucas could not let the moment pass without a silent prayer. He struggled to find the right words, although he had been brought up as a regular church goer, since he had been given the choice at the age of fourteen about whether to attend or not he had chosen to not go and worship a deity that he had so much trouble believing in, now when he needed a prayer no words were available; the few tears that rolled down his cheeks became his only eulogy for Charles.

The disturbed and troubled wannabe officer looked peaceful as he lay at rest on his single bed in a way that Lucas had never seen in The Colonel before, the face had lost its lines, the permanently furrowed brow now smooth as the creases of concern and bad memories had been erased, Charles was at peace. "You have earned forgiveness my friend, rest easy from now on." Time had now run out and Lucas needed to act if his friend's selfless act of death was to be of any use.

He pulled the body, sliding it from the bed to the floor as gently as he could, even though there was nothing to Charles the weight surprising him, as much as his lack of strength. Charles fell to the floor, crumpling as he hit the grey utility carpet. Lucas muttered an apology before rolling him into the drawer, as he manoeuvred the limp form of his friend, Lucas realised how frail he had been, while everyone else on the wing had been overweight and with a sizeable paunch Charles was rake like.

An image entered the silent mind of Lucas, it was of a girl, a girl with no name, and she was slim, gangly white legs sticking from a skirt bunched up to the thighs, her head, like Charles', twisted to one side, her cheek a bloody mass of damaged skin. A brown brogue was pushing her under a bench, its toe scuffed and muddy; the scene repeated as Lucas shoved Charles under his bed. A bead of cold sweat drizzled down his spine making Lucas shiver and a wave of guilt for two deaths raged within. First the fist, flying into an innocent face, then the shoe kicking, pushing, the body rolling under the bench; a pale moon over an imposing spire, a pale face round and looking at him, two faces merging into one dreamlike image, one skinny and smiling after finding some sort of peace at last, the other damaged and bloody, both dead. Blood on his hands…

Charles' head, its face staring blankly, lolled backwards as Lucas struggled to get it all in the under-bed drawer, the fierce red line, where the noose fashioned from one end of the knotted sheet had been looped to facilitate the hanging, showed itself angry and raw. Lucas knew it had been a painful way to go; for both of the people he saw as his victims. Both with necks bent in the effort of death.

He pushed the shell that was once Charles under his bed, he could not fail but see the similarity of the scene once again as he had shoved the unnamed girl under the park bench; Lucas was hurting, wondering if he was doing right in trying to escape and still questioning if he deserved to be here. The letter, the sacrifice of his friend, and the belief that he was ultimately innocent drove Lucas forward into the escape plan. He would truly grieve for the loss of a friend later, for now the instinct of survival took over.

The body stowed away Lucas lay on the narrow cot bed, a parallel reflection of the man beneath him, the two of them together for the last time, he pulled the sheet, carefully over his own body, beginning at the feet he drew it up and made it as neat as he could, working it all the way up his body until finally he lay back and covered his face and head. Carefully sliding his arms down and across his body to assume the cadaver position, the undead playing dead, and he willed the white shroud to be hopefully lying flat over his body.

It was hard work to calm his breathing and soften his body movement to almost non-existence and slow his pounding, fearful heart, the adrenaline caused by fear of discovery not allowing him to remain totally calm. In Dumas' tale Edmund thought he would be interred in the cemetery, but a cannonball is chained to his ankles and he is thrown to the sea. Edmond Dantes thrown from the ragged cliff top of the remote chateau island and into a stormy sea the final moments of escape in danger of failing as the tide threw his body toward the sharp edges of the rocks, his release from the sewn, canvas, body shroud if he could free himself, dangerous and time consuming, drowning a distinct option; but also a preferable one to being returned to his dismal cell. Lucas, as Edmond Dantes, felt he would rather die than fail and for a moment he also realised it would have been rough justice if he did.

But, Dumas had allowed his hero to survive, to overcome the difficulties of escape from the inescapable, Lucas would have to find a way of calming himself and in the last moments before discovery, just as Dantes had evaded the rocks in the final moments of his escape, so Lucas must evade to tidal surges of discovery and failure. In his moment of most danger Lucas recalled the meditation techniques taught to him by his Sensei in the Judo classes, he focused, slowed his breathing. Slowly inhaling through the nose, exhaling and emptying his lungs through his mouth.

Reaching a state of torpor he closed down his mind, restricted the trembling of his body caused by fear and adrenaline, breath by breath he made his breathing slow, become shallow, until it was little more than a sip of air for each delicate inhale of oxygen, his heart rate slowed, the pounding he could feel in his chest became a light tap, tap of a heartbeat. He could not remember the last time such a calmness had taken over his body and mind. Even the fear of how to get out of a mortuary fridge before he died locked and panic stricken in its confines for a whole weekend diminished, he would cross that bridge to freedom when he came to it. Like Dantes he would figure out how to avoid the tide and the rocks on the way to freedom.

As he meditated he also prayed there would be an internal door latch on the fridges, surely there must be a way out from inside for cleaning, maintenance and such like. At least he hoped that would be the case! It would only be later that the realisation would hit of the selfishness of his actions, first he hid the broken unnamed girl to avoid blame, and now he had hidden a man he called friend for the same, selfish, self-serving purpose.

Finally with his breathing slowed and as shallow as he could get it, his chest motionless, Lucas heard the rumble along the echoing corridors of the mortuary trolley and voices of the nurses accompanying it on its procession toward the deceased. As they passed each individual room, the doors were slammed shut, the limp curtains covering each of the door windows remained closed and ignored contrary to normal security rules as each nurse was thinking more of their future because of a suicide on their wing; their only immediate worry to remove the body and ensure the locks were turned on every room to ensure the inmates were locked in for the night; Lucas could mentally picture them just pulling each curtain back on the door windows to check on each of the inmates , sorry, patients. He had no idea that they had ignored that procedure and hoped that by fluffing up his quilt to make it look like he had already settled down for the evening it would be enough.

Lucas heard and felt the door open into Charles' cell, his eyes were closed, but the lids merely resting in that position under the thin sheet and Lucas realised he had controlled his body enough for it to seem that he had indeed stopped breathing, fear and meditation techniques had stilled him and it seemed his heartbeat was paused and his lung and chest were about to burst open and give him away in an explosion of breath.

"Your turn for the feet end, I've got the head end this time!" The unseen porters divided up the body in much the same way as the Christmas turkey would be portioned out, 'you have the leg, I'm having the breast'. Even in death the inmates were outnumbered by staff as one of the senior nurses, with his deep and rasping tone, told the junior staffers to, "Just get on with it!" Three to one even in death!

The sheet remained over his body as one pair of arms slid under his legs, the other slid under his torso, his senses were so heightened by the fear of being discovered Lucas was certain he could feel the coarse hairs on the nurse's arms as they brushed against his skin.

"I will never get used to the fact that dead people should be cold, but their backs are always warm when we do this." Head End said.

"You know that's because the blood pools at the lowest point, which is his back and arse, when it stops pumping round, it has to go somewhere and it will be warm for a little while. It will soon chill when we get him in the fridge." Replied Feet End.

"I know but it still feels wrong!" Lucas could almost feel the male nurse shudder at he thought.

Dumped without ceremony onto the trolley, the cold metal of the tray almost caused him to take a sharp breath inward. No sooner had the body dropped on the cold, bare metal of the trolley than it was instantly trundled out of the room, banging hard against the door frame as Feet- End porter lost control of the wheels that wobbled like those on a supermarket trolley. The vibrations coursing through the prone body under the sheet, which slipped slightly and the thin cloth began to drift off his body; before Head End pulled it back over. Lucas could feel his heart beating in time with the wobbling wheel, the thump, thump, thump of wheel against shiny floor was equalling the pounding in his chest as he lost concentration and normal service was resumed within his body. He felt certain they would see his chest heaving and pounding beneath the thin covering with the fear of being discovered.

As the trolley, with Lucas on board, thumped into another doorway, careless driving costs lives, he thought, he began to think that this escape was from a place where he deserved to be and maybe he should just step off the table and go back to his room. Death, it appeared, followed him around, there was now a second body to be put in the causal column alongside his name, first the thin girl with no name who he had pushed under the park bench, and now The Colonel, Charles. A man who had heroism snatched away from him when he crushed his leg between the hard Portland rocks denying him an army career so long desired; but who had now become a hero in death helping his new friend. Whether it was madness, or heroism, Lucas would never know but for now the counterfeit dead had to keep up the pretence and subterfuge to ensure the real dead had not had his final great and brave moment taken away from him. As he fought to control his breathing and heart rate Lucas saw once again the thin, but pretty face although hardened by troubles in her short life, of the girl in the Bishop's Garden, he saw it undamaged, cheeks rosy with evening chill instead of red with blood, he liked the face. As he listened to door after door being unlocked and the portals negotiated he promised himself that if, when his memory of that day emerged, he discovered that he had indeed killed the thin girl, then he would give himself up and take whatever came his way. Deep in his mind, and heart, he knew, just knew, that he could not have broken anyone's neck, let alone the neck of the young girl with the pale, scrawny legs. He was not that kind of person. Was he?

The vacuum seal of the large refrigerator door had popped and hissed as it was swung open.

"Eugh! His back is still warm, thought it would have cooled by now." Head-end said as he slid his arms under the torso once again.

The cadaver for his part in the unfolding drama held his breath and tried with all his mental agility to slow and still his rapidly beating heart. He felt his feet being held…

"And… lift." Feet End pall carrier called the action.

Lucas was hoisted from the trolley and over the sliding tray that would take him into the dark interior of the cold storage room and even before his back hit the new metal tray he could feel the icy cold radiate from its surface. This one would be a real shock to the system and Lucas knew he could not react. It is a hard thing to brace oneself and yet remain limp and impassive; Lucas needed to be both.

Head End commented, as much to ease his loathing of lifting dead bodies as to keep conversation going in a mortuary, that the fridge would soon take the last of the warmth from his charge's body. "It's weird." He said as he released the torso to its fate. "He still feels, well, almost sweaty, the skin is clammy, never known one feel like that!"

"They are all different; life, or death for that fact, would be boring if we were all the same." Feet End said in support, nodding in pride at his own wise and sage comment.

When the warm back hit the ice cold metal tray the breath really did almost leave Lucas' body. Mentally he fought hard to keep any physical sign of the sudden change in temperature hidden. It was like being plunged into an ice-cold pool, almost unbearable, his body wanting to scream, his mind wanted to join it but he was being strong, he had got this far. He felt the very flesh stick to the tray as if being glued there. Every ounce of his being was tearing at him to let it all out, the body had its own defence systems and he was overriding it, but weakening.

Suddenly he felt the tray being shoved hard into its narrow and low slot within the fridge, the dead did not need headroom. It slammed against its metal rail stoppers, shaking his body a lot harder than the argumentative trolley wheel had done.

The door closed with a dull thump against its rubber seals, he heard the echo of the door's handle as it caught in its retainer. Felt the air forced from the space he now occupied. Darkness filled his world and replaced the little amount of light that had been sneaking through the thin weave of the covering sheet. The feeling of debilitating cold hit him but was instantly replaced with the sensation of claustrophobia and imprisonment; no, interment. If Lucas thought his heart was beating fast before, after what seemed a stoppage of many seconds, it now tried to beat a way out of his chest.

He was alone, he never felt so isolated, so far from help. Lucas tried to move, but the cold metal beneath his back had 'glued' him to the metal tray that held him and his fellow cadavers in near-by frozen rows. Wriggling to try and free his body from the tray it felt as if the skin on his back, buttocks and backs of his thighs were tearing away from the bone, reaching up with shaking hands, now almost numb with cold, and within just inches they struck the cold metal underside of the tray above. Every movement was slowed down, every reaction stilted and stiff, and even the claustrophobic shock that now hit him took a moment to register as if in slow-motion. Lucas mentally saw a body lying prone in that space over his face. Reaching to the right his hand, now moving with a slow, purposeful, wariness, touched the linen shroud of yet another fridge inmate, he recoiled and banged his elbow against a metal upright, the sharp pain from the collision offering up yet another aspect of the panic that was beginning to enshroud him.

The thought crept into his mind, an unsettling predator stalking a prey of disquiet, slowly as with every other thought and movement in this icy tomb, 'is this to be the end?' Laying his hands back on the cold steel tray Lucas gathered his thoughts, an old expression springing to his mind, there was a need to 'gird his loins', and just get on with working out how to escape this new self-imposed prison of metal and debilitating cold. Escape the icy prison as Dantes had escaped the foaming sea and threatening rocks.

When he stopped to concentrate it came to him, meditation again. He brought his martial arts training to the fore once more and with short breaths he began to concentrate on his inner-self. Again he slowed his breathing, which had increased its rate with the panic of being in an enclosed space, the smell of death all around invasive despite the cold trying to disguise it. During one judo championship a couple of years ago he had suffered a broken rib, an opponent falling on him in the hope that injury would give him the bout; his ploy had failed, but Lucas still had several bouts to fight through in order to reach the final stages of the Championship. Then, as now, was not ready to give in, to submit to fate.

After each fight he had sat in a corner of the hall and meditated, telling his brain that he was not in pain and the injury meant nothing, if he had not been so cold he would have smiled at the thought as he went on that day to win a bronze medal for his trouble and pain. His brain went off into an almost trance-like state and yet he remained aware of his surroundings and situation; with each breath the shivering eased from his body, his teeth clenched, against the cold, opened slightly easing the tightness in his jaw, and he could almost feel the tray beneath him begin to thaw, his flesh begin to warm.

This was not going to be the last place he would remember; he would prevail...

Even though his mind was telling him something different, Lucas was shivering with a deep, internal cold he had never felt before that numbed body and brain, all the while gazing hard into the darkness waiting for his eyes to become accustomed to the little light that crept in through gaps where nothing else could find room for entry, it felt like a sci-fi prison where violent offenders were put into a frozen state for their prison term, only thawed upon their release.

Now that his meditation technique had lifted him from the doldrums of that cold he began to take in his cramped surroundings a little more earnestly, he began to look around his chiller coffin looking for an exit, a door release. Knowing he was about to, or at least hopefully, step back into the real world he became aware of his own nakedness. As a new born infant he was about to enter the world naked; a rebirth and a new beginning.

The only hope was that somewhere along one of the metallic and insulated walls there was an emergency escape button, they would have to have a way of getting in and cleaning the large fridge, which meant they would have to have a way out if the cleaner became trapped inside. And, that way out had to be a release button, or upright entry door, somewhere nearby.

As the light grew from total darkness to dim and then just murky Lucas saw it, his way out. Three bays across and two down he saw the red button, although it looked grey in the dull interior and with its layer of frost. Six letters, three across and two down; a crossword clue leapt to his wandering mind; 'A way out'... *escape*!

Like a potholer in a maze of tunnels within his metal cave he twisted from the plateau of tin where he had been placed, the top half of his body squirming, shoulders just managing to squeeze from his small cavern into the next awaiting portal. His body heat had melted the frosty surface of the tray and he now wriggled and moved in a shallow pool of icy cold water.

He gripped the cold uprights that connected each shelf and pulling his freezing and exhausted body from one part of the metallic grotto to the next. As he worked his way three across and two down, his human crossword, his mind took him elsewhere to a place that had terrified him almost a decade ago, but that had now, he realised, prepared him for this moment in time. As his body wriggled slowly forward his mind went back...

Lucas had become besotted with a half Chinese, half English girl who was stunning with her petite figure and semi-oriental look, wonderful cheekbones sharp and delicate beneath glorious dark eyes shaped like almonds had captivated him. He had always felt in awe of her and never quite comfortable in her company, it always felt as if he were tiptoeing through broken glass when with her, and this feeling was made worse when she turned out to have a low boredom threshold and a heightened sense of the adventurous. Although the family business was yacht brokerage he had only sailed dinghies at his local yacht club or small craft on coastal waters, she had talked him into taking a navigation course and then borrowing a 27 foot yacht to sail her across the English Channel to Guernsey and then onto St Malo in France. The return trip would take them via St Hellier in Jersey but two things brought the sailing adventure to an abrupt end.

A bad batch of mussels in St Malo and the rolling seas on their homeward journey meant that both skipper and girlfriend crew suffered seasickness and vomiting beyond belief. She had stayed in the cabin and he had to stay on deck to sail the yacht, called Moonfleet if he recalled correctly, into St Hellier. The worst part of the journey was during the last few hours of approach into the popular port.

Such are the rocks in this part of the English Channel, vessels have to sail within sight of the port, but running parallel with it, for a couple of hours before they can tack back and head into the safe haven. All the while the sea produced high rolling waves every time Moonfleet broached, and heaved its little white hull over the foaming crests, Lucas on deck would also heave in time, dry retching as there was nothing left for him to disgorge. It was a horrid cruise but worse was to come.

He should have changed girlfriends then and there. As they overnighted in St Hellier a storm blew in curtailing the sailing for a few days, something which Lucas was eternally grateful for. Instead they abandoned the yacht to a hired crew to sail it back to home port in Chichester while the sickly pair took a plane into Southampton airport; the only part of the adventure Lucas had enjoyed, aside from the wonderful pre-mussel-poisoning sex that they had performed on the deck of the yacht one warm evening in Guernsey.

Not having learned his lesson on that adventure when as well as changing plans, he should also have changed girlfriends; he went along with her when she organised their next escapade, her mention of The Red Devils first brought to mind a possible training session with Manchester United football club but as he hated football he quickly changed his thoughts to the Army freefall parachute team and knew he was in trouble! This surely would involve leaping from a perfectly good and serviceable airplane.

And so it was, in the name of charitable donations, that for two days the instructors, who had them leaping from platforms as high as table tops to practice falling and which seemed wholly inadequate, had continually told them nothing could go wrong or would go wrong. That was before the last part of the two day course where more than half a day was spent on what to do if it did go wrong! It was not a comfortable few hours.

All geared up they finally sat on the floor of the Brittain Norman Islander, a small plane that held eight jumpers and yet no door to stop them from falling out at any given moment. Lucas felt this was a particular unnecessary risk, not even having a door, but it did not seem to faze the Red Devils who rode in the plane with them.

The plane took off, circled tightly, climbing ever higher with each loop, until it reached just over 2000 feet and then the Jump Master ordered everyone out of the aircraft, one at a time, so as to plummet on faith alone that the chute would open as planned and leave the occupant of the straps to float toward the ground and safety. Terra firma never looked so good and on feeling the effect of ground rush, where the earth comes up to meet your dangling feet at a rapid rate of knots Lucas had to admit that he loved every moment.

He left the plane; "One thousand and one! One Thousand and two! One Thousand and three!" He counted down the seconds and screamed at the blue sky above him as he exited the doorway and plummeted away from the transport. "AND CHECK!" He yelled with grinning delight and feeling the incredible tug on the harness as he looked above to see the canopy open on its own, the umbilical cord between him and the aircraft having done its sole task of opening the chute for him.

As he drifted earthwards, steering the chute by pulling on the chords in his hands, he looked across the army town of Aldershot and revelled in the feeling of peacefulness and yet power as the ground still seemed a great distance away. Time spent hanging in the comfortable harness under the chute was not long enough and as he reached the treetop level his brain was able to equate height once more and the 'ground-rush' took over. He was no longer falling, mentally he was just hanging there as the earth rushed up to meet his legs, which training had instilled in him to hold in the right position for landing, and suddenly within a split second, or so it seemed, he had hit the ground, or rather the ground had hit his feet, and rolled as he had practiced so many times while leaping from the table top. Surprisingly uninjured he had leapt to his feet and rolled the chute up as he had been shown earlier that day. He had never felt so elated, so free, he had loved every moment of the experience.

He was first in the queue to take a second jump, and that queue was much shorter than the original flight that day.

The crunch moment came and finally he learned his lesson, enough was enough with the half-Chinese girl, and her marvellous almond shaped eyes and sharp cheekbones, following, what turned out to be, their final adventure together. Lucas always considered himself fairly brave and up for most things but their last adventure together he did not enjoy for one moment, not for one little second.

After walking for a mile, from a car park deep into the Welsh countryside, along a very precarious footpath that circled a mountain and then crawling through a small metal door hidden among rocks on the edge of that mountain, before spending the next six hours crawling through narrow gaps between rocks and through small crevices that existed far within the mountain itself along an ever narrowing channel. At one particularly nasty point, it meant scurrying through a thirty foot long tunnel, three feet in diameter and half full of water. And, this, according to the half-Chinese girl with her stunning smile, was for fun.

As he shivered in his frozen confine of the morgue, the cold numbed his brain and while remembering their final adventure he struggled to recall her name.

Preparation the previous evening had, like most outdoor adventures, begun in a small local pub drinking copious amounts of a dark beer that was more suited to Irish tastebuds than Welsh, and that had been followed by a take-away curry from the tiny Indian restaurant in the, laughably named, High Street. Bellies full and everyone in the team half drunk, the night for Lucas and his girlfriend had been spent in a glorious, deep and comfortable bed, the plumped quilt like a cloud settling over them and protecting them, situated on the first floor of a Welsh farmhouse where the view when they sat up in bed the next morning looked out, through a massive picture window, over a lush green valley and in the hollow below their window a stunning lake, its surface shimmering in the early morning sunshine, surrounded by a lofty forest of tall, dark green, pines that climbed all the way to the far ridge of the valley. He had enjoyed immensely that part of the adventure, he could have lain in that bed all day, but while safely snuggled under the quilt with a sexually adventurous girl, he was totally unaware of what was to come later that day.

They had arrived at the farmhouse in the dark after the session in the nearby pub, and the filling curry, and then had made energetic love on the deep and soft mattress and fallen asleep in each other's arms while watching the reflection of the bright and full moon in the lake below. On waking the next morning, within seconds of each other, they were left speechless, and emotional, by the scene that greeted them through the broad window at the foot of the bed. The sun was rising over the pine tree covered hillside and allowed its light to be danced across the surface of the still lake. It was magnificent. Sadly for Lucas that would not be the memory he would take home after the weekend away, the only things he would recall would be the narrow, panic instilling, passageways, the sharp rocks that cut flesh and bruised bodies, even before crawling through the flooded tunnel, propelled forward by his elbows and the tips of his toes.

The love-making, and the views, had been the last enjoyable thing that day and would prove to be the last adventure with that particular girlfriend.

Following the walk around the mountain path that at times required the attributes of a mountain goat, they had passed through the small hatchway and signed the visitors' book, as if booking into a cold and damp guest house, and then the fearful journey began. Dressed in a tight boiler suit, too short and therefore uncomfortable, eye-wateringly so around his groin area with Lucas' long body; a safety helmet perched tightly on his head with a taught strap under his chin and topped with a powerful torch, he felt like the miners he had seen in news reports being taken down to the dark shafts of coal; before the pits had been closed down and abandoned that was. Formalities done with the 'signing in', the dozen adventurers began to squeeze between rocks and hard places. The first few yards, were indeed an adventure, with the banter that always goes hand-in-hand when a group of intrepid explorers start out on their quest, and Lucas had to admit he was quietly enjoying himself; that was until he came upon a blank wall, craning his head in all directions on three sides all he could see was rough cave walls, the fourth side was the route which had brought them to this point. Puzzled Lucas turned to their guide; "Where to now?" It was an honest question as he could see no way forward.

"Through there." A finger pointed ahead and downward.

Lucas looked to where the shadowy digit of the guide was pointing, it was down, and into the shadows where the beam from his head-lamp had not reached, there, in the darkness, was a small hole in the rock face, round like the black pupil of an eye staring out. Big enough for rabbits, or whatever tiny animal lived in these caves, but way too small for a human or so he thought.

"How the hell do we get through there?" It was said with a throat constricted with panic and an octave or two higher than Lucas normally spoke.

"Quickly as possible!" Was the glib and unemotional reply.

It was the only instruction offered as the guide dropped to his knees, bent forward until he lay on his stomach, and then, with a push of toes and a pull of elbows, scurried away into the wet and rocky burrow, disappearing into the dark gaping mouth as if he had been food for the mountain and had been gratefully swallowed up, a sacrificial offering.

Two others of the group, bearded and hairy and looking like they enjoyed folk music and craft fairs, followed with undisguised enthusiasm, Suzi, *that was her name*, the soon to be ex-girlfriend, waited for Lucas to build up his courage. Afraid more of looking bad than looking scared it was with much trepidation he knelt and looked into the hole which swallowed up the light from his helmet in just a few feet, but in the all too short distance he saw the reflection of brackish water. He wanted to back out there and then, never being a lover of confined spaces, he wanted to sit on the hillside, in fresh air and sunshine, counting the sheep while waiting for them all to reappear, but with a girlfriend patiently waiting for the next move, that move had to be a brave one, even if the decision had been made at that moment that she was soon to be an ex!

As he had seen the others do it was to his knees first and then dropped to his belly and with his elbows doing the work of dragging him through the narrow, wet, confining tunnel, Lucas begin the thirty feet of hell which seemed like thirty yards and then thirty miles as it seemed to never reach a conclusion.

The elbows dug into the rough walls and floor of the tunnel while his feet, like a penguin pushing his way across an icy surface, moving so fast that ahead of him in the watery part of the tunnel he was forming a bow-wave. Lucas had begun the real journey into the cave, a trek that would take three hours of small, damp, dark and dangerous holes in order to reach one large dark, dank hole in the middle of this mountain, and all the while in his mind was the realisation that the only way back was to once again scuffle though that tunnel half filled with water and totally full of dread.

In the heart of the hole-riddled mountain there were not enough stalactites or stalagmites to make the cathedral sized cavity one of interest, to Lucas it was as advertised, a big, black, dank and dark hole. Disappointment joined fear on its day out!

When frightened Lucas always had the habit of talking, about anything and everything, just chattering away to no one in particular and about nothing in particular. Such was his mood and the depth of his fear he talked his way into the heart of the mountain... and then after a brief spell 'enjoying' the sensory deprivation of the large black hole, talked his way out again. Unlike the parachute jump where everything he did, he did without a word, so calm did he feel.

After six long and tortuous hours, they had signed out of the visitors' book and dragged sore and bruised bodies back through the metal hatchway. Those who treated this as sport relived every inch and every squeeze through crevice and tunnel, revelling in the shared, excited chatter about beating the cave. Lucas stopped talking at this point, looked at the glorious and sun brightened views from the side of the mountain then looked at the girlfriend, not even noticing the almond eyes and the marvellous cheekbones at this moment, and then the sheep that filled the very welcome hillside, and continued to graze in ignorance at the human adventure; those sheep, he thought with some venom, had more chance of being his next date.

It was in silence that Lucas and his girl with those great cheekbones, amazing eyes and spirit for adventure in and out of the bedroom headed back to the farmhouse. It was just a few hours previously that the farmer's wife had sliced delicious bacon rashers, thick and richly smoked, from the hock hanging from the kitchen ceiling beam, but it seemed like days ago to Lucas. They went to their room, packed and climbed into the car before she spoke. "Do I take it that was our last adventure together?" She had captured the vibe perfectly and the question was asked without too much emotion as she already knew what the answer would be.

"You do!" He said with finality.

Those were the last words spoken during the four and half hour journey home, Lucas hid his annoyance and did not even mention how much it irked him when she unilaterally retuned the radio to Radio One, which played the types of music he could not stand presented by banal and whining DJs that he liked even less than the music, he put up with it rather than speak, rather than step into confrontation. Outside her apartment there was a clipped farewell and a brushing kiss on one magnificent cheekbone before they parted company.

Nothing of value had been gained in his life with that trek into the mountain, but now the memory of the experience and the fear he felt held strange comfort for him as the thoughts of that final adventure with the girl with the almond eyes were now helping Lucas as he crawled and pulled his way across the inside of the large fridge. He muttered inane words to himself as he traversed three across and two down, a Knights move in Chess.

Squeezing between shelves and twisting his, slightly podgy, body he caught his rib cage on a sharp edge. He could only move forward, the lack of manoeuvrable room meant there was no reverse in this situation. He felt the skin on his side snag, tear and rip away as he forced his torso onward; the blood that oozed from the long, deep, scrape warm against his icy skin, the feeling a mixture of painful discomfort as the cold was numbing the wound slightly, and relief as the warmth of the blood coated and eased the coldness of his flesh.

Another sheet-covered cadaver to traverse, cold, stiff, he imagined it to be a rocky outcrop that had to be challenged and beaten; barred his progression to the escape button, it was inches away from his outstretched hands as he continued to navigate the metal cave. Fingers grasped for purchase to aid the movement forward and the white sheet, bright even in the dark of the man-made grotto, and that covered the body slid away revealing the haggard face, skin grey, its lips blue, and the blue/grey sagging breasts of an elderly woman; Lucas mentally apologised to her for the loss of dignity at the same time as he realised that death was no longer holding him with its twin grips of fear and revulsion. He saw the old lady as just another impediment to be overcome on his way to freedom and he slid, cold skin on cold skin over the body, he shuddered at the touch but it was something that had to be endured, his chest pressing and moving the soft flesh of breasts that, probably, her husband had once hefted and squeezed in passionate hands. Sliding from her body Lucas dropped back down to the tray below. It was a Crystal Maze exercise but instead of points at the end for his team there was freedom and a chance to prove, or disprove, his innocence.

Blood still running down his side and over his hip he now cracked his cold shin, hard and bruising, removing a shaving of skin against a sharp edged upright and cursed loudly, his own voice echoing like some ghostly spectre in the enclosed space. It was then that he realised he had been talking to himself, non-stop, from the moment he had moved from what should have been Charles' resting place in the fridge.

Despite the need to get away from this place with as much time to spare as possible, he hoped they would find his friend's body soon and treat it with the dignity and respect it deserved, instead of being stuffed in an under bed compartment like luggage unwanted on the journey! Instead of, like DEATH OF AN UNNAMED GIRL, shoved without dignity or thought, under a park bench because discovery would have been inconvenient!

Exhausted, fighting for every breath in the cold and near airless environment, it took one final effort, every unfit and out of condition sinew straining with the effort, he reached around one last upright, while lying on his side in the last row of the fridge trays, blood mixing with icy condensation. One more across and two up from the floor, he took a deep breath with which to steel himself for the final assault, it chilled and ripped at his throat and the inside of his lungs felt like frozen meat, it hurt his teeth and stung his gums as the cold air started its journey into him and Lucas also, in those final moments before release from this tomb, realised the smell that kept filling his nostrils was the smell of death. He recalled a mortician friend of his father's saying that he could never get bitten by a dog; no matter how much he showered or what cologne he wore the dogs could still smell death on him and they stayed well away, he was not a man who could have pets except for maybe a goldfish or two.

Panic once again helped him as he stretched, reached, pushed his hand ever nearer the button. He slapped at it, missed. Tiredness was attacking his every movement with a deliberate attempt at leaving him in the metallic grotto to die. He reached, so hard he could feel his shoulder wanting to dislocate, slapped again and felt like he had caught the half-round ball of plastic, his heart held a beat, he held his breath, nothing!

What felt like a final supreme effort, the arm fully extended, the tear in his side pulling open, shedding more blood, pains in his side, pain in the skinned shin and every muscle an aching mass, he produced a third slap into the semi darkness, his arm stretched out...

Something gave under his hand, something popped in his ears, like they do on an airplane as it takes to the skies. Then to complete the collection of popping sounds, every door puffed, as air being blown from cheeks, as the airtight seals were broken and the doors, in a single regimental movement of precision timing, all cocked open. Light and fresh air flooded in, even a wave of warmth seemed to pour into the enclosed space, but that may have been a welcome snippet of imagination. Lucas was sweating with exertion despite the cold of the fridge and he was free, he slid out from his final resting place, the last tray in the row, and stepping out onto the tiled floor of the mortuary he was away from that metal and cold, multi-tiered coffin that could well have been his demise, for a moment he felt more comfortable with the thought of real death in their rather than the living death of being confined to Broadmoor.

The cold room behind him he realised it would soon be the transit lounge for Charles' on his way to his own final resting place, that thought hit him with almost overwhelming sadness. Greater love hath no man than this; that a man lay down his life for his friends... Lucas could not recall where the quote came from, unsure but he thought it was the bible, but he knew that Charles had been and was, even in death, a true friend.

He had been leaning against the door, catching his breath, feeling his wounds, but with time of the essence he forced himself upright, dragged his cold, weary body away from its tomb. He shared the task of looking around the room for clothing of some sort with a quick gaze at his wounds, blood oozed down his side and he could see a flap of skin laying against his ribs. Tearing paper towels from a dispenser over the large, chrome sink he slid them up his torso and replaced the divot of flesh back into the hole that had been made, a good golfer always replaces his divots. Then he looked down at the blood stained leg and a long graze of a wound as if he had been attacked by a cheese grater, it was the lesser of the wounds and of little concern for now...

Looking around the clinical surroundings for clothing, and the next stage in his escape, he noted a telephone, he had never received the one call they always mentioned when arrested in the American movies, now he had only one call to make, only one person he trusted to act upon his call. He rang the White House, hoping Annie and not his brother would answer and at the same time hoped someone on the switchboard in the hospital had not noted a call was being made from an unmanned mortuary on a Friday evening. He decided to ring the number and not put a nine before it as you would when passing through a switchboard. He heard it connect in the cottage and imagined phones ringing around the house.

CHAPTER 14

She left the waterside cottage just before daylight had appeared over the marina and harbour, the sun still an hour or so away from raising its lazy head above the horizon. And, just over an hour, or so, away Lucas would be living every moment hard and frightened. Behind the wheel a nervous Annie too was counting the each and every minute, just like she had counted the miles on the seemingly unending journey up to Berkshire from Chichester, each mile had been endured and counted and now ever minute and every second was being lived in a surreal way and counted down.

The drive on visiting days was a different matter, those trips were accompanied by the slight thrill and joy at seeing Mr Lucas as the car ate up the miles on the way up; the journey home though was filled with no small amount of despair, but it was always a drive that offered beautiful scenery and that in some part made up for the disheartening reason for the regular trip, it was almost made enjoyable by the wonderful sight of nature as it sped past the windscreen.

As she drove lost in thought, Lucas lay under a concealing bush. A night, now giving way to weak morning light, spent listening to every crack of twig, every move of nocturnal creature, and he shivered as cold bit into every bone once again, escape now beyond the tall walls and razor wire, Lucas could not have known it but there was also tension and high blood pressure in the open spaces beyond his hiding place. Just a few hundred yards or so away from his hiding place Annie checked her watch for probably the ten thousandth time, nerves almost getting the better of her. She had reached their pre-arranged spot just as early rising dog walkers and families were setting out for early morning strolls, each taking a wary look at her sat in the car, Annie did not know how to act or react and so just sat there nodding at anyone who looked through her windscreen and at the elderly lady sitting there.

Meanwhile back at the cottage down on the edge of Chichester Harbour a livid Jacob ranted and raged in the kitchen, with no Annie there to cook breakfast or him he was reduced to heading out to the Boathouse restaurant for his bacon and eggs; Annie was going to be replaced after this weekend, the old crone would be out on the street, enough was enough with her disloyalty. So angry was he at her not being home to wait on him, that he never even thought about where she might be, even if he had aiding in his brother's escape would not have been one of the options.

Back in the car park that fed the wooded country park, every small noise and disturbance at the edge of the woods, caused Annie to be startled, her eyes felt as if they were standing out on stalks, a scratch of a branch, the trill of an morning bird heading seeking food, the argumentative laughter of the crows as they flew over the tree tops, every sound magnified by fear of being caught.

Now, hunkered down in her car trying to remain inconspicuous but by her actions achieving the opposite, she waited on the edge of Bramshill Forest, where, during one visit to Broadmoor a some weeks ago she had walked to shake of the malaise of visiting her young master, she told Mr Lucas it would be where she would wait for him during their brief phone call. When asked for her help she had not hesitated, not baulked at what was being asked of her; why would she?

Annie took her driving glasses off and rubbed the bridge of her nose. All she knew was that Lucas would, by some miracle, be arriving sometime soon. Always being a capable boy she watched as he grew into a confident, even cocky sometimes, young man. Annie had never a moment's doubt about Lucas and still had every faith in him, but, and it was a huge but, she could not help feeling this was a wasted journey an escape from the secure unit like trying to juggle smoke; all well and good in theory but impossible to implement.

By parking in the forest car park she, hoped, looked more like a forest walker rather than some suspicious character waiting for an escaped murderer, an insane one at that, to arrive after breaking out from Broadmoor. Would they be searching for him already? Her only hope was that being in a busy car park she would raise less suspicion and attention than waiting near housing or closer to the hospital.

As with anyone carrying out some sort of illicit act, part of Annie's conscience was most definitely pricked, her biggest guilt trip when she had eaten an entire Easter egg, and the two rich chocolate bars from the same box, in one quick sitting when she had put herself on a diet only days before and the biggest illegal action so far in her life had been stealing a bag of sweets from her local Woolworth store in the same week she had become a teenager. Dared by her, so-called, friends, she had thought it better to steal than to suffer the indignity and bullying she would surely receive if she had not fulfilled the dare. As it transpired the dangerous felon and big time thief had walked no more than two paces from the door before the store detective held onto the collar of her school blazer and quietly said, although there was little doubt in the forcefulness of the request, "I think we had better step back into the office don't you Miss!" Polite and authoritarian in one, heart stopping, sentence.

Her widowed mother was mortified to discover her little Annie, was now a hardened criminal. Annie for her part, although she never uttered this out loud, kept believing, it was just a bag of sweets so what was the big deal. It took her some time to realise the big deal was the fact that her mother carried the burden of shame for the both of them, and it took a promise of severe home penalties which included grounding and a whole fortnight of doing the washing up, before she was allowed to leave the store and go home, while the store manager content this was a just a one-off occurrence decided that no further action would be taken. Mother meted out the punishment and Annie never transgressed again, never broke the speed limit, or at least not by much, and never took anything ever again that did not belong to her. Now here she was sitting in a lay-by on the edge of a forest waiting for an escaped lunatic who, it was said, unbelievably, had beaten a young girl before leaving her to die under the slats of a hard park bench. But, there again this was her Lucas and she had been taking care of him since he was a young boy and she had always believed in him incapable of such an action.

There would be consequences, of that she was sure, there always were when one stepped out of line, no matter what the reason. For Annie the deepest of her concerns was not the law and its powers, it was the ire of Jacob when he got up and discovered she was not there to wait on him. Anger would fill the cottage while she sat waiting at the forest's edge. Compared to the resulting fallout of that cataclysmic event the full force of the law would pale into insignificance; the anger of Jacob when things did not go his way was far more frightening than any police action!

An hour had already passed since Annie had parked her car, it seemed like more. There was an almost overwhelming fear that someone would spot this little old lady sat in a car, in a lay-by at the edge of the woods – being a strange occurrence on its own. But the mere fact it was also just a few minutes away from a hospital for the criminally insane, a place she could well end up herself if not for the fact it was a men-only facility, and people would view everything out of the ordinary as suspicious.

Just once, feeling conscious of just sitting there, she had stepped from the car and walked around the parking area, skirting the line of trees, where shadows were growing shorter by the minute as the sun took the early start of a journey across the blue sky, that line signalled the edge of the forest. It seemed the sort of place that Annie would have loved to don her walking shoes and explore; the hidden paths and well-trodden walkways that make up the beautiful English countryside. Since childhood she had enjoyed the feeling of isolation and freedom as she walked, letting her mind wander along with her feet, taking in the lush green of her surroundings in summer months and the stark nakedness of the trees in the winter. Annie especially enjoyed being the first human footprints in new snowfall, she would get into tracking mode, following the slim prints of the fox or the slightly deeper cloven hoofed tread through the white landscape of the deer. One day she had followed the tracks of a small deer that she assumed was that of a delicate roe and as she turned a corner of the woodland sanctuary there was the deer, a young roebuck, which was hunkered down in a snow drift in much the same way as a dog snuggles down into its blanket. All that was on view was the deer's hind quarters at one end and its head and neck at the other. Her appearance did nothing to startle the young buck, he just stayed in his snowy den and they watched each other for more than thirty minutes until the cold began to make Annie shiver.

As she climbed back into her car, a little red hatchback that Mr Lucas had bought her as a birthday present two years ago, she noted the mud up the side panels, thrown there by agitated tires as she had pulled a little too quickly into the pot-holed lay-by after almost missing the ideal spot to wait for Lucas. As she pulled the door closed and the interior light faded to darkness she had a little shiver, partly to ward of the chill that still held sway in the weak morning light, partly out of nervous fear but mostly in memory of that cold morning stood watching the roebuck hunkered down in his snowy bed.

On the edge of the forest Annie checked her watch again, habit more than need; just a few minutes had passed since her last check and she began to believe that the escape bid had failed. There was also an awareness that visitors to the forest walk were arriving, exercising legs, dogs and children before returning to their cars and still the dotty old lady was sat in her car; one friendly soul had even knocked on the driver's door window to ask if she was okay and did she need any assistance. Annie had replied that she just enjoyed sitting out in the countryside. As for Lucas she did not know what to do; she just knew she would wait all day, and into the night, if she had to!

Cramped from sitting in the car for so long there was a need to stretch her legs but knew she could not stray too far from the car. There was always the fear that as she turned the curve in the path Lucas would emerge from the woodland that would surround her.

Both realised it would be a waiting game was no sure way of making this escape run like clockwork, too many variables, too many things that could go wrong. Lucas unsure if when, or how, the ruse would be uncovered, morning role call would reveal all but he had no way of knowing how time was passing.

Annie decided she would take a walk through the woodland so as not to arouse suspicions of anyone nosy enough to notice her; she also had no doubt that some of the staff from the hospital would walk their own dogs here. Despite the warmth of summer the chosen footpath was covered in a soft carpet of pine needles that had been shed by the towering conifers that, sentinel like, lined up for inspection on either side of the narrow path. The footway was muddy, soft underfoot, one of those that never dried out summer or winter as it was sheltered from the drying elements of the weather by the trees.

After some fifteen minutes of walking she reached a steep climb up a hillside that seemed to just spring up out of the forest, she looked at the imposing hill, and then down at her muddied walking shoes, enough mud had been collected to convince anyone that she had indeed visited the forest for the scenery. Returning to the safe haven of the car, the excess mud had been kicked from her shoes, against the driver's side front tyre, before she had climbed into her pristine car, it annoyed her slightly to see the remaining dirt and mud from her shoes flaking and caking on her carpets.

Annie settled down for the wait, a wait that would take as long as it would take, she looked through the windscreen, slightly grimy from the motorway dust, and saw the bushes ahead of her shake and move, it had been a windless day so it could not be the breeze, she held her breath, fear stalked her heart. She sat upright to enable a better view across the top of her steering wheel, peering out into the open space between woods and car, hoping, expectant.

The disappointment hit hard, she let the breath from her lungs out in one long, drawn out, gasp, feeling her heart begin to pound again in her chest. A young roebuck, brown, a pair of unicorn style straight antlers pointing skyward as he sniffed the air, alert to any danger, as he nervously stepped out onto the grass verge from the protection of the trees. He took a tentative look around before bending his head to the ground to forage and graze. A few steps away from the deer a pair of colourful jays, their cries a raucous screech, had joined forces with a small flock of a dozen or so wood pigeons to peck at the soft ground and seek food. The buck dipped his head again, and just as quickly lifted it to look at his surroundings, ever alert to danger; sensing, rather than seeing, there was a person sitting in the car just ten feet away his almond shaped, soft eyes glared toward Annie; it was only a deer but the look was accusatory and she felt pangs of extreme guilt about breaking the law, even if it was for Mr Lucas.

Feeling every bit the age, of her 64 years, she could not help but ponder at the contradictions that life threw up, here she was in the middle of so much beauty, such peacefulness and there, just on the other side of this stretch of woodland, with its wonderful flora and fauna, and within a mile or so was a place of such mental destruction, madness and violence; it did not make sense.

With one last glance the dun coloured deer looked around the clearing, turned his back on Annie, and her feelings of guilt, and nonchalantly walked back through a tiny opening in the shrubbery, hidden again in his own territory. A few yards to his right, as the bright, white flash on his hind quarters disappeared amid the greenery there was more rustling and Annie, although she had been expecting it was shocked to see the now round face of Lucas; who on seeing her in her car strolled from the woods like a walker who had just hid behind a tree to relieve himself; not that many walkers, even on a warm morning such as this, would be out in pale green hospital scrubs and white, short, wellington boots. As he crossed the clearing, with as much nonchalance as he could manage, the oversize boots flapping around his legs; the pair of jays and the pigeons took to the air in a flurry of activity and feathers.

Annie could not help herself, she had to get out of the car and greet him, despite the earnestness of the moment.

"Hi Annie." The voice was quiet but she recognised it instantly, a puffing, slightly heavier, Lucas stood just a foot away from her and they moved in over the last few inches and hugged like a long lost lovers so intense was the embrace and she felt the ID badge he was wearing dig into her scrawny chest even through her light overcoat., She took in the costume of hospital scrubs, pale green, freshly laundered but around the ankles damp circles and muddy patches where he had been running through woodland that separated them from the high walls. The rest of the pale green outfit was damp and creased, testament to a night spent in the open. Clipped to the breast pocket was the ID badge, the photo was of a grey-haired man well into his fifties and would have never beaten any sort of scrutiny.

Breaking away from the tight hug and looking down at the tight fitting outfit Lucas explained, "It's all I could find to wear."

Annie, still had a semblance of humour left in her, a little joke is useful when tension needs to be relieved; looking him up and down while still holding him at arms' length; "I thought you were inmate, not staff or did they promote you?"

Awkward smiles broke across both their faces. "The weird thing Annie is that the last bit, and these scrubs, was the easiest when I thought it would be the hardest part of getting out of there. I got out of the fridges..." he saw a puzzled look on her face. "I will explain all later as we drive. But, I wound up in the mortuary and folded up in the changing room was this set of scrubs and on top of them the ID badge, I looked in the lockers but there were no civvies' clothes in any of them, not even a pair of trainers." He looked down at the white, bright even though muddy wellies on his feet. "I just put the scrubs on and walked up to the exit door, swiped the ID on the security pad and a door opened out onto the car park. I couldn't believe it and walked to the edge of the grounds, jumped a small fence into the woods and ran all the way here. It was almost too easy, I expected to hear dogs at my heels any moment." Then as an afterthought as Lucas looked at his surroundings, nervously much as the young deer had done a few minutes earlier, expecting at any moment to be discovered and hunted down. "Do they still use dogs?"

"Of course they still use dogs, but I know from watching those TV shows about the police and chasing getaway vehicles they are more likely to have helicopters with that night vision stuff where it can still see you through trees; and as my little hatchback is now one of the aforementioned get-away vehicles; please can we get away from here;" She looked at Lucas and noted his weight gain. "Now, get in the car, if you can fit chubby!" A smile from Annie to say, no offense, and one returned to reply none taken!

"Glad to see you have lost none of our charm and humour while I have been away Annie!" Lucas slid his seat belt clip into its holder with a firm click. It felt so 'normal' being free and back in the world, it puzzled Lucas that he should feel it as such.

"You make it sound like you have been away on holiday, young man, been a bit more serious than that though hasn't it?"

"I suppose it was a bit like a strange holiday Annie, nothing to do all day except sit around reading, or just sitting..." Lucas' face took on a glazed quality as he thought of the last ten or eleven months, not even really remembering how long it had been since he was last free. "With nothing to do all day, it always surprised me that we had to get up at seven each morning, eight on Sundays; they were nothing if not generous with the hours in our days."

As he stated the time they were normally roused he noted the clock on the dashboard read 7:10, the ruse would be discovered. Sooner than he thought it would happen, a loud and piercing whine of sound began to rise from over the trees, it wound itself to a huge crescendo and filled the very air they were trying to breath. It echoed, sounded as if it were coming from several different directions; it was the siren warning the residents of surrounding villages around Broadmoor that one of its charges had escaped; children would be swept indoors, windows and doors locked, and everyone within a few mile radius would be mentally cowering. In primary schools they would be taking headcounts every few minutes to ensure every child was safe and accounted for.

Annie pushed the gear stick forward and hit the accelerator, the car lurched forward kicking dust and dirt out from behind its wheels, spewing out a cloud of getaway rubble. "I haven't heard that sound since my youth when towns would test their air raid sirens once a week, a left-over of the war." Annie stated, breathless, as she looked right and left before forcing her little hatchback out onto the main road.

"Keep the speed even Annie, we don't want to draw attention to ourselves." He put calming hand on her elbow, and she in turn dropped the speed just slightly.

With the sirens only just spouting and screeching their warning, the surrounding police had not yet been galvanised into action, and while Annie was expecting a car chase of Steve McQueen and Bullet proportions, Lucas was quite pleased to note that the early morning roads were actually quite quiet, the sirens putting the school run on hold; maniac on the loose.

As with his egress from the morgue, the escape still seemed to be going with ease, both silently worried about the simplicity of it all as the car kept just a mile or two over each speed limit. 32mph, 42mph and finally a steady sixty as they left the towns and followed the country roads.

As they drove, the sound of the incessant sirens now left behind, neither knew what to say to the other, conversation, like any art, is something that needs to be practiced and both people in the front of that little red hatchback were out of practice. Annie spending as much time as possible up in her rooms at the top of the cottage, so as to avoid the ever angrier outbursts from Jacob; and Lucas with no one except the criminally insane to talk to, which sadly included his friend Charles, who was so barking mad he had taken his life so Lucas could begin to live his own again. The conversation between driver and passenger dried and then died, Lucas gazed out of the window, sadness etched in his reflection which faded as the sun rose higher and the world the other side of the glass grew brighter and brighter, freedom had never seemed so alight, so clean and so clear. In contrast his thoughts were darker, a storm cloud over his escape, that cloud the depression of a lost friend. He may have felt storm clouds of doubt filling his mind but nothing was as dark as the despair he had been feeling about the days and months closed away from his world with no hope or joy.

As the countryside, green and lush, bright with new growth, flew by his window he thought all the way back, back to the Bishop's Garden and that poor girl who he had hidden under the bench in the park, he could not recall ever hearing her name so to him she was still just the girl in the park. He could see her now with her skinny legs, limp and white against the darkness of the evening grass, he could make out her untidy, stringy hair, blonde and plastered to her forehead with the blood from her torn and damaged cheek congealing on face and neck, a dark blemish clogged into blonde hair.

"Are you okay Lucas." Annie asked, flicking her eyes between the country lane unravelling in front of them and Lucas sitting alongside her and looking so troubled, she placed a reassuring hand on his forearm.

Without turning round he responded. "I was just thinking about that poor girl in the park Annie, did they ever tell you her name?" Annie just shook her head in response. "If I did kill her I deserve to be back in that place." Annie knew that Lucas needed to find answers and platitudes from her were not going to make him feel better so she chose not to respond. She would not normally condone self-pity, but felt that Lucas deserved a little, just this once.

Lucas continued to look out of the window and even though it was only a few months ago that he had lost his freedom he began to notice that around the new growth of nature with the pale green of new foliage there was a contrast, something he had not had call to notice before; but, now it stuck out like a proverbial sore thumb; what a dirty, untidy and grey dusty country England had become!

Inside Broadmoor it was always clinically clean, it looked dust free, always smelt antiseptic; the floors of corridors, common rooms and cells shone; he knew they were always called rooms as it was a hospital but to him and other inmates with a little of their sensibilities intact they were cells. They were small, claustrophobic and they were all locked in at night, and released in the mornings; that was the definition of a cell, surely!

In comparison, the roads and the villages they drove through, Lucas realised some miles ago they were not taking the busy A3 south and thought it sensible that Annie had chosen to take lesser roads through countryside and villages, but when they did pass through civilisation he noted the litter, the grey dusty roads, chip wrappers, fast food boxes, mini plastic rubbish sacks in various colours littered the gutters and roadsides. The English countryside had become a rubbish bin for its inhabitants.

Sandhurst, a place of conflict, a scruffy little town, run down and depressing, despite it being the home of the Royal Military Academy where trainee officers, in their highly polished boots and shining regalia, marched on a spotless and pristine parade ground, trained to become the elite in the British armed forces. The grubby town surrounding the Royal Military Academy appeared greyer and dirtier than everywhere else they had journeyed that morning. Even the trees and shrubs that lined roads and kept parallel with footpaths were not safe as thoughtless dog owners had been busy throwing their full dog poop bags into the branches to act like weird Christmas decorations that remained dangling in branches like pink and black testicles until some stranger decided it was time for them to come down and be disposed of properly.

A once beautiful England with its glorious countryside was now a litter bin for idle fast food eaters and dog owners to despoil, a place where council street-sweepers would not be seen from one year to the next, their brooms lying idle in some work's store. Lucas felt much like the streets he was viewing through the car window as they swiftly passed through village and farmland; his mind was cluttered with the dirty and dusty debris of life, his heart was littered with the rubbish and dirt of how his life had turned out this way; and all the while the monotone grey detritus of England continued to whizz past his eye-line leaving him sad for the loss of beauty, in a once green and pleasant land.

As it is wont to do, traffic built up around Farnham and the bustle and braking of the tail end of rush hour annoyed him and made him continually look around and behind, town centres and major road junctions seemed to him to be the most dangerous places to be recaptured. And, all the while the wailing drone of the sirens, that had now faded with the distance of travel, still filled his ears where early morning birdsong had lightened the mood of day; now, with each mile travelled the sound diminished to silence with distance.

It was not until the countryside opened up again with views of field, farmland and woods surrounded by the rolling hills of North Hampshire that Lucas began to relax once more. He took time to look at Annie, who was as intent on her driving as a Formula One racer at Monaco.

"You okay Annie." His voice seemed to startle her and the car veered slightly from its onward journey, before regaining its straight and true line.

"I am fine Lucas, just glad to see you again." She smiled the smile of a parent or carer who wished to ease a discomfort in their charge, and yet carried the stern countenance of a parent who had collected a recalcitrant child from school following a suspension for misbehaviour. "This is quite the adventure, isn't it?" She was enjoying the chase and the thrill of it all.

The constant rumble of the wheels over tarmac that hummed a repetitive tune, plus a sleepless night in the woods, soon had Lucas dropping into a drowsy state. Finally his head started to loll forward and his eyelids began to get heavy; with the smooth movement of the car, like a baby on a long journey, Lucas fell into a deep sleep, he would only wake when they reached the outskirts of Fareham as the sun reached higher in the sky and the car began to become stuffy, Annie continued driving east along the M27. The south coast motorway that carried holiday makers east and west among the green liveried trucks of haulier Eddie Stobbart and the red articulated trucks of Norbert Dentresangle, or Nobbies as they had called them as children. They seemed to be everywhere on England's roads. It had been an often played family game on long journeys to keep a wary eye open with Nobby and Stobbie spotting, and the one to spot the most would win a bar of chocolate at journey's end.

As they climbed the slip road and joined the traffic heading toward Portsmouth and the cross-channel ferries, Lucas opened his eyes as a spotlessly clean Eddie Stobbard truck thundered by in the middle lane. "Stobby." He said absentmindedly.

"One nil" Annie replied, and smiled at the memory of his childhood game.

"Where are we going Annie?" Lucas' voice was so soft Annie had to ask him to repeat. "Where are we going, you cannot take me to the cottage, that's the first place they will look."

"I have the keys to your dad's boat, it's still down in the marina."

"But, he left that to you, it's your boat." He continued to speak with a gentle wistful quality and continued to look out of his passenger side window, he pressed the button to open it and felt an afternoon coolness on the breeze that forced its way into the car's interior.

"And what have I ever done with that boat, it was very nice of him to leave it to me but I am hardly the boating type. You should be safe there, I have stocked it with supplies and I will have the marina people fuel it up, so you can go wherever you need. I also took the liberty of opening a bank account, it's in my name, but I have put funds in there for you, you will have to use the hole-in-the-wall to get access and use cash but maybe that is not such a bad thing when you are on the run!"

Lucas was stunned, he never even consider that he was, as Annie put it, on the run! His next statement shocked her. "Take me back Annie!"

"What!"

"Take me back, take me to the nearest police station. I will tell them I called you and you picked me up." Panic filled his face.

A gentle anger filled Annie as it always did when one of her boys tried to quit on anything. "You listen to me Mr Lucas," The first time she had used the 'Mr' since picking him up on the edge of the forest, "We have got this far and we are not going to give up now. I have been terrified about doing this, ever since you telephoned last evening." Lucas looked around and paid attention, as he always had as a boy when Annie put her serious voice on; the wind through the open window blew his hair into his eyes and he brushed it away without thought. "I must admit once I was up there waiting for you to come out of the woods I was frightened for both of us but the adrenaline was flowing and I had not had such excitement for years. So, no, I am not taking you back. Wouldn't dream of such a thing."

"What if I did it though, what if I did kill that poor girl, what if I did break her neck? I should be back there, I should be locked away." Tears appeared in the corner of his eyes.

Annie glanced from the road to him and back again, she had never seen Lucas so unsure of himself, so lacking in confidence. This boy child that she had raised, befriended, and watched grow into a fine young person was now almost shrinking in the seat beside her. She had never seen him scared of anything, growing up nothing was too much for him to cope with. He was a strong young man and not this troubled, confused individual. The institution and the bad luck that life had meted out in recent months had changed him almost beyond recognition and she longed to see that slightly cocky look, that he carried so well and the girls loved, in his eyes once again.

"You listen to me Mr Lucas, you did not kill that girl, I know you and it is not in you to do such violence. But, I will make a deal with you."

"What deal?"

"You tell me you want to discover what happened that night..." He nodded in response. "The boat when fully fuelled can take you anywhere abroad, as I said, I have set up bank accounts for you so you can get money wherever you are; but if I know you that boat will not go far, well not until you have discovered the truth."

"So, here is the deal, you find out what you can," Annie explained in her most serious Governess tone of voice. "I have no idea how you will do that as even the police say they are not totally sure what happened that night; but once they had you they did not look very far for anyone else. But if you discover it was you and you did cause that poor girl to suffer, I will drive you back to Broadmoor myself and leave you there, because, if you did murder that poor young girl, you are right, you deserve to be there." Her voice was harsh and scolding.

The subject of innocence or guilt was dropped there and then, Annie had always had a way of saying her piece and then everyone would be quiet. Lucas recalled his father once trying to have the last word in a heated discussion about something he and Jacob had done, but all it took was a withering glare from Annie's cold grey eyes and he stopped before he could get into more trouble. Annie had so many emotions in those eyes that one minute could be so warm and comforting, but if you crossed her they would freeze an opponent. Those eyes would have been great on a super hero, making good people smile and villains wilt before their gaze.

The journey, it seemed, with the ever present fear of discovery had taken them much longer than was thought or planned for, the bright midday sun had already crept across the still harbour waters, the sky a brilliant blue reflecting on the surface, sun and sky leaving its signature on the dappled waterway.

The burning orange orb that had taken over the day as they travelled toward the marina, it had lifted both their spirits.

The road into the Mediterranean style marina ran alongside a stretch of the Chichester canal where tall, yellow reeds hid families of swans and coots, a mixture of desirable and decrepit houseboats of varying styles and sizes lined both shores appearing as idyllic living to the outsider. Some were plush, five star waterside living, while others appeared dilapidated, struggling to remain afloat. Lucas always imagined creative artisans hidden behind the wooden and fibre -glass shells and being ultra-creative. Breaks in the reed beds revealed their front doors, most with a porthole for a window, and those on the far shore were reached by rafts connected by ropes to pull the residents across the narrow waterway to home, residents becoming their own ferryman.

Lucas and Annie both took in their surroundings, aware that discovery, or lack of it, of the runaway killer and his helper, was still just a matter of luck. Annie was glad to have arrived without challenge but still wished they had arrived beyond nightfall with its protective shroud of darkness, as she knew a young man wearing hospital scrubs and white boots would stand out like a sore thumb in the marina surroundings visitors there more used to deck shoes and salopettes.

What neither of them had failed to be aware of in their efforts to remain unseen and unnoticed was the fact they were indeed being watched; and watched closely.

Parking the car as near to the pontoon entrance as possible Annie went to open her driver's door but a staying hand from Lucas stopped her. "This is as far as you go Annie." She looked hurt. "You have done so much for me, but if I am going to be caught now it's because they know the family have a boat here and they are waiting for me. So, you get home and remember to look surprised when they come and tell you about my escape, I have no doubt they are already at the cottage. So make sure you have an alibi for today, what will you tell them?"

"You let me worry about what I will tell them, I have arranged for a couple of members of my bridge club to say I was with them all morning for coffee and a vicious hand or two of Bridge, they will back up my story and I trust them . In fact they got quite thrilled about the intrigue when I asked them; we olds don't get much adventure you know so when it comes along, we grab it with both hands." She gave a comforting smile to Lucas, which warmed him as well as easing, just slightly, his concerns.

She handed Lucas the keys to the boat and released her seat belt so she could reach across and hug him, she kissed his forehead, the way she had done to him child, boy and man and he smiled, it was an action that always brought a smile. "It may be some time before we see each other again Annie, and if I cannot discover what happened that night we may never be able to make contact again." The hug gained pressure.

"I have no doubt you will find the truth, you will find that you did not kill that young girl and then you can treat me to a slap up feed at a posh restaurant and thank me for today."

"I will never be able to thank you for what you have done for me, and not just for today, for my entire life." With that he stepped from the car and walked away towards the pontoon where his father's old yacht was moored

Annie quickly opened her door and the sun lit her face, it was such warm and comforting face, round and motherly. "Ten sixty six! Lucas." She yelled.

"What?"

"Ten sixty six, it's the code for the gate leading to the pontoon, t change it monthly."

He waved his thanks but that shout had further garnered the atter of their watcher; who at first had only been mildly interested in the odd couple in the hatchback, but now her antenna had been well and truly tickled into action.

Gill Harmon leant against the fence that surrounded the marina pool enjoying the warm rays of the summer sun, her eyes keen and sharp behind the shade of her pink-framed Ray Ban sunglasses. She had seen the car arrive, the couple inside hug after a brief conversation, nothing unusual so far. Then the voice of an elderly woman shouting the code to a young man in hospital scrubs of all things, and on his feet those white ankle high wellies shining new and brightly under day's bright gaze.

Her journalistic hackles had risen; there was a story here!

This could make her name! In the morning she would phone the paper and feign illness, a couple of days taking sickies would be time well spent. Of that she was sure! They would never allow her to follow the story herself, if they even thought there was a story, they would have sent a senior journalist, not left it to the new girl on obits. She found it strange how modern day journalists no longer followed hunches but followed instead the electronic press release.

She watched as the 'Doctor' as she had instantly nicknamed her subject and it seemed apt, certain in the belief that hospital scrubs were not a new fashion statement, especially for yachtie wear!

"Where are you going Doctor?" The rhetorical question muttered under her breath in a tone just above whisper. Like a great many people when deep in thought Gill spoke her thoughts, quietly, but spoke them aloud none the less.

The footpath on Gill's side of the coded gate ran parallel to the long finger of the pontoon where her quarry now walked, his head down, shoulders hunched as if trying to blend into his surroundings but with the bright sun above and the reflective water beneath he was caught in a spotlight of attention seeking light, he also strode along the wobbling walkway, struggling to become used to its constrained swaying, with a sense of urgency. His trying to be inconspicuous was achieving the exact opposite, this was not a man used to acting in a clandestine manner, but was actually standing out because of his trying to hide in plain sight. If he truly were prey and she were a hawk then the mouse would be frozen as the mighty bird stooped to its prey before holding it firmly in the talons.

The Bonnie Annie like many boats in the marina was underused, moored hard against the pontoon, her white fenders spaced equally down er side warding off scrapes and bumps, was a solid, seaworthy looking ssel, blue hulled with a wooden, dark and polished, rubbing strip half way up its hull's height, the superstructure was workmanlike, solid, white and it shone brightly, obviously a well-cared for craft; a family friend or heirloom handed down through generations since her launch. From her vantage point Gill wondered who the real 'Bonnie Annie' was, it was one of those boats that had to be named after someone special and not christened just on a whim, boats were more personal than that. She took her gaze from the boat and back to the man just as the Doctor took one last look around, watching his surroundings but not really seeing; the searching gaze failing to spot his observer just hidden behind the shadow of some bushes and overhanging trees; gentle twittering of near-fledgling birds was emanating from the shadowy foliage. Believing the coast to be clear he swiftly stepped onto the deck, holding the safety rail for just a moment as his legs became accustomed to the lazy movement of the boat that rocked in complaint under his weight, opening the door Lucas stepped into the cabin, stood for a moment to reacclimatise himself with the interior of the compact cabin area, before swiftly pulling the curtains across the small windows, but not before he had taken the irresistible one last look outside, his face framed portrait like in the frame of glass. Gill, who prided herself in a decent memory, had a vague tingle of recognition that ran up her spine and caused the hairs at the nape of her neck to stand on end; the goose-bumps on her bare arms had nothing to do with the drop in air temperature as the sun momentarily took cover behind a heavy cloud. She had no inkling as to who he was, this 'Doctor', but she knew that face was familiar, and then adding that familiarity to the strange medical clothing and the secret nature of his behaviour, and this was one character that would be newsworthy soon.

For a brief moment she had the urge to scamper along the pontoon and step on board, knock on the door and announce herself by just blurting out that she was reporter for The News and she would like to know why he was being so secretive and cautious. Sometimes the direct approach was best, but a lot less fun than finding out for yourself what he was about... and then confronting him! Stalk your prey before taking the kill, patience Gill; that was the answer.

With that thought she thought better of the direct approach, patience was definitely the key, however, walking past and trying to get a peek through the curtains couldn't hurt! Standing land side of the tall, barred gate, finger poised and ready to press buttons, it didn't take a second thought, she punched in the overheard code, 1066 and the electronic gate clicked and swung inwards!

Chapter 15

Annie had left Lucas safely on the boat, she thought unnoticed, even though deep in her heart she did believe he would be inaccessible to her for some time. Reunited, just to be parted again, but at least he was free for the time being. Annie smiled contentedly to herself as she drove the narrow lanes the short distance toward the cottage, the hatchback alternating between shadow and sunshine as it drove alongside the tall hedgerows weaving and meandering the way homeward. She was happy that even this deep into the young man's life she was still needed.

There was already the sensible mind-set that she may never see her surrogate son free again, that she would never be able to see him outside of the walls of that place, but they had succeeded in his escape, and although his freedom was illicit, and no matter how brief, Annie was pleased she had done her bit for Lucas; she felt no pangs of guilt, so certain was she of his innocence. There was always a strong belief in the boy; she had raised him after all and knew him better than anyone, and right or wrong in her actions of the last few hours she knew there had been no choice in the matter; her life for the last, almost thirty years, had been taking care of Mr Lucas; and she was not about to skip out on what she saw as her duty toward the him. He had never shown an angry bone in his nature, certain that as boys Jacob's regular complaints of Lucas being a bully toward him were more a matter of self-protection against the younger brother's behaviour, than any misdemeanour on his part.

Even the trepidation she felt as the front door key slid into the front door lock of the cottage with its usual familiarity, and turned, could do nothing to force the smile away from her kindly and aging face; she felt as if she had done a good thing; protected her charge as she had promised Mr Jonathan shortly before the cancer had taken its toll. Pushing the door open the smile was immediately sent on its way, dismissed without a second thought, and her expression sagged as if the air had been stolen and sucked from her surrounds. She felt the colour drain from her face and the hope and happiness seep from her soul.

He stood in the centre of the hallway, intimidating in pose and posture, feet apart, clenched fists hanging menacingly at his thighs, a face darker than the night-time waters in the harbour,

"Where the fuck have you been?" It was like lightening from a blue sky and the clap of its thunder and the violence in his voice scared Annie.

Deigning not to answer the forced query, in fact too afraid to speak at all, she walked around Jacob, as if he were a statue, and she headed for the staircase that led to her apartment and sanctuary. She could not look at him, she hoped that not seeing him meant she could sidle by! Like a child hiding behind its hands believing if they cannot see they cannot be seen; but life is not like that! Only one step had been gained beyond the anger that made his face so dark and bloated like a plague victim, she flinched as he grabbed her arm, vicious, the grip unbreakable, the skin just above the elbow pinched where his fingers met, the muscle squeezed, fingernails leaving a row of arched impressions in her elderly, pliable flesh.

"You are hurting me, how dare you! Let go!" She tried to pull away but the grip held fast; like the boat, her namesake, she was tethered and unable to sail away.

"How dare I?" He raged, his face thrust close to hers, so she could smell the malty aroma of a classic whisky on his fetid breath, felt the spittle land on her face. The pull on her arm lifting her up on to tip-toes "It's been on the news, I have had the police round here asking questions. The police, here; in *my* home…" The last two words yelled as if to give them even more impetuous.

"This is not your home, it is Lucas' home!" The instant retort left Annie surprised at her own bravery in answering back.

The fury that was released following her response was instant, unstoppable, shocking and it struck with the same unexpected ferocity of that lightning bolt, it burned her face as his clenched fist powered into her cheek, she felt the skin tear, the bone give, the chunky signet ring ripping into the soft flesh of her cheek! The blow should have knocked her to the floor but his grip on her arm remained and it held her up, limply, but keeping her in range for a second, even more powerful blow. This one catching her in the side of the head, pain driving in through the thin skin of her temple; she wished for unconsciousness because of the pain and fear that worse was to come. She felt the warmth of the blood running down her face. That dull ache in her head far worse than any migraine she had suffered, and she had been victim to some vicious, lying in a dark room, migraines! Annie ducked her head, hiding her face the best she knew how, tucking her chin into her chest and cowered, fearing and knowing there was more to violence to come, much more…

Blood dribbled out of the open wound on her face, she felt it seep and run over undamaged skin, so close to her nose she could pick up the unmistakeable aroma, it leaked from the torn area, over her cheek and into the corner of her mouth; the metallic taste added to the smell. From the second blow Annie felt another rivulet of blood, this time seeping into th frown lines and crows' feet that radiated out from her eyes on the aging b soft face. Blood flowed easily from the wounds where the ring, and t power of the venomous strikes, had torn the flesh apart.

Pain is strange bedfellow, one moment it is overwhelming before it becomes an almost euphoric state of mind, shutting down the body, where the whole being goes numb, a defence mechanism against further assaults on the senses. The feeling of mental rescue, escape from suffering, lasted only seconds.

The arm was released, Annie attempted to step away, trying to distance herself from the raging bull that confronted her, her legs wobbling and un-answering the call to move, weak like a punch-drunk boxer in the ring about to drop for an eight-count. Annie collapsed to the floor ready to take that count and find time to recover. Again the lightning thrust of power this time she was bent double, searing, sudden pain wracked her body as a foot, clad in an expensive, highly polished and tasselled deck shoe, burst into her midriff with true and undiluted malice. The difference in their heights as she was falling meant the kick struck her with explosive force in the ribs and removed the wind from her lungs in one harsh expulsion. She felt something give, break away in her chest and the pain was intense as a broken rib, shattered and sharp ended, dug into her lung and tore at the softness of the vital internal organ, an internal, unseen, dagger.

Gasping for breath, trying to draw in valuable oxygen, Annie fell, crumpled to the brightly polished hall floor, a floor she had taken great pride in keeping clean and shining, above the pain and fear for a brief second she was dismayed to see the blood from the facial wounds she had suffered sliding across its surface and despoiling her work; Annie was always house proud.

Hurting with an intensity she had never felt before she dared not look up at Jacob, afraid of what she would see in his raging face, she curled into an embryonic position, self-protection automatic.

If she had possessed the strength of will to look up at Jacob's face she would only have seen madness gazing back at her; his eyes bulging, the whites bloodshot. Amidst that uncontrolled anger and violence there was something worse, something far more terrifying. There was pleasure showing.

Jacob was smiling, he was enjoying the vehemence, accepting its adrenaline rush in the same way a man accepts the force of lust when making passionate love to someone he cares about. This was an embracing of the fervour, he loved his partner in this vicious dance of passion, it was encompassing him, defining him and possessed him with a fury as he thrust into her body with one painful kick after another, sexual as well as violent. Annie remained curled like a cat beneath his lunging limbs, almost accepting blow after blow as her mind closed out the pain.

"You give your help to that little shit of a brother of mine!" Breathless he forced out the words as he neared his climax, approached being satiated.

He has had all the privileges, he was given a house while me, *Me*, the bastard son of a bastard father had to make do with the scraps, not even knowing who my mother was after the lord and master, my father, deemed it not necessary to tell me." As the tirade continued Jacob circled around Annie, like a predator teasing its prey, the seducer tempting his muse. "I wanted you to be my mother, be with me the way you were with fucking Lucas, you were a mother to him, you loved him, adored him, but not me." The rant accompanied every verbal blow with a physical strike to Annie who was nearing the sought after comfort of unconsciousness. "Tell me where he is." He spat, "Or it will only get worse for you, I don't want the fucking police around here again. He belongs in that nuthouse, should be locked up after what he did to that girl; he does not deserve to be back here, it's mine now! My fucking house, you hear me!"

He screamed, spittle spraying with every word thrown; Annie heard nothing, felt nothing; not anymore!

Jacob dropped to one knee, not caring that he was kneeling in the blood of the woman who had raised him, cared for him, rubbed cooling butter into injuries to soothe bruises and squeezed antiseptic into cuts and scrapes, lovingly tending his childhood wounds. She had held him during illness and sung to him during sleepless nights, helped him with homework and sided with the mischievous boy when he had crossed his father. Now in return she received a smile that was drenched in wickedness, full of rancour. He put his sweating and venomous face close to hers and even over the fading pain, as life drained from her, foul emanations brushed her face and she felt every ounce of its evil.

"Where is he?" It was whispered and it was threatening; her own breathing was ragged, broken, rasping, but at least the physical pain had gone.

Suddenly, anger not quite satisfied, his fist once again flew into her face, it pounded, the first blow shattering her nose and sending shards of bone into her brain, the second tore the cheek again and she did not feel her head crushed between powerful fist and polished floor. If she had been conscious she would have once again felt the pride of her shining hallway floor; and before passing into full unconsciousness a sudden thought interrupted her final moments; 'this was going to be hell to clean tomorrow'.

The last thing that registered in the fading thoughts of Annie were the droplets of sweat being thrown from the perspiring brow of Jacob and landing on her face, as he landed blow after blow on her shattered features. Drifting in and out as she neared her last breath, Annie's last words, "My boy, I love you!" whispered through broken teeth and murmured with a bitten and bloody tongue...

Thankfully she was now totally unconscious, mind numb, her breathing shallow, laboured, and ebbing, the glorious daylight that she had shared on her drive with Lucas now replaced by darkness. Jacob was not yet finished. He grabbed a handful of her blood streaked grey hair and used the handhold to pound her head into the carefully polished floor, once, twice, three times and each time asking the same question...

"Where..." pound, "is he?"

"Where..." thud, "is he?"

"Where..." thump, "the fuck is he you old bitch?"

There would be no answer, the last breath had just bubbled from her throat. The blood from her shattered skull had splashed up his trouser legs, up the wall and across the floor. In one last act of uncontrolled rage he threw her limp head back to the floor, discarding it as if it were worthless trash, it whumped into the floor with the soft thud of a deflated ball, and finally Jacob stopped the onslaught, stood over the prone and still Annie, his lust and angered satiated.

Breathing heavily like a spent lover he gazed down at the curled body. "You asked for that you bitch; I will find him without you. And just guess who will get the blame for this...?" He paused to savour the moment. "Your fucking precious Lucas, that's who."

Jacob left her lying there, he went to the downstairs toilet and ran the hot tap before washing and scrubbing his bloodied hands and arms, he watched with amused pleasure as the 'red cordial' swirled around the pristine white basin and disappeared down and away, as with Annie's life just extinguished, like a reluctant stain to be removed and flushed away. He cared not about any mess he made, about the stains on the hallway floor, Annie would clear it up in the morning. Oh, that's right, she won't be able to. He chuckled.

Back in the hallway, after taking extra time over the sink to scrub the bloody evidence from his signet ring with the nailbrush whilst thinking absently - who used a nailbrush anymore? He looked down at her body before kneeling alongside her once more. To an onlooker it looked as if he were praying over a fallen friend, or about to offer CPR, saying a few words of comfort and peace, aiding the victim. When in fact he was merely coating the palms of his now clean hands in her blood, wiping that blood, smearing it down his shirt, making the evidence fit the story he would tell.

It wouldn't do to have spotless hands when the police arrived and he told the tale of how he arrived home to find the front door open and poor Annie lying in a pool of her own blood, give evidence of the shock her felt at seeing her blood staining a floor she had always taken such pride in. He would sadly tell of how he tried to revive her while all the time being afraid it was too little far too late. Of giving up trying to save her, feeling the revulsion of having her blood on his hands, the blood of someone so loved and valued as a family member for so many years, of giving up and calling the police and an ambulance. Too little too late he was afraid, the words would catch in his throat.

With one last thought to embellish his story even further, he bent even closer and kissed her bloodied lips, the action surprising him as erotic when it gave him the slight surge of an erection, he pulled away and wiped his mouth with the back of his hand. It would give credence to his story of trying to give her the kiss of life! It concerned him not at all that he had actually enjoyed the same metallic taste of blood on his lips that Annie had experienced, and felt that exciting sexual surge at the same time.

He would tell the very polite and respectful police officer about how he had rushed back to Chichester from his Southampton apartment when he had heard of his brother's escape from Broadmoor. Of how knowing of his brother's madness and history of violence toward women, he had worried for Annie's safety; she had raised him after all and it was the least he could do to rush along the A27 to protect her and ensure her safety. No, he had not had chance to see if anything was missing from the house and would they like him to look now.

In reality the kindly officer would say it could wait a while, and they remained in the kitchen waiting, he guessed, for the family liaison officer, who he hoped would be quite pretty, (note to self: bad form to hit on her too soon,) and she make them all tea. Tea was the answer to all ills and trauma.

He had dialled the triple nine number, and as he hit each button, the finer hitting as deliberate as any blow on Annie, he altered his mood and mind-set from exhilarated to fearful, bringing a hint of panic into his voice. So it was with, what he considered to be fine acting, blustered through the fact that he had arrived home to discover his beloved housekeeper lying dead on the hallway floor, beaten to a pulp by an imagined intruder. Help was needed and swiftly, he didn't know what to do, there was palpable fear that the intruder may still be in the house, blood everywhere.

Breathlessly Jacob added, "My brother has escaped Broadmoor, he is obviously unstable and is back in the area. Help me." He pleaded, with what he felt was just the right amount of throat constricting panic. At the other end of the phone the controller advised him to stay on the line as a car was on its way, the voice was a comfort, supportive.

The quiet harbour -side cottage, so long a family home and refuge from all that was bad in the world, with its white walls and rose lined footpath, was about to be shaken to its formerly peaceful foundations as police, paramedics and scenes of crime officers walked and investigated very inch of the property. Jacob paced outside, smoking cigarette after cigarette and took on board the comforting words of neighbours and police, he sat in the library, interviewed briefly by the first officer on the scene and then by a more senior detective, DS Kobie Kaan who's dark eyes did nothing to give away any sort of deductive thought, was back in the Tubb home, the intense detective wanted every gory detail, as well as much information as he could glean of the escaped brother. The violence that filled this house, and any scene of violence, always rankled and confused Kobie, his strong Muslim beliefs totally against any form of violence except in protection of himself or his family, meant that scenes like this caused him extra grief. He was also annoyed at having been forced to leave his one mortal sin, the love of a thick bacon sandwich, with tomato sauce, it could be days before he could sneak another.

To the professional and casual onlooker Jacob was the shattered and shocked victim coming to terms with the violent death of his much-loved housekeeper who had been more like a mother for all his life, he had explained to the DS who appeared to be listening sympathetically, but behind the shocked and shaken façade the lord and master of the White House was smiling and playing his part to perfection. In a rare quiet moment when no one else was within earshot, he muttered, "And the Oscar for Best Actor goes to..." Jacob even acted out the opening of the golden envelope until he realised anyone could walk into the library at any time and so replaced the veneer of the shattered demeanour.

Within an hour or so a, as hoped for - very pretty, Family Liaison Officer was really making tea in the kitchen along with the expected idle chatter. What was it with people and fucking cups of hot, sweet tea every time there was a tragedy! Someone dies, prepare a hot beverage, house burnt down, a nice cup of tea; it was the panacea for all traumatic ills, penicillin for the traumatised. He hated tea and could do with a proper drink but for appearances sake, and the keeping of a clear and alert mind, he sipped the offered brew, thunderous and dangerous eyes hidden behind the steam lifting from the brew, and nodded politely over the rim of the flower patterned china mug seemingly thankful for is healing properties.

Chapter 16

As Annie, lay alone, hurting, the pain beyond belief, curled up on her once shining hallway floor, semi-conscious and unaware that the savage beating she had taken was bleeding her out toward death, breathing her last, those breaths now shallow and insufficient, just a mile or so away Gill Harmon was feeling very much alive and alert as she revelled in the feeling of becoming intoxicated with excitement at her first real sniff of a scoop, it was better than any alcohol high. The story, whatever that may be, was drawing her in and like a well-bred tracker dog she had picked up the scent with nose to the ground; there was no choice now, in her mind she must run with it. Predator and prey with the victim totally unaware they were about to be fed upon.

She remembered the historic number that had been called out by the old lady, 1066, and somewhere in the recess of her mind recalled that a major company who make security gates was based in Hastings and set all their new keypads at the iconic date of the Battle of Hastings, it was the first number she always tried if she needed to get past any keypad gateway; but this would be the first time it had worked.

From the top of the sloping gangway she had clearly heard Annie call out the number; and she now gently punched them into the electronic mechanism, trying to remain calm and appear as if she belonged among the gleaming craft lining the pontoons, thankfully the gate gave an electronic click and swung open. A brief look around, a surge of adrenaline, hands pushed deep into the pockets of her blue quilted gilet, she strolled down the gangway towards the rows of bobbing, tethered, boats. Her weight on the pontoon agitating them at their slumber, where brightwork shone and reflected the sunlight along the wooden walkway. With a nonchalance she didn't feel she walked closer to the boat where she had seen the 'doctor' disappear just a short while earlier. With the weekend ahead she felt she had a couple of days to discover this man's secret, delve into his story, unearth the demons that had delivered him to this spot and begin her climb up the journalistic ladder. Anything to get her away from the numbing world of obituaries; if this worked out well by Monday lunchtime she could be a real journalist.

The Bonnie Annie, strong in name and strong in character, a gleaming but old-fashioned, some would say classic, cruiser sat still on the calm waters of the marina, its only movement the gentle rocking as Lucas moved about inside. It was one of the few craft with curtains pulled closing off the cabin interior from onlookers, as she approached Gill kept a wary eye on the windows while watching for the slightest movement of the thin curtains. She had locked onto her target and would not be diverted from her quest, determination and tenacity – by-words for a good journo.

Every step she drew nearer, nerves began to become unsettled. She dared herself to walk past it, within just feet of the 'doctor' hiding within, her heart pounding with fear of discovery and pumping adrenaline. Hoping to gain another glimpse of the man aboard, a closer look at the man in the green scrubs. The secretive sailor who looked and behaved like anything but! What was his story, if he had one, it was the first hint of doubt from the story-starved reporter. She told herself, nonsense! Scratch the surface and everyone had a story! Gill had the gut instinct that this was a fascinating one.

When the mind begins to feel fear it offers imaginary scenarios, some to settle the jangling nerves and others to heighten the senses, fear and flight, it was the safety valve for moments of danger. Gill's mind was currently diverted from the danger of discovery and set on comfort with nerve-settling thoughts of success, as she first imagined the headline, followed by the words 'Exclusive Report from News Reporter Gill Harmon, she saw the bold wording read *'Doctor of Death Discovered in Local Marina'*. Gill was aware she had an overactive imagination; she recalled her school reports, *'Intelligent but does not pay attention, overactive imagination causing her to lose track of lessons, seems to live with her head in the clouds.'* It was an overused phrase in nearly all her reports; thankfully her parents just shrugged those remarks away, they believed in a happy childhood, it was a time for fantasy not one bereft of dreams. She let an almost silent chuckle sneak from her lips – 'Doctor of Death' it was a ridiculous notion that had just leapt into her imagination – but then what if he really were a killer, here in the marina, just a foot or two away from where she now gingerly walked, trying to lessen the rocking motion of the floating pontoon. Her parents had always told her that the seriousness of life would soon be upon her so enjoy the moments of youth whenever she could, they had worked hard all their lives in humdrum employment designed to dull brains and bring home the pay. Their artistic desires buried under the duty of raising a family, they wanted more for their offspring. Was this what they wanted for her, to be stalking an anonymous man in a marina and deeming him, although probably totally innocent, a murderer! She thought maybe not.

Approaching the Bonnie Annie, Gill suddenly became aware that her attention on the boat and not her feet had meant those footsteps had the pontoon rocking from side to side on its floating concrete plinths; surely the headline grabbing 'Doctor of Death', his, probably undeserved, title growing with every step nearer, would feel the movement from inside the boat. The curtains were pulled tight together so she had no way of knowing, for all she was aware of he was now watching her; reaching the boat there was nothing to be seen between the minute cracks in the curtains, the risk had been worthless. She had slowed her walk, nonchalantly peered in; nothing! So, sticking to the centre of the gangway and treading lightly the journalistic sleuth put her feet in reverse and backed away from the craft, she felt defeat and then turned to make her way back to the electronic gate at the top of the gangway. This time her head was hung low, the footsteps heavier, less care being taken on the return journey.

Determined, Gill was not to be beaten at the opening moves, she would watch from a safer distance, keep vigil over the weekend, and, if need be, she could always take a sickie on Monday to keep ever watchful. It was a game of chess, although she had never learned to play the combative game, but she knew of the expression. For three days she watched, waited, saw exactly nothing, there was not even a visit to the cockpit from her elusive subject. She watched with diligence, only heading to her Emsworth home near the quay after The Boat House closed its doors and she would be back for their breakfast opening. At times she wondered if he had left the boat while she went home to sleep, shower and change. But the slight rocking movement of the Bonnie Annie each morning when she returned confirmed that at least someone was still on board. Her idle time of being on the stakeout, more boredom than the excitement she had expected, included a phone call to the office, telling the male in the Human Resources she would not be in for the week, feigning 'woman's problems', they never asked, political correctness was sometimes a handy tool to be used.

All the while Gill kept a faithful watch on the Bonnie Annie, her patience and determination never waning, in the hope that she would once again catch sight of the occupant who, it seemed, never left the confines of the cabin, never even opened the curtains. She was becoming impatient for her, supposed, story to unfold but the longer he stayed out of sight, the more she was convinced there was a tale to be reported.

Behind the pale beige curtains and on board the Bonnie Annie things were not quite so easy for Lucas, no longer under the watchful eye of the medical staff he was regaining his full mental capacity. He had taken no mood controlling drugs for two days and with his medication wearing off he was suffering, what felt like, the worst hangover of his life, a pampered life where he had suffered many a self-imposed hangover. This was different though, it was violent, all-consuming, bathed in sweat his head pounded, the light invaded, even in the dull interior of the cabin, his eyes hurt, his neck ached, every bone, muscle and joint cried out in pain and minute by minute the walls of the main cabin closed in around him. Lucas had exchange one cell for another!

In the few hours he did sleep, or rather nap restlessly, horrid and vivid dreams invaded his mind, bordering on hallucinatory. Every movement of the boat, every footfall on the pontoon meant discovery and a swift return to Broadmoor, he knew he was becoming paranoid.

To counter his withdrawal he tried to stay awake, alert, by replacing the antipsychotic drugs with copious amounts of coffee, drunk for the caffeine kick. This only served to make him vomit, regurgitating the brown liquid, seemingly quicker than he could consume it, and his throat burned with the effort of retching. Lucas realised his system had become used to institutional food, unused to excess of anything, apart from chocolate bars! Annie, had left him plenty of bottled water and so he drank that instead, it served to flush his system and the constant retching ceased, over the hours that followed not only did his stomach cramps ease and his urine begin to clear from the cloudy outpouring he had been producing, he had noticed but his brain power also sharpened. On occasions during the third night on the boat and under a waning moon he would risk stepping up on deck, enjoying the fresh chills of the slow moving sea air and the fresh, clean aromas that it offered during the higher tides, he even enjoyed the ozone that was thrown around during the hours of low tide. Lucas felt, almost, overwhelming fear each time he stepped out of the cabin lounge, drug-free paranoia quickly setting in he would quickly dive back inside and below deck to curl up in the unmade double bed of the aft cabin, the comfortable quilt left in an untidy shambles from his previous visit to the bed. Each time he slept fitfully without actually getting rest, before waking again from bad dreams of a battered girl laying twisted and bloody in a garden full of flowers, their petals all turning to blood red before falling from the parent plant,, and then waking in a cold sweat, beginning the process all over again.

As the weekend turned into Monday and weekend blue skies turned to sombre grey, all unnoticed by Lucas who had no idea what day it was, his head began to clear, his aches and pains were nagging a little less, the stress easing with each hour at large, and he was beginning to crave the sights and sounds of other people. The drug-free paranoia he had been feeling was being replaced in equal measure by the harshness of isolation and a growing craving for contact with a living world. Until now he had replaced one prison cell with another, imprisoned on the boat, also he had been locked up in his thoughts; thoughts and dreams of violence, but now it was time to escape both. It was time to shower, something he had not done since his break for freedom and he suddenly had a dread of what he must smell and look like, it was time to re-join the human race!

Seeing the boat move with increased agitation on its mooring Gill was imagining extra activity from within, would today be the day she would see the 'doctor' again?

She had taken another stroll along the pontoon that held the Bonnie

Anne to its wooden arm, something she did every couple of hours or so even knowing there was nothing to be seen, and despite not being able to see through the pulled curtains she was glad of the activity. It broke the monotony of just watching, felt like she was doing something pro-active.

Latest patrol carried out like a vigilant border guard, she once again decided to head back to the café at the harbour end of the marina, ready for another coffee, or maybe this time a mint tea, something more refreshing. Turning around to walk back she pondered on another potentially wasted day, she wondered how many sick days she could get away with before anyone actually noticed she was gone and began to ask questions. She could have called her news editor and explained to him about her 'possible' story, but what would he do with the information that she had been watching a boat with a man who stayed on board, a man, suspiciously she thought, had been dressed like a surgeon. In the cold light of day it did seem ridiculous, but she still thought she was onto something, anything to get her off the bloody obituary pages. And, if she had to be honest, she was enjoying the clandestine activity. A few paces past the Bonnie Annie she had failed to notice the curtains, so long closed to her closer inspection, being whipped open allowing the morning sun to flood into the cabin.

Deep in thought she reached the foot of the tilted walkway and began to climb the, now steep gangway as it allowed for the low tide drop of the pontoons. There appeared to be an alternating force on the pontoon as it felt to be swaying more than her gentle footsteps were causing, there was an acute awareness that another pair of feet were heading in the same direction as her and just a few paces behind her. She hoped, but dared not turn round and look, tried not to quicken her own steps. Fought the desire to take a look over her shoulder.

Up the sloping gangway she climbed, hearing the soft padding of someone behind her, and as she approached the gate, an invisible eye operated the mechanism making the gate swing away from her and open; she paused for a moment in the opening as if she had forgotten something and the man who had been behind her brushed past, his head lowered, his face hidden under a baseball cap, offered a muttered apology, indistinct but an apology none the less.

The suddenness of his being alongside her startled the young woman, and a moment's fear smothered her, causing breath to be held in anticipation of a forthcoming shock, and she just watched, a little afraid she would admit later, as the handsome man, handsome despite the dark bags under his eyes and the sallow complexion that were partially hidden by the peak of the dark cap, made his way brusquely past her and towards the restaurant and café, that overlooked the scenic harbour and where she had enjoyed so many coffees.

In for a penny, in for a pound, as her mother so full and fond of pithy sayings would have said - Gill followed him, staying a couple of yards behind but keeping pace, stalking her prey. On reaching The Boat House, he held the door open for her and even though he still kept his head down and his face in shadow she could not help but think he was now watching her. The voyeur had become the viewed. Had he observed her watching him from the pathway above the marina pool?

Inside the warm and friendly atmosphere of the cafe Lucas looked around and, after ordering a large cappuccino at the counter, found a two seat table in the corner parking himself with his back to the dining room; there was still plenty to look at to keep his mind off his problems as the wall was covered in framed photographs, all in tight groupings, some black and white, some sepia, and the odd colour image artistically faded by time.

Photos that adorned the wall in a modern and fashionable twist of seeking nostalgia toward the world of boating and the lifestyle that surrounds it, each image looking like an advert for Ralph Lauren prep-school clothing. Young men and women lounging around classic wooden yachts or attractive lakeside settings all trying to look natural and relaxed but in fact looking false and posed, happiness pasted onto model faces, a brief glimpse into a designers idyllic vision of an ideal life. Then there was the occasional real-life image, ancient and turned sepia with age, of groups of sailors casually dressed and standing on the deck of some long ago sunken, scrapped or abandoned yacht, the men all in roll-necked, oiled wool jumpers that protected against the intrusive weather. Hardy yachtsmen from a time when men were 'real' and the ropes that hoisted the sails were made of rough hemp, rather than the smooth, man-made fibres of today, ropes that slid through calloused hands and became wetter and harder to pull on as their journeys across angry seas continued. Back in a time when even the weekend sailor was a hardy sea-faring soul.

His coffee placed in front of him by a pretty young waitress dressed all in stylish and practical black that outlined a petite but curvy figure, Lucas realised it had been some time since he had gazed upon a pretty girl. That lax moment of minor lust was immediately replaced by the vision of the unnamed girl being pushed under the park bench, her skinny and white legs jutting from her pulled up skirt, her head at a weird angle. Lucas felt the bile rise in his throat as the guilt once again twisted at his thoughts.

Prior to those debilitating thoughts Lucas had been perusing the menu, had been tempted by a juicy sounding quarter pound burger, pure beef with herbs and a stilton centre, served in a sourdough bun and with sweet potato fries on the side; this was manna from heaven after the food of the past year served by uncaring cooks who were trying to work to pitiful NHS budgets, but his hunger pangs had vanished as quickly as the image of the girl had arrived. He knew, however that he needed to eat and prepared to order the food.

Sensing someone alongside the table, and presuming it to be a waitress, without looking up the order for the burger and a cold bottle of beer was made; the response he received was unexpected, drew a small amount of fear from somewhere in his gut, but it was, he noted, said with a smile attached.

"I would but I don't work here, and you need to go and order at the counter anyway. I was just wondering if I could share your table as it's rather busy in here this morning." Gill had never felt so brazen or bold. "Unless of course you are waiting for someone. We passed each other on the pontoon and there is nothing sadder than two people eating alone on either side of a restaurant when they could be getting to know each other. Wouldn't you agree?" A leading question asked with a raised eyebrow as if daring the handsome man to refuse her.

There was no time for Lucas to respond, ignore or deny her the company she seemed to crave as she slid onto the banquette that hugged the wall and immediately sat down opposite him offering her very best and engaging smile. "Of course, if you would rather be alone!" It was statement not a question, and gave him no chance of a negative response. He knew that he should have declined the company but something stopped him, starved for too long of both good food and decent company it felt as hard to resist as his medication had been over the last couple of days. He craved it, needed the fix. Could not resist its intoxicating pull. Whatever the reasoning, it could have been the desire for some intelligent companionship, or the fact it was a pretty girl in front of him, whichever it was, he just sat there and allowed Gill to take her place opposite him. She smiled a pretty and, he noted, slightly smug smile.

The volunteer dining partner introduced herself. "My name is Gill, Gill Harmon." A hand extended over the table for a handshake of friendship.

He stumbled in reply, tried to think of a name; and failed blushing, felt his cheeks burn as he succumbed to the pressure of his first human on human contact outside the institution. He was not good at this subterfuge and had not considered being put on the spot. Being on the run, he suddenly realised that was what he was, on the run, like some mastermind of a criminal, he had prepared no background story, no series of lies to keep him safe and away from prying eyes. Gill just stared, waited for the moment, now knowing that the first words from his lips would be lies. But, that was okay as it merely confirmed that she was on the trail of a serious story.

"Gill; Gill Harmon." She repeated her name in the hope of prompting him forward; for his part he wondered why people always repeated themselves such as with Bond, James Bond.

He spoke clearly and with a confidence he did not feel; "Charles Drayton." Lucas was sure his friend would feel complimented by the name's use. "I am sorry, just getting over a bad break up and I am just a little uncomfortable in company." Smooth; *not*, he berated himself mentally.

"I am starving!" Said the friendly, warm and slightly throaty voice from behind the menu held up opposite him. "I think I will go with what you are having; I hope you are not a vegan or something equally weird, I tried to be a vegetarian but I missed bacon sandwiches too much... and chicken and sausages and beef burgers. Is the food here any good?" She finally asked as if a stranger to the establishment, her babbling making her feel as if she were on a first date.

Charles, as he now realised he had to become, ordered for both of them, choosing the burgers, and ordering them 'naked' as he felt he needed to lose weight so he would forego the bun.

"Can I have sweet potato fries with mine please?" It was aimed at him not the waitress and he realised that he was being made the centre of attention whether he liked it or not.

"Make that twice please."

He looked up at the waitress from under the peak of his baseball cap, that carried just the white 'swoosh' of a famous sporting goods manufacturer, for conformation and she in turn stole away the menus, tucking them under her arm and left the couple to their conversation, which was stilted and mostly one sided.

After a few minutes of stumbling on, Gill stopped, and the table sat in silence. She looked at her companion and tried to recognise the pale, round, face, that had obviously seen no sun for some time, with its early growth of beard; she had to admit that even though his eyes looking tired, slightly bloodshot and with heavy dark bags under them, and even though his brow created a furrowed hood over them as if trying to shield the light reflected in the bright orbs, they still shone through bright blue , she was taking a fancy to him, there was something mysterious about the man before her and it was more than just a story. She mentally kicked herself for thinking like that.

"I am so glad it's not just me you are ignoring, you seem to have shut the world away." She said breaking the silence. "If you would rather be left alone I can find another table, I am sorry if I have intruded." She began to slide out of the seat but all the while hoping he would not call her on the bluff.

"No, please stay." Charles/Lucas said, keen to keep the company now it was sitting with him, and he laid a gentle hand on her wrist to emphasise his need for that companionship. That simple touch, that brush of affection; it was as if he had received an electric shock sending a wave of power through his fingers. For more than a year the only human contact had been when rough hands had placed handcuffs on his wrists, snapping them tightly on the skin or whenever drugs were introduced into his system in order to place manacles on his mind. This was different, smooth skin, warm, tender to the touch, stimulating.

"You were right, it would be shame to have us eating alone at separate tables. I am a little distracted and for that I apologise, I have not been sleeping well, some sort of bug I think." Lucas, no, Charles, he had to keep the falsehood in the front of his mind, tried to keep the nervous stutter from his voice his words were spoken softly, the tone of a well-educated man and without a local Sussex twang. Gill liked its tone and timbre; deep and manly, it suited its owner.

Suddenly the table appeared to lose its awkward atmosphere, as if a switch had been thrown, suddenly the two strangers were comfortable with each other and no longer foreigners. But, there was still something of a kind of an impasse as each realised the other was holding something back, it was a game of chess where each would move their pawns but would guard the important pieces to the bitter end; they held back emotionally rather than verbally; both with secrets and in turn feared being discovered as imposters for it would spoil the bond that had begun to build.

"You asked if the food was any good here and yet, when you sat down there was no staring around the room, no curious investigation of its décor, you sat down like someone who knows the place." Lucas kept a small smile on his face so as not to offend.

There was no offense showing on her soft face. "Was there a question in there somewhere?" Gill asked while giving herself time to think, but then, with a touch of the cavalier, thought that honesty was the best policy. "I was just trying to break the ice, I don't usually just approach strange men, hoping you are not strange, and just start to chat with them. I couldn't think of anything else to say." She shrugged and showed the palms of her hands in submission. "Actually it is one of my favourite places and I always come here if I have had a bad day at work. Which just lately seems to be most days"

"What do you do?"

"Well I am supposed to be a journalist," Sadness in her eyes was noted by Lucas but Gill in a lapse moment failed to notice the look of total shock on his face. "But most of the time write nothing but banal things about dead people for the obituary column. I joined the Fourth Estate to try and change the world but I suppose I should have been a little more realistic in my ambitions."

As she looked up she noted a shadow seemed to throw a darkness across the eyes of the man over the other side of the table, Gill decided to push her luck.

"I was stood on the quayside just watching the sun set as you got onto your boat the other day you looked an interesting man decked out in your hospital scrubs, not the normal attire for a yachtie, and I thought you may make an interesting story, let's just say you lifted my journalistic hackles and I thought you may be the scoop I had long dreamed about. Ridiculous, yeh?"

"That's why you sat down with me?" It was said a little sharper than he meant and he wished he could just slide from his seat and go back to hiding on the boat, this brashness and need to escape from every confine put upon him had put him into an awkward spot; his freedom at risk.

"No, that was because, despite your lack of sleep and the bags under your eyes, you are ruggedly handsome and I was feeling all alone and unwanted." A brief pause and a sideways glance at her companion to see if he had taken the bait. "Of course that's why, did you think I was desperate for a man." It was said with a smile that was on the side of wicked.

"Well I did wonder! You may be the type of girl to just follow men off their boats and hitch up with them thinking them to be rich." Gill noted the returned mischievous smile but also noted the eyes flicking furtively around the pictures above her head, Charles did have a secret and he was trying hard to hide it... "In case you are wondering, the boat was left me by my father, it was his pride and joy and I have never had the heart to sell it; so not rich at all if that's what you were hoping!"

Do I look like a gold digger, a money grabber?" It was said with mock indignation, it was a table tennis match with the small white ball of teasing being smacked back and forth over the net. Still Lucas spluttered and stalled over any sort of response.

"As a member of the hated profession of journalists I always thought I could make a difference, to influence as well as report just the facts; but, it seems, those above me have one criteria and one only in local press..."

"Ad revenue." He interrupted; adding. "What exactly is the Fourth Estate? You mentioned it earlier." He had to keep the conversation going as an early withdrawal from this encounter may raise her suspicions even higher; and he had nowhere to go without the protection of the boat.

"I don't suppose it is used that often nowadays but is was a term used just to refer to the news media, especially us technophobes who still work in the world of print. It began during the first chance the press had reporting from the House of Commons. I think and don't quote me, hum.., 1787." She said unsure of the date. "It was called the Fourth Estate because the press had become an unauthorised political influence on society from its press coverage of political matters."

"Not long out of college then and still remember the lectures?"

She replied taken at the boldness of the open question. "Just a few months, but I have this habit of just knowing stupid data, for instance, did you know that the record for climbing Mount Everest was a little over eight hours and at one time there was a seven year waiting list to climb it." Gill sat back, mildly impressed with herself for the useless snippet.

"Do you know that was something I did not know; and, really, just over eight hours?" His interest had been peaked in this attractive companion who now was nodding with confidence at her useless store of knowledge.

Charles gazed through the window at the sky as it changed colour. "My Grandpa Jonathan used to call skies like this 'nicotine skies' they were his favourite views across the harbour and he liked the way it changed the colour of the waters with its reflection." He said gazing out across the harbour at the sepia toned skies that threatened storms. Lucas almost smiled at the memory and his tense expression of a moment before began to relax and his face once again took on that handsome look that always smoothed Annie's annoyance at any mischief. A glimpse of the Lucas from before these troubles had started made the fear, trepidation and panic of the day all worthwhile. "I remember, grandpa, and my Father come to that, always used to sit out on the back patio watching the late afternoon sun cross the harbour, staying there until the sunsets, no matter what time of year. He called them tobacco skies, puffing on his pipe because he was not allowed in the house with that stinking chimney; that's probably why the evening skies reminded him of nicotine, it was the same colour as his fingertips!"

And, so they continued to chatter, not quite as if long lost friends but fairly close, their meal arrived and a bottle of a rich and ruby red wine opened, it seemed right to enjoy such classic and tasty burgers with a robust wine. Lucas enjoyed every mouthful of both having been starved of decent food and wine for so long; he felt the same with the conversation, much of which had also become quite rich and earthy as the wine had been consumed. It only took a couple of glasses before Lucas felt, what he would describe as 'squiffy', and he told himself to slow down, the last thing he needed was to get pissed and loose lipped in a moment of drunken weakness and inattention to details.

A little old fashioned, but they both had a vintage port after their plates had been cleared from the table, he could not recall ever meeting a girl who liked port and it pleased him; almost as much as that warm, all-encompassing glow that a good port always supplies to the inner being.

For the first time in as long as he could recall, Lucas felt at ease, he wriggled on his chair every now and again just to remind himself that not all seats were hard benches. After months of being under the close watch from all those around him, mad and sane, and under the constant gaze of security cameras this long and enjoyable afternoon he felt like he was not under scrutiny and yet there was something that continued to be sounding alarm bells in his consciousness; he knew she was a journalist but she could not know who he was or else she would have substituted another career when speaking of work and not been so candid with him. Or was that a double bluff.

As they enjoyed each other's company and time had gone the way of the tide the sun had crossed the sky and begun to dip lowering its head toward the harbour waters. Into evening and the day was still warm despite the fact the sun was slowly disappearing, unlike their comfort with each other as that had grown over the hours spent chattering. The two had really chatted about nothing, idle conversation had drawn them closer together. Head to head and face to face they had ignored the comings and goings of the restaurant, only interrupted by attentive staff. Finally on leaving The Boat House bar, she surprised he had paid his part of the bill with cash, nobody used cash these days, they strolled alongside the pontoons where the myriad collection of craft were almost level with them thanks to a very high equinoxal tide, and then without conversation, they walked toward the broad canal, with its lily pads, wild fowl and boathouses. Over the bridge that was once the lock gate for the canal longboats that plied their trade in Chichester and Portsmouth and then on through to the old and charming Birdham Marina; walking very near to the White House, but Lucas decided to avoid taking a look at the end of the cul-de-sac at his old home, even the thought of seeing his childhood home was heart breaking. The canal was originally built to take cargo along the south coast where it would join up with other canals to take precious loads to London and the markets. The advent of an efficient railway and then the network of ever improving roads meant that the canal system was killed off before it had even had a chance to thrive; it now offered a delightful route to walk and enjoy for leisure pursuits such as fishing and bird watching. The footpath opened out to the beautiful marina that was lightly bathed in pale, end of day sunlight, the light of which painted itself in a haphazard line across the open water area like the sweep of an artist's brush. The scene was charming and one could even say romantic, classic boats gleamed in the soft light, water sparkled and as afternoon rolled into evening it was a glorious, breathless, summer one.

Sometime during the late evening stroll their hands had just lightly brushed and then intertwined and without thought of the action they had been walking hand in hand; the laughing coughs of late night ducks surprised them as they walked the pathway that separated marina waters and the lake of a nature reserve, the entire length of which carried the long, broad, faint, white, rippling, reflection of the gently rising moon's illumination across its near still surface, the waters shimmered. Sun setting to the east, moon rising in the west, a double treat. They stopped as a startled duck lifted and flapped off across the water breaking up the perfect reflection in the process, they both laughed easily, and comfortably as the squawking mallard broke the silence.

Gill moved in closer as they stopped walking and leant against the rustic fencing, boats bobbed behind them. The odd few with the glow of nightlight producing elongated mirror images in the still waters of the marina.

The only sound now was that of a brief breeze that had picked up and ruffled the tops of the trees and, with the last of the ducks finally gone for the night, the waters of the lake sat in stillness along its grassy shoreline.

Emboldened by the copious wine, and that final glass of Port, Lucas pulled her closer and she lifted her face toward him, he removed his baseball cap and Gill, for the first time, gained a good look at the face she had thought of as ruggedly handsome, she had been right to think that. As the setting sun lit her face, the rising moon softening her pretty features even more; a brief moment was taken to ensure both were willing partners, a gentle peck, lip on lip, hers stiffly puckered as if to protect herself, his soft and wanting for more; a brief respite, a glimpse of eye to eye contact, Gill's with a small catch-light supplied by the bold gold of brightness of a rising moon, his dark and mysterious, but not threatening, in the shadow of her face.

Again lip touched lip and this time as they kissed the lips parted, her tongue flicking first to just touch his lower lip, sensuous; she eased her tongue against his lips in invitation and he following suit by gently pressing his tongue into her mouth to which she responded by placing her hand on the nape of his neck, where Lucas felt the hairs stiffen and react to her touch, followed by a gentle stiffening in a lower place as well, it had been a long time since he had felt this excited about anything. Drugs had kept any thoughts of erections and sexual activity away from idle minds, now there were no inhibitors to stimulation. And, he was being stimulated!

He pulled away first, gasping for breath as he was now unaccustomed to such intimacy, slightly embarrassed by his semi-erection, a schoolboy unconscious reaction to the sexual tension of the moment he knew he was blushing and was glad of the night hiding it, he hoped his excited member was as well-hidden as his blushes.

"That the keys to your boat or are you really pleased to see me?" She beamed a huge smile his way. All Lucas could do was continue to blush and bluster, trying to speak but his words of apology would not come. It was not helped by the fact that she had just reached down, unnoticed at first, and given his cock a quick squeeze through his trousers, he jumped a little startled by the intimate touch.

"Oh, right, pleased to see me it is then." Without speaking further she took his hand and the couple, which apparently they had now become, headed back toward the Bonnie Annie. With each step taken Gill berated herself in a mental battle of wills, sensible she knew had no chance of winning this battle; she wanted him! He hoped he was feeling the same.

For his part, Lucas was concerned, just for a moment that this had become a Mata Hari moment, but then that anxiety eased for two reasons, firstly he was not going to refuse the advances, it had been too long – far too long, and secondly there was something about this girl he trusted, he knew deep down she was neither callous nor so deeply committed into her desire to be a successful journalist that she would abuse this new-found friendship. At the end of the day his penis was doing the calculations for him and it was a powerful adversary when pitted against seeing common sense.

Gill was torn, go with the flow, as she was doing, or be the professional and hold back. She had introduced herself, gotten to know her prey and now was the time to strike, to get his story, or at least a foot in the doorway of his life. But - why was there always a 'but'? – this 'but' was saying, he was handsome, charming in a shy, nervous, sort of way, and interesting. She liked him! Dreams of the big story were drifting away, thinking that nobody could be this nice if they had horrid secrets to hide, Doctor Death had become Dr Dear...

Hand in hand the two of them had walked quickly toward the mooring as if time were of the essence, both frightened the other would change their mind before they reached the destination of the Bonnie Annie

The pontoon wobbled with their impatient walk, they stepped on board, Charles offering his hand to Gill in a moment of chivalry as she stepped up onto the gunwale of the craft, once on board Charles removed the key, that hung from a cork ball the size of a tennis ball that would keep it afloat should he drop it into the sea, and unlocked the door to the main cabin. Down the three steps into the main lounge they kissed deeply and held each other tightly. Impatience and passion not easy bedfellows! There was a hint, big hint, of poor practice as his hand reached up her back beneath the jumper in an attempt to reach the hook on her bra, his fingers fumbling for the hooks, he used to be able to unclip tem with just two fingers on one hand, now he even had trouble locating them.

"It's a front loader so you won't get anywhere by putting your hand up there, and anyway take your time, I am not going anywhere." Charles was enjoying being the alter ego of Lucas and this new person liked that Gill was taking control and once again he felt at ease, embarrassed because of the length of time since he was last in this position, and also aware that his body was now not as fit as it once was, but she had a positive effect on him and he felt like a young man being seduced by an experienced courtesan.

She broke away from the clinch, like a fighter hearing the bell clang for the end of the round. "Where is the, head, is that what it's called on a boat?"

"It is, or at least can be but not many people apart from the hard and fast traditional sailors, call it that anymore, the toilet is fine and it is just behind you by the main cabin.

"I take it you would be a single malt man? If so pour me a small glass will you, just for Dutch courage." She winked at him as she headed for the toilet.

As Gill closed the door to the toilet and wet room, Lucas lifted a decanter and two glasses from an ornately carved Tantalus and poured them both a small snifter, he downed his and poured another, feeling that he needed a touch more of the false courage at this moment. As he poured the second he felt the burning comfort of the first sliding down.

Sitting on the toilet, panties round her knees, she took the moment to think about what she was doing. From drug runner, bank robber or killer, or even all three, the subject of her big story was, if things continued the way they had begun, about to become lover as well. And, what if she went through with it and let her feelings take over from common sense, even if she did get a story it would be compromised because she could not keep her hands of the handsome villain's tackle, or her lips from his, and she did love the way he kissed, deeply, passionately!

It seemed to Charles that it was only the briefest of moments that she had been gone and then, with the breath held in his lungs unable to expel itself, Gill stepped back into the lounge area and she was wearing nothing but her blouse, unbuttoned, white satin against tanned skin, shapely legs on show and as she walked the material parted, showing just a brief glimpse of the triangle of dark hair at the top of her thighs. It seems her mind was already made up.

With a mischievous smile she walked right up to him, took one of the crystal glasses from his trembling hand, and lifting it to freshly painted lips sipped the oaky and smooth whisky and turned toward the bow of the boat. "Main cabin this way I suppose!" Lucas touched her shoulder as she walked past him, this time it was a glimpse of the perfect orb of just one buttock beneath the short shirt, he had just enough strength to gently turn her around and point to the rear of the boat. "Other way." He spoke through a fast drying mouth.

Lucas realised that his daring escape from Broadmoor and his flight to the coast, although traumatic and scary, was far less intimidating and frightening than this moment, he felt like a schoolboy on his first date.

Gill moved ahead of him leading the nervous man toward the aft cabin, she could feel a nervous tremor in his hand as she held it gently. He made his excuses and stopped on the way before releasing her hand from its soft grasp, stepping in and shutting the door of the toilet; he relieved himself and flushed, washed his hands, and splashed cooling and refreshing water onto his face, the coarseness of his fast growing beard still surprised him as his palms rubbed the course chin, he cleaned his teeth; the toothpaste tasting awful straight after a glass of malt. Finally he stepped from his chinos and washed himself, wanting to be clean when she played with him, he felt his erection rise again at the thoughts of what may happen and the fact he was washing it quite vigorously. He stopped and dried himself...

By the time he opened the cabin door, leaving his trousers on the floor outside, Gill was already under the quilt, moonlight and pontoon walkway lights gave just enough of a cabin glow for him to see her; and he looked down at himself. "I am sorry about the state of this body, it's a bit out of condition I am afraid, it's been a while..."

"Well it may have been a while," Gill replied with a nod downward. "But, it all seems to be working OK." It was a lascivious smile.

Lucas looked down and everything was indeed in full working order and before he could speak Gill just pulled back the quilt and told Lucas to climb in, he caught a brief glimpse of her body, her small and upturned breasts with their dark nipples, he was surprised to see one of them pierced and with a small bar through the brown protuberance, an almost flat stomach with just a little paunchy curve to it and a full bush of pubic hair. He took a mental note that she had avoided the current trend to be shaved or, at least landscaped into a narrow strip of fluff, if newspapers and magazine articles were to be believed.

Climbing in next to her, Charles realised that although this was his bed and his domain it was this confident woman that was taking control, in his past life that would have felt almost demeaning but now it felt right, it felt comfortable, and he was glad she was taking the lead. A schoolboy virgin again heading for promised lands.

As soon as the quilt was thrown back over his body Gill rolled into him and entwined legs and arms, crushing her body to his and trapping his erect penis between them, like finding the right piece in a box full of jigsaw pieces, they slotted together like old lovers, as if they were meant to be.

Despite a rush of impatient enthusiasm from Charles, thanks to Gill's self-control, their love making was slow, purposeful; he wanted to hurry, to climb atop her and mount her as soon as he felt the warmth of her flesh against his own body, but Gill retained control and gently eased him away without comment; she dictated the pace of their lovemaking.

Gill took him in her hand and rubbed him slowly but with a firm grip and Charles felt his toes curl into tight balls as he groaned with pleasure, she pulled on his cock and he groaned a little more, a purr, cat-like. In the half -darkness of the cabin Gill smiled at the effect she was having on her new lover, as she gripped him with one hand wrapped around his shaft and rubbed the palm of her other hand over the tip, Charles almost danced his way off the bed as his body responded to her ministrations, his back arched and the groans grew louder.

She was enjoying his reactions as much, or nearly, as he was but for a brief moment a pang of guilt crossed her mind; there was still a hint of journalistic assignment, she knew how unprofessional she was being but felt she had stepped on this roller coaster ride and now had to see it through every frightening drop, around every stomach churning bend and keep her hands inside the carriage at all times until the ride came to its conclusion, she realised there was no getting off half way through. All these doubts and feelings creeping into her thoughts now and again as she played with Charles, but the attraction she felt for this enigmatic man had quickly turned into something impossible to ignore.

There was also the fact that normally she would not even kiss on a first date, let alone end up in bed with a man who just hours before had been a total stranger. With caution at the front of her mind she was surprised to feel her legs parting at the slight insistence of one of his knees as it pushed against the soft flesh, Charles on his back and her on her side, his thigh pushed and slipped between her thighs and in between the grunts and purrs coming from Charles he found the wherewithal to make a gap for his hand to explore her body, which it did a little too roughly for her liking.

"Gently Charles, I prefer a soft touch, a feather, lightly." She whispered through laboured breathing and waited for his fingers to brush on just the right spot or even to enter her, she was willing, she was more than that, she was a desperate as it had been a while for her too but instead of feeling an intoxicating touch it was as if those words had broken a spell. Charles rolled away from her, pushed the quilt to one side and sat at the edge of the bed, elbows on knees, head in hands and cock dwindling quickly to lay useless between his thighs.

"Don't tell me it's all over already!" Gill tried with a humour she did not feel while placing a reassuring hand in the small of his back.

"I can't, you are too beautiful, too special and if we are going to end up going anywhere it cannot be based on lies..." Charles, in the depths of his mind was screaming 'FOOL', 'IDIOT', get back into bed. But the man that once was had changed, the playboy was now a gentler soul, no longer a player and there was something about this girl that said she would be around for some time to come, as long as he could remain free. He recalled the last girl he had been near, and she had ended up shoved beneath a park bench! He owed it to both the unnamed girl and Gill to be honest.

"Going anywhere!" Gill feigned shock, placed an arm around him and looked up from his lap where she had lain her head. "This was just a one-off date sailor, thought you could do with a pity shag while you were in port what with you looking so sulky in the restaurant, plus I have never done it on a small boat and I am intrigued to discover if it's the same as a waterbed."

Charles did not move, or smile at her frivolous remarks and getting the seriousness of his tone she rubbed his cooling flesh with one hand in the middle of his back; it felt good to him, reassuring. "Just kidding with ya, Charlie." Even though it was an assumed name he liked the familiarity of Charlie. "What's up?" There was no impatience or recrimination in the voice. "Tell me and then we can get back to our love-in."

He doubted she would want to do that with Lucas, now he would no longer be the mysterious Charles. "My name is not Charles." It was blurted out before the sensible half of him could object further to the confession. "It's Lucas, Lucas Tubb. You may have heard the name!" Recognition did hit Gill's brain but she could not put a story to it.

And, over the next thirty minutes or so and without interruption or turning round Charles, now

Lucas once again, told Gill the whole story, or at least the parts he could recall as there were still huge gaps in his recent history. All the while he remained sitting on the edge of the bed, Gill had not moved either, she fearful of breaking the spell that was allowing him to get the story out, not even removing the soothing hand from his back, gently stroking his soft skin with her thumb, she was listening to every word and surprised herself that there was not more fear, or indeed, disappointment being felt.

It surprised her that she did not have a strong feeling of animosity toward him, presuming it was because she knew there was a background story to the strange man on the boat, she had searched out the story only to discover the man behind it, and liking him. There was nothing but sympathy for the charming man that now sat on the side of the bed baring his soul, as well as a very nice bum she had noted; but she quickly brought her mind back to the current proceedings and not the lust she still felt.

"Did you kill her?" It was the obvious question if they were to move beyond this moment, and Gill had surprised herself that she was indeed thinking beyond this moment. The bluntness of the question did not surprise her as she had always been forthright and, maybe even a little too, forward.

"Honestly!" Finally he looked at her, eye to eye.

"Yes please, I think you owe me that." She blinked at the gaze but did not break the connection between them.

"To be totally truthful, I don't know. I don't think so. Its why they sent me to Broadmoor and not to trial, I showed no emotion over her death, no regret, there was nothing I could feel sorry for as I never recalled actually killing her, only trying to save her then leaving her in the park. I don't think I have it in me to kill, or injure anyone, I detest violence, always have done."

"And, you are on the run now."

"I escaped from Broadmoor Friday, a few days ago, blimey I have been on this boat for only a few days and I cannot even remember what day it is now. How long has it been? I presume you have been watching all along if you saw me in the hospital scrubs?"

"Yes, since Friday, today's Tuesday, that's when I first saw you being dropped off by your friend and I watched you in your doctor's garb heading for this boat. Well that explains the scrubs, you escaping from a hospital."

"They may call it a hospital, but anyplace where they lock you in a small, characterless cell is a prison to me, physically and mentally!" Gill caressed his back with her whole hand and not just her thumb to offer consolation; surprised at the strength of feeling she had for Charles... Lucas, she would have to get used to the new name, she tried it out.

"Well I will give you this Sailor, Lucas was it? You don't waste time getting back into the swing of things do you, bet you were a right charmer before you got locked up." Gill, surprising herself, attempted to lighten the mood.

"You seduced me if you recall, I was just sat in a restaurant with my face to the wall in the hope of not being spotted; lot of good that did me."

"Oh yes, so I did. Ah well never did have a good choice in men."

"You don't seem that bothered by what you have heard." Lucas looked her in the eye, trying to read her expression.

"Oh, I am bothered! Trust me!" Her voice remained calm and reassuring. "I broke my own rules about first dates, let my dream of a big story get the better of my usual good sense, but in saying that, I think if you were going to harm me I would have been in the marina waters by now, face down and not to watch the fish swim by!"

Later as they lay in the boat's aft, owner's, cabin, the Bonnie Annie rocked easily and lightly at its mooring, the gentle movement on the water hypnotic, but not enough to ease his mind and allow him sleep, Lucas pondered on how things changed so quickly.

A little under a year ago he was a man without a care, a wonderful home, all paid for, a housekeeper to keep it clean and him fed, flash car in the garage, a couple of holidays a year, one in sunshine the other skiing, and a lifestyle that many would kill for; (that one word of his thoughts caused a nauseous feeling to rise from the pit of his stomach); and a private income left to him by his father. What work he did do was in in brokering deals with used luxury boats and that could hardly be counted as hard work but it did add to the coffers every now and again.

He had a good circle of friends, which diminished with incredible rapidity upon his arrest and then his 'illness'; one or two had stayed close for a while but they soon dwindled into the never land where ex-friends go.

There had been one supporter who hung on till the end when madness took over, but she was only looking for marriage and to share the bed of someone wealthy, she had no doubt discovered another male nest egg by now; he smiled then as the thought that prostitution came in many forms crossed his mind. For several months following, what his mind now thought of as 'the incident', there was just a blur with many days lost to his memory, first by the breakdown and then by the drugs which dulled his mind and stilled his body; the daily cocktails taking away the desire to recall old memories, or the making of new ones.

Just a few days earlier he had been a patient in a high security facility for the criminally insane, as crazy as a box of frogs, as his friend Charles - The Colonel, Lucas smiling at the thought and affection for his friend, had described them all, no idea how crazy that actually was, and now he was lying in a bed, in an expensive yacht, moored in a south coast marina and with a very attractive woman curled up against his body making him feel warm, wanted and carefree. Or was this just another drug fuelled illusion, was he about to waken in his locked and secure room at Broadmoor and laugh at the nature of the world when it could play such a cruel trick as to free his mind through sleep only to slam the door shut on the illusion of freedom when he awoke.

He squeezed with his right arm and the warm body with her hair covering her face gave a little purr of pleasure, a brief snore, and she snuggled even tighter into him; a small fart released itself from her body and Lucas grinned broadly, her snoring had already made him chuckle to himself as it gave him a feeling of comfort and belonging, but with that little natural release he realised this was in fact reality. Not even a drug induced dream-like illusion would produce a fart as part of the story.

Laying there deep in thought he realised how shallow his previous life had been, his father and his father before him were both ex-Royal Navy, Lucas had spent his youth cosily tucked away in the University Student Union bar, while the men that had raised him had fought, risked life and limb in war zones during their youthful years and just because it was their duty. For Lucas it was his duty to get as hammered as possible every weekend. That lifestyle had led to this; on the run from a madhouse, accused, and still not sure if it were true, of violently taking a young girl's life. Finally a friend giving up his short, sad, life to allow him to escape and seek truth, whatever truth may be.

Lucas lay in the bed, covered by a warm quilt secure in the arms of a stunning woman, and pondered about his past, and promised himself a truer, more productive life. A private promise that could easily be reneged upon, but one he would endeavour to secure, with the help of this woman, he hoped. He wriggled to get a little closer and felt the roughness of her pubic hair against his buttocks, it was a strangely comforting feeling.

Where too now though, that was the big question? What was next in this adventure? And would Gill be coming with him?

Chapter 18

"Are you going to write this up?" Lucas enquired as he and Gill sat in morning sunshine, the harbour waters were glistening with a gold hue from the early day sun, a pair of swans drifted on the calm water, just allowing the tidal drift to carry them, their wings curved into ornate sails. A few yards away a cormorant perpetually dived for his breakfast, and seemed to be doomed to continue surfacing still hungry and unsuccessful, his plumage dark, sleek and shining with droplets of water. Keen sailors were already taking their boats through the lockgate for an early start to a day's exploits battling the elements and harnessing the power of the wind to drive them forward. Today's nautical battle would be insignificant as only light breezes had been forecast. Keen sailors would keep their masts full of sail, drawn in tightly, and hold the tiller firmly, eyes keenly searching for ripples on the water indicating a shift in the wind, hopes eternally raised for a prolonged gust. While the less traditional, and probably more practical among the sailing fraternity, would use the iron topsail, engine to landlubbers, to get their boat from an aimless 'a' to an equally pointless 'b' and back again, into the clubhouse to enjoy a deserved pint and some food while retelling their nautical exploits at the end of the day...

Lucas sipped on his cappuccino, the foam cool while the coffee offered a brief scalding of his lips, the caffeine gave him a little drug hit; something he felt he needed as he still adjusted to days that began without drugs. He was still waiting for a response to his question from his new companion it was slow in arriving but following a sip of her own coffee it was duly delivered.

"I should do, it is what I got into journalism for." She looked him in the eye, seriousness stamped across her face. "Are you ready to give me a full and frank interview, my deadline for the evening edition will be eleven at the latest?" Gill's facial expression gave little away, but she had a wicked glint in her eye and her body language was relaxed, not taut or ready to pounce, as an animal released to chase after its prey should be.

"You're a tease, aren't you?" Lucas responded with more confidence than he felt. "You are kidding with me; right!"

She could see the doubt in his eyes, doubt mixed with a hint of fear, and the need for reassurance as his fingers stroked the new growth of hair on his chin, a habit that had become a regular feature when deep in thought.

Gill leant back in her chair, sipped another hit of her Americano, and looked out across the harbour, noting that the cormorant was now on the end of the long jetty that poked out from marina into open water, his wings spread out, as a fisherman boasting of the size of his catch with arms spread wide, and drying in the warm summer's morning breeze while the pair of swans had paddled off into the distance in a pretty flotilla of two shining white craft. Her silence a tribute to the internal struggle going on within; one part so wanting to ask the questions, while the other waned to offer support to a man she had so swiftly grown fond of and with whom she now sat in comfortable silence as if they had been a couple for some time, despite the constricting mood of the situation they were easy with each other's company. Lucas appearing cool and strong while inside his worries fluttered around like annoyed butterflies; Gill torn between profession and personal; she liked him, would not have spent the night with him if she did not. He, despite what he was going though, was charismatic, and she was swiftly being drawn into his world, one part of her said to write the story, the angel on one shoulder speaking of common sense, of calling the police and handing him over while getting the story she craved, on the other shoulder a little devil, his trident tips burning with flame, telling her to go along for the ride, help Lucas and see what happens until if, and when, he recalls what happened that autumn night back in the Bishop's Garden.

Later, following a breakfast of fresh croissant and coffee, picked up from The Boat House, Lucas lingered in the shower, his skin wrinkling as he enjoyed the cleansing feeling of hot water. This was no timed washing session as per the norm during his incarceration, no one stood outside the shower stall watching, just him standing under the near-scalding waterfall and surrounded by the sweet smell of mango shower gel. It, and he, smelled of freedom and no longer of an institution. The aroma was of a good life and not of a life on hold. What everyone takes for granted as an everyday necessity Lucas took for a long wished sense of freedom and belonging. For the first time in many months he could step from the shower, choose what clothes he wished to wear and then step out into sunshine without hindrance. Once he had stepped out of the shower, wrapped in just a towel he stepped onto the deck, taking in his surroundings with renewed eyes, everything brighter, cleaner, clearer; then there came the aromas of his surroundings, the saltiness of the sea, ozone from the mud as the incoming tide covered it over and then the smells that made lips moist and stomachs growl in anticipation; that wonderful smell of the English breakfast. Sitting out on deck, his bare feet up on the gunwale, he heard Gill at work in the boat's galley.

"Have we not just had breakfast?" Lucas enquired in a loud voice without moving from his position on the deck.

"After that night of passion, a couple of croissants are not fulfilling enough, they just do not fill the desire to be fed." She poked her head from the galley area so Lucas could hear her response. "Plus if we are to set sail to wherever today we need to do it on a good solid meal." Her head ducked back into the galley but not before Lucas captured in his mind's eye how beautiful she was.

Her voice was replaced with the sounds of eggs bubbling, bacon sizzling and the toaster popping forth its warmed load of twin slices of wholemeal, Gill was struggling to hear the music from the cabin's radio and was in the mood for some busy rock sounds. Swapping spatula from right hand to left, keeping a wary eye on the eggs, she reached across and turned up the local radio station as it played some banal, but funky, pop tune from the charts, the beat was just enough to get her dancing while she flipped eggs, checked bacon and fed two more slices of bread into the toaster's hungry slots.

Floating from the twin speakers the presenter, in a slick, smooth voice reading from his studio script, teased his audience with the announcement of the tunes and songs that would be played following the news. Gill pictured him touching computer screens and working the sound desk sliders up and down, when with a slightly plummy voice the newsreader hit the air waves in serious tones with an introduction of who he was, even though knowing his name would add nothing to the value or importance of the news, although strangely it always added an imaginary face, she saw the voice as being owned by an upright man with well-trimmed hair that was slightly greying at the temples, clean shaven and with the look of a doctor or solicitor.

The second round of toast popped their browned heads out from the toaster trenches and egg yolks hardened as the albumen turned into brown lace, the bacon meanwhile, went beyond crisp to burnt-beyond-recognition. Spatula still in hand Gill stood in the narrow gangway between galley and dining area with mouth agape and ears tuned into the radio. Lucas was the lead story, but not only that, according to the erudite newsreader, following his escape from the secure unit at Broadmoor the escaped mental patient had killed again; and there was now a full blown manhunt for the escaped psychopath. "The public are warned not to approach this man as the police say he is extremely dangerous." The newsreader continued. "Any sighting of Lucas Tubb by the public, and there are images of the escaped psychopath on our website at www.spiritfm.net, should immediately be reported to the police."

She increased the volume a little further as the story was reported in a little more depth, on deck Lucas sat frozen, his coffee ignored, the sights and aromas around him vanished while he listened via the on deck speakers. "The well-known former local playboy Lucas Tubb, escaped from Broadmoor Hospital sometime late last Friday afternoon, he was being held in the secure unit following the murder of a, as of yet unidentified, young girl in a Chichester flower garden, (somehow the addition of the 'flower garden' to the report gave his crime added dastardliness) and a police spokesman has told Spirit FM news he has possibly killed again. The report confirmed that Lucas Tubb, aged 29, had indeed escaped from the maximum secure unit but that information had been suppressed at the request of the Police to minimize local alarm. The spokesperson confirmed that the housekeeper at the Tubb's marina side, half a million pound, family cottage, Annie Smith, aged 68, had been beaten to death. The body being discovered late last night by the escaped mental patient's brother, Jacob Tubb."

A millisecond of silence and then Jacobs's voice, a clear distinct sound bite. "I arrived home late last night to discover poor Annie's body in the front hall of our home, it was obvious she had been badly beaten but the police have asked that I do not give further details as their investigation continues, but suffice to say it was a shock to find her lying there. Again, at the police's request, I checked the house and several items have been taken such as my mother's jewellery, and some of Lucas' old clothing that was due to be taken to a charity shop, I have given the full list to the police." There was a theatrical sob to his voice to end his section of the report.

The newsreader again. "The police have advised that if the public suspect they have seen Lucas Tubb, not to approach him as he is deemed to be extremely dangerous."

"And in other news…"

Gill turned from the radio to return to the now ruined breakfast and she saw Lucas standing halfway down the short staircase that led to their aft, owner's cabin, he was clutching the towel around his waist, as if it were a protective shield; the look of loss, mingled with fear, on his face tore at Gill's heart strings.. "I didn't!" he began to say.

Gill held a hand up to stop him, and realised it was the one holding the spatula making her feel ridiculous at such a moment. Lucas felt panic rise like bile in the throat as the realisation was about to hit Gill that he was indeed a killer, and a double killer at that, nothing he had said the evening before meant anything of any worth as of his moment!

"You don't have to explain Lucas, I saw you arrive with Annie and then saw her drive away, I watched you go to your boat and have been around all weekend before I joined you in the restaurant; it could not have been you; you were in my eye line nearly, if not all, of the time Annie was away from you. I know it wasn't you!" Gill could not decide whether to smile with relief that this man, who had suddenly become a part of her life, was innocent or to be sad for him at the news his housekeeper and ex-nanny had been murdered.

Lucas just stood there nodding, face a storybook of confused emotions, tears gently welling in the corner of his eyes before breaking free and running down his cheeks, his expression was crippled with shock and despair. Gill walked to him and he dropped down the last two steps to get to her level, she took him in her arms and he buried his head into the soft skin of her neck; the towel dropping to the floor but neither noticing his nakedness as he was drawn into the the enfolding arms, they hugged, held each other. Gill let him sob gently, shoulder shaking with the effort, and she calmly stroked his still damp hair, at that moment he was childlike. Neither spoke; words would have been superfluous.

"We need to get away from here!" It was Gill breaking the silence of the moment with an urgency to her voice, realising that someone needed to take control!

"How, where?" Lucas was puzzled his mind still trying to function without the regular drug regime it had become used to, there was a still, at times a thick and swirling fog of confusion. "I don't even have a car, well I do but it's at the cottage and we can't go there." Words were just tumbling, he was babbling.

"Shush, calm, we have the perfect getaway vehicle right here, no one will be looking for you on the water, they will be looking for a man on his own and wearing prison clothes at best and bloodied clothes at worst, meanwhile we can just slip away as if for a day's sailing and not come back. Does anyone know you own a boat?"

"Um, no, the boat was really Annie's my father left it to her." Lucas was trying hard to get his thoughts and feelings in order. "I doubt Jacob will even remember it is here; but shouldn't I just give myself up?"

"They will send you back to Broadmoor and probably will not even consider anyone else but you for Annie's death." Gill suddenly thought of Lucas' feelings for his housekeeper. "I am sorry Lucas, this must be a shock for you on so many levels. I presume you two were really close, you must be hurting."

The look of the bereaved on his face spoke volumes, Lucas did not feel like talking about Annie and Gill respected the fact he needed space so as he could just remember her, and keep her to himself for a short while. Released from Gill's arms he turned and stepped into the aft cabin, where he had experienced so much joy just a couple of hours ago as he and Gill made love, he closed the cabin door. Gill turned to the galley and began to scrape the ruined breakfast into the rubbish bag.

So it was, less than an hour later, that the Bonnie Annie was released from the ropes binding her to the pontoon and he pushed a small wave of water ahead of her bow on join in the flotilla of yachts and cruisers that were readying to exit the haven through the lock-gate, just another craft moving toward open water, uneventful, without suspicion. The craft bobbed and strained at the leash, like an animal released to the wild after a long hibernation, she was keen to play again.

Gill told Lucas to stay in the wheelhouse and drive the boat while she handled the ropes that tied them to the pontoon. She was not totally at ease with boats but had done a little sailing in her teenage years, so knew what to do when it came to the routine stuff. As Gill stepped out of the cabin gangway and onto the grey diamond-patterned non-slip decking, this type of craft being designed as a working boat that now doubled, perfectly, as a leisure craft, beneath her bare feet she felt the engines throb with restrained life and watched as dark exhaust smoke choked from the aft end of the boat. The craft came alive beneath her even before she had reached the first cleat and untied the forward ropes, then scrambling along the side of the Bonnie Annie to release the aft tethers; all with seemingly expert smoothness. Lucas let the craft ease lazily away from the pontoon before nudging the twin throttle levers forward causing the boat to join the small throng driving towards the lock gate at a low five knots, left hand on the wheel, right hand resting lightly, and confidently on the twin throttle controls. Gill, on deck and standing like a broad-legged drunk to counter the movement of the boat, coiled the ropes best she could and left them in a tidy-(ish) heap on deck before, and with no small amount of relief that she had arrived there safely, standing at the cabin door, one hand gripping the rail at eye level, the grip firm even though they were still in the calm of the marina.

"I'll teach you how to stow ropes when get a little more time but for now I need you on deck and ready to take the lines from the Lock Keeper." Through a strong facial expression Lucas faked a confidence he was not really feeling but at least he knew about boats; Gill was less confident!

"I don't have to tie the boat off do I, or do one of those bowline thingy knots?" Her eyes darted between the cabin exterior and the man she was about to help stay free a second time, and then she gazed with a little apprehension at the approaching lock which seemed to narrow as they crept ever closer, like a stealthy cat closing on its prey, three boats already waited in the small basin of water before the lock and the Bonnie Annie joined the queue and waited patiently just bobbing on the water, throttles for the twin engines now in a neutral position... Gill, with unfelt confidence, stepped back up onto the deck, trying to look comfortable in her role as deck hand.

An incongruous traffic light at the lock entrance shone bright red, reflecting on the still water and even at a distance Gill could hear the clank and hum of the curved and sliding lock-gate as it began to open, the mechanical sound seeming to heighten her apprehension. The pair of gates reached their destination fully open with a deep clang that echoed across the marina like a distant clap of thunder and the traffic light flicked from red to green, it all seemed very civilised, it was a signal for them to go, to get them away from the world that was chasing them and sailing toward safety.

Wherever that was!

A flock of early geese in a small and ragged V formation flew overhead with military precision, these were early arrivals, the dull, grey coloured Brent Geese, which would eventually count in the thousands, were really autumn visitors, these skeins were the advance party seeking out expanses of lawns to graze on.

"All you have to do is take the lines from the lock keeper and keep us close to the wall as she drops to the level of the harbour waters on the other side of the gates. Go on!" Lucas urged her through the open window from the steering position below deck.

Gill held the rail as the 45 foot hull was manoeuvred with lazy ease into the last slot in the pool between the gates, Lucas avoided the natural urge to hold the wheel, instead he gave one hand to each of the throttle controls and manoeuvred the boat using its twin engines, each propeller doing its job of positioning the craft, the steering wheel virtually useless at such slow speeds.

On the lock wall just above them a smiling keeper greeted Gill, "Good morning", his short cut ginger hair bright in the morning sunlight, his face, round, freckled and pink, beamed contentment, a man happy in his work. "Nice to see this lovely craft being used again, been sat at her mooring for far too long, she has." Gill wondered why all boats were 'she', his voice carried a country burr making him sound just a touch piratical and even with his friendly, sun-wrinkled, face it seemed to suit him and his position in life. "Like dogs they are, need taking out for exercise every now and again."

Gill opened her mouth to reply at the same time as juggling the two lines that had been handed her, at first pulling hard on them but then relaxing as she realised that the Bonnie Anne was going nowhere, before being able to utter a word in response she watched the keeper as he climbed the external staircase into the lock-house to hit the red button to first close the back gates blocking off the marina basin behind them and then open the front sluice gate in order to let the level of water drop, like a lift designed by Archimedes, the boat slid effortlessly down the moss-covered wall, and struggled, just slightly like an impatient dog wanting to get off the lead, to move forward with the water's flow. Gill hung on, collision and disaster were averted by her firm hand on the ropes and she began to feel pleased with her small contribution.

The downward journey came to an end, the watery lift reaching basement level, the gates curved and swung back into their hiding space in the dock wall and the harbour opened out to them and the other craft in the lock; the open water offered them more freedom than the other sailors would ever realise that day. The first three boats, all yachts, their masts empty, with engines puttering, moved out into the vastness of Chichester Harbour, each with crew members scurrying over the deck readying sails, stowing fenders and coiling ropes. The two swans from earlier looked up from their spot on one side of the deep channel at all the commotion but then went back to their food foraging, first head up and then tail up in the water, Gill thought they looked quite comical with their white, tufty rear ends poking up out of the water, before they bobbed back upright, elegant heads and necks raised, water droplets dripping from their pristine plumage and large beaks; the two of them a couple for life, devoted and dedicated to each other.

The Bonnie Annie followed in the gentle wake of the other craft, her engines throbbing lowly and in time with each other, pushing the craft forward at an easy pace, the speed of a funeral cortege that linked to the mood on board. Lucas, wanting to open the throttles to get away as quickly as possible restrained the urge and just eased her into the open water and followed the marked channel at the required speed limit, even on watery roads there was a highway code to be adhered to, especially in a conservation harbour such as this where the wakes from speeding craft would damage the delicate banks and the eco-structure, it was a tricky balancing act to keep both leisure seekers and wildlife in harmony.

Lucas looked up from his position at the wheel, there was someone standing on the wall that separated Birdham Marina from the broad waters of the harbour, his body language one of anger and resentment, between them the long pontoon where boats moored waiting for the gates to favour them strained at their short leashes. It was a face Lucas recognised but there was no point in his hiding below the windows of the cabin, the boat was known and he had been already been seen, distant eyes were blazing in resentment and anger at him.

It was his brother; Lucas was looking straight at Jacob standing way above the low tide line, their eyes meeting. Jacobs filled with hate, Lucas' he could feel, were fearful. Without altering his gaze Jacob hefted his mobile phone from his pocket and began dialling; the chase, it seemed was over before freedom had even started, and Lucas looked on unable to stop him making the call.

Jacob held the phone to his ear and Gill, her eye-line following Lucas', as she realised his attention had been diverted. Jacob's lips formed several hellos. He looked at the face of the phone again, redialled the triple nine number, and again mouthed several greetings. There was no signal down at the water's edge, he was below the line of sight for the nearest tower! He looked at the face of the phone again, held it in front of him, held it high above his head before turning around in circles before looking again, performing pirouettes in some weird waterside dance routine. He hopped and spun and lifted his hands in desperation trying to fill the signal bars on his inert phone. His face reddened with ire, Lucas all the while looking on, terrified of his younger brother.

A shout, angry, venomous, carried over the water as Lucas opened the throttles just a little, the Bonnie Annie responded immediately and raised her nose, just a little, up out of the water; Lucas hearing the shouts but not the words that had been hollered. As the Bonnie Annie collected a little more speed he was aware it may well garner the attention of the Harbour Master in what was a wake free zone by driving the boat too fast, and yet he knew he had to get into open water as swiftly as possible, Jacob would not be too far away from a stronger signal.

Lucas finally heard the words spoken; "Get back here you murdering bastard," Jacob's voice amplified by the enclosed harbour. "You can't keep running they will get you, and that's my boat now, just like it's my house and my car, you have nothing you are nothing, except..."

"What is it Lucas?" Gill gazed across to where Lucas had his gaze fixed, his mouth hung open and he appeared to be struggling to catch his breath. She placed a hand on his arm. "Lucas you are scaring me, what is it?" Her voice had become timid and faltering.

Lucas could still hear Jacob's vicious vitriol as they motored far enough away for the angry voice for it just be a humming tirade of black noise from a red-faced aggressor. Looking back, he said, "It's Jacob, my brother, up there on the marina wall, he is trying to call the police, we won't get away." His voice was panic stricken, that of a frightened boy.

"Lucas, breathe, take a breath and look." She took his chin, gently cupping it in her right hand and turning his gaze to where he had been pointing. "There is no one there Lucas, I saw and heard no one. It is just your fear, probably the lack of medication, look Lucas, no Jacob, no one in sight."

Lucas looked again, eyes on the point on the waterside where he had seen and heard his brother, but there was no one, he cocked an ear to listen, no sound except of the gulls wheeling and screaming overhead. "But..." Gill held him. "I saw him, he was there." He added.

Gill explained that it was going to be hard coming off the heavy medication he had been on, telling Lucas just to concentrate on driving the boat. Although she tried to console him and convince him all would be well, she was unsure herself of what the future held for both of them, both physically and mentally; she had become embroiled in this man's world, almost without any say in the matter, it had all happened so quickly, so automatically, like a car parking itself, she had just been taken along for the ride.

The 'Victorian' looking boathouse and lock gate at Bosham Marina, pitch black wooden shuttering making up the old, character, buildings, drifted past them as the Bonnie Annie motored forward, this was the slowest getaway in running-from-the-police history.

"Does it go any quicker?" Enquired Gill, concerned with imminent capture and looking back over her shoulder toward the marina that they were leaving behind. "This would make a lousy film good-guy, bad-guy chase scene you know."

Lucas confirmed it did indeed go quicker but explained the reasons for his reluctance, now free of the lock gate Gill stood alongside him, co-conspirator next to co-conspirator, she squeezed his hand as a show of support, while inside her stomach was churning at the thought of how her life was turning out. She should have been at her desk, copying press releases and writing obituaries, but here she was on a boat, running from the police and falling for the man now holding the wheel and steering them to, to… wherever it was they were going. Following a big story did not entail being on the run with the subject of the story; and she realised that she was now part of the substance in her own scoop.

The channel narrowed slightly as at a lowly six knots they motored towards escape at little more than walking pace. Lucas had explained that a knot was the speed of one nautical mile an hour and that a nautical mile was approximately one point one land miles, it allowed for the curvature of the earth's surface. Lucas realised he was talking just for the sake of talking, something he always did when nervous or scared, and right now he was both! He decided not to tell her that their top speed would be little more than twenty four or five miles-per-hour, as he realised that she expected the boat to pull up her dowdy skirts and rocket off into the wild-blue-yonder. Boats like this were for cruising and not for rushing to distant destinations in the shortest possible time!

A group of pensioners sat on the viewing platform in front of the Chichester Harbour Conservation offices and waved as each boat went by, not wanting to be rude they both waved back causing much glee among the elderly audience who all smiled at the pair of sailors as if greeting long lost friends, before tucking back into their tuna fish sandwiches, the only suitable filling for a daytrip to the seaside, while one old man sucked toothlessly on the whipped ice cream atop its yellow cone, "Lovely couple." Offered one old lady who had finished her sandwich and was now picking cress from a small gap in her false teeth, before replacing the plate in her mouth.

Lucas peered beyond the geriatric gathering and looked up the road, expecting a flood of flashing blue lights accompanied by the echo of swirling sirens bouncing down the narrow street, as police rushed toward the water's edge to cut them off, he was relieved when none seemed to be arriving and he breathed a little easier, the harbour exit not too far away.

Onward they motored, ever closer to the open waters of the English

Channel, no conversation, each feeling far too tense and yet there was a comfort, and ease between them that both recognised. It was as if they were meant to be doing this together, fate was leading them. She trusted the 'murderer' with her heart, but her head was confused and cluttered with thought, as he fashioned his pedestrian paced escape and he, in tacit turn, trusted the journalist on the trail of her first big story.

A smile broke onto her face for the first time since starting the boat engines as Gill pointed out a Great Egret on the shoreline, four foot tall, lanky and bright white, head swivelling atop the long neck like a periscope's eye, as the boat cruised past it causing the gangly bird to lift into the air and flap away like a clumsy angel. A stunning array of sand dunes came into view and Lucas explained that this was Easthead, a National Trust property that was just beautiful with its rolling dunes and a great place to spend a summer evening picnic watching the sun set in the west. She playfully punched his arm and accused him of bringing many a girlfriend down to the dunes for a summer picnic and whatever else he could get, she realised that a smudge of jealousy had entered the banter, for his part Lucas merely shrugged his shoulders and blushed, his, now, bearded and slightly chubby cheeks, which he had become used to, glowing with embarrassment. He brushed his hair from his forehead, something else he was getting used to, in the past it would be gelled and swept back, now he allowed it to just hang loose and soft, he preferred the carefree cut.

The exit from the harbour curved gently around to the left and there before them lay the open sea with its white horses and lazily curling waves which in a never ending cycle lapped at the sandy shore, a beach popular with summer visitors. The boat began to dance, lively on top of the increasingly agitated water.

"Left, right or straight on?"

Lucas looked at her, scratched his whiskered chin and said... "I have absolutely no idea! I hadn't planned this far ahead!"

"So let me get this straight we are on the run from the police, you from both the police and a lunatic asylum, in a boat that so far has not exceeded the walking pace of a pensioner on a Zimmer frame and now there is no plan and not even any direction." Gill summed the situation up perfectly!

"Nope, not the foggiest!" Lucas responded as they both looked out of the cockpit at the open sea and wondered, what next!

"Well this has to be the greatest getaway of all time, certainly the slowest." Gill smiled broadly as she realised she was beginning to really enjoy this stuttering adventure with a man she only met recently who was now thought to be a double murderer. Both her mother and her editor, would be proud of her!

Chapter 19

Patience was not a trait familiar with Jacob Tubb, he sat at the refectory table that dominated the large, rustic styled, kitchen, units with doors of dark oak seeming to suck the light from the room, he was sipping on his fourth coffee of the morning. The caffeine hits giving him an early day high while easing another hangover headache, beneath the stripped and worn with age oak planks that made up the table top his left foot twitched and hammered in a rapid, repeat, drumming motion, the heel impacting with the flagstone flooring, while on the table surface his hands shook with rising anger, or the overdose of caffeine.

His ire this time aimed at the police, who still, two days after he had first called them, sifted through every room in the cottage and took away bag after bag of what, they said, was evidence. As if waiting to race away again some of the police cars lining the driveway to the cottage still had blue lights flashing and twirling, in readiness for rushing off to some as of yet unseen drama, they sent a strange blue glow drifting across the front of the white house and through the leadlight windows, lighting each room as if a television had been left with its screen flickering long after programmes had finished.

A support officer, had, on her arrival the day before, introduced herself as Jemma Costello with the unsolicited rider that, "my Grandfather was Italian". Her crisp white uniform shirt, neatly pressed and open at the neck, heightening the fictitious sexual tension which Jacob was feeling between them, as she sat at the far end of the heavy, oak refectory table. She sipped her tea, Earl Grey the choice, which had surprised Jacob when she made it herself a few minutes earlier, thinking her a simple girl with little taste or education, what did the working class know of style; although he would never consider himself a snob, he viewed her from the moment of their first meeting as someone beneath him, and making her all the more desirable for that – a bit of rough, as Jacob was thinking.

While the petite officer, with her dark and heavy eyebrows that shaded her eyes under a short fringe of jet-black shiny hair the colour of wet coal, had waited for the kettle to boil she chatted about time of day stuff, what a nice cottage, it must be nice living this close to the sea and what's it like on stormy days; each question greeted with silence as if the hired help were getting above their station in life. Jemma misread Jacob's silence. Non-communication from the bereaved was a problem she was used to and experience told her there was no point in either getting frustrated or annoyed at a lack of response. Everybody grieved differently, there were some visits to bereaved families where she could not get a word in edgeways, if truth be known she actually preferred the silent client and hoped the sound of her voice speaking of nothing in particular would ease their moments of sorrow.

A loose lock of hair fell from her pony tail and she tucked it behind her ear and quietly reflected that a little earlier, when asked, he had not even known where the tea was kept, let alone if they had Earl Grey. Part of her job as family liaison was to watch for behaviour patterns, spot inconsistencies and there was something about this client she definitely did not like, her instincts were raised like a warning flag; yet, despite being on guard, her demeanour remained impassive and professional. The fact he knew where nothing was in the kitchen meant the relationship between housekeeper and this obnoxious man, who continued to leer at her, was not one of beloved family retainer as he had portrayed, but more of one that bordered on master and slave.

It was her prime role to comfort and support, not involve personal feelings, but there was nothing in the manual said that you had to like the victim's relatives or those close to them; her job was just to empathise.

There was little more to this man than the character he was showing, he was a letch and a snob, and a dislike had been garnered from the moment she was introduced by the senior officer at the scene, DS Kaan. The escaped nut-job, sorry, she thought to herself and corrected her thought, mental patient, was primary to this investigation; political correctness in thought, speech and deed, any other way these days and your professional career was quickly down the nearest toilet!

From the moment of that introduction it had seemed as if the man's eyes had not left various parts of her anatomy, never looking her straight in the eye; while greetings were exchanged he had addressed her breasts, although small and tucked well into her slightly loose fitting shirt, he still found a pleasure in making the minimal amount of conversation aimed toward that area. When she had looked over her shoulder while making the hot beverages she noted the eyes were fixed and glazed upon her bum which was rounded and petite in tight police trousers. This man was making her skin crawl!

"Had Annie been with your family long?" She asked between sips of the aromatic and slightly dusty flavoured tea, as they now sat with the long and broad table as a barrier firmly between them, she felt protected by its solidity and size.

"Since I was born." The reply curt and almost spat at the enforced companion. "When will you all be out of here? I have a life to get on with you know!"

"Sorry Jacob, is it okay to call you Jacob or would you prefer Mr Tubb?" He had nodded in response but his eyes had showed even more annoyance and impatience. "It is always a long and painstaking effort to collect evidence after a killing, especially one as violent as this…"

The foot stopped drumming, the glare became ratcheted up in its intensity. "I don't know what for, we all know who did this, my maniac half-brother who, you remember, is the one your lot let walk out of a, so-called, secure mental facility. Easy, so he could come down her and continue his murderous campaign, who is next, me? Will he be coming after me? Will I have to lock myself away to stay safe? Certainly can't stay here. Can I?" The last two words were fired at the liaison officer as if it were all of her doing. "I am not safe. And it is hardly conducive to good living with her blood still staining the floor

Experienced in handling tricky clients, they were clients nowadays, not victims, accused or customers, they were clients; it was more like a corporate sales job sometimes, the human touch almost non-existent. She kept her voice level, low, pleasant and with a slight hint of huskiness that Jacob liked, if he closed his eyes he could imagine her on one of those sex chat-lines where the most inane comment was made with sexual undertones. "We believe that he would have left the area now Jacob, there is much, too much, of a police presence around your home for him to return here, it would not be safe, especially if he wants to remain free. Would there be an overriding reason for Lucas wanting to get to you." She may have been in the cottage with Jacob to offer support, as well as being a link with the investigation team, but she was still a police officer and she had a duty to discover things missed with previous interviews.

After the initial mad flurry of activity with paramedics, first police on the scene with their hurried questions and then the more calming and in depth interview with Detective Sergeant Kobie Kaan. Jacob had begun to explain what he had found on his return home. The Sergeant's, dark features and brooding eyes hid a shrewd and incisive mind and many a criminal had been fooled by his mellow, soft, Mediterranean looks. Behind that friendly face, with its brown eyes and round face, was a man who tended not to let go of a problem until he had solved the riddle. When frustrated he had a habit of rubbing his hand vigorously over his shave and dome-like pate. Riddles were his business and each day he would begin with a coffee and the crossword on the back page of his paper, it was his mental exercise to keep his brain sharp. Kobie, was a handsome, in an easy sort of way, never really looking youthful, his serious gaze always aging him and he was often underestimated, and that was a mistake.

"I knew something was wrong as soon as I arrived home." Jacob explained to the DS as a lone crocodile tear appeared in the corner of his left eye. "The front door was slightly open and Annie, poor Annie, I don't know what I will do without her, she has always been there in my life. Anyway Annie..." Jacob wiped at the rogue tear and felt he was putting on a great performance. "Well, she was always security conscious, always kept the house locked down, probably doing a better job at security than that fucking nuthouse. What's the matter with those pricks, who let my brother get away to do this?"

"Save your anger for later please Mr Tubb." The calming, but suspicious, voice of DS Kaan had urged. "It is important we find out exactly what has happened; it may be we discover it is just a vicious and weird coincidence, I personally doubt it, but we have to follow where the evidence takes us at the moment. So please bear with us! Now, you were telling me what you found when you arrived home. Try to think clearly because the smallest detail may turn out to be vital"

"Do I have to go through all this again, this is rather traumatic you know?" Jacob had every detail of his story already in mind and would let it out piece by piece when he felt it was needed; the fools in the police force these days were well below his intellect.

"Please." The experienced Kobie was ever the patient man, especially with people he had taken an instant dislike to, and he did not like the man in front of him one little bit. Men with that amount of arrogance were always the harbinger of their own downfall, they always thought they were better than those around them, almost as if baiting their own trap.

In impatient tones Jacob continued, "As I said, the door was open which I did not think was right but then briefly I thought she had seen the lights from my car and just unlatched the door for me. I left the car on the drive walked over and pushed the door all the way open, that is when I just saw her laying there on the floor." He turned his head toward the hallway to emphasise his story. "My first thought she had fallen down the stairs, she was getting on and not so nimble on her feet anymore, and tried to check for a pulse, but I never know where the right place is, so I just attempted to resuscitate her, like they do in the movies, you know by banging on her chest and stuff."

"Did you give her the kiss of life?"

"No I didn't, not at first, she was an old woman and who knows what disease she might be carrying! I just pumped on her chest and had to stop when I thought I heard one of her ribs break, I guess I must have been trying too hard, that's when I was left with no option but to try the kiss of life, lot of good that did and who knows what I have caught!" He wiped his mouth with the back of his hand, a reaction to the thought of her blood on his face, although in truth he had enjoyed the metallic taste, licking his lips with relish before washing the dried blood off some time ago. Jacob suddenly fearing he had taken things a little too far tried to step backwards slightly with his statement. "I hope that fact doesn't taint your evidence, you know a broken rib and stuff. I was only trying to help!" A small sob that caught in his throat he felt helped sell the story and his distress.

And so it went on, the tale was repeated several times to see if there were inaccuracies, and then finally he was left alone with the pretty little thing in the crisp uniform sitting opposite him now. The coffee had gone cold but he sipped it anyway, keen not to break the spell he thought he was binding around this young officer. He played out the drama of the shattered victim, lucky to have not been home at the time, although he may have been able to save poor Annie had he been there. Jacob was working her, slowly bending the pretty, dark haired officer to his will and charm.

"Have you ever lost anyone close, Officer?"

"Jem, Jacob, you can call me Jem."

In reply he managed to avoid the cliché of using her name as a tool to flirt. "Have you Jem? Lost anyone I mean."

"I lost my parents in a car crash two years ago, a drunk driver just ran through a red light and hit them, which is why I signed up for this part of the job, the officer that dealt with me after that tragedy was very helpful in allowing me to come to terms with my loss, so I suppose, it's a case of giving something back." The canny officer also knew that if you give a bit of yourself, you will always get something back. People did not realise it but whether innocent or guilty, they all wanted one thing, to talk about their experiences and once the talking began they rarely stopped before they gave something away, something personal or something to do with the case; conversation always led to one step too far. And, this guy, she hoped, was close to taking that step.

Jacob fidgeted and drummed on the table with his fingers, the thick planks soaking up the thrumming noise, Jem was unsure if this fidgeting habit was as result of far too much caffeine or the nervous twitch of a guilty mind.

In turn he pretended a little amount of confusion, the actor in him said this was something someone in his position would suffer. "Have they taken the body yet Jemma?" He looked toward the door into the hallway, each sentence spoken was clipped and delivered without emotion, strange if the housekeeper meant so much to him. "Or is she still out there, in the hallway?"

"No Jacob, she has been gone for some time now; the police surgeon pronounced her and the funeral company came and took her as soon as the forensic team had done what they needed to do." Her voice was calming, even toned, but there was a hint of the investigative about it as well and Jacob had noted that change in tenor.

"You think I had something to do with it, don't you?" The sudden flip from cooperative to annoyance caused Jemma to tense. The outburst was delivered harshly and globules of spittle darted out of his mouth, falling short of the teapot and leaving a dark spot on the oak. "I can tell from your snotty tone." He almost added, 'you bitch' but held back.

"Let me assure you Jacob that nothing of the sort…"

"Don't lie to me little lady, I know your sort!"

"There is no need for rudeness Mr Tubb, I have no opinion either way because I have no idea of the evidence that is being gathered, and even if I did…"

Jacob began to interrupt but she stopped him by just raising her voice one mark on the volume scale and by one octave on the annoyance scale; training for this type of scenario had been intense.

"Even if I did know what the rest of the squad have deduced I would still keep it to myself, I am here to support you and offer counselling should you need it. That is my job from start to finish!" As the sentence tailed off Jem returned her voice to its normal timbre and tone.

Jacob sulked into his cold remnant of coffee, wishing it was something much stronger, head hung low he seethed behind the cup sensing that now was a good time to shut up and keep his own council.

He wondered where his damn brother had got to, if they had caught him by now he would have no worries as they would not be looking for anyone else when it came to who killed Annie. Before calling the police Jacob had gone through Lucas' room, removing clothes and shoes, fresh underwear, his passport and various other personal items such as family photos; he had jammed them into the old suitcase that Lucas always insisted on travelling everywhere with, well before his incarceration anyway, and then he had stowed it in the boot of his car, in readiness for a later disposal. He presumed, with a certain amount of hope, that there would be no need to search his car. To all intents and purposes it appeared as if the murdering brother had returned to the cottage to get some of his belongings to help while on the run, he was disturbed by Annie and after being threatened with being reported he had beaten her to death. As he explained to that smarmy, darkie, sergeant; "He had always been a wild one, and everyone knew what he was capable of, but even then there was no reason to batter our beloved housekeeper; his mental state is beyond comprehension. What makes people like him do that sort of thing?" Jacob had cast his line on the water and hoped the bait and hook had been taken.

As he sat, and although he was now very wary of her and her agenda, with the sexy little police officer, who on any other day would have found it difficult to resist the mixture of his charm, good looks and presumed wealth, he imagined slowly unbuttoning that uniform shirt, creasing its perfection, to find a small lacy, black hopefully, bra underneath holding the white and firm orbs of her breasts constrained. He saw them in his mind's eye as pert, nipples erect at his touch. So lost was he in his reverie Jacob gave his brother no thought at all, thinking him to be miles away, when he did deign to think of him, and had no idea that at the time of his lustful daydreaming Lucas, along with his new and confused companion, were just a few miles away in the marina, and that, more importantly, that the companion had given him an alibi.

Chapter 20

They had both chosen right, they would head west out of Chichester Harbour, the forty five foot vessel handling the larger waves of open water easily. The coastline to their right had slid steadily, if not quickly, past them.

"Penny for them!" Lucas knew, or guessed, what she was thinking but needed to ask, to clear the air as the sturdy, well-built craft made easy going of the light seas as it left the open English Channel and entered the Solent with the mainland on the right, Isle of Wight on the left. The weather so far being good to them, seas slight and only the lightest of onshore breezes.

"What? Oh, sorry." Gill could not catch his eye, or would not. "Nothing, really, just stuff."

"Out with it, whatever the *stuff* may be."

There was a hint of fear in her tone and the words spilled in a hurried torrent. "What am I doing Lucas, I am on the run with a convicted killer, excuse my description but it's true." Lucas chose not to correct her at that moment, keen to let her get her feelings out into the open. He would remind her later that he had never been tried, just deemed unfit to plead and therefore never convicted. "I was always the sensible one in our family, the only daring thing I have done was to go back to college to learn journalism and now look what I have done to my career!" He reached out with a comforting hand but she moved to avoid it. "I am obviously attracted to you, never slept with anyone on a first date, or second or third come to that, and I certainly always drew the line at psychopathic killers." She breathed.

"Gill…"

"Shut up and let me finish." The anger in her tone directed back at herself and not at Lucas. He did as he was told and turned his eyes back to the seas that were sliding under the boat as they journeyed onward. "I am torn Lucas, one part of me says, even though it may be a bit late given what has happened, to hand you in and get my story written, while the other says I want to stay and help you discover what happened with that girl. My heart says stay while my head says to push you overboard and head for the nearest marina and call the police."

"At least give me chance to put a lifebelt on before you decide."

Even given the confusion and the circumstances that morning Gill could not help but smile; she punched him in the arm, eliciting a yelp of feigned pain. Lucas was charismatic and, she had to admit to herself, made her feel good. Now, neither knowing what to say they continued on their way in silence and each hidden behind their own thoughts.

To the port side the Bonnie Annie powered on past one of Palmerston's follies, a circular fort designed to protect England from French attack during the Napoleonic Wars, a threat that never occurred and two of those forts were now heritage time-capsules, while the other two were luxury hotels where the rich, famous and those with mini-delusions of grandeur retreated to get away from the crowds and enjoy a sojourn with a difference in the opulent rooms that once held mighty cannons, guns that were never fired in anger at a foe.

Looking to speak of anything but their predicament the forts offered the perfect diversion. "They have just what you need right now!" Said Gill as she nodded towards the first, and one of the biggest, of the Solent forts. "That's St Helen's Fort right there off the Isle of Wight, and soon we will be passing No Man's Fort and then Spitbank. Both those have been converted to hotels, I was lucky to be invited out to Spitbank for a press launch, one of the few jollies I got to go on."

"There you were wanting me to feel sorry for you stuck on the obit's desk, and all the time you are living it up in luxury!" He said it, unsmiling, but did not mean to sound harsh.

"That's not what I meant." Both suffered another uncomfortable silence for a full minute, but it seemed like an age, they were still getting used to one another.

He took his hand from the boat's wheel and squeezed hers before she broke the silence. "What I meant was that you need a bolthole, and these forts are where the expression comes from." She noted the inquisitive look and continued. "The brick forts have walls sixteen feet thick and they were reinforced with a belt of steel plates to protect them against the expected French gunfire, which never happened by the way which is why they are referred to as follies, around the wall. Inside the fort behind those plates runs a corridor or passageway where if the plates were damaged they would remove the nuts from the bolts that held them to the wall and just then push the damaged piece into the sea and crane another down to replace it; that narrow passageway was known as the 'bolthole' and it was reckoned to be the safest part of the fort because it was behind those protective plates."

"Ain't you just full of info!"

"Well how about this then, Spitbank Fort, which is now just ahead, the one with the lighthouse on the roof, has an artesian well that goes down over 400 feet and it draws up French water, the hotel bottles it and calls it Spit Water; and, they have proven that the water table is so deep that it actually comes from France. So the Marines who manned the Fort were drinking French water while defending it against a French invasion that never happened."

"So all those well-to-do visitors are actually drinking spit water?"

"Hey, aren't you one of those so-called, well-to-do people." She nudged him, shoulder to shoulder, enjoying the physical contact. That one simple action seemed to break down the barrier that had built between them.

"Seems not so anymore, escaping with some loose change on a borrowed boat, and with a strange woman to boot! But, you called them Palmerston's Follies, why?" Lucas was finding the information and conversation a good distraction away from his problems and the clouds of thoughts that would still not leave his head; for a brief moment he wished to be once again under the mind-numbing drugs that had kept those thoughts hidden away under a thick fog during his incarceration.

"Lord Palmerston was Prime Minister during Victoria's reign and the Royal Commission on the Defence of England in 1860 were concerned about the strength of the French Navy, so Palmerston ordered the building of forts along the English coast, we have these in the Solent and some up on the chalk hills behind Portsmouth. Despite the worries of the time the French never did attack though so the forts were a total folly."

"A bit like this little jaunt, I thought my escape was folly, but you joining in this little adventure and going on the run with me, well that beggars belief really. I don't understand what you are doing here; don't get me wrong I appreciate the fact that you are, but I have no idea why!"

"Me neither, as I said, I never kiss on the first date let alone sleep with someone, and now look what has happened!"

"Always been my cross to bear, this being irresistible." He smiled to show he was kidding.

As the boat beneath them dealt with the repetitive chop of the Solent, taking the bumpy road with little concern, and continued on its way at a steady 17 knots Gill sidled up to Lucas, lifted the raise-able arm of the chair, and shared the pilot's seat with him, leaning into his body and enjoying the feel of his arm around her. They were equally confused by their feelings as less than 24 hours earlier they both saw their lives as being in very different places, neither had spoken of love, it was far too early and seemed crass given their situation, but there was a strength behind their emotions that neither could explain.

All around them yachts, their sails full of wind, leaned into the sea and carved their way through the green waters, while powerboats with their gleaming white hulls charged forward impatient to get nowhere in a hurry, before heading back again with the same urgency. A giant tanker, hull black and threatening, seemed to fill the horizon as it waited its turn to take the one way street into the narrow confines of Southampton Water where it would moor up to a long pontoon and disgorge its load of crude oil into the refinery bowels.

Ahead of them the sun was still high in the sky, having recently begun its post midday dip and beginning its downward journey toward the horizon, the huge golden ball causing them to pinch their eyes and giving them furrowed brows which added even more to the puzzled and thoughtful looks that were already etched on their faces.

Regular waves rolled ceaselessly beneath the hull and the Midas sun drew them ever westward towards perceived freedom as wave after wave disappeared under the bow, the repetitive tump of the sea against the hull a comforting and rhythmic sound. All around gems of silver light reflected and danced on the surface of the water like nature's bling. Leaving the entrance to Portsmouth Harbour behind them and passing Gilkicker Point they both noted the white pylon of Spinnaker Tower that towered over Gunwharf Quay, a fashionable and popular retail and leisure destination built on the waters of the harbour, constructed to celebrate the Millennium but in practice arrived to its completion two years too late. Despite an inauspicious beginning it had become a well-recognised and popular landmark.

Knowing the waters reasonably well Lucas drove the boat away from the 'Cowes Road' channel and across the entrance of Southampton Water with its strange double tides. Conversation had died for the moment but the silence between them was comfortable, but Gill felt the need to warn. "Are you heading into Southampton? That could be a bit risky."

"Thought about it but I think Cowes would be a better place to spend some time, I never used the boat enough to be easy with night sailing and seeing as we have no idea how far we are going or even where we are heading. I thought Cowes would be better but there is a huge sandbank, the Ryde Middle, just here and we have to manoeuvre around it before we can head in towards the island. I have seen too many a yacht get stuck here because they cut it too close."

"I have a thought about where we can head, but I need to make a phone call first." Gill realised that the trust between them was not yet complete and so she quickly quantified her statement. "Don't worry Lucas, it's not the paper or the police." He smiled his support for her to continue. "I have friends who may help us, I have known the couple most of my life, they were friends of my parents, and I am sure they will say yes." She continued on with a brief smile to belay any concerns he may have. "I have to tell them the story, and the whole story though, it would be unfair to invite them to help without honesty." He was a little reluctant but nodded ascent. "If they say yes, then I have a plan for us to lose anyone following."

"If nothing else it will give us time to assess the situation and make some sort of plan, if your friends are willing to help." Lucas looked at her to make sure she got his message. "And, yes, tell them everything, I have put you in danger, poor Annie has been killed for helping me, of that I am sure, Charles died so I could get away. Enough people have been hurt because of me, they need to know." She smiled at him, he continued. "And, you need to have time to decide what you need to do. Maybe you should tell my story in your paper, at least that will give you a reason for being with me and may avoid you having to go to prison for helping me."

Nothing more was said, until the Bonnie Annie turned her nose in toward Cowes and its marinas.

Lucas explained that once in harbour she should go and settle the mooring fee, and that their biggest danger came from customs officers who would, as a matter of course, ask where they were from and where they were heading, but they would have to overcome that barrier when they came to it.

Turning back onto the well-known Cowes Roads, a body of water that every keen sailor in the world dreamed of sailing into at some time or another, Lucas pulled the throttles on the twin engines back and slowed to the speed limit of a sedate five knots as he radioed the harbour master for permission to dock and stay overnight, the reply gave him a mooring for the Bonnie Annie and a few minutes later, using the gear levers in varying gentle degrees of forward and reverse, again ignoring the wheel totally, which impressed Gill, he manoeuvred the long craft and gently nudged, or rather kissed, the allotted pontoon and brought the engines to an idle. An assistant harbour master was there to take the forward lines and help secure the craft while Gill just stepped down onto the pontoon and made secure the aft lines. The sun by now had begun to disappear behind the popular town, stuck between hillside and waterfront, leaving the marina in light shade and so Lucas was unconcerned about being noticed and recognised in the late afternoon, he donned his battered blue baseball cap, faded and mottled with white from too much sun and salt spray, and pulled the peak down over his eyes, the minimal disguise and then the late afternoon dullness meant he was hiding in plain sight.

They had already decided it would be no problem to stroll into bustling town centre to find a pub or restaurant to eat at; and the quaint Union Arms fitted the bill, a small and traditional pub sat at the top of a sloping alleyway that lead down to the sea, a TV, hung high in one corner of the bar flickered silently but with foreboding as it relayed the news by mute newsreader who had an ever scrolling headline banner beneath his serious face. A sigh of relief crossed their faces, followed by guilt, that was unspoken, as they both read the urgent alert which reported that a small girl had gone missing from a caravan park near Christchurch and police were very concerned for her safety, apparently, according to the scrolling banner, her mother had only been gone for a few minutes to the shop on the caravan park for some cigarettes, when she returned the caravan door was open and the small girl, Natalie Thompson, had disappeared. Police were appealing for information. A picture of a cute, but thin, girl with dirty blonde pigtails, filled the screen, her eyes, shining from a grubby playtime face, carrying sadness as if she had already known she was going to be the subject of something traumatic, either that or she hated having her picture taken. She carried a toothy grin and her fair hair hung limply in a scruffy fringe around her face, framing her cheeks which were puffed like a well fed hamsters.

"I know this is callous but at least that has gotten you out of the news headlines." She leant across and whispered in his ear, giving the soft lobe a gentle kiss before returning to her cod, with a crispy beer batter, and thick delicious chips that filled her oval plate. Illicit foods always tasted so much better! She paused, with chip laden fork midway between plate and mouth, as she realised how cold she must have sounded, putting a missing child beyond their own troubles. Lucas, realising where her thoughts had gone, squeezed her thigh and just said, "Eat. I know what you meant." The fork completed its journey and delivered its load.

The relief of someone else being headline news was short lived; as a photo of a handsome and thinner Lucas filled the screen, followed by a film of his cottage as a stretcher topped by a body in black bag was wheeled to a small black Volkswagen ambulance which was parked by the very recognisable white picket fence. Jacob, his face etched with concern stood at the gate flanked by a diminutive and dark-haired female police constable who stood erect in a crisp, white, crease-free shirt. His words, mouthed but silent on the pub's TV screen, from a pre-prepared statement scrolled across the bottom of the screen.

The newsreader's words were in white, 'Jacob Tubb, the owner of the waterside cottage spoke to Sky News following the discovery of his housekeeper who it has been reported was bludgeoned to death.' Jacobs words were in red, 'It is believed that my brother, Lucas Tubb, who escaped recently from a, so-called, secure mental unit, may have had something to do with my beloved housekeeper, Annie's death…' on the screen he choked back a tear or two, 'Lucas has killed before and police think Annie, who was a huge part of our family, may have disturbed him as he returned to the house to get some cash and some of his belongings while on the run from the authorities, an amount of Annie's jewellery has also gone missing as has some money from the house. I am appealing for my brother to give himself up to the police; he is ill and needs help urgently.' He mouthed a 'thank you', but the rolling script ignored that part of his media statement.

As the image on screen returned to that of a slimmer Lucas posing for the police camera, grim faced and gaunt, clean shaven, thinner and with eyes in the image seemingly dead; the banner headline advised people not to approach the dangerous young man and that anyone spotting him should immediately call the police, a number was advertised on the rolling banner which paused for the message to hit home. As the banner finished scrolling news and changed to the lighter mode of sport the bartender noticed, without concern or comment, that two servings of cod and chips had only been half consumed by the young couple who had ordered them and now departed, two pints of Guinness similarly remained only half consumed. The world of the pub landlord was full of strange characters, and he shook his head in wonderment of it all.

Chapter 21

The last of the police had left the charming cottage that held so many secrets, and tragedies, just one uniformed officer remained standing sentinel at the beginning of the communal driveway, a boring task for the officer but a necessary one, keeping the press and curious onlookers at bay. The final officer to actually leave the house was Jem, secretly glad to be on her way, exhausted due to long hours and also tired of being around Jacob, he had been hard work with his flirting and openly suggestive comments. In turn Jacob had felt a sweet pang of discontent as she informed him it was time to leave, her job done. He was annoyed at her senior officers ordering her away, in his mind he was guessing it would have only been a matter of time; oh, how Jacob would love to have got her naked, knowing that under that crisp white shirt and those black trousers there was an amazing body just aching to be abused! He would have found a good use for her handcuffs; and he watched with lascivious intent as her pert little bottom, the last and lasting image he had of her as she had climbed into the passenger seat of the police car. She never looked back as the car swept away from the house its swirling lights extinguished with a lack of further urgency.

Jacob had closed the door on them all some ten minutes earlier, he kept up the pretence of grieving a little longer, in case, just like in Colombo on the TV they would return to ask, 'Just one more thing?', but no one came. It was safe to drop the anguished look and open a bottle of fine red, a St Emilion Premiere Cru, something earthy and robust, something that reflected his mood, something rich, a palatable celebration. He took some stilton from the fridge and cut a wedge of red apple to go with it, a feast to go with wine.

His brother could run as far and as wide as he wanted, one day they would find him, he would be caught to face another case of justice or, even if he wasn't caught, his running would only strengthen the story of how he had caused Annie's death. Jacob now had the house to himself, the family fortune and best of all, the freedom to do as he pleased to whomever he pleased. It was wonderful feeling of power, of being untouchable! He sat in the leather, wing armchair in the library, glugging on the St Emilion while listening to a heavy rock CD from some indistinguishable American rock band. A broad smile on his face that said nobody will catch me, free and easy from here on in!

Back on board the Bonnie Annie there was confusion to say the least. The couple had left the Union Inn as soon as the photo of Lucas was seen shining out from the 50 inch flat screen TV that hung on the bar wall., Although he looked different now with his extra weight and the new and darkening daily facial growth, the result of just a few days of not shaving, or as Gill called it his 'chin-fungus'. Now they sat opposite sides of the galley table, hands holding hands in the middle, his left thumb caressing the back of her right hand as she looked at his worried face.

"You look so different these days, your face is cutely podgy and that fur you have on your chin, well you just look different. You were so thin in that photo in the news."

"I am not worried about me; it's poor Annie, I still wonder who could do that to her. We both know it was not me this time... But seeing Jacob on TV I cannot believe it was him; he is my brother. She raised him as well, in fact I always thought he was her favourite, she always seemed to dote on him so much more."

Gill was quick to keep her support of him to the fore. "As I said when we heard the news from the radio, I know it could not have been you, as the time they say it happened you were on the boat, so for sure, and I think it proves the questionable trust I have put in you."

"Questionable?" There was hurt in his eyes.

"Of course questionable, you are a convicted murderer..." Gill's voice had raised an octave or two, Lucas interrupted.

"You keep saying that but I have not been convicted! I was never convicted, I was too crazy to plead and so they just threw the key away." He was a little peeved, to say the least. "They assumed guilt because I had no answer to their questions, no excuses for the evidence and with all the attention my brain just shut down. I was assumed guilty." Realising he had probably overstepped the mark with Gill, who was still coming to terms with her own part in his story, he softened a bit. "I had gone a little mental after being with the girl in park, so maybe I did deserve to be in the nuthouse." He gave a mischievous grin at the description of Broadmoor and saw Gill visibly relax.

"Okay, I will give you that." The smile returned to her face. "Escaped Psychopath, if you prefer, and these last few hours, well since I followed you to The Boat House yesterday, it must bring my own sanity into question." He nodded affirming the question of her sanity. "What have I been doing with you? This has gone way past following a story as an intrepid and tenacious journalist. This is way beyond the call of duty; you were the story I always wanted; no, dreamed, I would discover, uncovering the truth that no one else could see, my big scoop, my name under the headline; but here I am suddenly a big part of the story I thought I was investigating. And now, suddenly I am on the run with a confirmed nutter. I must be the one who needs their head examined." She blew out a long breath of relief, she had gotten her misgivings and fear out in the open. "And to top it all, I went and slept with you!"

"Yes, that was a fun part! Wasn't it?" His smile filled with lust, eyes sparkling. She offered him a clenched fist as if to throw a playful punch, stopped as his tone turned serious. "Thank goodness you were a nosy journalist though, if you had not been keeping an eye on me I may well have believed that I had killed poor Annie, and forgotten it again, like with the girl. To tell the truth though, if I had any sense I would leave you here in Cowes, sensible for both of us; we know so little about each other and yet, we…" Careful thought was needed before speech. "We seem to have a connection, strange as it sounds when I say it out loud. There is a link between us that I have never felt with anyone before. Because of my recent pass and all the events that have led me, *us*, here, I don't even trust my own thoughts half the time, but for some reason I trust you; so much so that I have put my freedom in your hands; you could turn me in at any time and have the story you have always dreamed of." As he spoke the last few words his voice softened almost to a whisper and both deeply felt the emotion of the moment.

"I can see your headline now;" he added, voice returning to normal. "'I was Love Slave of the Broadmoor Murderer'!"

"Actually, that's quite good. Don't forget my by-line underneath it. 'News reporter tells how she was held hostage and taken on a hijacked boat as he made his escape, I feared my life could have ended at any time', Ace News reporter Gill Harmon writes! Ooh, I like that, it has a ring to it don't you think?"

For a brief second fear clutched a hard hand around his heart, blood draining from his face, but one look up at the impish eyes and the grin that broadened with every moment, which he was already becoming accustomed to, brought him back to being at ease with the girl in front of him. "You're a tease aren't you?" Lucas said and she nodded. "I am going to have to get used to that. Or start teasing back."

"I know I shouldn't tease you at a time like this, but you are so easy." The grin had broadened even further into a huge and carefree smile. "We both know that it could not have been you that killed poor Annie. I am sorry for your loss by the way, I know she meant a lot to you by the way you speak of her."

Lucas interrupted. "She was such a gentle soul, she did not deserve an end like that; Annie should have been able to die in her sleep; peacefully." The light that she noticed in his eyes a few seconds before was extinguished. "But, does it mean that the girl in the park was not me either? Could it be that I cannot recall killing her because, I didn't" Pleading eyes, wet with emotion and a tear for Annie.

"How old was she? Annie I mean not the girl." Gill did not want to bring that evening up just yet, partly in case she did not like what she would hear, but also partly to find out more about this enigmatic man's life, this man who had, without trying had involved himself so deeply into her own life, and in doing so changed her future irrevocably. She Found herself, strangely, falling in love with him, with his handsome face and his easy charm, a few hours in a restaurant and on this boat and to her great surprise that was what she felt, love, she had never been so smitten with someone before! She also felt turmoil, confusion, even a little panic, and yet, yet, she felt happiness welling up within her. She did not know it of course but Lucas was feeling exactly the same emotions and confusion. He had the additional feeling however, that his saving angel was sat opposite him.

In the back of her mind she knew who, and, more importantly, what he was and yet, she had fallen for him and his gentle eyes; likewise Lucas was on the run with a journalist who could easily have him back in his ten by ten cell before the day's end.

"Still young really," Lucas related in answer to age, and Annie's story was bringing them both back to the real world. "She was somewhere in her early sixties, I think, she had always seemed the same age to me, as a young boy she was really old when she was in her late twenties, but as I grew older she just aged along with me; it is as if she was a sweet, grey haired old lady all along. Sometimes she would not be quite so sweet, especially if Jacob or I were in trouble, she was scarier than the Old Man, my father, when we stepped out of line. But, like him, she had always been there, first as our nanny and then the housekeeper, the good old family retainer I suppose."

"I never knew my mother but Annie was a bloody good substitute, even with a ready hug of comfort should it be needed, always thought our father had a soft spot for her as well, but he never did anything about it; at least as far as I know, Dad said that after my mother another woman would never come up to scratch, she was irreplaceable as far as he was concerned, he loved her totally." With each word Lucas' voice softened with the memory. Shaking his head the thoughts of the past were taken away, the current situation needed to be clarified.

"But you said Jacob was your younger, but half-brother."

"That was always a strange one, Dad, when I had asked him much later, just said that he had a brief affair with a friend of the family and that the mother did not want the baby so he adopted Jacob, I never questioned it because I thought it was cool to suddenly have a kid brother and as far as I know Annie never questioned it either. I don't even recall hearing Jacob ever asking about his birth mother, he was always the selfish one and only ever thought of himself; he never really fitted in with the family unit, but we all loved him anyway, despite his shortcomings; he was my kid brother; and,

I often thought, Dad's favourite because of his hard start in life." There was a moment's silence where both were suddenly stuck for words.

It was Gill that broke that quietness and was the first to say what both had begun to think, "Should we get the hell out of here. You know, like now! We, and yes I meant we, are both on the run you know; and your face has been all over the tele. Won't be long before they realise there is a boat involved and then they will talk to the staff in the restaurant and discover you are not alone."

"You could always say I kidnapped you."

"Oh, yes, I can hear my story now. I was held hostage over Haddock and Chips in an Island pub and he was holding my hand so I could not run away."

"It was Cod and chips and we were not holding hands until we left the restaurant!" It was said in jest but both Gill and Lucas held their serious looks. "If they are coming for me they are coming for me, we would not be able to get out of Cowes and off the island if I was recognised so we may as well wait for dawn and the tide and then just slide out of here with everyone else heading out for a day's sailing. We have enough food for breakfast, so there is no need to go ashore again and we best get some sleep if we are going to figure this out; besides, you have a phone call to make…"

"So I do." Gill stepped out on the deck with her mobile phone in her hand, scrolling the contact's list as she did. Lucas could hear her voice drifting through the window, but he could not hear the actual words, it was a long call. He imagined her retelling his story.

As she ducked back into the cabin under the low door lintel, a nod of her head and a smile were all that was needed, her friends had agreed to help. Lucas felt things were starting to go his way. "We head for Studland Bay tomorrow, my friends will be there in the afternoon, ready for us." Gill could not help herself and moved in for a tight hug with her escaped lunatic! It felt good.

Chapter 22

The rocking motion and sound of footsteps on the wooden walkway woke them both at the same time, and both held their breath waiting, hearts pounding with synchronicity in their chests. They lay under the quilt, a protective barrier against the world, her head resting in the fold between his neck and arm, her arm that was wrapped over his chest pulled him closer, fear of discovery tightening its hold on them like a python crushing life from its next meal. They waited, breath held, for the boat to list with the weight of a fully armed and ready for action boarding party. The sudden movement of the boat never happened, a pair of footsteps on the pontoon walking further down the row of boats and as the Bonnie Annie levelled herself and settled back down slowly, the gentle rocking ceasing, they both exhaled; letting out breath and tension. Lucas kissed Gill's forehead, wrapped her in his arm a little closer, words not needed.

"You cook breakfast and I will get the boat ready for leaving." It was meant as a statement but came out as an order. Gill smiled.

"How about you do the breakfast and I ready the boat, Captain!"

"Well my cooking is awful and if your boat readying skills are on a par with my cooking then we are likely to be in deep trouble!"

"Like your eggs scrambled?" She turned toward the galley.

"Please." He patted her affectionately on her naked buttock as she bent to slide a pair of colourful Wonder Woman knickers up her legs, they were the shape and style he had worn as a small boy but he found he liked that style on her apple shaped bottom. "Nice pants. Sexy!"

"One, I didn't have time to pack much and two, I didn't realise that some strange man would be watching me dress this morning. And; C, if I don't find a shop soon to buy some clothes the only undies I will be wearing are your spare boxers."

"If we have to make Studland sometime this afternoon then there is no rush to leave the marina, and, let's face it, at the moment no one is looking for you so why not go ashore and get some bits and pieces." It was agreed, the beauty, or one of the beauties, of Cowes as a venue for the yachtie was the closeness of the High Street, with its close knit rows of shops just a few paces from the marina.

The new partnership divided their duties without further chatter, and food was prepared in the same length of time the boat took for readiness, then with just the fore and aft lines to release they would be heading out of the marina, heading west to uncertainty and a new chapter in their enforced adventure. There was a tacit agreement that they would not discuss the implications of Annie's death until they were under way and out of the Solent, passing through the Hurst Narrows, the weather that summer morning was reflecting their mood, dark and sombre; something, in the air and in their future, was brewing and broiling, dark clouds rolled overhead. The private thoughts of both, for differing reasons, were rolling toward darkness they knew a storm was heading their way but had no idea when and where it would hit them and those thoughts had nothing to do with the weather. Everything was going a little too smoothly, a little too well, somewhere along the line luck would turn against them, that storm would hit, it was just a matter of time.

Gill left him to clear away the breakfast things as she stepped ashore to shop, they shared a peck on the lips and she was gone as if heading off as if to the office for the day, casual, normal. As Lucas stood at the galley sink watching her rear end drift along the quay wall he could not help but wonder if she would return, not only that would she send reinforcements to arrest him. He put the last of the plates in the drying rack, poured the soapy water away and sat waiting for her return. Or the arrival of his re-captors!

As the couple had lain under the protection of the quilt in a Cowes marina over to the east in West Sussex it took Jacob a moment or two, as he woke from yet another drunken stupor, to realise that his morning coffee was not going to appear on his bedside table as normal, he lived alone now and had to fend for himself. Annie, of course, took the blame for that realization in his warped and angry mind! It was her own fault, she should have remained loyal to him and not his murdering brother. The police had let him return and live once again in the house but there were parts that still showed signs that it was a crime scene; there had been no Annie to clear that up either and apparently the police did not clear up behind them. Walking down the stairs he took a brief look at where Annie had bled out, a dark stain left on the polished floor; the spot where he told police he had 'found' her; a satisfied smile cracking his anger filled face, the sombre mood that had been showing disappeared. He needed coffee.

Jacob thought he would feel a little more elation, of having rid himself of that interfering housekeeper who had always shown favour to Lucas, admittedly he now had to fend for himself until he could find someone to take over Annie's duties, maybe one of those pretty little Polacks, or Romanians, wherever it was they came from, that he had seen in the town centre. They could do more than housework, the wicked smile and glint of eye returned. But, the more immediate call was for breakfast, he didn't even know if there were eggs in the fridge, and he had no intention of checking to see if there were.

Quickly dressed he grabbed a coat from the hall closet and slinging it over his shoulder in a nonchalant manner, he ran the fingers of his spare hand through his tousled hair, and swaggered out of the house and through the tree lined cut-way toward the marina. The footpath was still puddled in places from earlier rains, it never quite dried out in parts under the overhanging trees, and he cursed as his heavy, and expensive, deck shoes, that would never see a deck, picked up some clinging mud.

The narrow footbridge crossed the spot where canal met disused lockgate, he had no idea that his brother had recently crossed the self-same bridge. A solitary swan swam into the lock, realised there was nowhere to go and gently turned and drifted out again. Jacob looked up the canal toward Chichester, ducks, moorhens and coots mingled on the calm surface and swam in and out of the reedy banks, houseboats sat either side of the straight ribbon of water, all looked quiet and abandoned, there were residents but he always thought it strange he never saw or met anyone who lived in them. Through the car park he crossed the gravel toward The Boat House Café where, he had earlier decided, they would cook a far better breakfast than he could, he stepped through the door ignoring the outside tables and chairs, the grey skies negating the original desire to eat his morning meal al fresco.

The staff in the waterside bar and eatery were polite to all their customers, they were well trained and friendly, but it was hard work with customers such as Jacob, the rude and surly man just assumed they were at his beck and call, and he treated them as subservient to him. The regular staff who knew him always tried to avoid serving him, but when they did, they knew enough to keep up a charade of being polite and that meant trying, often failing, to engage him in simple conversation.

Standing at the chest-high counter, "Black coffee and an English breakfast." Manners were neither expected nor received as he delved into his wallet for banknotes and loyalty card.

"Is that a large coffee and would you like brown or white toast?" The smile on the young server was as false as her eyelashes and her enhanced breasts.

He handed over a twenty pound note. "Large and brown, and make the coffee strong, I don't want dishwater like you usually serve."

The server was petite in height and had to reach to place the coffee on the counter, her pretty little face continued to smile politely although the thought had crossed her mind to let the saucer catch on the counter edge and splash over this customer; but common sense said he was not worth the effort, instead she kept up the pleasant front, smiling politely but it was a smile that held sarcasm in its broadness. She flicked her blonde ponytail as she turned, in much the same way as a pony would flick its tail in a moment of disdain. Her face and tone hid her dislike.

"It was nice to see your brother in here yesterday, he has not been in for a while, has he been working away?" She inquired in all innocence and just for the sake of saying something.

The hand with the banknote in it froze just short of handing it over and his face darkened with a bigger threat of thunder than the skies outside.

"Excuse me!" He barked the question, startling both his server and the elderly couple stood just behind him in the queue, they took half a step backwards.

The thin face with its deep, blue eyeliner took on a worried expression causing the eye make up to resemble bruised and blackened eyes. "Your brother, he was in last night for dinner, with a lovely young lady. I was surprised because I had not seen him for some time. But I may have been mistaken, he was little more..." a pause to ensure she was not being rude about a customer. "...round faced than I remembered. So I might have been mistaken!" The look of sheer venom and hate on Jacob's face frightened her.

"But you are sure it was him? It was Lucas?" His aggressive tone was beginning to really scare her and she looked around for her manager in the hope of protection.

She explained that she had not spoken to him as he was not on one of her tables and he seemed too engrossed in the woman he was with to notice her when she smiled at him..." The server was talking to thin air; Jacob had gone, almost in the blink of her heavily made-up eyes.

Twenty pound note still in his hand and black coffee left behind on the counter Jacob rushed from the Boat House Café and headed down toward the pontoons, trying to recall which mooring belonged to the Bonnie Annie. In his hurry he almost toppled a line of family cyclists from their leisurely rides along a path that ran parallel to the canal.

All four wobbled and swerved to avoid the crazed and angry man who shouted at them to, "Get out of my way, fucking cyclists!" He was out of earshot before the father had the presence of mind to react and complain about the stranger's language in front of his wife and children.

Jacob stopped running, he grasped at the railing with sweaty palms, the knuckles on both hands white with the fierceness of his grip. He had no idea that he was stood where Gill Harmon had stood and watched Lucas when he had boarded the Bonnie Annie.

Jacob looked on, astounded and annoyed with himself, he had not considered it before, he assumed the cruiser sized gap between a classic wooden hulled yacht, its masts bereft of its canvas sails, and a tatty motorboat on the pontoon was where the Bonnie Annie had been, virtually ignored and unmoving for the last couple of years, the space it had inhabited was now empty. The Bonnie Annie was gone, and Jacob may not have known where, but he sure as hell knew whom! He crashed his clenched fist down onto the barrier, then cursed loudly as his fingers took the bruising pain of his anger. He cursed himself for forgetting about the boat, realising he could have sold it and made some serious money, now it appeared to have helped his maniac brother to get away...

Shaking the hand and fingers to get the feeling back into them with his good hand he reached into his pocket and drew out his mobile phone, like a gunslinger with a fast draw in a shoot-out, not noticing or not caring that somewhere between café and gripping the railings he had dropped a twenty pound note. Fury again erupted as he realized how poor the mobile reception was in the Marina; "Fucking phones!" He yelled at the sky. He held the phone high, danced a circular jig in an attempt at getting the signal bars to fill.

Gem, the liaison officer, had put her official number into his phone before she had left the night before, telling him if he needed anything to call at any time; and he pressed the call portion on the phone screen repeatedly, waving it around his head to get a signal, he danced like a native American trying for rain in the hope of gaining a signal, eventually the bars showed recognition of communications tower and connected to the number. The WPC, her voice tinny and weak, responded after only a couple of rings, Jacob wasted no time with niceties.

"He's on her fucking boat!" He was not to be interrupted. "You imbeciles have let him get away, he is probably in France by now and you idiots did not think to check on the boat!" He stopped briefly for breath.

Now she could speak, "But, we never knew there was a boat, what boat? You never said there was a boat." The reception was bad and the line crackling....

As the tirade continued from Jacob the WPC still managed to get the disjointed information from him and what the boat was like, etc. The marina would soon be flooded with police officers checking stories, asking questions and checking CCTV monitors. The chase was on again on for the double killer and whoever his new accomplice, or, unlikely as it seemed, a possible hostage, was.

Chapter 22

Shopping done, and new knickers stowed away in a drawer on board, Gill was beginning to feel as if this was a home away from home, but also felt disquiet at how quickly things were moving in this adventure as the Bonnie Annie made her way through the comparative calm waters of the Solent, a passage of water navigated by thousands of keen sailors, and ferry passengers, before them, back to the anonymity of open water to be lost among the summer's day flotilla of a thousand or more leisure craft. This story was unfolding without any conscious input from her, as with the boat it was beginning to seem as if she were just along for the ride.

Once free of the haven's protection the agitated surface of the busy channel had raised to an uncomfortable chop in a strengthening wind, it felt as if Mother Nature herself had woken in a bad mood. Gill thought it felt like driving along a rough road in an old car with flat tyres. Lucas, and the sturdy boat itself, felt the going easy and he handled the 45 foot craft with expertise while the sharp bow cut through the chop and handled the conditions with the trouble free air of a solid workhorse.

Along with the imposing and darkening clouds of an approaching summer storm came the heavier swells that can build quickly in the Solent, out past the Isle of Wight's lee side and into the English Channel it was blowing an easy force 4, but with the predominant south westerly wind blowing in through the slim entrance at the Hurst Narrows, it was hitting Force 5 or 6 in the Solent, a big selling point for those who preferred the thrill and skill of stick and rag to the engines of powered craft, the increased wind making for great sailing; a reason the Solent was such a popular sailing venue. Lucas knew that once through the narrow gap, which seemed like just a strong stone's throw from mainland to island, the going would be much easier, although the choppy surface would change to one of larger rolling waves that would make their way forward easier on both boat and crew. As they battled against the racing water, a swift tidal flow with the Venturi effect of the Narrows.

Gill gripped the chair with knuckles whitening. "I love the sea but is this going to get rough?" She asked.

Lucas could see the clouds breaking up ahead of them, a bluer sky in the distant west while the clouds that currently chilled the summer air were busy scudding eastward. "Blue skies up ahead, the storm, if it happens, is behind us now." He looked at her. "Should be easy sailing from here on in."

The look they gave each other said that life may not offer such a storm free future; but nothing was said.

As the boat, with Lucas at the helm and Gill behind him in the galley making more coffee, headed through the Narrows with its fortress on the mainland side the marine radio squawked out a message to all craft. Lucas had failed to heed the message on low volume as he concentrated on the tidal race that made this narrow channel so tricky to manoeuvre. It was barely half a league from mainland to Island at its narrowest point and the wind was not the only thing that increased its speed through the gap, the tide now raced and boiled and the Bonnie Annie's engines strained against the power of the tide. A week later and this stretch of famous water would be frighteningly full of sailing craft as the famous Round the Island Race took place, two thousand yachts would be fighting for position through this narrow channel and there would have been no room for an escaping motor launch.

Gill had heard the broadcast plea from where she was in the galley, stood with feet shoulder width apart and braced against the galley units, she was now becoming attuned to the thumps of the water against hull, the creaking and complaining of boat against conditions and the feel of its sways, its rocking and its movement in general, feet still slightly apart she staggered toward the wheel position where Lucas controlled the helm with deep concentration, she moved like a Saturday night drunk on his way home.

"Did you hear that Lucas?"

"What?" The spell of concentration was broken, they were almost through the gap and out into the freedom of the English Channel. Then he heard it repeated, Gill didn't have to explain. A general call put out on the radio for all craft to look out for the Bonnie Annie, a forty five foot Nelson built cruiser with two occupants, a man and a women. The leisurely escape that they had planned had now become an urgent flee from the authorities. They looked at each other, hoping for mutual support, but both sets of eyes held fear and trepidation in their gaze.

As they cleared the bumpy ride that was the Narrows, Lucas pushed both throttles as far forward as they would go, he even pushed the chrome levers against their stopping point in an attempt to take them beyond their designed limits, and the Bonnie Annie stretched herself with the force of fast throbbing, twin diesel engines to her 23 to 25 knot limit. Lucas felt it would not be enough, their luck seemed as if it were finally running out; but he was not yet ready to give up, they would have to catch him.

Gill wanted to ask about their chances, and would the boat be able to carry them to safety, but chose not to, keeping her own council just as

Lucas had retreated into his own thoughts. She already knew there was no point in breaking into whatever spell he was under at that moment. She just looked forward, out toward open water as the Bonnie Annie threw herself through rolling waves as the Island slowly unwound its craggy shoreline toward the lighthouse at the end of the string of rocks called The Needles.

"We may as well enjoy the freedom while we can." Lucas smiled at Gill as he swivelled from the pilot's chair and made his way out on deck to the fly-bridge steering position, she followed with two steaming mugs of coffee, both black, both sugar free, something else they agreed on. The storm clouds had cleared, the sea had levelled out and the sun shone down on them, warming, pleasing and tasting of freedom.

Distraction comes in many forms, but this was one image she had not expected as she looked toward the island, wondering why, it appeared, there were a crowd of people playing cricket in the middle of the channel. She so wanted to ask! Full grown men in cricket whites, some in lifejackets, seemed totally incongruous considering where they were, on a shingle and sand island, which stood a fair distance off shore.

"It's the Bramble Bank cricket match."

"Sorry!" She was so intent on taking in the strange, so typically eccentric English, scene before her that she did not realise that Lucas had been watching her watching the annual sporting anomaly "This weekend is becoming more and more surreal," Gill ruffled her fingers through her hair, just for the sensation. "I watch you sneak onto a boat dressed as a surgeon and looking as if you had just stepped from an operating theatre, and before I know it we are having dinner together, I let you seduce me." Lucas looked at her with a certain amount of disbelief, his meaning well noted without the use of words; Gill shrugged. "Okay, we seduced each other; then we sleep together before I end up going on the run with a person everyone thinks, except me that is, is a serial killer…"

"That takes three!"

"What does?"

"Three kills before you are a serial killer, I need one more."

"Oh, now you can joke about it." Shrugged shoulders again and this time a mischievous grin and twinkling eyes were aimed toward her from the driving seat, and she realised that was what had captured her heart the day before. "And as if things were not weird enough I am now watching a bunch of grown men playing cricket in the middle of the sea!"

"There are girls out there as well, and, if you look, they even have a clubhouse."

"Please don't tell me that."

As if on cue the skipping clouds parted a little more and took the cricket field from shadow, and the sun shone down on the cricketers and their small shed of a clubhouse. All across the coastline the clouds were now beginning to part showing first a blue and grey patchwork of sky and then more blue as patchy clouds moved away, the wind blowing them asunder and letting the sun through. It was a glorious day as the wind dropped and the sea around them began to sparkle with summer light, just as on the Bramble Bank one of the fielders dropped an easy catch and ended laying spread-eagled and face down in a sandy puddle of seawater, much to the friendly annoyance of his team mates, on board the Bonnie Annie they could hear the banter, and the groans of agony over the fumbled chance, and cries of 'Catch-It', drift across the sea toward them.

"Are they actually playing a match?" She asked, realising that other boat's owners and crews were so intent on the 'game' that they were ignoring the fleeing vessel that was among them.

"Sort of, they play for honour and the match lasts for a little more than an hour or two, one week each year and dependent on the state of the tide. Sometimes they have a huge playing field of sand and shingle and other years they just play in shallow water. It doesn't matter how many wickets each team takes or how many runs they get, it's always between the Royal Southern Yacht Club and the Island Sailing Club in, what they call, The Bramble Clash and the winners are pre-determined each year, they take turns, as the 'losing' team has to supply a slap up feast for the winners and that takes some organising."

"The good thing for us is that the eccentric English and their strange games is keeping everyone's eyes away from us." She squeezed his hand that held the wheel showing support and encouragement; his smile was enough to show appreciation. And the Bonnie Annie thundered on through the crowded waterway following the pattern of the mainland's shore toward the west.

While the new couple, their situation drawing them ever closer to each other with each nautical mile travelled, enjoyed the less than leisurely motor down toward the Jurassic coastline of Dorset, maybe enjoyment was the wrong term as both, with conversation now at a minimum, it gave time for the heavy thoughts on their minds, and worried looks on their faces to take centre stage. Until the facts could be proven one way or the other these obstacles would remain a wall of sorts between them, a seemingly insurmountable obstacle despite their, so far, short term closeness. Gill was troubled, career on hold, on the run, about to involve close friends, friends she considered family, and this man! This handsome, young-faced, charming man, who, despite his situation, exuded fun and confidence, showed just the right amount of affection and, deep within his eyes somehow showed a need to be trusted. He was a confusing enigma, deemed unfit to stand trial for the vicious murder of a girl who had never been traced or named, left under a bench like a piece of discarded rubbish, which Lucas had admitted to, but then there was the second killing, and he could not have done that... Her mind raced back and forth and yet she could not leave his side.

"You okay Gill?" Lucas rubbed the back of her hand as it rested on the arm of the pilot's seat.

She nodded. "Just deep in thought Lucas, just trying to figure out what I am doing here with you."

Lucas understood her dilemma. "I am just glad you are here." He squeezed her hand and she responded in kind.

Behind them back in the Chichester Marina the normal quiet and lazy lifestyle of the yachting and tourism communities were definitely on hold. Police cars filled the marina side, while other cars blocked the broad entrance to the marina, even the police launch was in attendance having made its way from Littlehampton. The local branch of the constabulary continually checked cars and their passengers as they passed in and out of the marina; none of them knowing quite why. As is usual at a busy crime scene an indeterminate number of uniformed officers wandered almost aimlessly in an attempt to at least appear to be involved in the hunt for the fugitive and his companion, while ostensibly solving the current murder case by stopping and chatting to every passer-by and walker; even the least experienced of the officers in the marina that morning knew that this was the perfect case of locking stable doors after bolting horses; several of them wondering why they were searching cars leaving the marina, when the man they were seeking was well away from the area and by boat. Such is the way of life that it was senior officers, university educated and not street wise, determined the orders of the day

Liaison officer, WPC Jemma Costello, although she wanted to be anywhere but there, stood at the marina edge alongside Jacob, she was dressed in plain clothes as she had been off duty when the call came on her personal mobile, trainers, leggings which hugged her legs and lower body and a sweatshirt with the West Sussex Police logo at the breast. She did not enjoy the fact that she had been brought back in so soon after thinking she had escaped the lecherous gazes of Jacob, but it was her job and now here she was at his side again trying to avoid his disconcerting gaze drifting like the fluttering burgees on the mast heads, from marina to her backside. Without thought she tugged downward on the hem of the sweatshirt in an attempt to keep her dignity. Both she and Jacob standing just a few inches apart were keeping their attention toward the empty pontoon space, when he could draw his gaze away from her arse!

"How did your marvellous boys in blue miss this?" Jacob asked with the anger in his voice barely disguised, although he was trying hard not to include Jem, in that list of incompetent officers as it could seriously damage his, deluded, chances of bedding her; he cared little that, in his imagination, it may just be, what he would call, a sympathy shag because of his predicament.

"It's down to manpower Jacob," she said in defensive response, he liked the easy tone of her voice, the well-practiced one she had learned to mollify agitated family members who were her charges. "It's not like on the TV in those crime dramas, there is no huge reaction force to flood the streets, create roadblocks and, well all hands to the pumps, kind of scenario. There just simply is not enough of us to go round."

"So, nothing was done?" It was a cross between statement and question. "A murderer escapes from what is supposed to be a secure unit for the criminally insane and nothing is done, he kills again and still nothing is done! And, then he escapes on the family boat that your lot never even knew existed."

Jem felt anger rising, but kept her own council, and decided not to state the obvious that even Jacob, a family member, had failed to mention the boat. Biting of tongues can only last for so long, Gem's patience was thin now.

"The local force at Broadmoor would have been out on a search, helicopters and all that and the home force, us, would have been contacted and a squad put together to investigate all his old haunts and his home and friends. We never knew that he, or indeed your family, had a boat; did you?" The question was accusatory. Jacob explained, for what he felt was the fortieth time that morning; that the boat, which had been his father's, had been forgotten because it was Annie's. He added this time, in the fabrication that continued to grow, that he thought Lucas must have visited the house to steal what money he could, pick up some clothes and find the key to the boat and that is when Annie, "poor Annie", he added for effect, discovered him, confronted him and been killed for just being at the house at the wrong time. "If only I had been there, I could have saved her; I blame myself."

He didn't have to look to discover she was looking at him with a slightly sympathetic eye; albeit a suspicious one. It turned out that the young police officer was not as gullible as Jacob had thought, nor would she ever be a sexual conquest for him as she was totally aware of the likes of Jacob Tubb. In her relatively short career she had met all sorts of men, both colleagues and criminals, who had tried to bed her, and a few women too because of her short haired, elfin looks. She was happy living with William, with her childhood sweetheart who also happened to be her best friend and confidant, he was the daily antidote to the hard job that she did and she enjoyed nothing better than getting home, sharing a bottle of Merlot and hearing of his day teaching teenagers the romantic joy of poetry. He was the calm to her life of tempests and troubles.

In the few hours away from her duties of supporting Jacob, the victim, she had been awake and discussing her assignment, as much as she could, with Will. In speaking her thoughts to him she had come more and more to realise that this was not a simple case and that there was more to Jacob Tubb than everyone thought, she had a good mind for figuring out people and to her, at least, it seemed as if everyone else involved were looking straight past Jacob and toward the obvious, rather than asking questions about the man right in front of them; sometimes the obvious really was just that, the obvious solution.

A squat plainclothes detective, his suit always appearing too big for his short, round frame approached the railing where they stood, as was habit Kobie reintroduced himself. "Good morning Mr Tubb, we met when I was at your house, DS Kaan." He gave a curt nod of recognition to Jem and she responded with a simple 'Sir' in reply. The DS did not wait for a response beyond a handshake to match his outstretched hand; Jacob almost kept his own hand back as a snub to the detective, but then quickly realised he needed to keep the police on his side. He gave a firm-gripped shake to show his confidence and in an ignored power play. "According to the lock-keeper, they went through at first light and there is no way to determine if they went left, right or straight on when they reached the mouth of the harbour, my best guess is that they would have headed for France."

"They?" Jacob had screwed his face up in confusion.

"Yes sir, apparently, and he is a cool one your brother…"

"Half-brother!"

"Sorry, your half-brother, he and a lady companion dined in the Boat House restaurant last night, and according to the staff they looked quite tight and involved with each other. Any idea who that could be, did your bro…, half-brother have a girlfriend from before his arrest that you knew of?" Kobie did the thing, without realising he was doing it, with his hand rubbing his head in appeared confusion.

Jacob admitted that he could think of no one, he said that Lucas had always had plenty of girlfriends but they had all disappeared after the murder of the young girl, no one trusted him after that, in fact all his friends had abandoned him so there was no one that came to mind that could be his current companion.

"Does this mean if they have made it to France there is no chance to get them back?" Jacob made it sound as if he was concerned that his brother would evade re-capture, but he now had a strong desire that his brother win the chase, avoid ever being caught again, or in fact ever heard from again. In hindsight he wished now that he had not been so quick to make the phone call with regard to the missing boat. His desire to see his brother back in the asylum had outweighed the sensible option of just letting him go while taking the blame for Annie's death, he may as well have been hung for a sheep as a lamb. If he was seen having dinner in the restaurant and spotted around the marina then the police would be aware that the timings may well give him an alibi for Annie's slaying; for Jacob to remain away from suspect status Lucas needed to stay free and away from England so that alibi, including the timings, could not be established. It was vital for his own freedom if Lucas remained a double murderer.

"We have already contacted our French counterparts Mr Tubb, and they are looking for him at all relevant marinas and ports, just as we still are on this side of the Channel." The DS had a gut feeling about Jacob, a nasty feeling there was more to this character than the act he was putting on for everyone around him, but for the moment he was keeping that feeling close to his chest; he always, but always, trusted his gut when it came to people. His hand rubbed across the dome of his shaven head once again, this time the habitual motion as a tool to casually look at the man, standing a good four inches taller than the detective, and note his demeanour. Kobie tried to keep his soft eyes passive, calm, a poker face to avoid giving alarm. It was not that he just did not like the man or his manner, which he didn't, there was the experience of close on a decade dealing with guilty people who pretended and professed innocence. Deep inside the police gut, which acted like a well-tuned radar for trouble, there was a bright signal flashing that something was not right here, DS Kobie Kaan kept his look soft and did nothing to reveal that foreboding.

Somebody, in some movie or other that Jacob had seen, said *I have long feared that my sins would return to haunt me, and the cost would be more than I could bear*, in the next few minutes he would understand that line from The Patriot in its entirety.

Chapter 23

"Mr Tubb?" It was a quizzical call from the DS.

They were away from friendly environment of the marina and back in the local police station; the monotone walls of the interview room replacing the bright colours of the waterfront. Jacob was once again sitting opposite the tenacious plain clothed policeman and this time, feeling decidedly uncomfortable, he did not feel like a victim any longer; he felt like he was a suspect and his protective barriers were raised. As long as he stayed calm Lucas would take blame, anything else was just guesswork and bluff. It was becoming hard to pretend he was suffering the lot of someone whose space had been viciously invaded, he felt guilty; he was guilty, and now, sitting in the cold atmosphere of an interview room rather than in more comfortable surroundings of a victims lounge, he was sure he even looked the part of offender rather than offended. Guilt, even on one without conscience, has a strange way of painting its colours on the faces of the culpable. Jacob strained to keep his breathing level, keeping eye to eye contact with the police officer who, now rather than the friendly investigating officer, carried the demeanour of an unhappy undertaker; his serious, rounded, face difficult to read.

The opening question came from nowhere and shocked him, hit him hard, a hammer blow to his rib cage that caused Jacob's heart to stall. "Why didn't you say that the deceased was your mother?" Kaan, thought he knew the effect it would have and from the look on Jacob's face he had measured the man, and that impact, perfectly.

For Jacob the floor had opened and he had dropped through into an endless abyss. Any composure he had acted was gone. There was no longer any façade, no pretence, he felt every inch of the shock, and bewilderment, and that was now etched on a face that was swiftly draining of colour.

"Mr Tubb, Jacob?" In a career spanning some fifteen years, ten of those with CID, a posting he had enjoyed every day since hanging up his uniform despite the horrors he had encountered, Kobie Kaan could never recall ever seeing a subject of his interviews, especially from just one question, lose colour and composure so quickly. Jacob's flesh was grey, the dull colour of the walls that were now closing in on him, as if the very blood that coursed through his veins had vaporised.

Flustered, confused and thrown off course as much as a small boat dismasted in a storm, Jacob tried to regain safe ground. "Sorry Sergeant, wh... wh ....what did you just say." He had difficulty forming his words as the realisation of what had just been asked became clearer.

The canny officer was not going to let him stall and regain level ground, there would be no time to take this damaged craft to shore. "Your mother, Jacob. Why did you not tell us that Annie was your birth mother?"

"No she was the Nanny and then the housekeeper, that's all! She took on the role of mother I suppose, over the years as the Old Man never remarried." Stalling for time.

Kobie Kaan almost took pleasure in the discomfort of the unlikable man in front of him as he slid a sheaf of paper across the table, parchment-like in colour, obviously it was an official document. "We found your birth certificate among Annie's things, we were surprised to see her name on there as mother, we already knew you were half-brother to Lucas, through your father, but it may well have helped if we had known about your maternal parent, it gives us another reason for Lucas to come back here." Bluff, while a full house was being held. "What! I mean why would that make Lucas come back?" Jacob was again stalling for an answer, for some sort of recognition toward what was happening, he was sliding down a decaying rock face, foothold after foothold crumbling, and needing to regain firm ground.

"Well, if he had discovered the truth while searching for money when he returned to the house, we can assume he found the document in Annie's bedside drawer, just as we did, while he was seeking anything he could take with him; and then realised that all the love he thought he garnered from her, his surrogate mother, was in fact aimed at you his brother; then who knows what snapped inside of him when he realised that." DS Kaan, was leading Jacob.

"She came back unexpectedly and when he saw her his anger just boiled over, as it did with that poor girl in the park, and all his frustration was taken out there and then." The DS said the words clearly but his thoughts were more complex. He tried to keep an open mind towards Jacob being the perpetrator, he felt anguish for Annie knowing that with her final breaths and thoughts, she was more than likely being beaten to death by her own son. Kobie had already worked out the timings, and knew, with fair certainty, that Lucas had been in the restaurant at the time of Annie's beating. That left only one likely option!

For his part, Jacob sat in astonished silence, partly because he was truly stunned by the revelation, but also because he knew that if he opened his mouth he could give himself away. It was a hard task as silent was not his normal modus operandi, but he needed time to think, to calculate.

The officer, an expression usually soft and friendly but now hard with an intensity in his dark eyes, continued, he appeared to be in control but he was also somewhat overwhelmed by Jacob's reaction, he hoped it did not show in his own eyes. He need not have worried, his own poker face was firmly in place. He had felt that Jacob must have surely known about the true relationship between him and Annie, but from the shocked reaction he now doubted that; Jacob had not known that Annie was his true mother.

"We know it was Lucas who beat Annie to death, the wounds in her left cheek were consistent with the wounds on his last victim's face the deep tearing on her cheek from his ring ripping apart the flesh were very similar." He explained, but as he spoke it was without his normal conviction, something was bothering him about his carefully sourced evidence.

Chapter 24

The team fielding crowded closer to the wicket as the unstoppable tide rapidly began recovering its rightful place over the playing area, as the cricket pitch shrank so sailors and cricketers, realising their short day was over, began to climb back into their various craft, stumps were drawn, the makeshift shed taken apart and put on one of the larger yachts, and scores ignored as the pre-planned 'victorious' team headed toward the vanquished sailing club for a slap up feast and a few ales by way of celebration, it would be a cheerful and drunken afternoon and evening among friends back in Cowes for the sporting elite.

On board the Bonnie Annie the escapee and the reporter sipped their steaming black coffee from enamel mugs sporting semaphore flags denoting 'England Expects', Nelson's famous message from Victory, and the sturdy craft headed on past the easily recognisable Needles lighthouse and out into the open sea of the English Channel.

"I have an idea!" Gill spoke as if a light had pinged on over her head as it did in cartoons.

"I am all ears."

"Oh, I wouldn't say that, they stick out a bit but they are not that large." A grin crossed her face.

"I am on the run from the police for two murders, one of which I know I didn't do, and you find it the right moment to tease me about my facial defects; I will have you know my ears were the subject of much bullying and teasing at school." His indignation false.

"I'll stop for now but I cannot promise not to continue teasing you once they lock you up again!"

Lucas chose to ignore a conversation he knew he would not win. "What's this cunning idea of yours then?"

"Naturism!"

"What?"

"Naturism, nudity, nudists on the nudist beach."

"You have seen the shape I am in, or lack of it, and you think that finding a nudist beach is a great idea for an escape, what happens when we have to leave and we have no clothes?" In the last 24 hours he had started to become used to her quirky ways and teasing; but this had him baffled. "I thought your friends would be there to meet us but I'll go along with it; any excuse to see you naked again; but?"

"I may have forgot to mention that Nathaniel and Pauline are confirmed naturists?" She gave that quirky little smile that he was fast becoming used to and Lucas just raised his eyes to the distant ceiling of the sky, now blue and bright, shaking his head in disbelief, but hoping this woman would always surprise him. "And, how much does this boat mean to you?" Gill added placing her hand on Lucas' arm, looking him in the eyes with genuine concern and affection. "What if we had to sink her?" She added, slightly fearful of his response.

"I had already considered that the Bonnie Annie may well have to be sacrificed or abandoned, and my freedom means more than a damn boat. So go on, what's your thinking."

Gill, took her hand from his arm and paced the small on-deck fly-bridge. "We are heading west toward Shell Bay in Dorset, right?" Lucas nodded his agreement. "Once in the bay it will be pretty certain that we will have garnered at least some attention, we may even have the police hot on our heels, after the radio and TV appeals, well, what if we set the autopilot to head the boat straight toward Old Harry Rock, the waters are pretty deep around there. Cut the fuel lines and open the cooking gas bottle valves so the slightest spark will blow the boat apart and we will slip over the side, naked, and swim to shore."

"If they have put out a description of you, or even picked up some CCTV camera footage from any one of the places you, and we, have been, then you may be recognised with the clothes you are wearing. We swim ashore, just looking like any of the naturists already there, and trust me there will be plenty; we look as shocked as everyone else at the small boat exploding against Old Harry Rock, then with any luck, and it is about time we had some; my friends Nathaniel and Pamela Jones will be there, in their normal place among the dunes, as planned."

"Is it likely they will be there? I know they said they would but it is a big ask to help me given the circumstances." Lucas queried as he headed the lazy craft toward its final destination the far side of Christchurch Bay. Even with their position some way off shore they could make out the tourists arriving on the sandy beaches to enjoy the summer sunshine and packing themselves in between the twin piers of Boscombe and Bournemouth, each claiming their little stretch of sand like prospectors claiming their land rights in a gold rush; only these spaces in summer sunshine were much more highly prized than gold nuggets.

"They said they would and, trust me I know them well, they would not have promised and then changed their minds, now the cloud has cleared away with the late sun breaking through it will be totally natural to be on a nudist beach, where people naturally avert their gaze, except for the odd pervert or two and they won't be looking at our faces. Nate and Pauline worship the sunshine and have been avid naturists all their lives, any chance they get on a non-race day and…"

"Non-race day?" Lucas interrupted, puzzled by the expression.

"Nate is a trackside bookmaker, my dad loved the gee-gees and, in a very small way, loved to have a flutter on the horses. Just a pound here and a fiver there when he really fancied a horse and over the years he and Nate, great name for a bookie Nathaniel Jones, yeah?" She did not wait for an answer. "Well, he and Dad became friends. Nate liked the way Dad would act like a big spender and cool gambler, and Dad loved this wonderful character with a broad grey handlebar moustache and an even broader grin. They were like schoolboys together."

"So, what you are saying is that we crash the boat into an ancient and well-loved chalky outcrop and while it explodes and bursts into flame, leaving the assumption that we perished in the ensuing inferno or at the bottom of Davy Jones' locker, we swim to shore buck-naked and walk up the beach as if we belong in the hope that a grandly moustachioed bookmaker with the unlikely name of Nathaniel Jones and his wife Pauline are sunbathing among the dunes and that they have not only spare clothes that they have brought with them but they are willing to help an escaped lunatic and his equally crazy partner to evade the clutches of the law." Lucas looked at Gill with an incredulous smile.

"Yep, that about sums it up." Both took their gaze back to the sea in front of them as the Bonnie Annie cavorted over shallow waves and carved her way ever onward toward Studland. "That is if you can swim!" Gill added without looking back at him.

"I can swim, it's the walking up the beach naked and with my old chap swinging in the wind so everyone will notice that I am worried about." Lucas kept his eyes on the watery road ahead.

Gill watched him. "Trust me, I have seen your old chap, and there won't be that much swinging and I am certain that no one will notice!"

Their idle banter, which had in such a short span of time become so easy and natural, continued as the boat, with throttles eased back just a touch, cruised at a steady 17 to 18 knots across the blue-green sea, the rhythm of the craft beneath them seemed to be keeping both minds off the dread truth of their situation. Lucas looked around the vast seascape that surrounded them, gazed at the various surrounding leisure craft as they sailed and powered their way across the agitated surface. The tall, slightly curved, chrome levers of the throttles were kept just short of home and Lucas grasped, with quick confidence, the black tops and pulled the levers back to neutral. The Bonnie Annie rocked to a halt and she was lifted and dropped on each gentle wave that rolled by and as they massaged the hull beneath them and rocked her in a mesmerising way, Gill looked at her companion expecting to see angst etched on his face; but there was no panic, no fear, just a quietness, a calmness. Slipping from the driver's seat he stood for a second next to Gill, hugged her easily and kissed her on the cheek, he let go and she followed him from the flybridge and on to the forward deck area.

She let him go ahead as he shuffled on the side walkway, careful to hold the handrail atop the cabin structure, remembering the old sailing adage, one hand for you and one for the boat. Reaching the bow of the Bonnie Annie he stepped to the chrome pulpit and sat himself down with his feet dangling over the bow of the boat, the weighty grey anchor alongside him. Every now and again a wave would wash over his bare feet as the easy sea rose and boat dipped; each time relishing the sudden cold brush of nature against the bare feet dangling over the side. Gill watched carefully, suddenly realising what was going on. Lucas had been locked away for too long, first in his own mind creating his very own inescapable imprisonment and then as the healing had begun he had been held behind high walls and razor wire; accompanied and surrounded for every step he took away from his small cell-like room. Even his first few days of relative freedom had been spent cooped up below decks on the Bonnie Annie, too scared to step onto the deck and out into fresh, clean and free air.

This was the first moment he had found to truly enjoy the feeling of being in open air, the world around him; just soaking up that feeling of freedom that so many of us take for granted. For the moment he was free to take in his surroundings, to feel wind on his face, the sea on his feet and the sheer joy of the freedom to just look around at open vistas, of blue skies with the odd white clouds scudding across its vastness, of seagulls swirling, circling and crying out; Lucas wondered if they just flew for fun or if there was always a purpose to their sweeping activity, he envied their freedom.

"Are you okay?" It was asked softly but it still startled him just a little as he was so lost in his surroundings; Gill had joined him at the bow but he had not noticed her approach.

"Mmm, fine thank you, I know we do not have time to spare but if I get caught again then it would be a very long time before I would ever be able to breathe clean and salty air again and to see clear blue skies without interruption. I just wanted a moment to drink in nature."

Gill did not believe in love at first sight, but what she was feeling had to be damn close to that right now. And she also now believed, without doubt, that she was with an innocent man.

As with every dream moment there is a wake-up call, an alarm to pull one back from the brink of the unfolding of those dreams. In this instance it was the distant, but still audible on the quiet sea air, clatter of rotor blades carried on the wind from some distance away, that put the urgency back into their day. The pair of them looking aft toward the striped colours of the sand cliffs of Alum Bay at the most western end of the Isle of Wight now in the distance Lucas could clearly see the deep blue colour of a police helicopter as it zig-zagged a search corridor over the sea where he imagined the navigator intently watching a camera screen while the pilot searched the stretches of water beneath them for the missing boat and runaway prisoner.

The romance of the moment gone and without a word he leapt from the pulpit, taking a second to settle himself with one hand on the rail before gaining his balance and working his way back to the wheelhouse, he brushed, carefully, past Gill and she followed him back to the sanctuary of the cabin, with discovery in sight he once again took the wheel in the cabin rather than out on the flybridge.

Squeezing between the seat and the consul with its dials, depth gauges and radar, he pushed both levers forward once again, the engines immediately responded to the urgency of the moment, till once again they hit the end of their respective slots, before Lucas even began thinking of sitting at the helm. They felt the vibration beneath their feet as the throbbing diesels kicked and roared back into full life, pounding like resuscitated hearts, and through the fast spinning propellers the Bonnie Annie was forced forward, she in turn lifting her bow clear of the water and surged once again through the foaming sea and leaving a long, white, double, wake behind her as he propellers pushed her onward.

Gill took the deep leather seat on the opposite side of the gangway from the driver's chair, she looked across at the man who was holding the helm as if his life depended on it, and noticed a small smile on his face despite the desperate nature of their situation. It was a while before Lucas realised he was being watched.

"What?" As he stared at his onlooker.

"You, sitting there with a little smirk on your face."

"I don't smirk." The look with one raised eyebrow was enough for him not to argue the point. "It seemed that I was destined to spend the rest of my days going from one hard bench or plastic chair to the next. The park with that poor girl, I cannot fathom why she is still unnamed and unknown…" The smirk left his face and a sadness entered his eyes and he paused for a moment's thought.

"Anyway, what?" She broke the moment.

"Anyway," a huge sigh. "I was sitting on a hard bench, I recall going to a pub and having to sit on a hard bar stool because a bulldog, with his tongue out, was asleep on the comfy leather couch. Then that police officer woke me in the park after I fell into a drunken sleep on another bench. The hard bench in the police cell and hard plastic chairs in Broadmoor, now here I am bouncing around the ocean on a deep leather seat and I was just enjoying the feel of it against my buttocks and back. Feels good to be in a nice seat but then I feel guilty for thinking like that when that girl will never sit anywhere again."

The following silence made him feel uncomfortable, a feeling he had not noticed in the time he had spent with Gill. He glanced across to her to see if he could read anything in her expression.

"For what it's worth I don't think you did it, I don't think you are capable otherwise I would have jumped ship at the first opportunity, if you will excuse a bad pun?"

The discomfort gone they settled down to each think about what the future held, where would they end up, the day was getting old and the afternoon sun beginning its downward journey toward the western horizon, its setting point directly ahead of them. The bright golden orb their guiding star with its reflections dancing with a host of diamond echoes on the sea's surface. If it were not for the fact that the boat held an escaped lunatic and his accomplice who were both on the run from a fast approaching police force, it would have been a magical and romantic moment.

Chapter 25

Every chance he had back in the outskirts of Chichester Jacob listened to news reports, in the car, on his radio on TV, each thirty minute bulletin and hourly broadcast brought a new mixture of disappointment, and, it has to be said, hope with the lack of capture of his brother; one part of him wanted him caught and safely back in a secure unit, fully aware that the rantings of innocence from a madman would hardly be listened to, while the other wanted him to remain free, on the run and well away from the police so he would remain the prime, and only, suspect for Annie's brutal slaying. With each report though it seemed the escape and evasion of one deranged killer was becoming less and less newsworthy as the story fell from grace as the lead, to second string story and now as there was nothing new to report dropped even further down the end with every opportunity it could fall off the end of the tree minute news programmes with very little trouble.

The headline story in all the news programmes now had him fuming, all about the lost small girl missing in Dorset, little Natalie Thompson missing from her holiday caravan, was the lead story on all bulletins, local and national as the police became increasingly concerned for her safety. Lucas Tubb and his flight from justice were actually relegated to the third, then the fourth, story as a major supermarket posted catastrophic losses in their annual report. What was wrong with people, money over murder; and the police, could they not find anyone these days! They had sophisticated equipment, tracking devices, dogs for goodness sake, tracker dogs with keen noses, and yet a missing girl, and profit and loss, were taking the news interest and manpower away from catching a murderer.

"Stay lost little girl, stay lost!" Jacob begged the radio, her misfortune could be his saving grace.

The longer Lucas remained free the less likely the spotlight would return to Jacob for the death of Annie, the meddling witch. Or was it better that Lucas be caught in the hope his alibi would not be believed and fall apart; these thoughts ploughed through his mind as he flicked off the car radio, almost pushing the dial through the facia. His mind was in turmoil, Lucas left to evade authorities or captured, the sudden revelation from that detective that it was his own mother that he had beaten to death; he was finding that a hard fact to file away amidst all his anger. All the while the bile of loathing and fear were all building in him, taking over, the violent calmness he felt when he was totally in control of the situation now quickly diminishing.

How he hated her for keeping that from him for all his life, his own mother denying her son while living under the same roof! Pretending to be just the nanny while she bedded the old man and had his love child, mentally he scoffed at that thought. Even more he was now believing she got what she deserved, and yet, he still felt guilt, that burden was an alien feeling to him!

So consumed was he with all these little problems building into one solid wall of trouble that Jacob never took the time to realise, or even consider for one moment, but a certain Detective Sergeant was already looking in his direction for the housekeeper's, murder. Something was at the back of Kobie Kaan's mind, pricking like an annoying thorn caught just beneath the skin's surface. Every now and again something stung, something raw and painful, no matter how hard he sucked on it he could not bring the offending sharpness to the surface, the splinter was tearing into him deeper and harsher every moment.

There was something, he had seen it, registered it in his own mental inventory, buried among the evidence that would alter the course of investigation, if only he could grasp it, pull the thorn out of the skin! Unveil that one clue that would turn things around.

Kobie sat at a borrowed desk in the shining new block-built glass tower that was Southampton's police HQ, the Lego inspired faceless edifice replacing the charming old Portland stone station. The old building had now been vacated, its old cells and offices transformed into a modern museum and exhibition space. From outside the windows of the new headquarters, that sat to one side of the main road carrying a busy influx of traffic from the west and into the city. The sunlight reflected in a blue tint from the windows, while from inside Kobie gazed outward to view parts of Southampton Water, its grey, cold waters leading out to the Solent. He watched but could do nothing from the office as his awareness grew that somewhere out there on a boat, and fleeing westward half of his conundrum was now fleeing while the other half, and fast becoming the more interesting half, was back in Sussex. He was beginning to believe in Lucas a little more with each passing hour and trusting Jacob a little less. Like his current location, he was halfway between the two protagonists in this story and midway between home base and escaping Lucas.

The neighbouring Hampshire force was offering the West Sussex detective every facility to help in the recapture of Lucas Tubb, they had a fairly fast police boat on standby, as did the Dorset force, and the Hampshire helicopter was airborne every moment it could be looking for the Bonnie Anne. The boat, and its runaway crew, had last been reported spotted off the Needles, amidst a whole flotilla of vessels, and Kobie began to think he would soon be leaving this glass box and heading into Dorset territory. How far west was Lucas going, and why was he heading along the coast and not toward France, or the Channel Islands, giving himself a bigger chance of avoiding capture. So much of this case annoyed and bothered him, irked his normal smooth thought process.

Dorset was the last place he wanted Lucas to head, with a small girl missing and the whole county on, what the Americans would call an Amber Alert, he knew that manpower would be severely restricted. All efforts in the county would be centred, as it should be, on finding little Natalie alive and well, Kobie had a guilty pang as he wished for the little girls return more for his own investigation rather than a child being returned to her family. "Sometimes you just have to be cold and calculating, it's part of your job." He said to no one and shaking his head at his own poor thoughts. His normally soft eyes had taken on a tired intensity, the placid policeman was being driven. A uniformed officer, a stranger to the interloper, passing his work station responded but DS Kaan merely shrugged and explained he had been talking to himself. "Job will drive us all nuts in the end." Was the response and the DS merely nodded.

Back on the outskirts of Chichester, Jacob parked his Range Rover by the cottage's white picket fence but he did not get out straight away, he sat with both hands on the wheel and wondered about his next course of action. He realised he was in a difficult chess game, 'Mate' was near and he had to choose his next move carefully, use every gambit, with a smart strategy he could move his pieces wisely and keep efforts focused several moves ahead. He was brighter than all of them put together!

For some reason he could not think in linear mode, it had been a while since he had taken any sort of stimulant, he needed something special but had, sensibly so he thought at the time, flushed his stash shortly before the police arrived after Annie's death. He could do with a line or two now, just to help him think, he didn't need it, but it would help the metal process. His thoughts were fogged, someone had moved a Knight near his King, 'Check', but far from closing the game, the board in his mind had been clouded by the information that Annie had been his birth-mother, he never had an inkling and only his sheer arrogance stopped the guilt from totally flooding his being. Guilt was an alien feeling for Jacob, and he had no idea how to handle it, or even understand its power.

It was her own fault, she should have told him, maybe he would have turned out differently if he had known; maybe, just maybe, he would not have been so hard on her. Somewhere inside his thoughts he held Annie, he could still not refer to her or think of her as mother, in sheer contempt for the fact that he was actually the offspring of the hired help. It came as a great relief to his way of thinking that that little snippet was not public knowledge. The Old Man had stooped low enough to screw the staff and get her pregnant. Were there no fucking standards anymore, why didn't people know their place in life? No wonder Lucas had got the bulk of the attention and of the Old Man's estate, he was the blue-eyed full blood son while he, Jacob, was nothing more than a dirty secret, son of the servant! His anger seethed and any small feeling of guilt over the old woman's death diminished into the rage. The housekeeper had gotten what she deserved!

Chapter 26

"We need to get as close to shore as we dare, but it will still be a bit of a swim, are you up for it." Gill looked across from her seat to Lucas, eyes travelling up and down at his unfit body; but there was no hint of meanness in the gaze. Despite it being a glorious day now the clouds of the morning had been burned away, bright sunshine and blue skies, Lucas had been driving the craft from the cabin set of controls since spotting the police helicopter weaving its search pattern in the skies behind them, the downdraft from the whirling rotors forming a fine spray over the surface of the sea. Down in the cabin he felt hidden from the world.

As they had driven the Bonnie Annie out beyond the Needles, leaving the strange band of cricketers to up-stumps behind them, he had stepped back into the cabin from the flybridge and now both thought it better to stay inside and out of sight, a move that took willpower for Lucas after having spent the last year or so hidden away from fresh air and sunlight. For the short time on deck he had enjoyed the feeling of wind in his hair, licked his lips at the salt-tasting sea breezes and lifted his face to the freedom of being on the deck of a moving boat.

"I was always a decent swimmer growing up next to the sea, summer days were always spent in or on the water."

"I meant because of…" Thoughts of hurting his feelings stopped her and he in turn noted the concern in her eyes.

"Because of the extra weight and being generally out of condition you mean." He patted his slight paunch. "I will be okay, the only thing that concerns me is that if Greenpeace are on the beach they will try and re-float me as soon as I crawl up onto the shore."

"Oh, being a funny man are we, once again, I am on the run with an escaped lunatic and he is cracking jokes."

"What, may I ask, is the purpose of being a lunatic if you cannot at least act mad?" Lucas thought he noted the slight look of concern and fear on her face, this girl who in the last twenty four hours had come to mean so much to him, but then realised that it was a wry smile she had broadcast and not a note of mistrust. "Hey, I know you are scared and what you're putting on the line for me. And, trust me, I am taking this all very seriously but I cannot help but see the lunacy of the last couple of days. I was set to spend the rest of my life in an asylum…"

"Secure unit for the criminally insane."

"What?"

"They don't use the term asylum anymore, not politically correct, they are worried it may hurt the feelings of the mad people!" The cheeky smile and the sparkle in her eyes meant she was playing with him yet again, this teasing side of her took some getting used to after so long with people who had long ago lost their sense of humour; it was a serious thing to be mad and living with lunatics.

"As I was saying before being so rudely interrupted… I was set to spend my time in the 'secure unit for the criminally insane'…" He paused, Gill nodded in much the same way as a school teacher would to a pupil who was on the right track; Lucas continued. "Then a friend, a man I barely knew, gives his life for me; the first person to believe in my innocence and sanity. Mind you he was also barking. Then Annie, my beautiful Annie," Lucas paused for a second, remembering the beautiful old lady who had raised him in lieu of a real mother, and stayed with him throughout his life, even when she should have disowned him. "She aids my escape, someone who has always believed in me and cared for me, and she dies, again because of me. Then I meet you and, as if there was nothing wrong with the situation, we end up sleeping together... Like that's not surreal enough on its own?" His smile disappeared at the thought of the two people who had contributed so much to his freedom and what would happen to Gill if it all went wrong and he were recaptured. "And now I am putting you at risk!"

"Thinking about last night, I don't recall much sleep, and by the way you were totally out of puff after the first twenty minutes, so, I hold little hope in you lasting a long swim." Again, despite the urgency of what they were about to do Gill smiled broadly.

"You were timing us?"

"I happened to glance at the clock."

"Before and during by the sound of it."

"Before and after, don't kid yourself, stud!"

Resigned to the fact he was never going to win one of these verbal exchanges ever again he just carried on talking. "I just don't want you to get hurt Gill, that's all I am saying. Yes I am enjoying every feeling that comes my way both physically and mentally, being with you, being free and back on the water, watching the sun slide toward the horizon, the breeze on my skin, the feel of the boat, so many experiences that for so long I took for granted and now seem so condensed and marvellous. Sounds a bit cheesy, but it is like a rebirth. And if that was not enough I think I am falling in love with you"

"Bit cheesy?" There was that school teacher look again. "And, if it helps, I feel the same way about you as well."

"You do?"

"Of course you silly bugger. Now let's get back to the task at hand, you can get all soppy with me later."

Hand steady on the helm, the Bonnie Annie continued on her relentless drive toward the beautiful peninsula of Studland with its curving soft, sandy beaches, painted a pale yellow that afternoon by the bright sunshine, the dunes, natural mounds of drifted sand where naturists bared all to the sun and nature lovers trained their binoculars and long camera lenses toward the diverse wildlife that inhabited this unique headland. No matter what the season there were things to attract all types of visitors to the National Trust area of outstanding natural beauty.

Early morning riders exercised their horses along the beach and galloped in the shallows throwing sprays of water over rider and mount, families picnicked on glorious summer days that would be recalled long after childhood had disappeared and walkers strolled the sands morning, noon and night.

Studland had long been a popular spot for so many people and now it would give Lucas, and Gill, the chance of getting away from pursuers that, if the sound of the rotors were to be believed, were not that far behind them.

As if as a reminder to their plight he looked out over the aft rail where the wake of the boat curled itself with furrows of white foam like the soil being turned by tractor and plough back on land, and saw the police helicopter continuing its sweep from side to side seeking their boat, it was growing ever nearer. As they left the confines of Bournemouth's bay and swept past the expensive millionaires row of houses that lined the shores of Sandbanks Lucas saw in the distance the unmistakeable row of white cliffs and the chalky outcrop climbing from the sea of Old Harry Rock, the beautiful part of the coast that would become the final resting place of the Bonnie Annie. That part of the coast had once seen dinosaurs roaming across the land, now it would have a minor blip in history that would be forgotten the moment the day's newspapers were confined to the recycling bin.

"Can't I wear a wetsuit, we have one below?"

"Yes, of course you can. If you want to look odd, and definitely out of place. That is if you can fit into it now!" Gill had this way of speaking as if dealing with a recalcitrant child and she gave him one of her looks that he was already learning to read. "You, like me, won't be wearing anything; we are swimming onto the nudist part of the beach." Just his look made her laugh. "Prude!"

"How are we supposed to make a clean get away without a stitch on, and taking of standing out, my lily-white skin will stand out like a sore thumb among all those tanned and sun-wrinkled bodies?"

"All part of my cunning plan from when I called Nate and Pauline. They are expecting us to arrive naked and they will have clothes for us, so stop fretting, Nate and Pauline Jones are committed nudists and they will be in their usual spot today, I have often been there with them. And they will be there for us…"

"You're a nudist too? Anything else I should know about you?" Both eyebrows were raised on his rounded face, the flesh on his cheeks and forehead already turning pink from sun and wind burn, the tip of his nose shining like a Christmas reindeer.

"Plenty, but you will pick it up as we go along." That smile again, every time Lucas saw it across her shining face there was a true belief that everything would be alright. "As we get near enough to swim for it, I have packed important stuff into a waterproof bag, at least I hope its waterproof, money and phone and stuff, you aim the boat just short of Old Harry Rocks, but try not to hit Old Harry himself Lucas, his base is eroding enough as it is, aim it to hit the cliffs in one of the little bays. The water is deep enough there to delay them with ample time to discover we are not with the boat and by then we will be long gone."

"Is there any way to not sink the Bonnie Annie, she is like part of the family, another part that has to die?" The cost of his escape seemed to be getting higher and higher. "Maybe it would have been better if I had just stayed put!"

So intent was he with the morose feelings that engulfed him from time to time and with listening to the plan that there was a failure on his part to notice Gill had left her seat and now stood alongside him in the driver's chair. With a scowl, she thumped him hard on his upper arm, a punch boxer Amir Khan would have been proud of, and Lucas yelped in pain while rubbing the numbed muscle. "Ouch, you keep doing that."

"Stop feeling sorry for yourself and pay attention." Lucas' look asked if she was always going to be this bossy and demanding; he received a strong nod and an even stronger "YES! Before you ask, I am gonna be bossy!" In reply to his facial query, Gill clenched her fist and prepared for a second blow to his arm, Lucas wisely capitulated into surrender holding both hands up in defence mode.

As the Bonnie Annie swept as near to shore as was possible without ploughing into swimmers; the sea seemingly filled with them, the shallower area close to shore busy with bathers naked and semi-naked, heads bobbing everywhere like a harem of seals, strongest bathers furthest out from the shore, families and children splashing and frolicking in the safe shallows nearer to the beach a distance off from the boat.

Just twenty yards or so from the dark blue hull of the Bonnie Annie, Lucas noticed a surgically enhanced, bikini clad, blonde floating on her back, arms spread so she formed a floating crucifix, her globe breasts unmoving in the waves like twin islands, nipples, through the thin almost non-existent fabric, ever pointing skyward. As if in some kind of animalistic mating ritual she seemed to be surrounded by a pod of several men trying very hard to pretend they were just swimming by and not paying her any attention at all while their eyes were actually riveted to the surgeon's skilful work.

"It's time to say goodbye to the Bonnie Annie, Lucas." He simply nodded, stroked the control consul as if the boat were a living thing, and engaged the auto-pilot while shutting back on the twin throttles just a touch to allow them a safe egress from the fast moving craft. Water may seem a forgiving surface, but hit it at speed it is akin to hitting concrete!

With the controls set Lucas turned and just watched as Gill slipped her legs from her trousers and pulled her sweat shirt over her head, naked she slung the waterproof bag across her shoulders, the strap cutting diagonally between her perky breasts, and for the first time he noticed they were lightly tanned like the rest of her body, there were no white patches. He realised he was staring but could not take his eyes from her.

She struck a pose, to show off her body. "Your turn." Lucas did not have the same level of confidence, so, self-consciously, he began to strip, still embarrassed by his out of condition body. "Stop worrying, I am not bothered by that cuddly little belly of yours." He smiled but it was a coy unbelieving smile. "Anyway, more interested in that cute little cock of yours before it shrivels up in the cold sea." She reached forward and before he could move away she gently cupped his balls.

"Little?"

"Get over yourself, you are no Errol Flynn. Although, your swordsmanship was pretty good!" She smiled wickedly.

"We need to go." Was his only response, he was ready, Gill was ready and the boat was set on its course to destruction.

Before stepping out on deck they both searched the sky seeking the helicopter and then the sea for the presence of nearby boats, all seemed clear, no one was watching them, especially the nearby swimmers who were still engrossed in the blonde's unnatural assets. Gill, ever the confident one, stepped quickly up onto the rail of the boat, the side furthest from shore, which was still travelling in excess of twelve knots and carving its way through the offshore chop, and dived into the sea without hesitation and with a certain amount of gracefulness.

The cold water hit her senses hard and seemed to shrivel her skin, the impact and the wake of the craft turned an elegant dive into a floundering crash into the hard surface. She was pushed under as if on the rinse cycle of a washing machine, and it took a moment for her head to break the surface of that blue green sea; she took a large gulp of breath, as she broached the surface then watched as Lucas almost slid from the side of the boat, inelegant, clumsy and she noted he was watching it disappear away from him as leapt from the safety of her deck. She had a slight moment of panic, afraid he may be too close to the twin propellers as he entered the water, but the forward movement of the boat took the spinning blades away from his flailing limbs.

They swam to each other and hugged in the water, a sign of their complicity and togetherness, legs kicking out under the surface, both thankful for the other's safety. Skin sensors already on high alert because of the sudden immersion in cold water were further excited by their skin to skin closeness. Lucas, felt a slight arousal below the surface of the water, he kissed Gill, just lightly, on the lips and without words they broke their hold on each other and began to swim for shore. Lucas began to strike out in a fast Australian crawl, keen to show off his skill and manhood, but Gill called him back before he had gone but a few strokes, her voice drifted over the surface of the waves and he trod water and turned to face her.

"Pace yourself Lucas, breaststroke." He avoided responding to the obvious cliché. "We are supposed to be enjoying the swim, don't draw attention by trying to be Mark Spitz; plus it is further than you think to shore"

Lucas bobbed in the water, a wave briefly washed over his head causing him to swallow a mouthful of salty brine, he spat it out and coughed, waiting for a second or two until Gill was alongside him. They both began a slow and easy breaststroke toward shore, keeping just that arm's length away from each other to avoid clashing like the oars in a close run boat race.

As he made for shore he pondered on two things as he began to enjoy the physicality of the exercise; what would he have done if Gill had not found him and helped him, and who the hell was Mark Spitz? The water, its enshrouding coldness, felt good against his naked body. It was a feeling of complete freedom.

A loud clatter of rotor blades, seemingly directly above them, woke both from their reverie. The rolling waves were whipped into fine spray by the downdraft. It would have looked strange if they had ignored the nearing helicopter and so, in tacit agreement, they stopped swimming, turned onto their backs and like everyone else in the water on that bright day the gazed into the burning blue sky, while treading water, and watched as the low flying aircraft flew a direct route towards the, by now, disappearing and doomed Bonnie Annie. Even the staring men turned their gazes away from the surgically enhanced breasts as the chopper flew low overhead.

The fast disappearing boat went from bright blue craft to a mere silhouette as it passed under the sun, its colour and form were eclipsed against the ball of golden light. From his low level in the water Lucas could now only see just the white radar bowl on the chrome superstructure of the well-loved craft, the Bonnie Annie was on her last ride.

It seemed they were in a watery grandstand as they heard swimmers around them comment on the chase with questions of why, what and whom; several people guessing, in loud voices, it was smugglers or illegal immigrants; the type of miscreant equally shared between people or drug being the illicit import. While treading water Gill positioned herself behind Lucas, wrapping her arms around his neck and legs around his waist and gave him a squeeze; these moments of strong affection something she was beginning to do on a regular basis and he liked it, liked the security it gave him. Chin on his shoulder she whispered in his ear, "I thought this may look more natural for anyone who may be watching!" He imagined her mischievous grin and replied it was good thinking. She squeezed harder with her legs and nibbled his ear lobe; Lucas was falling deeply in love with this woman who, even in a moment of danger, relaxed him and thrilled him all in one go.

Their beautiful boat was now out of sight but there was no mistaking the sound when they heard the deep crunch of impact echoing across the surface of the bay as the Bonnie Annie became the latest victim to die in the cause of his attempt at freedom and redemption. Her demise was lucky for the craft at anchor in the shallow bays of the white cliffs, Lucas had not taken into account the leisure craft that always moored offshore in that area, but the Bonnie Annie had passed through them without causing harm, except for some spilled drinks on a small yacht as she rocked it with her outward wash.

It was an inanimate object but it held memories and affection, it had been a small part of his family, of his growing up, and now it was lost. A few seconds after the crash of impact with the white cliff face came a loud thump of sound which almost punched the air from the very space around them with its shockwave, ears popped with the change in pressure, and a ball of flame lit the chalky cliffs and reflected in anger across the water's surface. They watched the funeral pyre lift and roll into the sky, a fitting epitaph.

Gill apologised, softness in her voice. "Sorry Lucas, I had to open the valves on the gas cylinders, we knew she was going to blow."

Gill had responded as the explosion had been bigger than either had anticipated. The helicopter, its crew still searching the sea's surface, dipped its nose, like a sprinter in the blocks, and swooped forward as if responding to the crack of the starter's pistol. Within seconds it was over the burning and, fast sinking, wreck of a boat and the surrounding debris, floating and abandoned to the sea.

"It was a good idea. You said you would." It was said unsmiling, with sad meaning and he stroked her arm to emphasise his words. Gill released her octopus like grip and drifted away to form a gap between their two bodies. Seeing enough Lucas rolled over in the gentle waves and now face down in the water he began to strike out for shore, his breaststroke at a steady pace; the sea driving over his face and body hiding tears that had begun to sting his eyes, parts of the old Lucas Tubb and his former life were disappearing daily. Gill immediately took to his side and at arm's length they both headed for shore, needing the energy sapping swim to counteract the mood they changed their stroke and kicked out with a crawl, hands, palms flat and pointing cutting into the sea before acting like paddles and driving their bodies forward, legs kicking and splashing the surface as they drove the swimmers toward the beach. The increased energy needed and spent was a comfort in itself.

Reaching the shallows Gill stood knee deep in the sea, hardly out of breath and with water droplets just running down over her lithe body, stretched up arms over her head and with fingers spread like the tines of a comb her hands swept back her wet hair, dark and lustrous, the extra water cascading down her back and running over her buttocks. Lucas was mesmerised on reaching the same part of the shallows just yards from the sandy shore, he stopped swimming but instead of standing he remained on his knees in the shallows, gasping for breath, trying to catch every atom of air in his burning lungs, water dripping from his dark hair and running down his face unattended, hands on knees. His back arched, chest aching with the effort of trying to take in oxygen, he coughed up some of the seawater he had swallowed or breathed into his lungs. Every muscle from his arms and legs, down his back and across his abdomen throbbed, even, he noted, his buttocks ached with effort. He was definitely out of condition. But in the moment he looked up his pain dissipated, forgotten. He was gazing, at eye level, at Gill's backside, rounded, perfect, glistening with running dribbles of water, now all Lucas could feel was his heart pounding in   his   chest.

Gill, who was not someone who took great stock in how she looked, knew what she was doing, she knew her body was fit and toned, she knew the effect she would be having on her exhausted partner. Without turning her head, with a knee high walk, she began to step out of the soft surf, "Seen enough? If you want any more you will have to get up and follow me!"

It was an old fashioned phrase but all Lucas could think was 'Minx'!

First one leg, then the other he stood, but his legs were trembling, the muscles over worked and the lactose no longer running over the muscles to keep them working, his thighs throbbed, calves burned and he struggled to move forward as the sea seemed intent on offering resistance to forward movement.

Chapter 27

"Is that him then? Doesn't look much like an escaped lunatic to me." Lucas heard the resonant, baritone, booming voice as he tried to regain the normal ability of just standing and breathing, something he had, until now, always taken for granted, but his legs wobbled with tiredness and he wanted, no needed, to drop to his knees once again, to return to the water and collapse in the lazy surf and let the waves wash him out to sea again; his body did not want to walk.

"Shush Nate." Gill admonished gently. "Don't want the whole beach to hear." Lucas stared on, not a little stunned as Gill hugged her friend, and there was no embarrassment given their nakedness, he kissed her on both cheeks before they parted. Lucas found it hard to equate the intimate nature of the affection, given they were nude and on a public beach, with mere friendship.

"Hello gorgeous girl, are you okay?" Again the voice was deep and rich in tone, the sound as if emanating from a deep cave carried across the sandy landscape.

"I am fine Nate, its Aquaman there I am worried about!" Her thumb hooked and indicated the gasping Lucas.

"Don't worry about me, I am fit as a fiddle." As he coughed up more water; feeling nowhere near like an aquatic super hero. He took a deep breath and with great effort, stood upright and strong and strode the several paces needed to reach the stranger who held his freedom in his hands. His hand reached out for a polite handshake but Nathaniel, being a free spirit all his life, took Gill's friend into a manly hug, using one hand to slap a hearty greeting on Lucas' shoulder blade. Stepping back he introduced himself, "Nathaniel my dear boy, but call me Nate if you prefer. Welcome." Now a couple of feet apart Lucas was able to take in the detail of the ebullient man in front of him. It could not be helped but the eyes automatically began their search just below the waist, he had after all just felt that region brush thigh against thigh. A small, shrivelled cock that resembled a left over cocktail sausage on a long abandoned buffet and a pair of balls like dark sun-ripened prunes, the body that was attached to the those three sad Musketeers, was cooked to a deep and wrinkled brown, the stomach that with its loose aging flesh slightly overhung the male equipment. "Pleasure Nate." Lucas said as he looked at the face, somewhat glad to find a different viewpoint.

"That said, I do prefer Nathaniel if that's okay, only this lovely lady and my dear wife get away with the shortened version; could never stop them." The face that belonged to the aging and sun wrinkled body came as a surprise. It was handsome, in a cavalier sort of way, a salt and pepper coloured goatee sat below youthful and full lips and they in turn were topped by a devilish and gallant moustache that swept away in both directions under a keen and pointed nose. The emerald green eyes were strong, friendly, and inquisitive and the greying hair on his head, a receding hairline a short way back from his tanned forehead gave way to a wave of hair as strong as any he had just swum through, it was swept back and washed its way down the back of his neck. Lucas liked the face immediately, as well as the man that sported it, it was strong, friendly and although of advancing years it still held a youthful quality and a trusting gaze.

"Pleased to meet you Nathaniel, Lucas Tubb." This time the handshake was accepted and shared, the grip firm and a bond began between the two, there was trust in that one gentlemanly act.

"Likewise Lucas." The voice again seemed to boom but there was a quietness to it as well, like a controlled explosion.

With the introductions done Lucas turned to see what remained of the Bonnie Annie, and took a moment to mourn another loss. All that was left of the craft was a pall of black smoke clawing at the sky but just as it cleared the upper lip of the cliffs the spiralling growth was thrown to the elements by the violent wash of the helicopter's rotor blades as it hovered over the scene, around the pall of dark smoke was a small, but ever growing, flotilla of craft circling the impact point under the acrid and dark pyre that seemed to settle over them creating a storm cloud that blotted out the blue sky of summer. Above it all, still searching for movement and survivors, the hovering police helicopter, from the viewpoint of the beach where the three compatriots stood, just a dark blot against those once chalk white cliffs. The three naked people, unheeded by all around them, turned and walked through the soft sand away from the sea and the crash-site and headed, unnoticed, toward the safety of the dunes.

Midway between those dunes and the gentle waves of the sea Lucas stopped curled and unfurled his toes in the sand, feeling the soft grains running between his toes; Gill watched and realised what he was doing. "Something else you needed to feel?"

"Every sensation, every breath of breeze massaging my body, touch on the skin, smell and sound; just everything feels as if someone has turned the volume up on life. I have taken so much for granted, ignored it and my feelings just got so busy with life I forgot to live. Forgot to feel. When it is all taken away from you, for whatever reason, at first you do not miss it or mourn its loss, simply because you have gone through life ignoring the obvious and the simple things, only as time goes by do they each come to mind, sights, smells, tastes, sounds and the textures of life; even feelings that take us over are forgotten, such as love, and sometimes even hate, are washed away so easily when you are too busy to take note, then suddenly they are all gone, taken away from you, your life becomes as bland as the beige walls that hold you imprisoned. Then, suddenly, when it's given back it is stronger, louder and clearer than you ever remembered. The colours are brighter, the aromas sweeter, every taste bud fights for flavour and voices become music. The sand feels pretty good between my toes too." Lucas smiled, the expression of a free man who cherished everything around him, and they continued to follow Nathaniel into the dunes.

A few feet up the slope of the yellow drifts, where each footstep was dragged a few inches backward by the soft, sliding sand, Lucas was once again out of breath, puffing hard with every muscle in thigh and calf, still tired from the long swim, begin to burn with the effort. Diet and gym were called for; if he ever got the chance to work out again.

As they crested the rise, Gill's hand helping him up the last few feet, Lucas looked behind, expecting to see an Everest of a dune below him as he stood at the summit, he was ready to plant his nation's flag into the surface and claim the mountain for England, but beneath his feet it was just a few yards of effort; an unfit body creating the false feeling of size. He took in the scene around him, his eyes scanning 360 degrees, and in the divot of each dune, where they could be seen, there were naked bodies of all shapes and sizes. In a few of the dunes along the outer edge of the sandy vista stood naked men, lonely, sentinel like and intent on showing off their withering manhood. It was a strange, even sad and pathetic, sight to say the least, sun worshippers slightly hidden from view and, what appeared to be, strange men standing in full view, wanting to be seen and maybe even applauded for the size of their equipment and bravery at showing it off.

Lucas had no idea what to expect on meeting Pauline after coming so close to Nathaniel and his bodily attributes, he predicted seeing a wrinkled prune of an aging woman, to match the skin tone and build of the male part of the partnership but as they stepped, or rather slid, down into a hollow in the dunes he was introduced to an unabashed Pauline. She did not stand from her prone position on the coloured striped towel, which had gone totally unnoticed by Lucas, she could have been laying on a bed of writhing snakes and he would not have noticed, but she rather leant up on one elbow and offered a delicate and slender hand in greeting. Self-consciously, both of his nudity and her nakedness, he shook it and said hello to a woman who was, to say the least, stunning.

"Not what you expected ah?" It was a mischievous question from Nathaniel. Gill giggled.

"Stop it Nate." The two girls spoke in unison. Nate shrugged with a gleeful look on his face.

Pauline was certainly not as expected. After meeting Nathaniel, although he had not analysed it too deeply, he expected the wife, Pauline to be similar in shape and age, firmly tanned with an equally leathery skin.

Instead there was this long, he imagined as tall as his six foot one inch, beautifully tanned and visually amazing woman. Her legs would grace any fashion magazine clad in nylons, her stomach flat and toned, beneath it a small and neatly trimmed triangle of pubic hair, above it a pair of neat, curving breasts with strong, seemingly hard, nipples. Eyes travelling further upward he noted a long and slender neck with long jet black shining hair wrapping itself around a face that held a strong chin. Soft but slightly thin lips boasting a smile that said she knew she was being admired, a tiny upturned nose and the most amazing almond shaped and coloured eyes completed the picture.

"You can close your mouth now Lucas; I am still here you know." A nudge in his ribs from Gill's sharp elbow brought Lucas back to the here and now. He apologised straight away for staring.

"It's okay Lucas, I am used to it." Explained Nathaniel, "People meet me and expect me to be married to some old dragon the same age as me, but I am a very lucky man to have the heart of such a beauty, don't ask me how, I don't know, just grateful for having her in my life. I look at myself in the mirror and I see this out of shape, funny looking old fart, and wonder how? But I thank a higher being, if there is one, every day for my good fortune and for the love of a beautiful and clever woman… And, best of all, she is a bloody amazing cook."

"That's all you want me for Nate Jones." The voice was gentle, melodic, slightly reproachful. "My stunning Yorkshire puddings and my fish pies."

"That's true." The laughter flowing easily between the foursome before the serious baritone of a voice took over the relaxed proceedings, his words stole the smiles as a thief would pick a pocket. "Now let's hear your story Lucas. Because although Gill has spoken for you, I will decide for myself if we help any further or just leave you here with the clothes we have brought you. I will do anything for this girl," He draped an arm around her shoulder. "But I will not put me and mine at risk for someone I do not trust, like, or who deserves what the world has handed out to them. Am I clear?" The strength of his words were matched by his bodily demeanour, the man, despite the lack of clothing, was no longer naked!

"Perfectly, and feeling the way I do about Gill I would not expect anything else, Sir." Lucas without thought showed the same respect as he would to his father. "I already appreciate that you have gone this far to help me just on her word. In fact I am amazed at everyone who has befriended me on trust alone and have helped me. Before I tell all though can I ask one question that is bothering me and I would love to know the answer before you throw me out of your dune?"

Nate nodded for him to go ahead.

"This nudist thing, I can guess, just about why those guys standing in the other dunes do it, but you three, is it about the sex."

"Good God no!" Nathaniel's voice boomed across the dunes with a peel of laughter that originated deep within his body, bringing looks from the nude sentinels, it seemed to carry over dune, across the beach and out to sea, powerful and yet with a gentle charm. Returning to his usual sonorous tone he explained. "If it was about sex, as beautiful as Pauline is, I would wear my glasses, can't see a bloody thing without them. It is simply the fact we dislike the feeling of being cooped up in clothing all day every day, it feels - feels, kind of claustrophobic if you like. Then when we come down to the beach it seems ridiculous to put cloth between our bodies and that glorious sunshine. It just feels good on the skin, like you said down on the beach about taking time to live life and enjoy the sensations it offers, to us this is like fine wine, good food, the love of a beautiful woman, it feels good and allows us to take those feelings and revel in them. We just like it in the same way some people like to dress up and put on all their finery, we like to dress down and enjoy the finery that nature gave us, although some of us are finer than others." He finished with a look at first Pauline and then Gill. "Your turn." With this request there was no argument and Lucas, sitting down in the sand on the downslope of the dune and feeling the sand slide between the crack between his buttocks, began to tell his tale from the unnamed girl in the park that he so callously pushed under the bench to hide her from a guilty conscience, right up to setting the, now destroyed, Bonnie Annie onto autopilot for her final voyage.

"Did you do it? The unnamed girl under the bench?" Was the expected response after nearly forty five minutes of uninterrupted talking; it was Pauline that asked from her position on the striped towel where, Lucas noticed with embarrassment and with great difficulty in averting his gaze that she had moved in order to listen intently to his tale, and now sat cross legged, straight backed, and totally exposed.

He stuttered a little, "All, all, I can say is that I don't think I did. I don't know for sure, I wish I did, but I don't think I am capable of such a thing. Although if you had asked me before all this happened if I could shove the dead body of some poor girl under a bench I would have said no to that as well! What I am sure of, because I have proof, is I know I didn't kill poor Annie, I was under the watchful gaze of Gill when she was beaten to death." He took a moment, a pause for the still raw shock of Annie's death; and no one else spoke allowing him time to compose himself. "And, as they both met a similar violent end I can only think it was the same person that did it and sadly for my family, or what little is left of it, that person could only have been my brother Jacob, although, of course, I don't want to believe it, there is no other option that makes sense."

There was silence around the dune, nobody had anything to add, Lucas could not even hear the small world that surrounded them, no gulls crying and squabbling, no sea brushing its waves at the sandy shore, no holiday makers screeching and shouting. Gill easily slid across the soft sand, placed her hand around the thickened waist of Lucas and gave him a hug while resting her head on his shoulder. It seemed to have become a tacit agreement that Nathaniel and Pauline Jones had just become his latest allies; they had said nothing to the contrary.

Lucas realised that goose-bumps had appeared on his chilling skin, the effort of the past twenty four hours was beginning to tell on him, even though there was still plenty of warmth in the, now, fast setting sun that they had followed to this location and this point in time; he felt tired, drained of all physical and mental resources, all he wanted to do was sleep for a good many hours and awake in a world where he was neither murderer nor lunatic.

"That's good enough for me dear boy." And, so it was with a simple nod from Nathaniel the girls began to pack up belongings and don clothes. Pauline's idea of replacing clothes was simply to wrap herself in an almost sheer, but beautifully patterned, sarong, knotted just above her pointed breasts and slightly round from her right protuberance, and seemed even sexier for the addition. Gill pulled on a dark sweatshirt and jeans but she held on to the rush-soled and canvas espadrilles to avoid getting sand in them while she walked from the dunes. When Lucas looked up as he was handed the clothing he was to wear, he saw that Nate was now in a tied at the waist sarong and a loose fitting T-shirt, he remained bare footed.

"I had no idea of your size Lucas so bought stuff that would probably fill every need."

Lucas slipped on the elastic waisted lounging pants that were black with batman images spread across the material. Not his normal attire, but he liked them, they were fun and comfortable, a touch of levity following the last few serious hours. He too put on a baggy, white T-shirt and a pair of brown leather thong flip-flops completed the strange ensemble.

"Sexy." Gill eyed him up and down.

"Teasing right, you just love the chance to take the piss, I bet this is what you asked Nathaniel to bring!" He smiled at her, and realised he had never smiled so much in his life as he had since meeting her in that marina just and over a day ago. It seemed she had been part of his life for so much longer, and hoped she felt the same.

"Every chance I get and I asked him just to bring clothes, although looking at you I wish I had suggested it. Nice one Nate." The foursome once again laughed, the first time humour had taken over since Lucas began to tell his sorry tale.

Leaving the dunes, and the dwindling number of sentinels who had disappeared in equal numbers due to the diminishing daylight and temperature of the day, they walked to the car park where from some unseen pocket, as a magician producing a dove, Nathaniel flourished a car key. Pressing the button the hazard lights on a bright red Volvo X90 blinked on and off and the doors clicked unlocked. Carrying nothing but shoes and the one waterproof bag that held their meagre belongings Lucas and Gill climbed into the soft leathery comfort of the rear seats while Nathaniel and Pauline threw their bags and towels into the spacious rear load area. Within minutes they were out of the car park, around the small roundabout and joining the queue for the quaint chain ferry that was the link between the peninsula and the mainland at Sandbanks.

"We could go round but it is a long journey and I guess you are pretty much exhausted Lucas." Nate said looking over his shoulder while waiting for the queue to move forward.

"Not much left in the tank I must admit." Was the reply as he lay his head back onto the softness of the head restraint and he allowed the tiredness to wash over him. Lucas felt it was the first time he had truly felt relaxed in many months. Even the concern that police would be waiting on the other side of the short crossing was a mild one, the strength of worry just taken from his mind by fatigue.

Finally the car moved forward with purpose and four lanes of vehicles quickly filled the deck of the strange little chain ferry that ran every day of the year, even Christmas Day as Pauline informed him, but he barely heard her voice.

The bump of joining the ramp up to the small car deck jolted him from sleep that had already begun to claim him, he would not feel the corresponding thump as Nathaniel drove up the off ramp and into Sandbanks, the mesmeric sound and feel of the mighty chain's clanking as the ferry fed it through the machinery that drove it across the fast flowing tidal race lulled him to sleep. Each day that narrow entrance into Poole Harbour saw ferries, fishing boats and leisure craft of all shapes and sizes pass to and fro. As the old ferry pulled from shore a black ball was raised to the small masthead over the pilot's viewpoint to indicate that it was moving across the busy flow of watery traffic, it had right of way.

It was the crunching sound of broad tyres on sharp gravel that stirred and woke Lucas, with unconscious thought he wiped spittle from his chin where he had dribbled during his deep sleep, and rubbed his face with both palms to rid it of sleepiness.

"Welcome back stranger." Gill's voice was soft, reassuring. "Good timing, we have just arrived home."

A pang dug deep into the soul of Lucas as he realised with that one harmless comment, which was supposed to be encouraging, he was homeless; in fact apart from the people in this car he was friendless and without family as well. He had no place in this world except his enclosed, beige room at a facility for the criminally insane that almost, for just a second or two seemed inviting. His only friend, apart from those in the car with him, now lay on a mortician's slab probably cut up and examined to see if he was a third victim of his murderous exploits, they would try and make up the numbers, elevate him to the ranks of serial killer.

Gill took his silence and lack of excitement on arriving at their destination as the tiredness and the remaining hold that sleep had on him, she would only discover later when they were in their room and alone that his thoughts were sombre; a serious bout of crippling depression was beginning to take hold.

Lucas knew he had placed three wonderful and trusting souls in grave danger, their lives would implode if they were discovered to be harbouring him, and he had to find a way to protect them. There was no way they deserved any kind of bad karma because of what they were doing to help him. Two people had already paid the ultimate price for his temporary freedom.

That was more than enough of a cost!

Chapter 28

Through the small square window panes of his bedroom in the waterside cottage, half hidden by the rainbow striped curtains, Jacob watched as the compact police car, a Ford Escort, pulled up beside the picket fence, the blue, domed, light stuck out of the roof like the pointed police helmets of old on a skinny officer. He thought that there was little less intimidating than a tiny police hatchback, why did we not use big impressive cars like the Americans, cars that made a statement when they pulled up oozing authority and power, to protect and serve, not to pootle around with a hunched officer inside its cramped cabin!

As he watched through the window a smile appeared on his narrow face, it was the liaison officer Jem stepping, elegantly, from the car, to Jacob she looked wonderful with her tight blue pants and white, slightly loose, blouse with its dark blue epaulets. As she walked through the gate, he heard the dry creaking complaint of its hinges, and wondered, just maybe, as he looked down at her navigating the pathway if a gap may appear in the top of her blouse so he catch a glimpse of the lace on her bra. He had no doubt she was wearing one, but was disappointed to note that all but the top button of her shirt was securely fastened.

Disenchanted, and on hearing the door bell's chimes he turned and headed downstairs; either they had caught Lucas and his trollop or she was just here to see him, he had been certain that there had been a lasting impression on her part toward him, and assumed that she merely needed decent time between a work and pleasure visit. Now she was here, in the guise of uniform, but he knew it was to extend their burgeoning relationship.

Opening the door he smiled his most charming smile, was about to offer a compliment or two, but Jem just walked past him and into the hallway without invite, brushing shoulder to shoulder as she squeezed through the narrow doorway, he felt a frisson of excitement at the brief touch. Her hair was perfectly mounted atop her head, not one stray strand out of place, he liked neatness. At the end of the hallway she turned left into the kitchen and waited for Jacob to catch up. Her radio, the microphone attached to a loop on the pocket of her blouse, squawked a garbled message, and without thought she turned the volume down.

Her face was a serious picture, no hint of playfulness, which halted

Jacob in mid-stride. "Jacob, I have news." She began. "You may need to sit down it is not good I am afraid." As instructed he drew a stool out from under the breakfast bar and straddled it, there was a brief moment when he thought he may have left evidence on Annie's body, but then double checked himself when realising a more senior officer would be here for something like that, probably that bastard DS Kaan, with that dark smarmy smile of his, all white teeth and olive skin; his bald head pointing up from that short body. Jacob, mentally shook the thought from his mind, ensured his face matched her serious demeanour, but inside he was smiling, heart pounding with the thrill of what he hoped to hear.

Jem continued. "The police helicopter searching for your brother followed the boat from Cowes toward the Dorset coastline, at first doing a sweeping search but then after spotting the Bonnie Annie, keeping a reasonable distance so as not to startle or pre-warn Lucas, the pilot kept up a search pattern but it was just a ruse to see where your brother was heading."

"Can we get to the crux of why you are here please? I don't need the whole sorry story." Jacob was impatient for a result that would suit him.

"Sorry, yes of course." Jem was polite but well trained in dealing with bereaved family. "The pilot thought Lucas was heading into Poole Harbour which would have been ideal as he would have been easier to contain and capture in there, but instead the boat veered away and ran straight into the cliffs by Old Harry Rock, there was an explosion and, although it is fairly shallow at low tide the boat sank quickly under the high spring tides. It is a fairly inaccessible place at the foot of the cliffs but divers are searching both the sea bed and the small beach for wreckage, and of course for your brother and his friend. But, we believe, very strongly, that they were lost in the incident. I am so sorry for your loss." As with any trauma tea was called for, as much as a diversion as anything, so she plucked the kettle from its stand and turned to fill it with water. "It seems to be all I have to say to you lately. 'Sorry for your loss.'" Tap turned off she placed it back on its pedestal and flicked the switch, the glass side glowed blue and the water began to heat.

Jacob's face showed the emotion of shock, his eyes began to well with a single tear, and the acting masterclass had begun, once again. Behind the façade one single thought crossed his mind; 'Fucking tea again, what is it with these people and fucking tea!' Instead he said, "The rock was named after a notorious local pirate you know. Harry Paye, he and his crew were based in Poole Harbour and sailed past the cliffs each time he did a marauding raid on French ports. He died in fourteen nineteen."

"That's really interesting, I often wondered why it had the name," The liaison officer turned and opened the cupboard containing the tea bags, her one thought was to keep busy as well as keeping a safe distance from this man, she knew people well enough to catch his act of distress and the lascivious looks he gave her, Jacob did nothing but send shivers of distaste down her spine.

What Jacob did not realise was that Jem was in the cottage under strict instruction from Kobie Kaan; the fact was, this was not a visit from a Family Liaison Officer as Jacob hopefully thought, but a call from an experienced and wily police constable. She was to watch his every move, take mental note of every word uttered; Kaan did not trust this man. More than that he disliked this man immensely and felt very strongly that the answer to all these deaths and tragedies was coming from the direction of Jacob and not, so it seemed now, Lucas. An old-fashioned copper's gut instinct and Kaan's very rarely let him down.

Although during the morning briefing some two hours before he admitted that he had no explanation for the unnamed girl's death, or even an identity and therefore no link to the brothers, but he was certain the squad did not have the whole story or anything near the truth.

Earl Grey teabags deposited in mugs, Jem thought confining such a fine tea in teabags a crime in itself, she turned back to face Jacob, certain she caught the remnants of a triumphant smirk disappear from his face. Jacob mentally berated himself for letting his feelings slip into a pleased expression; but thought he had got away with the deception.

"I know he was a troubled soul, but I cannot help but feel sorry for him. My brother and I did not always see eye to eye..." Give a little of the truth in every lie. "But, he was still my brother, my big brother at that, and I always looked up to him. When we were children I wanted to be just like him." He turned his back as if overtaken with emotion and wiped an imaginary tear from his eye; the rubbing with the knuckle on the back of his hand would serve to redden the socket and add credence to his grief. With a well thought out sigh, which dropped his shoulders, he turned back to face Jem, the light through the kitchen window caught the right profile of her face and he felt a pang of lust, she was so petite and so pretty, he was also certain, in his own warped mind, that under that uniform this was an energetic and sexually alive woman. "When will they know for sure, you know, whether they went down with the boat? There can be no real closure without bodies right; I don't care about the girl, don't mean to be cold but I do not even know who she could be, but I would like to put an end to this family tragedy, I can bury my family and move on, once and for all."

"That's not cold sir, I understand fully." Jem responded. "We, as of yet, have no idea who the girl is either, we just have the vague description of the staff from the Boat House restaurant to go on, and as of yet we have no reports of a missing person matching her description." She continued to be business like, brusque even, still with, she hoped, the right amount of tender support. Jacob was not the only one who could act. For a minute or two, in silence, they sipped their tea; it gave Jem a further chance to study this obnoxious man. A man she considered, to be her opponent. It was reminiscent of a tennis match where the opponents sit either side of the umpires chair sipping their energy boosting drinks and planning their next move, the ace serve, the hard returned volley.

While Gem considered how to trip him up and gain a confession, or even a minor tongue slip of information, Jacob took the chance to plan how best to make his move on what he perceived as a naïve girl.

From the pocket of her trousers Jem felt her mobile phone, set on silent, vibrate; it would usually be clipped to the left breast pocket of her stab vest and she wished she was wearing it now, she felt naked and unprotected without it. DS Kaan had insisted she wear the vest but she thought as a liaison officer it would look odd, and maybe even a little aggressive, if she were to gain Jacob Tubb's confidence and reluctantly the DS had to agree but with some trepidation and he gave his okay to the move. The phone continued to vibrate and she slid it from her pocket and checked the screen.

"Would you excuse me while I take this, it's my control room and it may be news about your brother." Without waiting for a response she stepped from the kitchen into the hallway. "Guv…" Jacob heard her answer the phone and used that moment to pour the rest of the disgusting tea down the sink, he rinsed the cup, as well as the chrome sink, to hide his wasteful sin. He rounded the breakfast bar and reclaimed his stool at the same time as Jem stepped back into the kitchen, Jacob failed to discern her demeanour; suddenly she was a closed book, something was going on! He could feel it.

"No news I am afraid Jacob, they were just checking there was nothing new at this end."

"New at this end? Why would there be anything new, at this end?" Annoyance filled his voice, his eyes quickly began to glare with anger, he was walking a fine line and he knew it, losing control bothered Jacob, he had to rein his ire in.

"Well we have to check every line of enquiry we can, you said so yourself when the search first began. If your brother, had somehow escaped the boat, or even not been on it to start with, he may have contacted the house." She was struggling to keep the story straight and Jacob happy with her being there in his kitchen, especially following what she had been told on the phone.

At the same time as Lucas had woken when the red Volvo had crunched onto the gravel driveway of Nathaniel and Pauline's country home, something had clicked in the mental filing cabinet that was Kobie Kaan's mind. The thing that had been bothering and annoying him, the one piece of evidence that was eluding him. It had been stored away somewhere and refused to budge, but like a name on the tip of the tongue, when you stop thinking on it, it suddenly appears, when least expected, in bold neon lights.

That name he mentally sought, the snippet that would change his thinking, had leapt out at him as if it had been waiting to ambush his thoughts, the neon lights of memory had flashed and blinked, brightening what before had been darkness. The chase and the boat crash had refocused his thoughts and when he least expected it, there it was, as bright as day.

Following the phone call Jem knew she had to stall for an hour or two while DS Kaan raced back from Dorset Police Headquarters on the outskirts of Wimborne; she knew he would be blue lighting it all the way back to West Sussex. With the new information on its way she wished even more she had put her stab vest on; it was too late now and would be too suspicious if she did. Risk was part of the job, but fear was not, and right now she was frightened, scared but determined; this was her job, what she had joined the force for; that buzz of being a police officer. She also knew that her boss would have called for back-up, but even officers never knew how long it would be till a car was free to respond, especially on the hunch of an DS who was some sixty miles away at the time.

Reaching across the breakfast bar from where she stood, and knowing she was taking a huge chance, she took his right hand in her left, she meant it to be just inquisitive, Jacob took it to be a signal of affection. "Your ring, it is so unique, is it the one that Lucas used to wear, I recall seeing it in photos from the original case." As she spoke she knew her approach on the subject had been clumsy.

"No, Lucas had his own, they were designed by the old man for our eighteenth birthdays. We both have one."

Chapter 29

The exterior of the house was bright pink, every wall, bright, glaring, clean and fresh, pink! As if designed by a small girl infatuated with My Little Pony and Barbie dolls' bedroom, it was a shocking pink. Lucas could not believe the bad taste until he recalled his host was a bookie and sported a broad, handlebar moustache, maybe bad taste came with the territory.

"I know, bright isn't it?" Acknowledged Pauline as if reading his thoughts; she had walked around his side of the car and stood next to him.

"It's very…" Lucas stopped himself, not wanting to be rude to these people who were helping him.

"Pink; I know." She shrugged. "We moved here three years ago and each spring we have told ourselves to re-paint; but when we begin to plan, and we both think why, it was pink when we first saw the house and fell in love with it and its location, it was pink when we moved in, it's been pink for the three years we have lived here. I guess what I am saying is that we would never paint a house pink but we have grown to love it and its quirky colour, it sort of suits us."

"Mind you, with my skin that has not seen sun for a couple of years, and a day on a boat and naked on a beach, I think I may be that colour come morning." Lucas confessed.

"Ooh, a pink willy, what fun!" At her quip Lucas readily did turn pink; this time with embarrassment.

As she walked away toward the front door, hips swinging in an hypnotic way, the low early evening sun shone through Pauline's sarong making it transparent and showing of the gap in her thighs, for some reason Lucas found this far more of a sexual turn-on than when he had seen her, in all her naked glory, sitting cross-legged, back in the sand dunes; he began to understand a little more about Nate's defence that naturism was not about sex. His attention was immediately taken away from the silhouetted outline of Pauline's stunning body by a sharp pain in his ear lobe. As the fingertip and thumb squeezed hard, he cried out in pain. "Ow!"

He had not realised he was staring and had been caught. "Eyes off the competition mister, unless you want to lose valuable parts of your body." Gill was dragging him, ear first, toward the front door and from the new position of his twisted head all he could see were the pink painted eaves of the house.

"I was just looking…"

"Oh, I know what you were doing, and I am here to tell you to stop." Gill playfully continued to squeeze his ear lobe, Lucas continued to yelp in pain.

"Looking was he?" Nathaniel queried from across the bonnet of the Volvo without a hint of annoyance. "Don't worry Lucas, I find I cannot take my eyes off her either." He added.

"I didn't mean, I mean, I didn't realise I was being that obvious."

Gill enjoyed his discomfort and she continued to lead him by his ear toward the front entrance. Through the jet black and glossy door, as keenly painted and as black as the door to 10 Downing Street, the foursome gathered in the vast hallway where bags and towels were just dumped on the attractive tiled floor, a mosaic of colours and swirls, the furnishings and walls were mock-Victorian and cluttered with knick-knacks and pictures, a not un-pleasant sight and Lucas scanned very inch of it, taking in every picture, every mini sculpture and piece of porcelain; all the while hoping his punishment for staring was complete.

"Was he checking out my arse Gill?" Pauline now joined in the teasing and Lucas realised he was being mocked so raised his hands in surrender, his cheeks still red from blushing

"What a beautiful home." He said genuinely and in a successful attempt to change the subject and received thanks for his observation.

"I think after the thrills and spills of today a single malt is called for." Said a jovial Nate as he walked through a stripped pine, heavy, door into a comfortable room with leather wing armchairs and a highly ornate and dominant Chinese cabinet. It glowed with the low sheen of its highly lacquered surface and behind its brass hinged doors adorned with swirling dragons it housed the drinks. The room was softly lit by table lamps and one beautifully curved lamp that rose from floor to near ceiling, it looked so out of place with the other furnishings and yet, it suited, Lucas dated the lamp from somewhere in the seventies whereas everything else was Victorian, pre-war French and, of course, that dominant Chinese cabinet with its brass handles and curling dragons in gold relief. It was a mishmash of styles and yet tasteful and relaxing; like its owners, full of character. Over the ornate fireplace of tiles and dark wood surround, there was an imposing portrait of Pauline in ball gown and pearls.

"Pour me one will you Hun, I am going for a quick shower." Pauline disappeared from the room and Gill asked for a gin and tonic.

"Malt for you Lucas?" Enquired Nathaniel who had already begun to pour three malts without checking for a response; Lucas was happy with the choice as the amber liquid splashed in the base of a weighty looking crystal tumbler.

Chapter 30

"When will we know if they have found the bodies?" Jacob asked, while sidling round the breakfast bar to get closer to the WPC. The touch of her hand as she had reached for his ring finger offering him encouragement.

"Well, that was one of the things my Governor wanted to explain when he was on the phone." She responded while bracing herself to push Jacob away should he get any closer. "The thing is, and you may not have heard with everything else going on, a small child has gone missing in Dorset and the DS let me know that all their divers have now been diverted away from the Studland Bay search and are being used in local rivers and lakes to search for the little girl. As with any missing child they know they only have a small window of time if they hope to find her alive, and so all their efforts are going into finding the living. With no sign or expectation of survivors our case I am afraid is taking a weak second place."

Jacob wanted to rage, needed to vent his anger, finding Lucas at the bottom of Studland Bay would clear him of any wrongdoing, once he was declared dead the case would be closed; a delay, any delay, would make things harder. It was tough, to hold back, to still his temper, not to let any sign of rage show, hard to keep a straight face, in order to keep his story intact.

To help keep composure he leant down, placing his elbows on the breakfast bar, his shoulder gently brushing against Jem's upper arm; he felt another small spark of excitement. In contrast Jem felt her skin crawl, goose-bumps and not the nice variety, covered the bare skin on her forearms, she doubted it, but hoped the touch was accidental. Again she wished she had donned her protective stab vest, instead it remained useless in the boot of the car, along with her utility belt and asp, the extendable baton modern police use in place of the old fashioned truncheon, she felt vulnerable and as each minute passed began to feel more and more that she was in harm's way.

By twisting on her stool and turning slightly to face him she removed her arm from his glancing touch; while lifting her foot and placing it on the rung of the stool she raised her knee to form a slim barrier; Jem tried to make the movement as natural as possible without alienating Jacob, her body language screaming self-protection. "Is there anything I can get you, something to eat maybe while we wait?" It was defensive waffle but she was fast feeling out of her depth and beginning to flounder.

Jacob in response placed his hand on the nape of her neck, on the flesh that showed beneath her hair, the gap in her shirt between neck and collar. "I think we both know what is happening here, don't we?" He almost whispered, it was what he called his sex voice, Jem would have called it frightening; a cold shiver of sweat trickled down and tickled her spine; it was not a comfortable feeling.

Placing her hand around his wrist she was about to stand and twist it into an arm-lock. Training taught her to make the move in one fluid movement. She spoke firmly to try and calm the situation and to make her assailant, for that was how his advances felt, understand as she feared she may have inadvertently given out mixed messages. "This is inappropriate Jacob, sex is not on the cards here. I am just doing my job so please remove your hand!"

Instead of the expected response of his hand being taken away she was shocked when suddenly the grip tightened; Jacob clenched hard on the muscles of her neck; the speed from caress to violence shocked her but that surprise lasted just a split second as he shoved hard with the strength of a madman and forced her head down with great velocity, the delicate features of Jem's face were smashed down onto the cold marble surface of the worktop, was held there. The work surface was hard, it was rock, and at the moment of impact the bone in her nose broke, shattered, she could feel the shards part and splinter, the cartilage drove upward splitting blood vessels and through the pain she could feel the warm gore flow over her top lip, and into her mouth, she began to swallow blood. If there was a cry of pain she never heard it or realised it, there was just the fog of extreme physical trauma.

Jacob never uttered a word, and it increased her fear factor tenfold, as he continued to grip her neck in a vice-like hold, her delicate flesh pressed hard into the cold marble. As suddenly as he had driven her face downward he now lifted her head from the worktop, bright, red, blood dripping down onto the hard surface thickened by mucus, globules of warm blood dropping onto cold marble, her nose crushed against her face. He held it for a second, examined the damage as an engineer checking for faults, held her neck just long enough for Jem to see through her blurred vision the hate and venom in her assailants eyes. In turn Jacob could see the fear and shock in her green eyes, and he could see his own reflection in the emerald pools. It heightened the sexual urge he was getting from the violence.

Again he pushed with all his power, drove her head down once more, Jem's eyes now watching the swift ascent of the hard surface, unable to do anything about it. Despite the speed of the action she saw it in slow-motion, like a movie. Her face and nose once again driven into the unforgiving marble. The blood already spilled now mixed with new blood as her nose flattened against her face, she felt something give around her eye sockets as more bones splintered, unconsciousness wavered tried to find a hold, but did not find her.

"You thought I wanted to seduce you, you sanctimonious, stuck up little bitch, if I wanted you I would just take you; a rough fuck is all you are worth. And I still might unless you tell me what Mr DS bloody Kaan wanted, what sort of name is that anyway is he one of those fucking Muslims? What did he say when he phoned, what did he want to know about my ring for?"

Jem needed to respond, but bitter, metallic flavoured blood flooded her mouth choking her as she tried to swallow it or spit it out, tried to talk but her lips were split, sore, and she could not spit. Blood continued to seep from her damaged face and mouth, part from her wrecked nose but now from the second source as much of it poured through a split top lip where her front teeth had been driven through the soft flesh. Her teeth felt loose as her tongue, almost bitten in half by the impact, brushed across them.

She tried to speak but merely uttered a groan, she felt a small piece of something soft drifting around her mouth, it took a moment for her to realise it was the tip of her tongue which was hanging by a loose thread of flesh, separated as her teeth were slammed shut on impact. Pain flooded every part of her head and she was almost unaware of her body that hung limply from the counter, her arms useless, her legs soft jelly that had no hope of holding her up, only Jacob's grip was keeping her from crumpling to the floor; he was holding her there with the weight of his hand on the back of her neck, a warm blooded human noose.

"Suddenly nothing to say bitch!" Spittle flew from his mouth onto the back of her head and stuck in her black hair which was becoming clogged with drying blood. Clear snot, dribbled from his nose, his entire being was wrapped in rage and as he held the damaged girl he felt his cock harden; he was finding the experience erotic and stimulating. God it was good to be so powerful. Maybe a good fucking that would make her talk and tell him what he needed to know!

Leaning against her, she was trapped between him and the counter top. Jacob with his free hand reached round his victim and gripped the, no-longer, white uniform shirt. With one sharp tug it tore away from the front of her body, another tug and it was pulled down her arms to her wrists, trapping her hands together as well as any pair of handcuffs would; not that she could have fought back, even if she had wanted to. He noted for the first time that Jem could have had mixed blood as the skin of her back was the colour of latte. With her make-up and the contrast between bright white shirts and slightly dark skin, he just assumed she was olive toned, that sudden awareness excited him further and he felt his cock fighting to push its way from his clothes.

"A Paki, you are fucking Paki..." his voice joyful "It's been a while since

I had one of your kind, I am going to enjoy this. Unless you have something to tell me about that phone call." In her haze of pain there was no response, Jem tried to clear her head, she did not want to die, and she certainly did not want this animal inside her. Through the agony she tried to speak, knowing that any words she could utter would delay his attack and hopefully save her life, but nothing apart from painful squeaks were forthcoming; her damaged mouth and tongue refused to form coherent words.

His free hand once again reached round her body and this time he merely pulled her bra cups down from her tiny breasts, the material too strong and well made to give way, even with his anger pulling at the cups. He felt the lacy surround and smiled a wicked grin. Even above the waves of pain that kept rolling across her face she yelped as he gripped and twisted her breast, the dark nipple held tight between thumb and forefinger, he pulled it, twisted and revelled in the softness of her skin giving way to his lust.

Bravery comes in many forms, sometimes it gives physical strength, the power to overcome any trial, but other times heroism comes as a silent power which makes the subject find an inner strength, a power beyond their immediate surroundings and Jem found that now. It would mean succumbing to his onslaught, to his deviant sexual assault and to the beating she knew would end her life – the one thing she would not give this animal was the perverse pleasure of hearing her suffer. As he once more tore at the flesh of her tiny breast, twisting, almost ripping the nipple away, she offered no sound, no murmur of pain, no bodily reaction. Jem shut down her mind, and half lay across the cold marble of the worktop, that chill, hard, material offering her no solace and comfort, nor something to attune her mind to as Jacob ended her short life.

"Anything yet bitch!"

Jem, knew she had little time left. She knew she was about to be raped, and she knew through the pain and without doubt, that she could no longer stall for time; she would be dead by the time the DS arrived at the house, she knew it was a long drive from Wimborne to Chichester. Self-preservation was not an option any more, but the thought of holding on to, at least some of, her dignity was kicking in over the pain.

While he was busy groping and pulling at her intimate parts Jem allowed one arm to drop by her side, the hand snaking into her trouser pocket, fingers fumbling with the mobile phone, her thumb hitting buttons, in the hope they would be the right ones. On the M27, eastbound side, Kobie Kaan heard his phone play his favourite Ry Cooder tune, the harsh blues guitar drifting in and filling the cockpit of the car. He hit the phone button on the steering wheel with his thumb. "DS Kaan." There was no response but through the car speakers he could hear what he thought was the ranting tone of Jacob Tubb's voice. He checked the screen and noted it was Jem calling him; his foot pressed a little harder on the throttle pedal.

As an incensed and aroused Jacob pulled at her body and flesh she went from victim to police officer, she tried to act like an officer and stall proceedings until help arrived. "The wing, it's your wing!" She tried to form the words but her damaged tongue, broken teeth and split lip would not form her 'R's properly. Every uttered word was agony; but Jacob would not know that.

Power, of sorts, flowed through her body, Jem was now invincible and unbeatable, beyond true pain now, there was nothing he could do to defeat her.

With one hand still on her neck, pushing her face ever harder into the marble surface, and the other still gripping her breast in a vice like grip that was forcing his sharp finger nails into the soft flesh, blood appearing around the arched indentations, he bent his head low to her ear. The vile whispering and taunting voice again, spittle wet her lobe. "The wing, the wing? What the fuck you talking about girl? Oh, you mean my ring, what is it about my ring that is so fucking important?"

Forty miles away the question was heard in the car. Kobie screamed at the consul where the phone symbol and Jem's number were being advertised.

Every sound muffled he heard her as she drew in a large breath, the inrush of air passed over the open nerves of a broken tooth and another shock of pain hit her senses, although she showed nothing to her assailant.

Jem ignored the searing pain. "It wath bothering the D Eth." She lisped. "The woundth on both the girl and Annie were thimilar, the cutth on their cheeks, and he thought that it was the thame wing that cauthed it." Jacob was straining to decipher the words, but he was getting the gist, but why should the ring cause confusion. Every moment of time, every pause in the attack, meant that the DS was one mile closer, she may survive this yet! The DS in his onward rush had the premonition that it would not end well.

"What about the ring, what difference does it make?" Reluctantly removing the hand from her breast he twisted and pushed her head back down in her own blood and mucus on the counter, she felt the warm fluid touch and then enter her ear.

"Mmmth..." Pushing too hard it stopped her talking and so he eased the pressure a little so she could speak again. "Thomethin bugged him and today he remembered that Lucath wing wath thtill in evidenth. Yourth wath the only wing it could have been that thplit Annie'th cheek open." Slowly she exhaled, let the breath ease from her body, tried to relax and rise once again above the pain, and, hoped the information would placate him and send him on the run, leaving her with a small chance of staying alive. "You are done," A deep breath knowing that baiting him it may be her last. "You murdering bastard!" It took all her remaining mental strength to utter the last few words as if nothing were wrong with her mouth; she relaxed, empty and unafraid with the knowledge her time was done.

"Good girl." Uttered Kobie, still 35 miles from the rescue. "Stand up to the bastard, I am on my way." He said knowing she could not hear him.

With the miles being stretched between Kobie Kaan and his escaped lunatic as he headed back eastward along the coastal motorway Lucas was settling into life in the lurid pink house and he sipped on his third malt, his mind and body now nicely numbed to the exertions and worries of the last few days. He had wanted to watch the news, only to discover that this odd, but lovely, couple did not own a TV, preferring each other's company, fine music and a wonderful library of books. Nobody thought of turning the radio on as Barbers Adagio for Strings was floating from the record player, the black disc of vinyl turning hypnotically at 33 (and a third) rpm and adding to the mellow atmosphere that pervaded the room. Nate had admitted to trying an I-player, just the once, and that somewhere in drawer, abandoned, it now lay waiting for him to catch up to the 21st Century, but he preferred the crackle and scratch of vinyl, and he sure had a wide and varied collection of LPs.

They didn't know it of course, what with the violent world at large being left back on a sandy beach, but as they relaxed and chatted about nothing in particular, a pretty young police officer's looks were being destroyed as her face was being firmly planted, repeatedly, into a marble counter top.

Blissfully unaware of what was happening in that ferocious real world two counties away they had been sipping finest Talisker Malt Whisky while listening to varied and great music, now it was the turn of a rock classic from Pink Floyd, the familiar opening notes, the distinctive and plaintive cry of Dave Gilmour's guitar drifting from the speakers and filling the room, The Dark Side of the Moon.

Pauline, who now sat in a wing armchair, hair wet and hanging loose, dressed in short denim shorts and a loose T-shirt, professed that Talisker because of its smoky, malt flavour and slight saltiness was perfect sprinkled, not too liberally, over fish and chips. Nate had nodded in agreement and added that they would prove it sometime in the next few days when everyone was in the mood for such a feast. Lucas could not believe they would be pouring such a glorious nectar over fish and chips!

Feeling totally relaxed, and not a little drunk, Lucas' eyes began to droop, the lids closing of their own volition, despite his attempts to keep them open, his head dropping forward, the neck no longer with the strength to hold it up. The lazy cries of the guitar, the warm hugs of the malt whisky and his head nodded down, suddenly, its involuntary drop to his chest brought him back to the conversation. Gill was talking to him. She was sat on the floor at his feet, her elbow resting over his knees, head resting in his lap.

"You smell." It was a casual comment, spoken quietly but loud enough for the room to hear. Nate and Pauline looked at each other and smiled, recognising the same comfortable air that was shared between the two of them.

"What, I don't!" Lucas was shocked, and now awake. "Do I?" He asked with a hint of pity in his voice and sniffing in an attempt to capture the odour for himself. A yawn escaped, forcing his mouth wide open.

"Baby, it been a tough couple of days and we left Cowes with such panic in our hearts, we both forgot to shower. Adrenaline smells, you know, and a quick dip in the sea does not constitute a bath."

Pauline saved the day and the embarrassment. "Actually, you both niff a bit, and we have kept you up long enough, we can all catch up again over breakfast, unless you two have become addicted to being on the run and want to sneak out before Nate and I are up."

Lucas realised the sunlight that had earlier bathed the garden with is end of day golden hues had all but disappeared and through the window now stood nothing but darkening shadows. "Not sure if I am pissed or just exhausted, but a shower and a comfortable bed does sound like a good idea." Lucas ran his fingers, slowly and affectionately, through Gill's hair as he spoke, a second unstoppable yawn proved the point, Gill swiftly followed with an infectious, wide mouthed, yawn of her own.

Nathaniel told them that there was an en-suite to their room with a gorgeously deep bath. "I often use it myself as its one of those lovely claw-footed, roll-top baths; we picked it up for a song at an auction." He added.

With the goodnights, and genuine heartfelt thanks, said and hand in hand, still each with a tumbler of Talisker only half drunk in their free hands, they wearily climbed the stairs for an early night. Dusk was still a slightly distant ally, shadowed areas were bathed in grey but some late remnants of evening sunlight still poured through the south facing window and lit the bedroom with a golden, reddish hue. Lucas sat on the bed while Gill ran the bath, the sound of running water further relaxing him, easing the stress even before thinking of lowering his body into the deep, hot water.

With uncontrolled sadness he felt himself begin to cry, sudden tears, unstoppable, ran down his cheeks. He bowed forward and hung his head in the palms of his hands his body shuddered, wracked with mental anguish. On leaving the bathroom Gill saw him shaking with sobs and rushed to sit at his side; climbed onto the bed behind him and keeling wrapped an arm of comfort around his shoulders and neck. Her head pulled in close to the nape of his pink skinned neck.

"Lucas, Lucas, what is it, Baby?" He kept his head buried his head into his cupped hands, tried to speak, but just gasped for air as the sobs grew heavier and gave up. He just let it all go, releasing all the emotions that had been imprisoned within him for so long! Incarceration was a state of mind as well as a restriction on the movement of the physical being.

Chapter 31

In the White House, behind the pretty picket fence, it had become a tableau, a moment frozen in time. Jem attempted to slide out from beneath the hand that held her down while he was distracted with thought; but, despite his lack of awareness of the moment his grip and hold remained firm. From the corner of her bruised and bloodshot right eye, the left one had swollen and closed with the second blow of face to counter, she saw the puddle of blood from her nose continue to spread, oozing out in a lake of crimson, an ever-growing dark tide across the counter top. The calmness that now coursed through her body came as a surprise as did her clarity of thought; it was as if the pain had become its own anaesthetic. She wanted to speak, to become her own hostage negotiator, but the effort was too painful and with the damage to her mouth she knew any further words would be incoherent, she had let loose the last of her words on that final insult; and hoped that someone on the other end had heard something, anything.

From the wild, loud ranting and threats just a minute or two before, Jacob suddenly had a calmness about him. Time had slowed for assailant and victim. The urgency of the attack may have diminished but the venom of the assault was about to increase.

"I suppose I am buggered now, whatever happens." Jacob said with calmness, as if ordering food from a menu.

Thirty miles away, and still getting closer, Kobie muttered, "Keep your hands of my officer you bastard." A voice only heard by the car's hidden microphone.

Jacob's calmly spoken statement and the momentary stillness of her crazed attacker scared Jem more than anything that had gone before, it was more threatening and, without any doubt now, potentially lethal for her. There was a finality to the tone. Any hope that he would just walk away and leave her to slide to the floor quickly fell from her thoughts as she felt an arm snake around her waist, felt his fingers begin to fumble with her belt buckle. The two ends of the belt fell free and as if watching a silent movie she watched, in her mind's eye, as he unbuttoned her waistband, pulled down the zip on her black uniform trousers. With her arm still dangling at her side after engaging the phone she tried to claw his hands away from her clothes, but there was no strength left in her grip and Jacob brushed it to one side with ease.

Jem's face was still lying in her own, ever growing, pool of blood, and mucus, and she could feel her body losing strength as it lost more of life's essential fluid, Jacob's left hand still held her head down firmly by the nape of her neck, and with her weight being left on her neck that was beginning to become the most painful part of her body. The right hand meanwhile was busy dragging the loose trousers, and her pale blue boxer shorts, down over her buttocks, she had always preferred boxers while working, thongs were for off duty. Once free of waist and hips they slid down her thighs, there came the clear realisation for Jem of what was about to happen, she had guessed this was his aim, but until now her muddled mind had refused to accept it as fact. She wanted to scream, more than anything she wanted to vent her rage with a blood curdling screech, but no sound, apart from a muffled groan that she could not hold back, came from her. She would not give him the satisfaction of hearing her scream, of vocalising her fear and dread! Even if she had screamed, there was no one to hear, except her DS who was still 28 miles away.

"If I am done for, then I may as well enjoy my final moments." Again the calmness in the voice was terrifying, she could hear that Jacob was smiling. The whispered, confident menace was always more effective than the shouted threat. Jacob held her firm to the counter but he took just half a step away to make room for his hand. From somewhere he heard someone curse him, he was not sure if he had imagined the voice or not – there it was again. The muffled voice was coming from her trouser pocket and he let her go for a second while he reached down to the material crumpled around her ankles; discovered the phone, and spoke into it.

"Ah, DS Kaan, on the way to the rescue" The voice gloating. "Too late Kobie Kaan, wherever you are you are too late!"

Kobie thumped the steering wheel with frustration, knowing that Jacob had spoken the truth.

In the kitchen 25 miles away, Jacob dropped the phone to the flagstone floor and stomped on its glass face, smashing case and internal works.

He reached back for Jem as she began to slide to the floor, he caught her by her short black hair, and the furtive fumbling was gone and a strong hand just tore the boxer shorts away from her body; Jem had always found that style of underwear more comfortable under her uniform, sexy at work was not an option. It took two rough, strong tugs to get them hanging from one thigh, her skin burned where the material had rubbed so violently. The extra pain was fine by her, because every new area of discomfort took thought away from her forthcoming trauma, she used the pain as a target for meditative thoughts. Jem concentrated on just breathing, even and deep breaths, keeping sanity and staying alive her foremost thoughts.

"I thought you had begun to fancy me, thought I was in with a chance, but you were just a teasing bitch, well maybe this will teach you not to use your sex to get what you want." She had not realised, or felt anything, as he had undone his own trousers, but she soon knew as he roughly entered her, his hard cock forcing its way in. No foreplay, no romance, no kind words or affection, it was just a brutal thrusting, she was dry, tense and his erection tore at the delicate skin. Jem tried to block out the physical pain but there was no way of hiding the mental anguish, she felt blood begin its tickling and trickling path down along her thigh, concentrating on the warm river.

After that first, hard, forced entry, she also felt wetness from his drooling mouth drip onto her back, drops of shuddering warmth on cold skin, Jem managed to take her mind to a far-away place where it never rained, where sun played on her pale skin and darkened it to a gorgeous tan, thankfully she no longer felt anything in the harsh brutality of the real world; mentally or physically, she was on a beach in Barbados, a place where she had enjoyed her last holiday laying in the sun and windsurfing across the reef into azure blue seas.

The only true sensation left was the feeling of her body rocking rubbing against the marble, now puddled with her sweat. Pushed forward with each thrust against the breakfast bar. In her numbness she could still, just, feel the broken bones in her face grinding together with each forceful drive forward as it was rubbed into the hard stone, sliding easily in the greasiness of her blood. Her mind had shut down, closed out the assault, her ears, with the trauma of the rape, had closed themselves to sound, apart from the whisper of wind in the bright coloured sail of her sailboard and the waves as the sped underneath the fibreglass plank, she heard the sound of rushing waves through an imagined conch shell held close to the ear. Her one good eye continued to watch and concentrate on the pool of blood that reflected the sparkling, star shaped reflections of the overhead kitchen lights; but what Jem saw was a shimmering dark pool of water at night, a sky full of stars dancing with their reflections in the spreading pool, the flash of green across the surface of a darkened sea as the sun set beyond a perfect horizon. Jacob, grunted and thrust into what was essentially a dead body, Jem offered no response.

*

Lucas had closed his eyes, but despite his, almost, overwhelming tiredness, sleep was avoiding him, thankfully he thought, as the warm bathwater embraced and soothed his aching body. Sliding down into the glorious depth of the Victorian roll-topped bath, the bubble covered water just an inch or two from the creamy coloured roll of enamel that gave the bath its name, Lucas enjoyed the feel of the water as the heat rippled around his neck, cool bubbles glancing against the underside of his chin.

"Are you going to keep the beard?" Gill's voice as soft, sensual and inviting as the suds that covered his body. He had not thought about its future, even forgotten that he had not shaved in days. "I rather like it, makes you look ruggedly handsome." She added as she stroked his hirsute cheek with her hand.

Lucas replied without opening his eyes. "I am ruggedly handsome with or without it." He boasted.

"Well you might have been before you got so pudgy, but now, not so sure." No offence was given and none was taken, he merely smiled under the gentle stroking that his face was receiving from the woman who sat, naked in readiness for her own bath, on the rolled edge. He was enjoying the affection as his body relaxed even further into the tub, he could feel his aches and pains drifting to the bubbly surface, the tension being washed away, freeing itself from his body; and his mind, drowsy with fatigue and the warmth of the bathwater, washed away some of the negative cares of the last year or so. If not for the trouble that he knew awaited in the world outside the garish pink house he would have felt truly happy and content; Gill had that effect on him. Well her, and the dual but distinctive warms of malt whisky and hot baths!

Gill was beginning to have another effect and she had noticed it the same time as he felt it. The hand stroking his face disappeared, the touch missed by its absence the moment the hand moved away. That feeling soon passed as he felt that same hand stroke down his thigh, which because of his height, and bent legs, stayed above the bubbly surface. Gill's hand slowly but surely dipped below the surface of the water and reached his groin, cupped his balls, gently, for just a second before releasing, much to Lucas' disappointment, but then it ran down the other thigh and repeated the ball cupping; the smile returning to his face.

Lucas fought his fatigue with all his being he wanted to remain awake for this, he felt her hand stroke the length of his hardness, once, twice, she picked up the soap tablet and rubbing it, filled her hands with suds before once again stroking and washing his erection...

Then he felt no more, not until her soft voice, and the hand shaking his shoulder, made him aware that the water had cooled and was no longer offering that comfortable warmth and bonhomie that only a hot bath can supply... his disappointment palpable.

"Well, is that the sort of compliment a girl gets when she begins her best bathroom seduction technique?" She feigned hurt in her expression, it fooled no one. But, he apologised anyway. "Come on you, out of the bath and into bed, I think we could both do with some sleep." Gill said stating the obvious.

Lucas apologised again. "I am sorry, you wanted a bath as well and now I have let it get cold."

Gill explained that once he had nodded off she had gone along the hallway and had a shower, it was then Lucas noticed she was wrapped in a cream towel that not only emphasised her tan, but also heightened her shape and sexuality. "I like you in just a towel, it's sexy."

"Half asleep and totally knackered and you still think smooth talking will win me over!" The towel was hoisted up slightly to keep her breasts under cover, the coyness wasted as it only served to make the other end ride further up her legs and display even more of her body. Lucas just smiled.

"Shame, I thought the smooth one-liners would work for me." His eyes devoured, in a nice way, her towel wrapped body.

"Oh, they did, but I just want you to think that you have to work harder." She gave him her coyest expression.

Hands gripping the rolled edges he lifted himself from the cooling water, the last remnants of bubbles sliding down his skin, and he stepped from the bath and stood on the bath mat, water dripping from his no-longer aching body. Gill had the towel ready for him and he just stood there, conscious of his slightly pot belly and frighteningly, he noted, the beginnings of 'man-boobs'. "I am growing tits, damn it!" He hoisted the man-flesh in the palms of his hands.

"Don't worry, I have spare bras and we can go underwear shopping together now, cool!" In reality she seemed not to notice his, supposed faults as she rubbed his body dry, lifting his arms as a mother would a child to dry the pits, first one then the other.

"Taking the piss, right!" Lucas shook his head, knowing when he was beaten by a smarter person.

Then as she worked her way down his body Lucas parted his feet slightly so she could dry his crotch, enjoying the sensation of roughish towel on delicate parts, as she did so. Finally she knelt before him and dried his legs, his mind thought, but his mouth kept it to himself, 'while you are there', and as if having read mind read he saw her dip her head forward. Gill merely kissed the tip of his flaccid penis and said; "That's all you're getting." Before flouncing out of the bathroom and leaving him standing there imagining what might have been.

By the time he had walked past her towel, now abandoned on the stripped oak floorboards, and reached the side of the bed she was already under the luxurious deep quilt. Gill held the corner up on his side of the bed, inviting him in. He was surprised that they had already determined, without consultation, whose side of the bed belonged to who. He climbed onto the deep, soft mattress. He lay beside her, they folded their bodies together, legs wrapped around thighs, skin on skin, warmth against warmth, protected, comfortable, both enjoying a feeling of permanence and safety.

Further thought alluded both of them as sleep swiftly took over. Gill just had time to hear the soft, husky and even breaths of Lucas before she too succumbed to sleep.

As they slept and held each other close just a few miles from the protection of the bright walls of the pink house a small girl, frightened and alone, apart from a grey furry rabbit, its head flopped to one side with its stitched smile hidden by darkness and a coating of mud, curled up in a derelict brick shack and shivered with both cold and fear. Every noise and screech of nature after dark terrifying her so much that sleep would not find her that night.

The shivering went on unabated, uncontrollable as she tried to let sleep claim her. Every ghostly rustle of the undergrowth, hoot of an owl and sharp squeal of distant fox cubs terrified her; but still she did not cry. Any tears had been used up over the past two nights of being abandoned and lost in deep woods, too frightened to venture out of the 'house' she had discovered that first night as darkness fell. She cuddled Bunny, he in return offered little comfort, apart from the stitched and permanent smile.

Chapter 32

Of the lost people that night Jem, more than any, longed for the peaceful release of sleep, or any form of unconsciousness to overtake her. When Jacob had finished with her, withdrew his flaccid member from within her body, she had no idea how long ago that had been, he had just let her go, withdrew from her, letting his wilting cock just 'pop' from her body before stepping back, releasing her bruised neck, and letting her slide to the floor, her ruined mouth clashing, once more, with the edge of the worktop, another tooth breaking on the marble edge but pain now something she welcomed as it meant she was alive.

Just for good measure as she crumpled into a bloody, damaged heap, he had planted one more vicious, unnecessary kick into her midriff. He did it just for the pleasure as he wiped traces of her blood from his cock in a handy tea towel, before straightening his clothes and re-zipping up his pants.

Jem had no way of knowing if it had been said out loud, or just a strong thought deep in her mind, a mind that was now as damaged as her body felt. "You have no way of getting away with this now, there is nowhere to go Jacob."

There was a hope, of course, that it had just been a mental note and not a spoken fact. That, she was sure, would have been a death sentence or at least invited another blow from his smart deck shoes, which now sported her drying blood.

Although as she mentally travelled the length her body in an attempt to find a small part of her physical being that did not hurt so she could focus on that, she knew that death would be a quick release from the suffering and torment she felt. Violated, beaten, the damage done was not like a bruise or a cut that would heal and not feel so bad tomorrow, it could not be kissed better or soothed with comforting words. A bandage or a plaster may hide the cuts, broken bones would mend, even if slowly, but damaged goods would always be damaged goods and people, even good people, could not be returned to the factory for an exchange, people came with no guarantee to last a lifetime. Plus when others looked at damaged people, they could only see the devastation, they would not see the woman still locked within. At that moment in time Jem believed she was broken beyond repair!

Under the haze of earned self-pity, shrouding her like a sea-mist rolling in from offshore to hide the coast from view, and self-recrimination she thought she heard a car door slam, its thump resonating through the empty and quiet cottage, Jacob was getting away. Holding onto the rungs of the stool, where, it seemed, just a short while ago she had been sitting sipping tea, she tried to lift herself up. The pain as a broken rib dug into her vital organs was excruciating, she screamed, the opening of her mouth throwing new pains into her head, the intake of breath across broken teeth agonising, and flopped back onto the floor which drove another sharp pain up through her core. Up or down it mattered not, everything hurt. Weakened and frightened, she shuddered when another lightening blow of pain accompanied the stress in her body as it tensed on hearing the front door crash back on its hinges.

"HELLO, this is the police; Jacob Tubb please show yourself." It was shouted, harsh, urgent, bellowing through the house like a lions' roar across an empty African landscape, but it was the best words she had ever heard. She tried to respond but there was nothing left, no strength, no willpower. Now she heard footsteps.

"Jem, Jesus, Jem." Out of her one good eye she saw the sensible black shoes of a copper who enjoyed comfort on his feet stop beside her.

She felt comforting hands just touch her arm, and there was the realisation that bit did not hurt, he could hold that one small area all he wanted, at last a touch of comfort and not violence. Recognition struck home, DS Kaan, a little late but better late than never. "Kobie?" she whispered with her broken mouth. "Is that you Guv?"

Blood had caked on the lid of her one good eye, making it difficult to blink and she had trouble opening it fully. Through the haze she saw his face, and even though blurred, and it was the best face she had ever seen, his dark features and friendly eyes telling her that she was safe from any more damage.

Soothing words followed amid promises of an ambulance and the fact that everything would be alright, she was safe now, she heard the words but could not form them into anything coherent as he phoned for support and an ambulance, experience kept panic out of his voice although his heart pounded and his thoughts for Jem were a jumble of friend, senior officer and just being a human and caring for someone close to death. In the midst of the pain she realised she had survived, she may be damaged, but she had beaten Jacob, she would live, he would get his comeuppance!

"I need you to tell me who did this Jem. Did Lucas do this to you?" With a calmness he did not feel, he asked the question; first and foremost he was a policeman and he had a job to do although every fibre was telling him to comfort first investigate second. He wanted to pull her trousers up to preserve her dignity but realised he would be tampering with a crime scene, and, so he sensibly thought, it may also hurt her or injure her more to move her, instead he took his jacket off and just lay it over the lower half of her body. Her hand reached out, for something, anything to hold, and Kobie took it, stroking her fingers with his thumb. For Jem the distraction felt really good, he had found another small part of her body that did not hurt.

Thinking on the question just asked of her, was that just a second or two ago, time was playing tricks. With a painful movement that took every ounce of remaining willpower she had, she moved her head from side to side, a firm 'no' to the inquiry. "Jacob?" and with the same restriction of movement and the same deliberate speed she nodded an affirmative. "Yeth, Jacob!" She answered, every simple movement of her mouth a knife to her nerve endings.

Sitting on the floor beside her, unconcerned with the blood that was staining his own trousers, but noting the blood that had already collected on his hand was now staining his pale blue shirt a light claret, he used his mobile to call for further help, to get everyone he had available and some of those that officially were not available, to search for one Jacob Tubb, wanted for the serious assault and the attempted murder of a fellow officer, there was no need to mention the sexual attack that had also obviously also taken place.

The viciousness of the beating would be enough to have every officer on the West Sussex force keen eyed and diligent in their search for Jacob Tubb. Kobie, whose face was normally one of a peaceful calmness, something that unnerved many an interview victim, now was riven with rage, his eyes dark and hooded, he no longer exuded the calm exterior he was well known for, anger; no rage, filled his very core.

The final words Jem heard, before she let herself go and allowed her mind to shut down completely in submission to the pain, were an apology from Kobie, "Sorry Jem, I should have got here sooner." She held no malice against her senior officer, she was just glad he had arrived, and made it while she was still alive, she did not have the strength to reply to him...

The combined might of the West Sussex police force need not have looked far for Jacob, he had not journeyed any distance or, for that fact, rushed to get there.

When he had finished his attack, his energy and anger spent, he had watched the once pretty WPC slide to the floor before pulling up his trousers and zipping them closed, as he cinched the belt, there was a pause as he felt that need to lay into her just one more time. He threw his right foot forward and planted in her side, he felt the ribs give and break through the thin leather of his stylish shoes; strangely that one last blow had given him no pleasure, he was done, he had fulfilled his desire for violence and lust; he had taken his desire to the extreme. With the main show over, the final chords played at the end of yet another encore, he realised he had not been left wanting more, his madness had been satiated, for now!

He wasn't sorry for the final kick, it needed to be done, it just did not please him in the way he had hoped.

Although she had not heard him he had muttered a goodbye. "Bye Jem, hope you recover soon." Violence satiated he had no desire to kill her. See, he was not all cold and unfeeling. One last look down at her beaten and bloodied body he strode from the kitchen and walked from the house, looked at his smart Range Rover that made the police car alongside it look even more insignificant and ridiculous, gazed at the police hatchback with its stupid blue light on the roof, thought for a moment about which one to take but then decided a walk would be better, it was a pleasant summer's evening and the fresh air would do him good. He followed the footpath back around the marina and as he crossed the familiar lock gate bridge one last time he failed to notice a cormorant dipping and diving below the waters of the canal for his piscine tea or the ducks that circled him quaking their displeasure at the larger bird's feeding habits.

On beyond the Boat House Café where he had enjoyed the odd meal or two and even enjoyed one of the waitresses who worked there. He looked down the vast basin of the marina and could see the empty berth where the Bonnie Annie would never be tied off again.

The lock gate that took vessels in and out of the marina was in the closed position and he strolled across it, taking time to look west and see the bright orb of a setting summer sun dipping toward its horizon, the lower the sun became so the temperature seemed to drop and he wished he had put a light jacket on.

Finally Jem had felt a calmness return as back in Jacob's kitchen she was rescued, in a sympathetic moment Jacob also now felt a calmness as he began his escape, his evasion of capture. Over the lock and the path worked its way around a dense portion of woodland where the shore of the narrowing harbour appeared and disappeared between gaps in the foliage. With the tide coming in the last few of the feathered and long legged waders searched for crustaceans in the shallows, their day of feeding would soon be done and they would return to their roost for the night, only for the searching and feeding to resume early tomorrow as the tide once more relented and uncovered the mud with its bountiful harvest.

He walked on, nobody paid him any heed, no one looked close enough to see the blood that stained his shirt, arms and trousers, and he ignored late walkers and strollers, this was a route not only for the confirmed rambler complete with heavy walking shoes and, incongruously, ski-poles and tiny rucksacks clipped firmly with shoulder and waist straps to their bodies, but also for families and those out for just an evening stroll. He absorbed the occasional 'good evening' and 'fine evening, isn't it?', none of them noted the dried blood staining clothes and shoes, and walked on without really catching anyone's eyes or attention.

Dusk was now taking over and no more walkers overtook him or walked past him, now was the time and this was the place.

Every road off the peninsula and leading back to Chichester were blocked, evening traffic took on the guise of the worst of holiday traffic combining with rush hour. The roads were a slow moving tailback of irritated drivers, angry passengers and the occasional reluctant car engine not wanting to continue with the treatment and boil over. Tempers too boiled over and only when reading the news at some time over the next 24 hours would those impatient souls behind the wheels of slow moving vehicles understand, such was the state of the world many would still not care as their journey home had been interrupted, but others would mourn the violence that now infected our everyday lives. While most would comprehend and sympathise, it would be sad to say many would also gloat and cheer over what had happened to that bloody copper, they all got what they deserved and for a brief moment, a very brief moment, and among the idiots of this world, Jacob Tubb would take on the mantel of hero; gain the same folk hero status as a Robin Hood, but without the good press!

Jacob would not hear the news though, would not be around to revel in his cult status or read the social media sites that would cheer on his bravery for fighting against the system and the man, he was not about to stumble into a road block or be caught in a house to house search. Nor would he sail through the exit from Chichester Harbour as the police, once bitten and twice shy by that route, had two boats blockading the route, causing an unusual tailback of leisure craft in and out of the harbour; some would miss the tide and be stranded, but that was just their bad luck.

With a calmness that Jacob had long wished for in his turbulent life he stood on the water's edge; breathing easily and deeply while taking in the stunning surroundings in the last light of day. He was stood at a favourite scenic spot, popular with dog walkers and ramblers, that looked north east to Dell Quay and south west to the pretty village of Bosham, where, it is said, that Canute told the waves to halt in an effort to show his followers that he was not infallible, but Jacob just looked across the water to the distance woodland shore his thoughts on anything but legend or history. A pair of white swans, brilliant white against the darkening sky flew past a few feet above the water's surface, their wings whumping through the air; their reflections flying in a mirror image across the darkening surface of the harbour's calm waters.

Jacob thought back on the last few weeks, he had always believed half the house should have been his, but finally he had got to live there; Master of the household! He had always wondered who his mother was, never suspecting that she and Annie were one and the same person, and he had always been jealous of his half-brother and his normal upbringing. Well he had suffered in the end and that pleased Jacob's warped mind, no end. And, finally, he had got to have his way with that pretty little police woman, he knew he would convince her to give in to his charms...

Jacob walked forward, his deck shoes quickly filling with the cold waters of the harbour and chilling his feet, for a brief instance the water felt painfully cold as it soaked through his jeans and bit at his legs, almost forcing him to turn back. But, the cold didn't matter, feelings of any sort would not matter any time soon. He walked on, fighting the muddy floor of the harbour bed as it tried to stick to his feet and obstruct his progress, he lost one shoe and then the other to the tug of the mud.

Then he was gone, swallowed by the cold, unstoppable, in-coming tide!

They would not find him for another two days, not until the fish had feasted on his body, and Jem would not be able to see him, through what would be her one remaining good eye, stand in a court and rue his actions.

Jacob Tubb had escaped.

Chapter 33

Sharp rapping on the bedroom door awoke them, echoing drum-like as a woodpecker deep in the woods hammering at a dead tree trunk, startled them both from the deep sleep they had been in, their bodies still wrapped in the position they had been the night before, they untangled their legs and quickly sat up, Gill without trouble but Lucas with an aching and unyielding body that needed to be forced into a seated position, it was as if his head was too heavy to leave the soft folds of the pillow. It was Nathaniel's voice, its tone carrying notes of urgency.

"Lucas, Gill, sorry to wake you guys but I think you need to hear the news." Pulling the quilt up to cover herself, which was a strange action Lucas thought for a naturist, Gill called out for Nate to come in.

The door creaked, its age showing, and the grey-haired head poked around its bleached wood. "The eight o'clock news has just been on the radio, it's nothing urgent and there is no one here looking for you, but there are some things you need to hear Lucas; come on down Pauline has some breakfast ready.

Thanks were offered and they both leapt from bed; Lucas too hyper to worry about a shower, so he just dressed in some old jeans of Nate's that were loose on him but stayed up with a pulled-tight belt, and the same T-shirt he had worn the evening before. Feeling a little sweaty and sticky from a night of close contact Gill dived in the shower but dressed while still a little damp and with wet hair cascading down the nape of her neck. Lucas waited patiently sitting on the edge of the bed; over the past 24 hours, or so, he seemed to have gained a new-found peacefulness in the world. He was hurrying nowhere, not for a while at least.

Both ready and with one last look into the others' eyes they headed down to the kitchen. On the Welsh dresser was a plate of still warm croissants, full, puffy and delicate; and a half filled jar of home produced marmalade. As soon as the couple had entered the oak beamed and low ceilinged room Pauline poured coffee. "Black or white?" She asked. Black was the double response.

"What is it, what's happened?" Lucas was desperate, the new-found patience with a short expiry date. Luck had gone his way so much over the past week or so, and so much had happened that fear gripped him that not only had his good fortune come to an end but also three lovely people would now suffer for helping him. He could not help but think that here had been too much misfortune caused to those surrounding him. The unnamed girl in the park, Drayton-Farlington from his fantasy world and into his one final heroic act, Gill with the love and trust she had given him, Annie with the ultimate sacrifice and now Nathaniel and Pauline who were harbouring an escaped lunatic with so much calm and unquestioned trust it humbled him. At that moment he even believed Jacob had suffered because of him.

They both greeted Pauline with a "Good morning." Lucas found it strange to note that they were both fully dressed, Nathaniel in a pair of heavy cord trousers and open necked white shirt, his feet still bare on the flagstone floor; Pauline in leggings and a baggy T-shirt, that still managed to highlight her small breasts through its thin material, and pair of thin espadrilles hugging her tiny feet.

"The news was just on, it's about the only time we listen to the radio, in the mornings." Nathaniel explained, but was hurried onto the story from Pauline who told him in no uncertain terms to stop waffling. "I'm getting there woman! Anyway, I am not sure if this is bad news or good news for you, but I am afraid Lucas, your brother has gone on the run and police have launched a massive manhunt for him."

"Jacob, why? What? Did they say, why Jacob?" His head was full of questions of who, what, why, how and when and Gill laid a comforting hand on his arm that also carried the note to let Nate continue with what he knew.

"It was not the main story, that little girl that is lost is still on everyone's minds, so I am not sure how much weight it actually carries. But, police sources say…"

"You are so bloody pedantic." Pauline said with mock annoyance and took over with the tale. "The report said that police were looking for your brother in connection with a serious physical and sexual assault on a police family liaison officer, who had been with him following your slaying of Annie, your housekeeper. The reporter also said that police were now taking another look at the evidence concerning the death of Annie but the spokesperson would say nothing further."

Lucas sat in stunned silence, his thoughts a jumble of unanswered questions "Do you think this means that it all could be on Jacob, I can't believe it of my brother, he was always the wild one of the two of us, but murder and assault?"

"I would believe that more than I would of you being the murderer of that poor girl in the park, and I have never met Jacob." It was Gill, offering her support.

"Do you think it could have been him, he was in the pub that night when I got there, the night that poor girl was murdered in the Bishop's Garden?"

"And, don't forget we both know it was not you who killed Annie, I wish I had met her she sounded like a lovely lady. So it had to be Jacob, and if that's true then why not the rest."

Nate took up the support. "Plus the violence seems to have stayed in the house even after you were taken away from it, first, Annie, Was it?" He looked for a nod of agreement before continuing with his analysis. "Now that police woman, I assume it was a WPC, they didn't say." That thought sent a shiver through all of them.

"Should I give myself in? See if I can clear my name." He looked around his friends, a new circle of friends admittedly, but he would trust their judgement.

Gill gripped the crook of his arm forcefully, as if he was about to be snatched from her. "No, what if they just send you back to Broadmoor while they search for Jacob, if they don't find him they still have you as the one who killed that girl, that would be convenient for them to have at least one crime solved." She looked him in the eye so there was no mistaking her intent. "I can't lose you now Lucas." Regardless of the feelings that were coursing through every fibre of his thoughts he smiled at her.

"She may have a point." Added Pauline as Nathaniel nodded his physical nod of a vote to the quorum.

"I need to think, to be, sorry Gill, alone for a while to figure this out." Lucas' brow furrowed, confusion was king at the moment and he was its subject.

"If a walk would help the woods at the rear of the house have some wonderful footpaths and are pretty quiet on weekday mornings, when I need to get away from him." Pauline prodded a thumb toward Nate, but added a warm, and slightly seductive, smile so as not to hurt his feelings. "I find it the perfect spot."

"She's lying of course Lucas, she never needs to get away from me but she goes there to photograph the wildlife, its teeming with it." Nate draped his arms around Pauline's neck and hugged as a sign of closeness, planting a kiss on the top of her head. She in turn confirmed it was in fact a lovely little nature reserve and perfect for some quiet moments.

"Would you mind Gill?"

She told him to go, "But take the mobile in case we hear any more news, you need time to come to terms with everything that has happened and we will all be here waiting for you when you are ready…" she urged.

Nate, supplied a pair of stout walking shoes, slightly too big but a thick pair of socks ensured their comfort, and Lucas headed for the rear gate to the property and with hands deep in the pocket of his, two sizes too big, jeans and chin down on his chest, he entered the woods with his thoughts and feelings as tangled and deep as the foliage that suddenly surrounded him.

The morning sun shone through the thick and leafy canopy, leaving dappled patterns on the woodland floor, birdsong filled the air around him and that same air smelled fresh, clean and with a hint of dampness from last autumns' rotting leaf fall. It did not take long for his surroundings to take over, it had been a long time since he had exposed himself to nature; even before the life changing events had begun he had ignored and forgotten what a wonderful thing the outdoors was.

Now, in a time where there was need of mental repair and acceptance, nature was coming to his aid, another friend he had to thank and the moment caused him to make the promise that no more, whatever happened, would he take life, the freedom to come and go as he pleased and friends for granted.

The ground beneath his feet was soft and he could not even hear his own footfall above the musical sounds of the woods, the raucous cry of a magpie, the singsong chirrup of a robin, the repetitive huff of a chiff-chaff; there were other birdsongs but he could not put a name or a picture to them. This was what he needed, lost in thought, catching up with events, examining not only his own actions, but, now, more importantly those of his brother. All around him the woodland symphony continued, movement in the foliage above him brushing branch against branch as a slight breeze annoyed the tree tops, the plaintive mewling of a buzzard way above the canopy and out of sight to anyone in the woods. Lucas felt the isolation of the moment, but it was a different loneliness to that which had been his constant companion for the past year or so, this one was welcome and comforting, the other was dulled by drugs and blunted by his situation and surroundings, this was fresh, alive and self-inflicted.

A different cry caught his attention and he stopped on the track, a fox cub, maybe! Would a deer make that sort of call, how beautiful would that be, a rustle, that cry again, almost like a sob. Lucas, stopped, searching the bushes with busy eyes, where he stood in an attempt to spot the responsible animal, or to seek out those seeking him, had they found him already? The guys had been right, the woods were teaming with life, and at that moment he decided that there would be no giving up, he could not go back to his cell and to the drug induced calm. He wanted to remain free in body and mind; he would wait until they caught Jacob and had his own innocence confirmed.

He heard the noise again, was it an owl's soft hoot? He stood still, hardly breathing listening for the sound, its direction. A flap and harsh rustle in a tree close by as a pigeon startled by the presence of man leapt into the sky and moved on to another part of the woods, its wings flapping wildly.

Back in the pink painted house the three friends had done little else except hold a circular conversation. Round and round the words went. Should he go and give himself up to the police and take whatever was coming? Should he wait till Jacob was caught? Should he stay where he was for a while? How long could Nathaniel and Pauline hide him without putting their own freedom at risk? Gill did not want to lose him, even for a short time and both Nate and Pauline did not want their friend hurt, but they could not deduce any other option except for Lucas to give himself up.

"If he is innocent at least now they have a way of clearing him, and if he is guilty…" Nate left the question hanging in mid-air.

"I know Nate. Lucas would be the first to agree, that if he did kill that girl in the park…" Gill began to add, but left the end of the statement hanging.

"Strange how they have never identified her." Interrupted Pauline. "I mean, it was sad she died and all that, but to die and not have anyone miss you or claim you, what sort of a sad little life did she lead to be so alone?"

"I know, I feel for her and so does Lucas, he is ashamed of the fact that he just shoved her under the bench and left her there alone, even though he knew she was already dead. But he said that something switched off in him that night, always leaving him with the thought that he had to have been the one who killed her, even though he did try and resuscitate her, but as he says, who else was there in the park that night and capable of doing it?"

"I think that may have been answered on the news this morning, and Lucas did say that his brother was in the area that evening."

And, so the conversation continued, there was no outcome, no comfortable summary of the facts, only conjecture, hopes and definitely no solutions. What happened next had to be Lucas' decision, and Lucas', alone with no pressure of influence from anyone around that kitchen table as they awaited the next news broadcast on the hour.

Lucas waited, frozen in place on the footpath, he had once read somewhere that the best form of camouflage was patience, to just remain still and let the wildlife come to you. Again that sound, a sob, carried toward him through the foliage, almost a gentle cough of air, it came from Lucas' left, from behind the wall of a creeper covered brick, and virtually derelict, square and shed-like building. Now his senses were focussed, it sounded to Lucas more like a human cry, than that of a young or injured animal.

Slowly and with more stealth than he felt, he moved towards the nearest wall, where a window frame, made up of rusted squares, stubbornly remaining intact while its glass had abandoned the building many years ago.

The interior was dark, there was no roof anymore but a light-sapping canopy of vines covered it from corner to corner. Still the sobs came again, like an injured animal breathing slowly and softly to avoid being noticed, but there was only darkness in the far corner except for one brief beam of thin light which highlighted the twin floppy and grey fur ears, of a well hugged and grubby toy rabbit.

Gill's mobile phone rang and vibrated on the kitchen table, gaining everyone's attention with a start. She snatched it up, without looking or hearing a voice, knowing it was Lucas.

"Gill you need to call the police and an ambulance, now, I have found that little girl."

For a brief moment Gill was confused, it was not what she was expecting to hear. She asked him to repeat, he did so without annoyance. The sobs from the old building had been the small girl missing from the caravan park, and he was sitting with her, talking softly to the child between explaining all to Gill. Apparently a strange lady had taken her from the caravan park asking her if she wanted to see the puppy, "She is more scared that something has happened to the puppy." Lucas explained, before quickly adding that the woman just dumped her in the woods and she found this old shelter and was too scared to move, "She is cold, wet and dirty but otherwise okay. I think. But get help quickly please, I am sure she has hypothermia and her family must be frantic!"

Gill relayed the call to Nathaniel and Pauline, Nate grabbed a pair of grubby trainers and rushed out of the door, while Pauline explained to Gill swiftly, that the buildings had been office blocks during the war and that POWs had been kept in camps within the woods, the camp huts had long gone but the brick support buildings had just been abandoned. Gill spoke again to Lucas, who was still connected via the phone.

"Baby, the guys know where you are, Nathaniel is on his way, get out of there now before the police arrive."

"I can't!" Just those two words in response, quietly spoken but firm in tone.

"Lucas if you want to stay free you have to." Tears, she realised, were streaming down her face. I have Pauline's car keys, I will meet you on the far side of the woods." Desperation for her man transcended all other concerns; she knew the child was now safe.

"I can't Gill, and I don't think she will let me go even if I wanted to, she is just clinging onto me, and her battered grey rabbit, afraid I am going to leave her like the bad lady did." There was a change of tone in his voice and Gill could hear the determination.

"I left the last young girl who needed me under a park bench Gill, I am not leaving this one, not when she needs me I cannot brush her away like so much rubbish. I can hear Nate coming and calling, I will see you soon. I love you." He shut the phone down without waiting for a response and called for Nate. "In here Nate, in the first hut." His voice clear and strong. Lucas felt a strength of character that he never knew he possessed before.

A moustachioed head appeared at the same glassless window that Lucas had looked through a few minutes before. "Hey Lucas, found trouble again I see." Lucas felt the tiny girl shrink against him, and he shushed her in gentle tones of support, while pulling her a little closer to him. Nat entered the old square building slowly so as not to startle the child further. Lucas, with soft words that Nate could not hear but understood, calmed the tiny girl's fears. A warming, and soft fleece, blanket, which Nat had grabbed on his way out of the garish pink house, was handed to him.

"Well done Lucas; if ever there was Karma to be had for that little girl, you were it."

Lucas smiled up at the man he now considered friend and held the child closer, offering warmth as well as comfort.

Chapter 34

The ambulance pulled from the driveway outside the house, spitting some of the gravel from beneath its rear wheels as it went, flashing blue lights bouncing off pink walls, and its two tones blaring, there was no real urgency to their exit, but a small child suffering from hypothermia and fear had requested the sirens. The paramedics had said she would suffer no further physical harm, but did say that another night or two in the open and it may well have been a different story, now the biggest task was to get her thoroughly checked and to reunite her with two very distraught, but now relieved parents.

In the kitchen Lucas, in handcuffs, sat opposite DS Kobie Khan, the officer having now driven from West Sussex to Dorset in record time; it seemed that in the last week or so he had covered that coastal journey more times than he cared to recall and the tiredness showed in the grey pallor that seemed to coat his face, his eyes dull and bloodshot. The cuffs shone brightly with the reflection of the overhead kitchen lights and Lucas realised he was able to twist his wrists, slightly, the cuffs were only on loosely.

"Are they really necessary?" Gill had queried as a local uniformed bobby, one of the first on the scene, had put them on. His response was that it was procedure, but adding an apology as a rider to the fact.

Now DS Kaan, needed the full story of the last few days, he would not wait until the man he had chased back and forth across three counties was in custody and in the interview suite. Both men were sipping on scalding black coffee, both needing the hit of caffeine, and Lucas needed the heat despite it being another warm summer's day, it was as if the small child had drawn all the body-warmth from him and the effort of the last few days and all that it had brought him had sapped his energy. For Lucas it seemed the end of one horrid journey was ending while another actually now had a hope of beginning, a life with Gill. For the weary DS it was a case of the coffee keeping him awake, it had been days of little sleep over the past week or so, and of trauma at seeing a friend and colleague injured, while feeling the guilt of having let her down. He had not slept at all last night, not since finding Jem the evening before.

"Well, it's been an unusual and busy few days, that is for sure." Kobie began after his first sip of coffee, apart from that his only words had been in introduction and identification. Nobody had even glanced at the proffered warrant card, his presence and demeanour the only proof needed; Lucas did not recall their previous meeting in the company of his Godfather at the Chichester interview room.

"You always the master of the understatement?" Lucas responded, not in sarcasm though as he felt strangely at ease and relaxed, now resigned to whatever was about to happen and feeling at peace because of it.

Fate had taken destiny from his hands the moment he discovered where the sobs were coming from and looked inside that brick outbuilding, and there was no point fighting any more, no more need for running away. The child had clung to him right up until she was placed in the ambulance, and only the received promise from the paramedics of the loud 'Nee-naws' during the ride to the hospital had she finally relinquished her grip. Nobody was watching over him as he stepped back from ambulance to the kitchen, the local police officer had seemed at ease, but then became 'efficient officer' when he 'slapped on' the cuffs before his superiors arrived.

The handcuff situation was quickly resolved with everyone who needed to be in the room now gathered. "I think they can come off now." Kobie nodded toward the cuffs. "You aren't going anywhere are you Lucas?"

Lucas shook his head, "Not any more, no!" Cuffs removed, wrists rubbed, as if they had been in tight shackles for days on end, it was an unconscious reaction to being restrained.

"Want to begin at the beginning." A preventive hand was held up between the two men to stop Lucas before he started. "I don't mean in the park, we can do that later, just start at the escape, and get me through to today's little adventure."

"What about Gill and my friends? Are they in trouble?"

"As you realise that is not down to me; that will be for those higher up and the CPS, but given this morning's events, I cannot see much beyond a slap on the wrists." He smiled up at the three other people around the table.

And, so it was, for the next few hours Lucas replayed the story of the last few days, not once but repeatedly, Kobie interrupting occasionally for clarification of some point or other. Even Lucas had not realised so much had happened, in such a short time, or that so many people had been involved. He was allowed to go through it all once, in its entirety, from Charles' note to finding the child. Step after step, meeting Gill, crashing the boat, swimming ashore and going on the run naked; even the batman lounging pants were included in his story. All the while Kaan listened intently, asking questions every now and again, but still intent on letting Lucas' tale unfold.

The only pause in proceedings were as Lucas mentioned the house, and he stopped his own story to ask after the injured police woman, who had been attacked by Jacob. Kobie Kaan told him she was in a bad way but stable, it would take time! Kobie thanked him for asking.

Twice more he told his tale, each of these times being interrupted for clarification, for confirmation of dates and times and for note-taking. His three companions not interrupting, not adding or embellishing, but all the time Gill sat close, her hand on Lucas' thigh under the table and Pauline pouring coffee whenever it was needed. Nathaniel was just an innocent bystander, a role he seemed very comfortable with as he listened to the drama unfolding in his kitchen.

"I think that is all we need for now Lucas, you look tired." The detective also looked tired, his shirt was rumpled, the collar a little stained with sweat, and there were still traces of Jem's bloodstains on its front, there had been no time to change as the last few hours had unravelled. Kobie now craved the hot ministrations of a shower and a change of clothes; he felt grimy and weary; it had been the toughest and strangest two or three days of his career; he also wanted to pop by the hospital back in Chichester to see how Jem was doing, he would not admit it but he felt a fondness and a responsibility there for the young officer.

"So, what happens to me now? Lucas queried, but resigned for the worst. Gill slid a little closer along the pew they were sharing and wrapped her hand around his thigh to stop him from being pulled from her, concern made her clench a little too hard, but he said nothing.

"This bit I am sorry about Lucas." More bad news had to leave his lips, too much information of that type had been passed from his mouth this weekend and it wearied him further. "The press are crowding round outside." Everyone looked around, as if someone had said, 'don't look behind you but…' "And they will want to see justice being done and safety returned to their streets. I will put the cuffs back on but we will put a jumper or coat across your hands to hide that fact from them. A car is ready to take you to the local nick, probably just for tonight, and then in the morning back to Broadmoor…"

"Does he have to go back to that horrible place?" Gill had dread in her voice.

"Until we get a judge to release him I am afraid so, he is there by court order after all." Kobie turned his attention back to Lucas. "But, you will not be going back onto the secure section; I have already spoken with the head nurse there with that regard. We still have to work a few things out but we are pretty sure that Jacob, when we find him, will be proved to be the killer of the unnamed girl, there are too many similarities with the two other attacks for it not to have been him. Quite what you were doing in the park apart from trying to revive her we may never know, unless you remember anything else about that evening."

Although it was not a question, Lucas shook his head in response anyway.

"Can I go with him?" Gill asked, the response was a negative but Nate and Pauline offered to take her up there right behind the police car later that morning.

DS Kaan, finished up by telling Lucas that after a few formalities and a written statement from him it was almost certain his barrister could bring about his freedom within a couple of days and Broadmoor staff would be alerted to treat you gently. "You never know you may even get ice cream after your dinner." Kobie said with tongue in cheek.

"You have obviously never tasted cheap institutional ice cream, or you would not have said that like it was a treat." Offered Lucas.

As it transpired Lucas never reached Broadmoor. Early the next morning a body was discovered face down in one of the many creeks that abounded Chichester Harbour and he was needed for the identification of his shoeless brother, the expensive deck shoes left stuck in the harbour's muddy bed.

To avoid the going to and from Broadmoor a magistrate was called and a release on Police Bail was agreed by all concerned, this time Robert Berry QC, Retired, arrived resplendent in a dark blue pinstripe suit, the jacket pinching a little as he had gained weight since he had last donned his court suit. He looked the part with his grey hair swept back over his ears and serious air while he explained to the magistrate how the story had unfolded over the past week or so. The police solicitor offered no objections and no evidence against Lucas.

The magistrate being the officious kind took time out of the day's schedule to severely reprimand Lucas for having escaped the institution of Broadmoor, stating, "It belittled the 'secure' status in the eyes of the public if any of the inmates thought it acceptable to just walk out of the front door so to speak." He sounded pompous as he lectured from up on the bench, his pinched features and pointed nose making him seem like a vulture on a perch waiting to come down and pick the carcass.

Robert stood to his full, and imposing height, and assured the magistrate, while placing a firm hand on the shoulder of the seated Lucas, that his client was particularly contrite for having exposed the weakness in the hospital's security.

Lucas for his part wished, just for once, to have a comfortable seat to sit on, the bench in the dock being hard and unforgiving; but he was free and as he walked from the Chichester Magistrates Court he realised there was no boat to go to and he had absolutely no desire to return to the White House where so many horrors had happened. So following warm and heart felt goodbyes and promises between them and Nate and Pauline to meet again soon, Gill took him home with her.

Over the next few months he was officially ruled out of the investigation of the original murder and it was recorded that all the deaths, apart from the wonderful alias of Colonel Drayton-Farlington, who was recorded by the coroner as committing suicide while the balance of his mind was disturbed, were down to his brother Jacob.

The part that weighed heaviest however with Lucas, was that Jacob had not just killed Annie, but also his birth mother. A fact that had never even crossed the mind of Lucas through boyhood or manhood and it saddened him even further to discover that previously uncovered nugget of truth.

To him though, Charles would always be the true hero in this sorry tale, the friend who gave up his life for his friend.

One year on.

Gill had lost the job she had worked so hard to win, it was not the fact that she had lied about being ill the week she had taken off to go on the run with an escaped lunatic, or the second week that she took as unpaid leave, to spend with that same now freed and exonerated psychopath.

It was the fact she refused to either write, or even give, the whole story to the newspaper she worked for, their much sought after scoop eluded them and their were not best pleased with this decision despite attempts at bribery of elevated status within the paper or a chance to join the national press through one of its other titles. Even the offer of a much higher salary, and promise of bonuses when the story was syndicated held no sway. If anyone was going to write the story, it was going to be the people who lived it, Gill had informed them as she resigned.

Lucas sold the pretty White House that sat so idyllically near the Chichester canal, its previously clean walls were tainted, its floor stained with the memory of blood, its picket fence bars around a violent past; too many bad recollections, too many ghosts.

With the influx of funds he and Gill purchased a charming little ex-farmhouse just a few miles from the garish pink house and they settled into domestic bliss. The only part of their new life together that left Lucas still feeling a little uncomfortable with came that following summer when the foursome, who had now become firm friends headed for the beach at Shell Bay for some more naturism.

Even with the weight gone and getting back to his fit and toned former self did not help, he could not but feel mindful of being naked; he also could not get used to sitting alongside the stunning Pauline without having the odd glimpse at her long tan legs and where they ended up. For her part Gill felt no jealousy at his odd admiring glance toward her friend, she just used it, whenever he was caught, to her own teasing advantage.

Life for the pair of them had become relaxed and worry-free. After a suitable gap of a few months Gill felt the need, the desire to write something and so the manuscript began and every morning, for at least three hours a day, the two of them sat in the spare bedroom of their farmhouse, now converted to an office, and wrote their story. The story of a small family that had greeted carnage in an idyllic waterside cottage with white walls and rose bushes.

There was no thought of it being published at first, it was just cathartic, the process of telling the tale word by word and seeing it produced on the computer screen, black text on a white background, every word that had been lived, every ordeal suffered, even the tale of the hard seats, although talk of them left Lucas with an aching behind! Evenings would be spent curled together on their beaten up old couch that had been sourced at a local furniture auction, the cushions were soft , it hugged them as they sat entwined every evening, like their relationship it was deep and comfortable, and they would read and chat about what had been written that day. Lucas found the process truly cleansing.

Come their first Christmas in the remote farmhouse they received a joyous greeting card, a fat and jolly Santa on the front, from a very grateful young girl and her even more grateful mother, both were responding well to therapy sessions and they hoped one day soon to be comfortable enough with the traumatic memory to visit; but like many such promises, life would get in the way of it actually happening, but that was okay as they all had new lives to begin; quieter lives and less dramatic hopefully.

For one week in the summer a small cottage in the pretty village of Singleton, at the foot of the South Downs and next door to a charming church was rented by the foursome. Pauline enjoying country walks, Lucas and Gill putting the finishing touches to the rewrite of their book and Nathaniel plying his bookmaking trade throughout the week that is Glorious Goodwood, the premier race meet on the south coast. On Ladies Day the girls put on their finery, Lucas purchased a new suit and a very pink shirt, and they joined Nate trackside; with a successful day for Gill picking three winners the evening was spent quaffing fresh oysters and sipping champagne, paid for out of the winnings, and being consumed pitch-side at the Cowdray Park polo. The sun shone, the days were warm and trouble free, life was good.

With the manuscript complete and the story told Lucas and Gill met with a friend of Nate's. He was a literary agent and he thought the book would be a best seller, but they would need to move quickly while the public still recalled all the scandals and tales of family intrigue. And so, the book, after much haggling and bargaining between two very keen publishers bidding handsomely for the rights was published, to critical as well as public acclaim. It flew off the shelves and one rainy day a week into its release the four musketeers sat in a Waterstones cafe and watched as a pile of the books diminished in the middle of the sales floor.

It was true, with a best seller's sales figures confirming the fact, that everyone loves a good scandal. The title they chose; 'Memory of DEATH OF AN UNNAMED GIRL'. On the flyleaf a paragraph about her, that also asked that if anyone knew of who she might be then to call the number publicised.

Police sources believed her to be a sex slave brought over from one of the Eastern Bloc countries, probably Romanian and despite exhaustive inquiries, her identity was never discovered.

One other mention in the book, the dedication on the flyleaf read simply 'The Colonel'.

Quickly on the 'best-seller' list the book became big news and began to take over their lives, radio chats, newspaper interviews, including a serialisation in The Mail on Sunday, and finally the TV talk show, the morning show host with a soft Scottish burr, was desperate to interview them both and despite their reluctance to continue the bandwagon ride, their publishers talked them into appearing on the show.

Their reluctance was because Lucas was getting tired and Gill noticed that the more interviews and the bigger the success the more withdrawn he was becoming, she had seen him grow from his protective shell and did not want to see him return there.

While recording a Radio Four interview, the book now being dramatized for a radio play, Gill had done most of the talking as Lucas had begun to retreat once again into that protective shell. She had asked him if he was alright during the taxi ride back to Waterloo Station, but he had merely responded, with a weak smile, that he was just exhausted.

A promise was made between themselves that the breakfast chat show would be the last.

They both wanted to get back to their farm cottage and some sort of anonymity; the ride had gone on long enough and they wanted the life that was ahead of them and not keep reliving the one they were trying to leave behind.

They waited in the wings, a make-up girl fussed over Lucas' sweating brow with a powder pad that he could feel clogging his pores, Gill was afraid to let go of his hand and she looked on concerned, the grip on Lucas' hand was clammy and yet cool.

Unusually the affectionate gaze was not returned, his eyes seemed empty, a little glazed, she had not seen this look since the day she first saw him in his surgical scrubs as he climbed aboard the Bonnie Annie.

The lights from the studio floor glared, a red light appeared on top of Camera One and the host of the show looked directly into the single eye of the lens. "Ladies and Gentleman, with a fascinating story that only Hollywood could think up, but my next guests actually lived through it…" Her joviality was what had made her so popular but the happiness of the introduction of such a tragic tale seemed incongruous with real life.

"Gill Harmon and Lucas Tubb" The small studio audience applauded and strained forward in their tiered seats to get a better look at the couple, who in return waved back to the audience in a coy, uncomfortable way. Fame was not a comfortable companion for either.

They wriggled slightly in the pair of chairs opposite a smiling host, her lipstick highlighting her bee-sting lips, and the questions quickly began. Each time one was directed to Lucas silence became the response and Gill would answer, in the best way she could but she was becoming increasingly concerned about the mentally retreating Lucas.

Then came the crunch question, and it was one that, oddly, had not been asked before on any of the other chat shows. The host repeated it, and aimed it specifically at Lucas. "Lucas, Lucas;" Trying to gain a connection with his blank stare, "…the unnamed girl was it ever proved beyond doubt, I mean did the police ever continue their investigation into whether it was your brother Jacob, who so brutally killed her?" The question, delivered as it was from behind the friendly face of the TV presenter seemed to come out all wrong, he heard the words as they were spoken but the tacit question seemed to be 'Lucas did you kill that girl?'

Lucas felt something kick in his memory, like an automatic car jumping another gear.

Gill was about to respond but the squeezing of her hand from Lucas stopped her and she looked at the man she had grown to love totally and trust completely and he in turn looked across the glass coffee table that made the set look like the presenter's home, and gazed into the female host's eyes, but he did so with a cold stare. The audience in the studio and on their couches at home could see the discomfort it was causing from her expression, the gaze she was caught up in from Lucas seemed to be filled with ice.

His voice was cold, emotionless and flat, he was on remote! "I don't think Jacob did it, not that one, not that girl, the unnamed girl." Lucas dragged in a huge breath, stared out into the burning studio lights. "She was offering to have sex, in the park, with me. Said she needed money. She was knelt in front of me as I sat on that bench. I didn't want her there, she started to undo my trousers and told me she was hungry and that it was okay and she would make me feel good. Her face, she was so young…"

He twisted the signet ring on the second finger of his right hand. He looked down at the ring! "It did so much damage to her face, there was so much blood, her head hit the seat and her neck bent at a funny angle!"

Gill, standing just behind camera one gazed on stunned, unsure of what she was hearing. Tears began to form in the corners of her eyes.

THE END

DAVID ROSE-MASSOM

ABOUT THE AUTHOR

David Rose-Massom worked as a photojournalist for over 20 years and has long had the desire for creative writing. Retired from journalism he now has time to write daily while sitting in his favourite café.

Born in Hampshire a county on the south coast of England David has a real love of the area where his novels are set. He has driven the roads, sailed the coastal waters and walked the South Downs, the New Forest and the beaches where his stories take place.

Death of an Unnamed Girl is the first in a series of novels featuring Kobie Kaan, a quiet family man who works hard to be a good copper while balancing his Muslim beliefs and a love of bacon sandwiches.

Being a photographer gives David a good eye when it comes to landscapes and seascapes and he uses this fine eye for detail throughout the book's journey.

Printed in Great Britain
by Amazon

38542352R00149